THE LION OF VENICE

An Historical Novel

Richard Cusden

UPFRONT PUBLISHING
LEICESTERSHIRE

THE LION OF VENICE: *An Historical Novel*

ISBN 1 84426 027 5

First Published 2002 by
MINERVA PRESS

Second Edition 2002 by
UPFRONT PUBLISHING
Leicestershire

THE LION OF VENICE

An Historical Novel

Foreword

Richard Cusden
1927–1988

Richard Cusden, born a century after the death of Beethoven, was brought up in London where he became a student at St Martin's School of Art.

He studied painting for three years under the remnants of The Euston Road Group and formed a lifelong interest in hand-lettering, which he pursued as a professional scribe and heraldic artist.

He completed his education at London University where he discovered a penchant for Art History. He was Art Master at Salisbury's Bishop Wordsworth School until 1965 when he joined the staff at Salisbury College of Art where he lectured in the History of Art.

It was early in the 1970s that he began his television career with the BBC, starting with his *One Man Show* series, teaching how to draw and paint. This was followed by *Private View* – a series of programmes filmed at some of his especially favourite spots around the south. In 1981 he made *Cusden On Location* and in 1983 *Cusden On Avon*.

He was passionate about Salisbury Cathedral and was commissioned to do a considerable amount of work for it, notably the historic notes on the tombs, the Book of Remembrance for the Prisoner of Conscience window, and the entire fundraising display for the Spire Appeal.

He died suddenly in his spectacular rose garden in 1988 aged sixty-one.

To view some of Richard Cusden's work visit www.cusden.com or www.cusden.co.uk.

Glossary

cartoon	A working drawing made of the same size as the final painting.
fresco, –oes	A method of painting in watercolour on freshly laid plaster; as both dry together, a chemical change fixes the colour.
glazes	Thin washes of oil paint which allow the colours underneath to show through; transparent paint, thinned with oil or spirit.
gravità	A deep seriousness of intention or achievement.
grotesques	A decoration which formalises flowers, foliage, human figures and heads in continuous patterns; derived from excavated Roman sources.
impasto	Oil paint applied thickly and not worked over, thus retaining the original shape of the brush mark, and giving the paint some relief.
lapis (lazuli)	A semi-precious stone which, when ground, gives ultramarine; a blue pigment of great beauty and durability.
lay figure	A wooden model of a figure which is jointed so that various poses may be set for drawing when a live model is not available.
orpiment	A bright yellow pigment which is no longer used.
pietre dure	An Italian technique of inlaying coloured stones and marbles for decorative purposes; parquetry in stone.

pigments	The coloured raw material of paint which is ground into a powder.
priming	A non-absorbent layer applied to a canvas to receive the paint.
stretcher	A wooden frame over which canvas may be stretched taut.
terra verde	A dullish green pigment, dug out of the ground, and hence durable.
terrazzo	A manufactured stone flooring made from chips, cemented together.
terribilità	The quality of horror contained in, and induced by, a work of art. Michelangelo's *Last Judgement* in the Sistine Chapel is the most striking example.
velaturas	Semi-transparent glazes, prepared by adding white to the colour, producing a softened effect to the painting beneath.

Contents

Part One
Youth

Pigeon Flight

The bells of the campanile scattered the pigeons that had roosted together on a ledge since the sun had dropped imperceptibly into the lagoon. A black priest scurried like an alarmed beetle from the presbytery, fumbling under his cassock, and disappeared into the blacker interior of the church.

Shutters were opened and wicker cages of singing birds were thrust out into the spring sunshine and hung on hooks by the window.

A dog stretched and yawned in a doorway, shaking the dust from his eyes, his ears joining the applause of the pigeons' wings.

Bedding cascaded down from the sills of a dozen houses. The *campo* stretched itself like the dog, who now relieved himself on the church step, affecting protestant malice.

Voices.

Thin wisps of smoke crept reluctantly from the chimneys and vanished against the sky.

It was morning in the Most Serene Republic of Venice.

Down a flight of stone steps, two by two, clattered the hard soles of leather sandals, thongs whipping round the brown ankles of a small boy who shot back the bolts of the door and, with long strides, ran across the flags to the fountain. Dipping his hands in the water, he gulped a cupped palmful and threw another across the back of his head. Luminous drops trembled at the end of his nose and chin, then splashed into the bowl. Another mouthful, and he was running again into a narrow, shaded alley.

Sandals smacking the pavement in even beats, he leaped the steps of a bridge and down the other side as smoothly as a cat. He wiped his mouth with the back of his hand and he tasted salt. He recited to himself in a breathless staccato, 'Open the windows, sweep the floor, dry the brushes in the sun, skin the oil, grind the umber and the resin, tidy the Maestro's table.'

Near the canalazzo he heard the boatmen's shouts and the gritty laughter of the fishermen on the way to the market. At the foot of a deep stone crevasse, he ricocheted round corners, his hands palming off the masonry walls and swinging him round columns at giddy speed. He stopped, panting, spreadeagled across an iron gate, crucified on the scrolls, one hand tugging a bronze handle from the white stone gatepost. His breath had made a moist patch on the cold iron. He looked at it and traced his initial in the dew. He curled the tail of the 'G' like the scrolls of iron into an arabesque.

'Is that you, Giovanni?' called a fragile voice from the other side of the courtyard. 'You're late,' it continued, without waiting for an answer.

'Yes, Maria, it's Giovanni.'

Looking through the serpentine coils, he saw the bent, frail figure of a woman scuffing between the pots of shrubs and palms, wiping her hands on an apron.

'You're late,' she repeated as she turned the key and let him in.

'Only a little, Maria.'

'But the Maestro would beat you if I told him.'

'But you won't, will you?' He stared back into her withered face with a saucy expression, his eyes full of mischief and mock apprehension. She wound her skinny arm round his neck and buried her cheekbone in his wet hair. Nothing more was said. The gate clanged and reverberated behind them and they walked slowly between the leaves towards an open door.

The bell was dancing silently on its spring as they passed into a dark passage. At the foot of a marble staircase carved with swags of fruit, Giovanni disentangled himself from the old woman's embrace and bounded up, his sandals slapping the treads with resounding whip cracks.

'Ssssh!' she hissed, her crooked finger trembling before her lips. 'The Maestro's still asleep.'

Imitating the exaggerated stealth of Scaramouche, he tiptoed down a wide landing, and waved a glib hand at Maria who waited, her neck twisted vertical, till he was gone.

He pushed open the door into a vast room that was heavy with the incense smell of oil and varnish. It was as dark as a womb, and he was afraid of the dark. Thin rods of light marked the windows and slit the floor in long diagonal shafts which, he noticed, got weaker as they got wider. He climbed on to a bench and undid the shutters, fastening them carefully against the wall. Then the windows. This was his favourite chore. He liked to be the first one into the studio, before the noise of the assistants, the laughter and chatter of visiting patrons relegated him to a position of no importance. This was his time of day, when he could imagine that it belonged to him, and that he was the Maestro. He liked to sit in the great chair, and he liked to gaze out of the windows of the house on to the ordinary folk down below in the square or on the canal.

His elbows spread wide on the Istrian stone sill and his chin in his palms, he gazed down into the water which lapped against the steps below. How green it was! How would the Maestro mix that colour? He put together a recipe in his head – terra verde, lapis, orpiment – and was pleased to know that it was probably right. He wouldn't have known that five months ago when his father first brought him to this room.

Then he remembered his duties. The catalogue went through his head again faster than he could recite it. He reached for the broom in the corner automatically; his mind was engaged on recollection. The things he had learned! He had to learn how to sweep a studio without making dust, he had to learn that some pigments had to be ground over and over again till they could be no finer, that others would spoil if they were ground too much. He knew that a brush needed to be cosseted, cleaned and dried with reverential care, or it would lose its particular attraction for the painter. At first, Giovanni thought this was absurdly pernickety, but now he understood that a paintbrush was in no way like a broom.

The bells had stopped now, but the world below made its own ripieno of sounds against the bubbling concertino of the pigeons basking on the tracery above the windows. He swept and daydreamed. He remembered the smell of Maria's apron. It reminded him of his mother. She was a tender woman who rarely needed to use words. She spoke in a whisper, and sometimes didn't speak at all, simply making eloquent gestures. He remembered how she would place her cupped hand under his cheek when he was tired or sad; he remembered dozing on her knee, his face buried in her apron, rocking. The little unexpected treats she made for him, the ribbons for his stockings on Feast Days, the nutty, crunchy morsels that came from the gridiron on baking days, delicately arranged on his own small plate. He remembered her long, brown hair and how it shone with blue lights as he ran his fingers over it. He remembered that her hair was the last he saw of her as she was carried out of the house on the day she died. Her face and body were covered by a sheet, and he didn't want to look, but as they took her through the door, he opened his fingers and recognised the shape of her feet and folded arms. Her hair had strayed from under the hem of the sheet and a strand hung loose, the curl at the end bouncing in rhythm with the footfall of the bearers. He was ten years old and he cried for a week. He was alone for the first time and the house was dark and silent. His father told him he would forget, but behind the tears Giovanni promised himself that he would always remember her. It was his first resolution. Four years had passed and it still hurt.

The sweeping done, he brushed the back of his hand roughly across his eyes and stood the broom in the corner again. He collected the brushes he had cleaned the night before and stood them in jars on the sill. He stroked the stiff hair and coaxed them into shape with suit.

'Hi, Giovanni!' called a voice from the water. He looked up and saw a neighbour leaning on a bent oar at the stern of a boat. He raised a brown hand in a masculine salute to the boy whose head barely showed at the foot of one long, dark window.

'See you this evening,' he called over his shoulder. Giovanni waved frantically. But he became conscious that his juvenile excitement was an unworthy reciprocation of the mature economy of Luca's salute. He paused and flushed, then imitated the man's gesture to his retreating back. He recalled that he and his father were going to have supper with Luca and his fat wife that night.

Sophenisba was enormous; she loved good food and laughter and expected everyone to love it too. She filled Giovanni with savoury pastas, grilled fish and sticky cakes till he could burst, and as they ate, she chattered and howled with demonic laughter. She teased all men with a good-natured impudence, and because she was so good-natured, she was indulged by all her male victims. With her own sex, she merely quarrelled; torrents of abuse and indignation flailed her unfortunate neighbours into stunned silence. They retired to a prudent distance and muttered the vilest imprecations. Perhaps they had success, for five of Sophenisba's seven children had died; two at childbirth, two in infancy and one of the plague that had killed Giovanni's mother. Of the survivors, Giorgio was married to a quiet wife and Maddelena was a nun.

Giovanni was fond of Luca and slightly afraid of his wife. She was as coarse as she was corpulent. But Luca would protect him from excessive embarrassment by applying a massive blow to Sophenisba's rump. The sound was deafening, and it never failed to halt all thought and conversation – even Sophenisba's. Their weekly visits always exceeded the pleasure of the anticipation. It was noisy, hot and confined; no room that held Sophenisba was not, but this was an excursion into family life that Giovanni and his father could not otherwise enjoy.

Giovanni had coasted through most of his tasks without giving them much thought. They demanded no concentration and gave him little reward for doing them conscientiously. While his hands were busy, his mind flitted from fantasy to recollection in uninhibited freedom. He ground the ochre for today's work. He cleaned the stones and began on the umbers. Without thinking, the order was right.

Voices on the stairs heralded company. The door shuddered open and the assistants exploded the peace of the morning.

'Haven't you finished yet?' asked one dark-bearded fellow who stood with his thumbs stuck in his belt.

'Very nearly; I've only got to crush the resin, then I'm finished.'

'Are my brushes ready?' asked another. 'And don't forget to call me Maestro,' he added with measured emphasis.

'They're all ready – Maestro.' The last word was barely audible. Giovanni's complaisance expressed his timidity more than his consent.

'Where are they then?'

'In the window.'

'In the window, *Maestro*.'

'Well, they shouldn't be in the window; they should be by my easel.'

The bearded one winked at Giovanni, who was not sure whether he was still being teased or not. Gathering reassurance from a friendly gesture, his courage rose sufficiently for him to say, 'I wanted to be sure they were dry.' The implied defiance surprised him. It had come out wrong, and he hardly recognised his own voice. There was silence. Suddenly all the assistants chorused in laughter.

'Good for you, sonny,' roared the beard. 'You're a good lad.'

They dispersed, each to his own part of the studio. The laughter and the talk died away as each settled to his own task. Giovanni ground on, the stones squeaking as the umber became finer.

One of the assistants belched, having breakfasted too fast or too well. He dragged an easel into a better light, nearer the window. He tapped his teeth thoughtfully with a brush handle as he viewed the progress of the picture he had worked on the day before. With a sharp dyspeptic gasp, he redrew a line with the butt end of the brush into the wet paint.

'Christ!' he said. 'I just cannot get that leg right. Who ever heard of a crippled Magdalen?'

No one answered. He belched again.

Another assistant was busily drawing a squared grid on a canvas before transferring a sketch. He counted the squares out loud, accentuating the counting when someone spoke. A row of tacks at the top of the stretcher had been equidistantly spaced, and he hooked the loop of a chalked string over each in turn, held the string taut at a corresponding mark at the bottom and plucked it so that it left a clean white line of dust on the red priming.

The chief assistant sat at a high desk in the corner, entering figures into the columns of a battered ledger. He scratched his ear with the end of his quill.

'Someone didn't get paid last week. Who was it?'

'Me!' they chorused, guffawing.

'Don't be stupid,' he said scornfully, 'I would remember not paying you all, but I seem to have missed one.'

'It must have been Giovanni, then, because if it had been me, I would have reminded you.'

'No, it's too much; it's not that. Anyway, I remember giving him his wages. Didn't I, Giovanni?'

The boy looked up and nodded. He did not want to repeat an indiscreet remark or inflexion, for the risk of mock wrath any of them made him feel vulnerable. He had not found a way to cope with their teasing, and it seemed foolish to provoke it unnecessarily.

'Well, my accounts don't balance, and I'm over.'

'Let's have a party, then. We'll soon put your books right.'

More laughter and private comments. Then they settled to work again.

The beard was drawing in black chalk a figure of a woman with head turned and arms raised in astonishment. The lines glided across the paper in long, flowing sweeps. His hand paused occasionally as he squinted through half-closed eyes, his lashes trembling. The hand moved rhythmically in the air, rehearsing the line before dropping to leave a curved thigh here, a fold of drapery there. With the impassive assurance of a boatman with his oar, the rustic with his scythe, he built the figure from the bones outward towards the skin and the drapery.

As he ground the resin in a mortar, Giovanni watched him creating a living woman on paper. Every touch of the chalk added more vitality, until the woman seemed more alive than the rigid stance of her creator. Giovanni was mesmerised by this miracle of evolution. He heard his name called and he automatically started grinding again.

'Giovanni,' the voice repeated, 'I want you over here.' It was the voice of the beard. 'Come and stand here with your arms like this.' He pointed at the drawing which Giovanni knew line by line.

He stood in the same pose as the figure, his head tilted, his arms raised. He watched the pigeons in the window tracery. One launched itself off a cusp, flapped twice and sailed across the water. Another followed. He waited for a third.

'Now spread your fingers a little more,' coaxed the beard. 'That's fine.'

He drew at the side of the figure a loose square from which two radiating lines issued. He made small marks between them to plot the spaces between the fingers.

Before Giovanni could succeed in inciting another pigeon to glide from the window, the beard said, 'That's all, I've done it now.'

'Can I see?' asked Giovanni.

'Of course.'

Giovanni gazed at the hand on the paper. The palm was small and slightly creased in the form of an 'M'. The fingers curled inwards with the little finger foreshortened, each joint clearly defined. The soft parts were smooth and rounded, the bones accentuated with darker, crisper lines.

'How do you do it?' he asked, not expecting an answer.

'Well, it's easy if you practise,' said the beard. 'But you must remember to let your arm move naturally. You mustn't force it.'

He drew as he talked. The line snaked up, slowed round a tight curve and flowed gently down in a full, floating ellipse.

'You mean, like pigeons flying?' ventured Giovanni.

The beard sat back on his stool and looked at him wide-eyed.

'My God, yes! Exactly like that. The lines must fly. If they do, the drawing is right.'

He paused and drew a pigeon, but his eyes, Giovanni noticed, were not on the paper, but beyond it. Contact between man and boy had been broken: the current flowed no more.

Alone in the hiatus that was not of his making or to his liking, Giovanni moved over to the Maestro's table. He arranged the quills neatly in a bronze tray, the sticks of chalk in a wooden box. He fingered one of them thoughtfully. Was there some kind of magic pent up in this unpromising material? He felt no mystical power. He laid it in the box and wiped the black residue on the back of his breeches. He picked up a scrap of pigeon's down off a pile of letters and with his sleeve rubbed the blue glass sphere which weighted them down. He removed the spent candles from the silver candlestick. He ran his finger round the fat belly of one of the cherubs, more to feel the shape than to dust it. The curve was just like the one the beard had drawn, just like the flight of a swooping bird.

He experienced a moment of joy, of illumination and realisation. He knew that art and nature were one. At last he knew why he could never kill a pigeon when the boys in the campo had managed to trap one. He knew why the tail of the dog outside his own door at home gave him pleasure to look at. He knew why the curve of the Grand Canal was beautiful. He knew why that strand of his mother's hair against the white sheet was unbearably sad and beautiful as well.

Acceptance

The door swung open, framing the square figure of Maestro Jacopo Robusti. He was greeted by his elder son, Domenico, who was his chief assistant, accountant and businessman of the studio.

'Good morning,' the Maestro said softly, pulling the deep fur of his cloak collar up to his ears.

His voice was always a surprise. It was velvety, with an almost musical timbre, as smooth as a tenor chanting melismas in St Mark's. His head was almost bald and it was always covered with a cap indoors and a brimmed hat when he went out. His spherical face was enclosed by a rough beard, striated with grey, and his dark eyes were never still. They moved around the studio, scanning his assistants, his furniture, his canvases, his table. It was a scene of industry and order.

'Good morning, Maestro.'

He sat heavily in his chair, stretched his legs under the table and yawned. He was not yet geared to the momentum of a working day. His head rested on the carved cartouche while he gazed at the ceiling. Europa smiled down at him from the broad back of a flower-decked bull. Daphne looked entreatingly into his eyes in suspended metamorphosis, her fingers sprouting leaves and her hair streaming down to her dimpled buttocks. In, half engulfed in grey vapour, struggled ineffectually, her lips forever parted in a silent cry. As a painting, it was far inferior to his own work.

'Giovanni,' he said, 'come here. I want to talk to you.'

The boy rested the pestle quietly against the mortar's rim and crossed to the table, his fingers entwined behind his back. They felt damp and his pulse hammered in his throat. What had he done wrong? What had he forgotten?

'Yes, Maestro.' He licked his dry lips and tasted salt again.

Jacopo shifted his head, with movements like a broody hen, into a familiar hollow where the foliage was comfortable, and still studying the ceiling, continued, 'You've been here nearly half a year now, and I promised your father that I would consider your indenture.' He paused and looked critically at the hindquarters of the bull. The modelling was wrong. His eye followed the shape, but the pelvis wasn't near the surface anywhere. It was smooth and rounded like Daphne's buttocks. He grunted and without interrupting his cursory inspection of the pictures overhead, added, 'You have worked well. You're punctual and diligent. You're obedient and intelligent. Domenico and Maria tell me that you are a good boy.'

Giovanni shifted his weight nervously. His fingers were still moist but the hammering in his throat had subsided. He smiled with relief and gratification. He wanted to tell the Maestro that he wasn't always punctual – like this morning. He wanted to thank him for the praise he had received. He wished he could say that he was eager to learn to paint, to be successful, to wear a gold chain, to live in a great house, But the words weren't there.

The Maestro looked at Giovanni thoughtfully.

'Tell your father to come and see me and I will get the notary to draw up the document. If we can agree, you will come and live here. Domenico will teach you the business and perspective. Bruno will teach you anatomy and drawing. Marco will show you how to prepare canvases, primings and glues. And later, if you learn well, I will teach you painting.'

The promises and praise reeled through Giovanni's head in a bacchanalian disorder. The simple phrases he had heard tumbled around uncontrollably. It was as if the world he knew had been shaken up in a bag and spilled out at random about him.

'Well, will you tell your father what I have said?'

Giovanni struggled to keep himself upright, to find a handhold on something stable, a point of anchorage in the dizzy vortex. He clutched at the table, but as a handhold it was useless; his fingers slipped off the edge.

'Yes, Maestro. Thank you, Maestro.'

Jacopo smiled sympathetically and his mind snapped back to his own acceptance in the studio of Titian. Forty years ago he was talented and ambitious. He learned quickly and easily, and he always exceeded the standards required of him. His master's pleasure was marked with generosity and pride as the orders poured in, first from the Republic, then from elsewhere in Italy, and finally from the courts of Europe. Patrons began to specify the participation of the assistant in major works. As the warmth of adulation increased, the chill of his master's jealousy began to make his position intolerable. Reminiscence no longer gave him pleasure.

The ascent to mastery, the spores of envy settling around him like the dust of corruption, the ostracism, the isolation and the fungus of bitterness; this was the private story of his success which he had confided to no one. For him, fame had been soured by loneliness. Was that web due to be spun a second time and enmesh the child that stood before him? He looked into the excited face across the table and saw himself. The same dark eyes and olive skin, the same enquiring tilt to the head, the same diffidence, and, God help him, an even greater sensitivity.

'You can go and tell Maria, if you like.'

He turned to the letters at his elbow and, tilting the glass sphere, drew out a sheet of vellum. The beauty of the script and the flourishes of the initial letters delighted his eyes but he did not read what was written. When he looked up, Giovanni was gone.

'Maria, I'm going to be the Maestro's new apprentice,' he chanted, gyrating round her like a light crazed moth. He wound her apron into a spiral which nearly pulled her over. She revolved unsteadily and somehow managed to halt the pirouetting.

Her feeling for this motherless child was strong and genuine, but like all good mothers and grandmothers – and she had been both – she knew very well the dangers of a love expressed in overindulgence. Her love was demonstrated in responsible concern and in gentle petting which most boys of his age would have found embarrassing or suffocating. He didn't mind acting the part of her infant. In fact, he rather liked it.

Their mutual affection was never more cheerfully enjoyed than it was at this moment. Each felt the comfort of fulfilment and each was invigorated with the promise of the future. Instinctively, they submerged themselves in each other, sharing a common joy in secret. Silently, they swayed together like a mother and child.

Never in those four yawning years had Giovanni known a happiness like this. The sun had risen inside him, warm and bright. He felt secure again and strong, strong enough to support the frail woman who clung to him. Time and sorrow had melted away in the warmth of their contact and affection.

Giovanni' father was pleased to hear the news, and said so. He squeezed his son's shoulder to reinforce the satisfaction he felt, but could not communicate.

'I'll see Maestro Jacopo tomorrow or the day after,' he said.

But later that evening, he loosened his belt against the ravages of Sophenisba's prodigious meal and announced that Giovanni was to be apprenticed to the second greatest painter in Venice, perhaps even the greatest, since Titian was now very old. His tongue was lubricated by the wine, and the rein of his pride loosened by congenial company. He forecast that one day his son would be surrounded by servants and be rowed in his own gilded gondola, patronised by the nobility as the Maestro was today.

'Giovanni is a good boy,' he added. 'It wouldn't be right for him to do heavy work, or to fight, or to work in a rat-infested ship with brutal men. He's like his mother – gentle and delicate, too refined for this world…'

His voice tapered away, heavy with wine and reminiscence. They waited for him to go on, but he had nothing more to say. The moment of silent remembrance that followed was desecrated by Sophenisba, who crowed like a cockerel declaring his potency to an impotent world.

'Poor little sod!' she cackled. 'How's he going to manage if he's like his mother? She couldn't say "go" to a mouse in her own kitchen.'

Sophenisba's candour was often tactless and even cruel, and this ill-timed observation was rewarded by a well-timed, well-aimed clout across her massive stern from her husband. The fat of her arms and chins recorded the itinerary of the shock waves seconds later.

'It's a good thing we're not all the same,' Luca bawled at her. 'I'm only fit to row a boat, and you're only fit to mattress a man.

Giovanni is going to be a painter, and that needs more skill and patience than we'll ever have.' He looked at Giovanni. 'We're all proud of you, lad,' he said softly. 'Don't take any notice of my old cow; even if she can cook better than anyone else in Venice.'

Giovanni was going to say something, but before the thought could be transposed into words, Sophenisba recovered her wits and her equilibrium and turned on Luca, her breasts like a battering ram.

'Old cow indeed! May the Archangel Michael geld you this very night,' she screamed. 'Or perhaps he did it five years ago, for all the good on are to me.'

Luca allowed this to pass. She was fiercest when she was lying. Satisfied that she had won the bout, she quietened and started to pile the dishes on the corner of the table. It was time to be magnanimous. She patted Giovanni's head and lowered her lips to his ear.

'Take no notice of me. Your mother was a saint and an angel, the only good woman in the parish. When she was taken, I cried for her more than I cried for my own babies; and that's the truth.' The acid tang of her sweat stung Giovanni's nostrils and destroyed the sincerity of her confidence. She crossed herself and her lips moved in silence. She seemed pacified by her confession. She finished clearing the table and emptied the flagon into the men's cups equally. The episode was closed.

'You will still come and see us when you're living in that grand palazzo, won't you,' Luca stated. There was no hint of questioning in his voice.

'Of course I will.' He studied the firm brown hand that gripped the cup. The black hairs curled from his fingers and round his wrist. The tendons branched out, each one terminating in a perfectly modelled knuckle. Blue veins meandered under the skin in a network of pulsating canals. He glanced at his own. It was like a girl's, and he despised his tender body and the fourteen years of wear and tear it evinced.

Luca put his cup to his mouth and threw back his head to drain the contents in one mouthful. It was a natural gesture of masculine power and casual dignity. He banged the cup on the table, swallowed and held out his hand to Giovanni, who took it rather sheepishly.

'Good luck, lad,' he said, making a small, but eloquent nod of the head that signified both pride and envy.

Giovanni's father, Gentile, was apprehensive about his interview with Jacopo Robusti, whom he had met only briefly before. In the first place, he was overawed by the reputation of the great man; his business as a clerk to a cloth merchant did not provide much opportunity to meet the illustrious. And secondly, he was really too poor to pay the premium normally demanded when indentures were drawn up.

As a father, he had done what he could for his only son. He had taught him to read and write, an accomplishment he believed would be useful when the time came for the boy to find employment. But by nature, he was quiet and reserved, and the pain of his bereavement had made him even more withdrawn, so much so that he had no affinity with children and no patience for their natural exuberance. When his brother had suggested that Giovanni might go to live in his house and be looked after by his wife, he was both relieved and grateful that a responsibility which he could not fulfil should be taken up by others more experienced and more capable.

Father and son met fairly frequently, but there was very little they had in common, and each reminded the other of the early and tragic death which afflicted them both. Everyone observed that there was no warmth in the relationship, and Gentile was deeply aware of his emotional aridity, but was powerless to irrigate it with open affection. Nevertheless, he was conscious of his parental duty to see to the boy's future and safeguard his interests as long as he was able.

Domenico met him at the door and welcomed him generously. 'Thank you for coming. My father wishes to talk with you about Giovanni, as I expect you know, but he is with a patron at the moment, so perhaps you would like some wine while you wait.'

'Thank you, sir. That is very kind of you.'

Domenico poured two goblets and offered one to Gentile.

'Saluté!'

'Saluté!'

'We all hope you will agree to Giovanni's apprenticeship here. He is a good boy and everyone likes him enormously.'

'It's kind of you to say so, sir.' He sipped again to conceal his awkwardness.

'This is a busy studio, and there will always be plenty for him to do.'

Gentile had neither knowledge nor experience of the working of a studio, but he did not wish to betray his ignorance. What he had picked up from Giovanni was too fragmentary to give him much confidence. There was nothing for him to say. He sipped again.

Domenico sensed the man's discomfort and chatted on about trivial matters until Jacopo appeared.

'Father, this is Giovanni's father.'

Jacopo advanced vastly, holding out a hand of greeting.

'Good morning to you, sir,' he said warmly, 'I am pleased to see you again. It was good of you to come so promptly.'

'Good morning, Maestro.'

'I'm glad you have had some refreshment. I think I will join you.'

He refilled Gentile's and poured himself a glass.

'Now, let's get down to business. I am sure your time is as precious as mine.'

He settled himself at his desk and moved the correspondence and the blue glass weight to make room for his goblet.

'I'm not sure how much you know of the legal side of the matter, but we can come to that later, if you like,' he began. 'The important thing is that I would very much like your son to be my apprentice. He has proved to be a splendid worker, quite the best I've ever had. He's conscientious, quiet and courteous; three vital qualities, but there is something else, more difficult to define. I believe he has a real aptitude for the work, and if I'm right, he might go very far in this trade. It's possible that, one day, he may continue my work when I am gone.'

He looked at Gentile seriously.

'Well, Maestro, I am most surprised to hear you say that, and I am sure he could not have a better master. I hope you are right.'

'Of course, it's only a guess and I could be wrong, but he has a remarkable sensitivity coupled with a disciplined mind, and that is rare in men, but common in great artists.'

Gentile had no way of knowing whether or not this was true, but he accepted it as fact confidently and without question. Furthermore, he had already observed the combination in the Maestro.

'You would want him to come and live here, I believe,' he said.

'That is customary and convenient, but I understand that you are a widower and may not want to part with him.'

'Giovanni does not live with me. After my wife died, my brother and sister-in-law took him in. Their children were grown up and the arrangement suited us all.'

'I see,' said Jacopo, tightening his index finger around his beard, 'so you would have no objection to him living in this house?'

'None whatever, Maestro. It would be very good for him, I'm sure.'

'And when do you suppose he could move in?'

'Just as soon as you please.'

'That's fine!'

Gentile wanted to ask about the life and training of a painter's apprentice, but judged that it would seem impertinent.

'Of course, you may see your son as often as you like. We do not keep our apprentices chained to the wall, you know.'

'How much time off would he get, Maestro? I wouldn't want to interrupt his work, of course, but we do like to meet once a week.'

'The day begins at six o'clock, eight in winter. The morning ends at midday, and we rest until three, two in winter, and then we work on till the light dies. Of course, we don't work on Sundays and Feast Days. But here, we don't keep very regular hours, and as long as the apprentices get through their work, we don't expect them to stick to the clock. My son, Domenico, whom you met, runs the studio and is responsible for the apprentices, and he's more punctilious than me, but not much. We're an easygoing bunch.'

'Maestro, I am a poor man and I cannot pay you the premium

for the indenture…'

'That doesn't matter,' Jacopo interrupted. 'I don't need payment; any nominal sum will keep the lawyers happy. Make it as little as you like.'

'That is most generous of you, Maestro, and I appreciate it. I will, however, pay for his keep, just as I do now. I don't expect you to train him and feed him and house him for nothing.'

'Look, sir,' said Jacopo, leaning forward and spreading his fingers, 'there are five assistants, two apprentices, my wife, two daughters…' he paused, having run out of fingers for his computation, 'myself and four servants living in this house, so feeding one small boy won't make any difference. I appreciate your offer, but I cannot accept it.'

Gentile was struck by the Maestro's generosity and candour. He had no misgivings about entrusting his son's future to such a man, who could teach him much more than the art of painting.

'I'll get the document drawn up right away and I'll send you a message by Giovanni when they are ready for us to sign.'

They shook hands again, testifying to mutual admiration and gratitude, and in token of a mutually beneficial agreement which only had to be legalised by a scrap of parchment.

Apprenticed Pair

Much to his surprise, Giovanni found that he was not the only apprentice to be taken into the studio. The Maestro's daughter, Marietta, appeared shortly after the indenture was signed and cut. It was a domestic rather than a legal arrangement, for Jacopo had two sons as assistants, and he was determined to maintain his workshop as a family business as far as possible.

His own father was a dyer by trade and all his children, except Jacopo, had participated in the work, enjoying an atmosphere of relaxed gaiety which they accepted as commonplace. The attraction and benefits of such an arrangement had been part of his upbringing, and the formality and imposed discipline of Titian's studio had confirmed his predilection for a family enterprise.

He often repeated his favourite maxim to his children, 'The only good discipline is self-discipline, and that is a pleasure, not a burden.'

Marietta understood this as an injunction, rather than from experience. A facet of her nature was wild and wilful, and her good intentions were often eclipsed by exuberance. Jacopo found it necessary to restrain her quite frequently, but he did so with reluctance and lenience.

On the morning he brought her into the studio to meet his assistants and her fellow apprentices, she darted round the room giggling and prying into everything, more out of idle curiosity than genuine interest. She lifted all the stoppers from the oil jars and left them askew, she spilt the spirit, dipped her fingers into the pigments and demolished a lay figure. When her father saw that her skirt was gashed with crimson paint, his patience was overwhelmed by exasperation.

'Young woman!' he bawled, 'sit down and stop thrashing around.' She sat instantly. 'You've caused more havoc in five minutes than Giovanni has in five months, or will do in five years.

If you are going to be a useful part of this workshop, you must remember, first, to be quiet; second, to do as you are told by everyone, including the boy; third, to walk – this is not a stadium or a ballroom; and fourth, God forgive me, to wear *breeches*!'

Marietta followed the catalogue of instructions calmly, nodding in acquiescence and trying to commit them all to memory, until he reached the final point. Her dignity, her childhood training and her whole nature would be disgraced. Her hands shot to her cheeks in an involuntary gesture of outraged modesty. Her femininity would have been less threatened if she had been required to wear nothing at all. Jacopo had delivered a double volley which annihilated Marietta and demonstrated his total authority.

'Marco, go and get her a pair of breeches that one of you has grown out of.'

The smirk on her brother's face was almost as humiliating as her father's callousness. She pouted and her lip quivered.

'I will not have a prima donna in my workshop. Now, take off that dress, and your petticoats.'

Dutifully, she turned to go to the door, gathering up her precious skirts in front of her.

'Do it here and now,' he insisted.

She glanced at the faces around her; the men's were amused, her father's resolute and Giovanni's flaming with embarrassment. In his alone was any indication of sympathy. Her natural defiance drained away and tears filled her eyes.

Jacopo interpreted them as tears of contrition, and he regretted his severity. He had always found the tenderness of women irresistible; it was a flaw in his masculinity which was often exploited by Marietta's mother and his sisters many years ago. He could not deny his remorse.

'All right, then, go behind the screen. But in future, remember that you won't be treated differently from Giovanni.'

Marietta unfastened the stiff bodice and wriggled out of her dress. She bent to step out of her petticoats. The under bodice fell loosely in front of her and she peered through the neck, between her breasts and down to her belly. The same curiosity that had infuriated her father had returned and her attention was absorbed in her own body. She stroked her hips and stretched her back in an ecstasy of self-approbation. Her neck strained backwards, and facing the ceiling, she saw above her head the undulating form of a nymph. An arm was raised to grasp the branch of a tree, the fingers of the other decorously clutched a white veil that looped up to her groin, revealing as much as it concealed. Below her knees, a brown faun sprawled lasciviously, one hand reaching up to grasp the hand that held the delicate veil. His pointed ears were stiff against black curls.

Marietta identified with the erotic image and copied the nymph's pose with affected grace. She closed her eyes as the sensation of desire transported her beyond the ceiling to an ancient grove where lecherous fauns peered through the leaves. Demented by her beauty and their lust, they fought over her, their grinning mouths salivating as she lay mute and helpless.

She became semi-conscious in her self-induced darkness. Her spirit floated freely, and from above she looked down on her own nakedness and desperate vulnerability. It was the most thrilling experience she knew.

Suddenly, the breeches were thrown over the screen. The laces flicked across her face. She screamed at the shock of her collision with reality. Had her fantasy been observed? Reality was unkind to her. She was vulnerable here too, but not to the gorgeous violence of her carnal delights. That familiar dream world was very precious to her, for there, she was always mature, always successful. But in fact, she was awkward, small and silly, floundering in situations which adults seemed to have fashioned for their gratification and her discomfiture.

She hoisted the breeches up her legs and found, to her surprise, that her buttocks were parted by the seam. It was hard and inflexible, not moulded by, but moulding her form. The piquancy was doubled when she pulled them tight in front. She recalled the forgotten pleasure of riding a broomstick in the courtyard. Her fears of indignity were groundless after all and she revelled in the generosity of this unexpected compensation. The cloth stretched taut around her, its support pressed in on her thighs and torso like a new glove. She tucked in the under bodice and tightened the knots at her waist. She was enclosed in a vice of voluptuous discomfort.

It was with pride, not the mortification she had expected, that she presented herself for inspection.

'You make a pretty boy,' said her father, relieved that his harshness had not been too severe. The men looked up from their work and nodded in approval. Marco dismissed a ribald comment, sensing that the situation was fragile. Giovanni was mystified by the transformation. Before, she had seemed remote and unapproachable, and he couldn't imagine how trey could work together, bound by equality, but now, her jaunty gait, her brown arms and saucy expression were curiously magnetic.

She turned neatly to display her back, shook her hair and looked over her shoulder, her legs apart and her fingers drumming impatiently on her hips. She waited for another compliment, but none came.

Words evaded Giovanni. His reticence permitted a smile in which Marietta read more than approval, and this time she was right.

The exhibition was interrupted by Domenico whose instinct for industry was never diverted by trivia for very long. He faced Giovanni.

'We need some more colours from the Rialto,' he said. 'I have written a list for you. You'd better take Marietta and show her where old Giulio's shop is.' He handed over the paper and added, 'There's quite a lot, so you'll need a basket.'

They went down to the kitchen together to find one. Maria greeted them with mock deference. It was she who had found the breeches for Marco.

'What do you two young gentlemen want?' she enquired. Marietta giggled uncontrollably. 'I don't believe my eyes,' she went on. 'You're like two eggs from the same nest. But you will need a stitch or two in that bodice, young lady. If you hiccup, you'll pop out.' Marietta stuck out her chest and shook her breasts at the old woman.

'I don't want it sewn up,' she protested. 'I like it as it is.'

'You look like a courtesan,' sneered the indignant Maria.

'I don't care.'

'But your father will. You're a slut!'

'And you're a silly old woman!'

Giovanni busied himself choosing a basket while the two parried and riposted on a subject he was neither qualified nor inclined to comment upon. Above all, he feared a demand for support from either of them.

In the colour man's shop the leather bags of raw pigment were weighed and laid in the basket in the listed order; four bags of lead white, the heaviest of them all; hard chunks of yellow ochre and red ochre; the famous Venetian red, two bags each; one each of burnt sienna, malachite green and madder; one bag of ready ground ivory black, light and fine; and most precious of all, a small bag of ultramarine powdered lapis lazuli in a white kid bag, its gathered neck whipped tight with silver wire which was braided into a loop around an ivory plug. The plug hung loose on a virgin bag, but was provided to bung the pouring hole once the skin was punctured.

Marietta was bored by the proceedings in the dismal shop until the ultramarine was produced. She grabbed at the bag and studied it.

'Isn't that pretty,' she said, placing the leather against her cheek.

'Be careful with that,' pleaded Giovanni. 'It costs four times more than all the rest together.'

'What is it then?'

'It's the finest, most beautiful blue there is. You can make the colour of the sky when it's mixed with white; or on its own, the colour of the Virgin's robe. However you use it, it will never change its colour. It will last for ever. When it is ground into varnish, it dries like blue glass from Murano.'

The information he had picked up from the studio gushed out in a torrent of undigested facts. Marietta was impressed, but she only wanted to know what colour was concealed in the tiny bag. Somehow she had gained some measure of its value from Giovanni's enthusiasm and knowledge.

'Can I see inside?'

'No, of course not. Your father would be furious if the bag was punctured. But you'll see when we get back to the studio.'

'Can I carry it, then?'

'Oh yes, if you like. But don't drop it, or I will get a beating.'

'Who beats you?' she asked with real concern.

'Well, no one has yet,' he confessed, 'but I don't want to find out, so be careful.'

Giovanni stuck Giulio's account into his belt and they climbed the Rialto Bridge again. They paused at the centre of the wooden arch and looked along the sweep of noble buildings. Arch and column were bound together with gilded tracery. Red and ochre alternated with inlaid marbles veined with green and blue. Dark windows were framed in stone. Ogival arches flickered like frozen flames around oval quatrefoils. Armorial bearings tricked out in gold and tinctures, and attendant mooring posts which echoed the tinctures in spirals. Golden finials and elaborate lamps flanked the wave-washed steps. Arbitrary patterns of reflected light animated the sheer walls and flashed in the dark shadows under arch and lintel.

Marietta pointed to the gold and white façade of the Palazzo Soranzo, frescoed with lively figures.

'My father painted that one when he was young. Twice he stepped back on the scaffolding and fell into the canal.' She started to snigger. 'And he can't sw—'

Their heads rolled together, speechless with laughter at the Maestro's misfortune. Weak and breathless from mild hysteria, they watched the boats passing below. Some carried huge blocks of Istrian stone, the crystals sparkling like sugar in the sun; some, long baulks of timber nearing the end of their journey from the mainland. Another, heavy with fruit neatly stacked in pyramids, was rowed by four men singing a bawdy song. Each sang a line in sequence – a parody of Venetian antiphony.

'I squeezed her lemons in my hand…' sang the bass.

'She trod my grapes and pressed the wine…' answered the tenor.

'I ploughed and sowed and reaped all day…'

The third voice rang hollow as the boat slid beneath their feet. Marietta giggled and raised a pert eyebrow at Giovanni from the crook of her arm. The rough joke was shared, each moulting a little of the down of innocence.

A friendship was launched from the slipway of modest guilt.

A familiar voice hailed from the water, 'Hi, Giovanni, what are you doing up there?' It was Luca, his oar trailing idly in the water, curling a hollow wave on the surface.

'We're going back to the Maestro's.'

'Want a ride?'

'Yes, please, Luca – come on, Marietta. It's my friend, Luca.'

They raced to the other side of the bridge to a small platform towards which Luca steered his boat. A twist of his oar and the boat turned alongside and stopped. He held out his free hand to help them aboard.

The long, rippling hair and dancing bodice of his second passenger contradicted the breeches and sleeveless shirt of the boy he had seen on the bridge. Luca was confused.

'This is my friend, Marietta,' explained Giovanni. 'She is the Maestro's daughter. We're apprentices together in the studio.'

'Does he want you to be a boy?' asked Luca.

He struck out into the middle of the channel. Marietta settled herself on a roll of canvas, her ankles crossed under her like a folding stool.

'Well, yes. You see, skirts are a nuisance in a studio, and I got mine covered in paint, so...' She shaded her eyes against the blinding light behind him.

'So you had to dress like Giovanni.' Luca smiled at the simplicity of the explanation. '*That* makes sense, now.' He smiled and rowed on. 'But how on earth does your father know which of you is which?' he asked, staring pointedly at the bodice. He feathered the oar and looked at them quizzically.

The trio's shouts of laughter echoed back across the water. Marietta slipped off her canvas perch and lay convulsed in the bottom of the boat.

Domenico checked the contents of the basket against the list and recorded the cost in his ledger. He explained the need to be neat and methodical, but he suspected that the significance of his advice was lost on the two whose attention seemed to be trapped by a private joke.

'Well, you appear to be getting on together,' he said. 'Bruno is going to give you some instruction in drawing, so run along.'

Giovanni forgot the jokes they had shared. The promise of a lesson from the bearded one cut off the past at a stroke.

Bruno sat between them and demonstrated how free lines of different lengths should be made with movements from the wrist, the elbow and the shoulder. Then he showed how the beginning, the middle or the end of the line could be accented by varying the pressure of the charcoal. They practised in silence, interrupted only by Bruno's advice and approval. The only sound was the soft hiss of the charcoal. He showed them how to erase lines with the herl of a feather which lifted off the dust without smudging. For two hours they were absorbed in the adventure of discovery as Bruno coaxed them along in easy exercises. They graduated to drawing clumps of reeds and water birds. But he demanded that every inferior line should be drawn again till it satisfied his eye. 'That's not right,' he would say, pointing at the offence with the feather. 'Do it again.'

Marietta tired first, and although Giovanni could go on till the light faded, Bruno insisted that they clean up, first the work area which was thick with black dust, then themselves.

On the ground floor was a washing room with basins, pitchers, brass cans for hot water and a huge copper bowl with a fire beneath it. Strings of clean washing hung from the ceiling; shirts, petticoats, stockings and bodices hung like banners at the regatta. Giovanni removed the wooden lid from the copper and baled two scoopfuls of steaming water into a basin, which he carried carefully to a marble shelf.

'There,' he said, 'you first, Marietta.'

She drew in her stomach and pulled her bodice out of the top of her breeches, crossed her arms and pulled it over her head. She paused with her arms high, exposing her taut bosom and armpits for Giovanni's approval. She watched his face change to absorbed admiration as his eyes ran over her skin, pausing occasionally in mute astonishment.

'Do you think I'm pretty?' she asked ingenuously. Her face and arms were streaked with dark smudges, a black aureole circled her left eye. She threw the bodice on the floor and waited for his inspection to be completed. She stretched her arms wide, drawing her breasts further apart. Giovanni felt the pulse again in his throat.

'I think you are the most beautiful thing I have ever seen.'

She flew at him like a gliding bird, and on impact, threw her arms round his neck, gripping him fast, pressing her mouth into his face in a frenzy. Her grip relaxed as she felt the coma of desire and desirability liquidate her. His hands slid up her back to steady her as he felt the strength fail in her body. The nuzzling, the clumsy kissing and the uncultured passion covered them both with shining black smears.

'Wash me, Giovanni,' she said feebly, 'and I'll wash you.'

With maternal tenderness they sponged each other's bodies, each marvelling at the revelation of the other's secrets. There was a sacramental dignity, a languid ritual of discovery in which the purest sensual pleasure was offered and accepted in silence, witnessed only by the washing.

Their friendship, which had germinated in guilt, had thrown its first exotic bloom. Their affection was like a yellow lily, a new flower appeared each day. Their discoveries in the studio were matched by mutual discoveries in secret places. Their artistic and amorous experiments grew in parallel more assured, more elegant, more harmonious.

To Parnassus

Their innocence was damaged, but not defiled and they were unaware of any need to conceal their mutual affection from the men. Their susceptibility to and consideration for each other, their expressive glances and their transparent joy in being together would have been obvious to the most boorish observer, but their lives were passed in the company of those whose appreciation of natural beauty and subtlety was burnished by constant use.

The studio had a penchant for nicknames. The precedent of the Maestro, who was known outside as 'the little dyer', or Tintoretto, undoubtedly fostered the fancy. Domenico was affectionately called Tintorettino, or more usually, Tino. Marco was facetiously dubbed Tintorettissimo, but that was too unwieldy to be used. The name he earned when he first joined the studio was 'the tap', from a noticeable weakness of his bladder, so the soubriquet Rubinetto had remained with him, even though the affliction had not. There was nothing subtle or witty about the nicknames given to Marietta and Giovanni. Their inseparability demanded a single name for daily use, and 'the doves' they had become, not from a conscious decision, but from a tacit recognition that no other was appropriate. They responded with childish delight, and they cooed at each other for the entertainment of the rest. Jacopo was equally amused by their imitation, and he took pleasure at the joy and tenderness they personified, as much as at their progress in the studio.

He had discussed a plan with Marco which would test their ability and application, and he had decided that the time was right to verify his own judgement.

'I have a job for you doves,' he began. 'You've been here for two years now, and it's about time you did some real work.'

Marietta scowled indignantly. 'We work very hard every day, don't we, Giovanni?'

'Yes, Maestro, we do. We thought you were satisfied...'

'Domenico said only yesterday that we were the best apprentices you've ever had,' protested Marietta.

'Domenico was quite right. Now, before you get angry with me, listen again to what I said: "It's about time you did some *real* work."'

Marietta was about to interrupt again, but Giovanni, sensitive to the Maestro's inflexion, put his hand over Marietta's mouth. She regretted her haste and waited for her father to continue.

'As you know, Marco usually does all the cassoni orders, but we've got a lot of work on at the moment, and another order has come in for a marriage chest. There's not much time to do the job, and Marco is busy working on the ceiling panels for San Rocco. So I thought you ought to do it between you.'

They looked at each other, eyes and mouths open in surprise.

'Do you mean on our own?' Marietta asked.

'Well, you can have some help if you need it, and I will want to see your cartoons before you start. But apart from that, the job is yours. There are five square panels and two oblongs, they will be delivered tomorrow. But there's no reason why you shouldn't start on the designs today. Do the squares first, because we don't know the proportion of the lid.'

Marietta didn't wait for him to finish. As physical and impulsive as ever, she wound her arms around his neck and covered his face with frantic kisses.

'Thank you. Thank you,' she whispered, punctuating each fresh assault. She knocked his cap awry and he pushed her away gently to regain his composure.

'I'm glad you are pleased, but there's no need to eat me.'

Marietta still had a huge residue of gratitude and excitement which remained unexpressed, so she poured it on Giovanni, whom she knew to have a greater capacity for her rapture than her father.

Cassoni orders were bread and butter jobs in a workshop like Tintoretto's. The Maestro rarely, if ever, painted them himself once he was established, even though they were accredited to him. Marco enjoyed the smaller scale they offered and the studio's current reputation in this field hung entirely on his ability.

The finest cassoni were the marriage chests which contained the bride's clothes and linen, and, sometimes, the portable items of her dowry. They were carried from her parents' house as she left it, arriving in her new home with her goods and, often, her fortune. The ceremony of which they formed a part and the public gaze they were subjected to had encouraged a richness in their workmanship and decoration which reflected the prestige of the bride's family. If the families were armigerous, their coats of arms formed a prominent feature of the decorative scheme. Time and custom had conferred upon them the status of works of art.

The confidence of the Maestro and the practical way he had chosen to show it was a generous reward for their efforts in the studio. But the thrill of working together on something permanent, something of commercial value and something that would bear the name of Tintoretto was overwhelming.

'Let's decide what we are going to do,' said Giovanni.

He remembered the urgency and he knew that Marietta's excitement might be tamed by a methodical, workmanlike approach.

'I can't think clearly,' she confessed.

'Well, we can do something traditional or something new.'

Mythological subjects were customary, and often they illustrated the amorous adventures of classical deities and mythical beings, surrounded by cherubs.

'What about Venus and Adonis,' he suggested. 'Or Paris and Helen.'

'...Or Dido and Aeneas,' volunteered Marietta.

Their ideas were hardly stimulating, and before long, a cloud of gloom settled over them which obscured their enthusiasm and their confidence. The more they thought, the more mundane their ideas seemed.

'Let's walk along to the molo,' said Giovanni.

'If you like.'

Their frustration was a depressing anticlimax to the Maestro's suggestion. Imaginative impotence was a chilling novelty.

'I suppose we had better talk to Marco.' Marietta blurted out the conclusion that had stalked their floundering imagination with such hungry persistence.

'Don't let's talk about it any more. We'll decide what to do later.'

They walked across the campo in silence, seeing neither the people who were there nor the colour and grace of the buildings. They were impervious to their accustomed pleasures. Without noticing, they walked through a flock of pecking pigeons who scattered irritably before their feet and closed in behind them. Marietta put her arm round Giovanni's back and fitted her head under his chin like a violin craving to be played.

They crossed over a small bridge and into a dark alley that smelled stale and damp. The paving was green and moist. They were alerted by their sliding feet. Giovanni stopped and lifted Marietta's head gently upwards from the pleats of his doublet. Her cheeks and lashes were wet and a strand of hair was caught in the corner of her mouth. He placed his mouth over hers and breathed into her body. He felt her ribs expand against his as her lungs gathered his air. They exchanged breath silently and rhythmically, obliterating the hostile world, relinquishing life.

The alley turned suddenly and opened into a small campo full of light and people. One side of the square was filled by the simple façade of a church. In the doorway stood a smiling couple, the girl dressed in white, her hair enmeshed in a golden net, encrusted with pearls and small white flowers. She clung to her new husband whose doublet hung with coloured ribbons. He kissed her forehead and the crowd responded with encouraging murmurs. He kissed her again on the mouth amid delighted laughter. A vulgar call floated across the jostling heads. Small children scurried around the steps gathering handfuls of white petals. A path was cleared through the crowd and the pair walked down the aisle of joyful neighbours to a waiting gondola.

Marietta managed a tearful smile which registered some gratitude for the diversion rather than relief from her misery. They wandered on towards the molo, untouched by the charm or the high spirits of the occasion. By the time they reached San Marco, their introspection had grown less morbid. The variety and ebullience of their city had begun to work its subtle magic, enriching and uplifting.

In the piazzetta, their pace quickened imperceptibly, their stride became more elastic as if in concert with the unbroken arcades of the ducal palace. At ground level, the rhythm was stately and processional; above, the ogee arches doubled the tempo, allegretto; at the top, the diapered rose and white marble shimmered in a brilliant vivace. Giovanni suddenly stopped and gripped her shoulders.

'I've got an idea.' His eyes were wide with enthusiasm. 'Let's make Venice the setting for the pairs of lovers – not mythical ones, but real ones.'

'Like us,' Marietta added, infected with excitement.

'Yes, and the bride and groom back there.'

'And instead of cherubs, we'll have doves…'

'Grey and white ones against an azure sky. And we'll use gold leaf…'

'Like church pictures in the old days…'

'Carpaccio and gold.'

'We'll gild all the details on the buildings.'

'The lid can have its setting right here.' He waved an arm in an arc around the piazzetta. 'It's the right shape.'

'And inside the lid we can have two lovers lying together on a marriage bed. They ought to fit too,' she giggled.

'We'll paint the coat of arms in perspective on the pavement of the Piazza San Marco, as if it were inlaid in pietre dure.'

'With the bride standing on her family's side and the groom on his.'

'Real portraits of them.'

'They'd have to be very small, like miniatures.'

'We could try.'

They did not get as far as the molo. Their problem solved, they headed back to the studio, exchanging ideas, refining them, seeing each one in imagination and locking them together like marquetry patterns.

They started to draw as soon as they got back. Giovanni ruled the squares while Marietta gathered chalks and quills and some meat pasties from the kitchen. The studio was empty. All the men were at San Rocco. They began by sketching the architectural backgrounds in red, crisp and precise, and over the grid of wall, door and window, string course, roof and cornice, they placed pairs of figures, male and female, slender and pliant. The contrasting black chalk lines owed much to Bruno's example; the ethereal figures floated serenely, transfused by love. The doves hung in the sky like wisps of cloud. All five square designs were completed as the light in the studio faded. They tidied up in silence. The conviction that their work was good could not be strengthened or qualified by words.

In her small chamber at the top of the house, they lay together, fatigued and fulfilled. Giovanni caressed her hair in the dark. The quiet house, the gentle movements of his hands lulled Marietta's vibrant spirit into a cradle of tranquillity.

Giovanni was unable to keep any private thought in his head, unless it would cause her pain. All others were shared.

'I wonder if the Maestro will like our roughs.' There was no answer. Marietta's eyes were closed in sleep, and contentment had left a trace of a smile at the corners of her lips.

By the light of a new day, the drawings seemed less successful. The contrast between the figures and the buildings was abrupt and crude. They wished now that they had used just one colour instead of two; perhaps then the disunity might not be so obvious. The figures themselves seemed too insubstantial, too mannered. Their feet hovered above the ground like stockings hanging on a line. They tried to correct some of the shortcomings before the Maestro came in, but their success was only partial and some of the erasures were messy. They were disappointed and fearful of the criticism they knew would be justified.

Jacopo leafed through the drawings without saying anything. Their anxiety became unbearable, and Marietta, forthright and yet apprehensive, announced, 'They're awful, aren't they?'

He sat back and studied the doves, sensitive to the poignancy of their feelings. 'No, they're not awful – a bit clumsy, perhaps, but your biggest mistake was that you tried too hard. You tried to make beautiful drawings of your roughs, and that's not what they're for. They are meant to help you think more clearly. Roughs are thoughts on paper, that's all.'

He shuffled through them again. 'But these have plenty of

energy and they are full of genuine feelings. I like your idea for the heraldry; I've never seen it done like that before. It's good, very good. You will have to get the figures and the backgrounds more…' he paused and made a gesture with his hands, dovetailing his fingers, '…more integrated. That's your main problem.'

'We wanted to use gold leaf on the buildings,' said Giovanni, 'but won't that make matters worse?'

'It might,' said Jacopo, 'but you can use a colour link to help you. That is, if you use ochre in the buildings, put a bit in the figures; or pick up the pink of the flesh in the walls behind. Then it should work. It looks worse in the drawing than it will when it's painted.'

'Do you mean we can go ahead?' asked Marietta.

'Of course. Don't worry about the mistakes in the roughs. You can get rid of them in the cartoons. No, I think you have done very well.'

The two were relieved that their work was not a total fiasco, and they were thankful that they had not received the rebuke they had expected. But the Maestro had not finished.

'I had the same sort of problem with figures and architecture when I did *The Legend of St Mark*. You might go along to the Scuola di San Marco and have a look at them. The custodian is a kind man and he will let you see them. There are all sorts of tricks in two of them; and in one, I don't think I was clever enough. But go and see what you think and we'll talk about it later.'

They were consoled and disarmed by this admission of doubt. If the Maestro had them, perhaps they need not feel too downcast.

The custodian introduced them to Tommaso Rangone, physician and scholar, and Chancellor of the Confraternity. It was he who had commissioned the young Tintoretto to paint a magnificent canvas of St Mark rescuing a slave, which he then presented to the Scuola. At the time, it aroused admiration for its excellence and opposition for its modernity, but the opposition faded before the adulation of established connoisseurs, and later, the Scuola had commissioned further paintings of their patron saint, at Rangone's suggestion. These were strikingly more modern in spirit than the original picture.

Rangone greeted them handsomely. He was a small, nervous man whose hands fluttered independently of what he was saying or doing. They were never still. His body gave the impression that it was continually wriggling inside his clothes, as if animated by a maniacal puppeteer. The costume, however, maintained the dignity of its wearer's responsible position.

'Come and see the first of Maestro Tintoretto's pictures. It is superb.'

They followed him down the hall.

'There now, the Maestro was only thirty when he painted this, and I believe it is one of his finest paintings.' The hands whirled excitedly. 'Aretino thought so too. He was a brute and a libertine, but he did know a good picture when he saw it. He was the most talented ape I have ever met…' His words died with disgust. He pointed to the left corner.

'There you see the Maestro's self-portrait. Very strange! He has grown more like it as he has got older.'

It was true. Marietta and Giovanni recognised him immediately. It was as if it were painted yesterday.

'Fortunately,' he went on, 'the members didn't spot it, or there would have been a fuss about that too.'

'Was there a fuss?' asked Giovanni.

'Oh yes! Some complained that it had been painted too hastily, too roughly. They didn't like to see brush marks. Others thought the lighting was too stark. Some thought there were too many figures showing their backs, and that was an affront to their precious dignity. Such stupidity!' His head rocked violently. 'All the complaints showed the ignorance of the complainants, but there were enough of them and the Maestro took it back in contempt, and we nearly lost a great treasure. Finally, a few of us managed to persuade him to return it, and fortunately, he did.' He paused in renewed admiration. 'But you wanted to see the others, didn't you?'

He conducted them to the series depicting the legends surrounding St Mark.

'I am proud to say that it was I who persuaded the Scuola to commission these, ten… no, twelve years ago,' he twittered.

'Maestro Tintoretto painted my portrait into them as a gesture of gratitude, but the members thought it was a sacrilege and sent them back to be removed. A great pity, a great pity…' His voice trailed away, the hands flicking imaginary dust. 'I will leave you now, but call me if I can be of some further service.'

The puppeteer became more demented.

'Thank you, sir. You have been most kind,' said Giovanni.

Marietta sniggered explosively. 'Do you think he has got fleas?' she whispered to Giovanni.

'Of course he has, silly!'

She leaned against him for support.

'Shut up, Marietta! He will hear you if you don't control yourself. I wouldn't want to hurt his feelings, he has been very kind to us.'

'I know, but he is very odd, isn't he?'

'I suppose so, but he's no fool. He thinks a great deal of your father, so he cannot be that odd, can he?'

The giggling subsided.

'No, you're quite right. But I thought his head would fall off once or twice…' She sniggered again, and Giovanni could not resist a smile of agreement.

'Now, we came to look at these pictures. What did your father say? He didn't think he had been very clever in relating the figures to the architecture – was that it?'

'Yes, I think so. But what did he mean?'

'I'm not sure.'

They stood before the huge canvases which represented the finding and the removal of the body of St Mark from Alexandria. The Venetians were very proud of their patron saint and prouder that his body had lain in the basilica that bore his name since it was stolen by Venetian adventurers seven centuries ago. The great church itself had been embellished to form a worthy reliquary for the sacred remains. The piety and the patriotism of the thieves was honoured by the Scuola and recorded by Tintoretto in these dramatic pictures.

Marietta and Giovanni had not seen them before. The sharpness of the drawing and the steely colour came as a surprise to them. The figures were modelled in strong light and shade with hardly any half-tones, and their movements and gestures were more reminiscent of statues than flesh and blood. In one, an interior, the architecture behind the figures was like a stage setting made of canvas and battens. It shone with an eerie light that came from nowhere; more appropriate to a religious ecstasy than to a record of an historical event. In another, in which a noble square was drawn in immaculate perspective, the buildings were transformed to glass by a lightning flash; only the foreground figures, who were lifting the body on to a camel, were solid.

The strange spell wrought by the pictures was broken by Giovanni's whisper.

'I can see what the Maestro meant, can't you?'

'Yes, I think so. The light in the foreground doesn't match the light behind.'

'But if it did, the pictures would look pretty ordinary, wouldn't they?'

'I suppose they would.'

They discussed every aspect of the two paintings; the imbalance of the compositions, the elongated figures, the mysterious light and colour. As they left the building, they were still perplexed, still amazed and bemused by what they had seen. Giovanni summed up his understanding and his reaction rather clumsily, 'They're odd, but they work, not in spite of it, but *because* of it.'

'That's very clever of you.'

'I'm not, but your father is,' said Giovanni emphatically.

The panels were delivered and prepared during the next few days. The cartoons were finely drawn in ink and the outlines pricked with a bodkin, then the paper attached to the wood. They put a small heap of raw umber in a circle of linen and tied it up to form a pad of brown powder. The transfer of the drawing was ready to begin. This was an operation they had done many times for Marco, but they felt a special exhilaration in doing it for themselves. Gently, they dabbed the bag over the paper and the powder passed through the pinpricks, leaving a trail of brown dots on the panel. The pounced cartoons were thrown away, ragged and soiled. With a fine brush they joined the dots, redrawing the lines.

The outlines stood clear and bland on the white gesso, inviting the washing-in of the shadows and dark areas. Marco examined the work carefully and approved.

While the under painting was set in the sun to dry, they started on the sketches for the long panels of the lid. Giovanni did the one for the outside with the background filled with the arches and domes of San Marco. Marietta had persuaded him to allow her to do the secret nudes for the inside. Their problems were different and, as they searched for the best solutions, their concentration forced them further apart.

Marietta finished first. Two voluptuous figures lay contiguous in erotic suspense. The heaving rhythms of their forms were complemented by the rise and fall of the draperies which held them together securely like the setting of a jewelled crown. Each limb, each joint o the woman was supported by her partner. She seemed half-drowned in his embrace and her own passion. Marietta's body was stirred by the image she had created. She felt her breathing quicken and her legs dissolve before she had finished. The tingling sensation under her bodice distracted her and distorted the drawing. The final lines whipped across the paper like a whirlwind. It was nothing if not authentic.

She grew impatient with Giovanni who worked on at a leisurely pace, ignorant of her consuming desire. He did not notice that she had unfastened her bodice, and this irritated her. Great waves of passion pounded her; the fragile defences were swept away. She hurled the wreckage on Giovanni, clutching for something stable, yet craving for her destruction to be consummated without delay.

He was never less prepared to relieve her anguish as he was at this moment, though he had witnessed and welcomed this endearing impetuosity of hers many times before. But deprived of the overtures, the suspense and the desire, his response was totally inadequate. His gestures were clumsy and meaningless, his reaction sullen wad sterile. The butting and writhing of Marietta's body seemed grotesque. He remained limp and indifferent.

She was not so bewitched that she didn't notice the torpor of his response. Her frustration flared to anger and she beat his head with clenched fists.

'You're useless and stupid,' she screamed. 'What's the matter with you?' The battering continued with greater ferocity. 'You're loathsome. You slug, you toad!'

The words cut into Giovanni like an axe. The humiliation and the pain released something infinitely gentle inside him. He rose and placed his arms around her shoulders to restrain the flailing fists, and to enclose her in the cocoon of helplessness she revelled in. She threw back her head defiantly, her eyes and teeth clenched, her face drenched with tears. She became as rigid as Lot's wife. He buried his head and face in her neck and murmured to soothe her and reduce the awful tension.

'I'm sorry, Marietta. Forgive me. I am sorry.'

He wiped her face and preened her hair. Gradually the sobbing subsided.

'You're right,' he went on, 'I *am* useless and stupid.'

'No, you're not.'

Her contradiction brought them closer together again.

Jacopo watched the progress of the cassone with critical interest, without once interfering. Any suggestion or amendment was passed on anonymously through Marco. There was no conscious division of work, except in the two pictures for the lid. Otherwise, their techniques blended perfectly. The only distinction Jacopo could detect lay marginally in Giovanni's favour; his lines seemed a little more elegant, his colour slightly more delicate than Marietta's. Hers was more masculine, or was it more impulsive? He wasn't sure, and he gave it no thought. But there was no indication that the pictures were the work of two hands, to the casual observer at least, and that pleased him.

When the painting was finished, the panels were displayed in the studio before they were fitted into the gilded frame of the cassone. Jacopo was to give his final verdict. It was the culmination of seven weeks' concentrated labour, although the other duties they were responsible for had continued throughout. It was an occasion which they looked forward to without reservations, because they knew that the Maestro had watched their progress with approval. It was more of a celebration than a critical inspection, and there would be no formality.

The Maestro promenaded backwards and forwards in front of the row of pictures, pausing frequently to bend and investigate more closely. An ewer of wine stood on his table and a set of ruby goblets was grouped around it. His smile of approval was a smile of duality; it recorded his appreciation of what he saw and gratification that his confidence had been so handsomely vindicated.

'You have done very well,' he said at last. 'The work is quite splendid.' He poured the wine and distributed the goblets. 'You have succeeded in combining freedom with discipline, energy and repose, in a way I would not have thought possible. It's a perfect marriage of Tintoretto and Andrea Palladio. It will be a great success.'

He lifted his glass. 'Let's drink to the doves; to their talents and to their marriage, if they so choose.'

Marietta and Giovanni bathed in the showers of congratulation and hung together, unable to express their elation. Marietta broke the silence with a rippling imitation of a cooing pigeon; Giovanni returned the call amid joyous laughter. Marietta kissed her father and her brothers and then the other assistants, moving from one embrace to the next. Giovanni's back was slapped with considerable ardour and, finally, he was embraced by the Maestro himself.

'On this occasion, an important one for the studio and a crucial one for our doves,' he began formally, 'it is appropriate that I should make a gesture to show my pleasure and esteem. It should not pass unsung or unmarked by a show of reckless generosity. I want them to receive half of the payment for the work when our account is paid.'

This was a dramatic announcement and it was greeted with gasps of astonishment from everyone. Domenico looked worried.

'But that is almost a hundred ducats, Father,' he said, looking into his goblet. 'It's an awful lot of money.'

He knew all too well that his father was naive and casual about money from the way he had conducted his business before he had made Domenico responsible for the finances.

Jacopo felt good. The celebration, the wine, his unprecedented idea and his deep affection for the two young ones had made his whole being feel expansive and slightly tipsy.

'Tino doesn't think the studio can afford to forego the payment,' he said with sham pomposity, 'that's rubbish. If it were not for these two, we shouldn't have been able to do the work at all. Paolo Veronese would have got the job.'

An idea came to him.

'So if we cannot afford half, then I give them the whole. It shall be my betrothal gift, in the hope that the gift will promote the deed.'

Domenico was stunned by the chaotic logic, but he knew that his father would not admit to extravagance, and he knew that he had already said more than was prudent.

'Will you arrange that for me, Tino?'

'Yes, Father, of course.'

The Maestro put down his goblet and opened his arms, inviting his doves to share the warmth of his affection. If he was drunk, he was drunk with pleasure and sentiment, he assured himself.

As drunk as him, they complied.

The Annealing Furnace

Alone in his chamber, Giovanni recalled the events of the day. The high spirits, the praise they had received, and the satisfaction they had both enjoyed had made him aware that he belonged to a real family. He felt like a Robusti and he was treated like one. He didn't merely work here and live here – he belonged here. All he needed and all he wanted was contained within this house.

Then there was the Maestro's beneficence. There was sufficient money coming his way to dress well, to buy gifts for Marietta and to marry her. He felt enormously flattered that the Maestro should want to give him his daughter. They had talked of marriage, of course, but, until now, it had to be kept impersonal, for Giovanni could not have presumed to ask his master for his daughter's hand. Now it was offered openly and generously. He recalled the Maestro's words and the sincerity of their expression.

But what of Marietta as a wife? His love for her had never been stronger, but the incident in the studio had troubled him frequently. It was a virus that plagued his solitude. He could not resolve the complexities, the implications of that sudden realisation that his adorable Marietta was somehow coarse and ridiculous, that she was able to repel him at the very moment she advanced her love for him.

He could not talk about it to anyone. He could not divulge a secret that involved Marietta. The sacred trust could not be dishonoured. Who should he consult, anyway? His father? Luca? Bruno? A priest? He realised that this single stain on an otherwise flawless relationship must be his concern, and his alone. He tried to arrange all the facts, all the circumstances, all the emotions in order, and then to follow them like a child learning to read, however painful, however degrading the result might be. But it did not help. Like a struggling child, he recognised the words and read them, but did not understand. His mind was as black as his room.

His tormented introspection was disturbed by the sound of voices far below in the campo. He lay still to adjust himself to the abrupt change from the silent world of his forebodings to the clatter of feet and shutters, the banging of doors. He got up from his bed and opened his own shutters. The cause of the commotion was there before him. The domes and campanile of St Mark's were silhouetted against a vicious orange sky. He climbed through the window on to the roof and saw that the crenulations of the ducal palace were engulfed in flames. He ran through the house calling, 'There's a fire! Wake up! Fire!' Drowsy figures appeared in doorways. 'Hurry up! There's a fire!'

'Where is it? Here?'

'Where?'

'The ducal palace is on fire!'

Without waiting for the others, he ran out of the house, through the lanes, dodging and darting among the crowds who poured forward, as relentless as lava.

Snaking lines of men swinging buckets from hand to hand stretched between the canal and the palace. Their shouts were almost drowned by the roar of the flames and spasmodic reports that sent plumes of sparks spewing into the sky. The roof was ablaze and molten lead ran down the walls in rivers of silver. Three windows on the third floor shimmered like the mouth of a glass furnace.

Another stream of men staggered out into the piazzetta carrying chests, bundles, golden plates, candlesticks and treasures of every kind. But there was no panic. Fires were common in the city, and the organisation of able men was spontaneous and efficient.

Giovanni filled a gap in the bucket chain when an elderly man fell to the ground.

The buckets looped from arm to arm in a continuous shuttle. Very little was spilled because the chain had ample links and there was a minimum of exertion; the rhythm was maintained, so as not to overtax the volunteers. The very young and the aged were marked by new arrivals, and the chain was never broken. The men at the water's edge worked in short shifts, as did those at the face of the fire, some of whom were perilously perched atop swaying ladders.

'Looks pretty bad... doesn't it?' said the next link to Giovanni.

'It certainly... does,' he replied in rhythm. 'Do you... know if... anyone was... hurt?'

'No... I don't think... so...'

Burning and smouldering timbers which had fallen, were pushed along the pavement by men with metal shod poles to the water's edge, where they were rolled, hissing and hammering, into the canal. The men, with wet scarves wound round their faces, were silent and efficient. Those who were unprotected in this way hardly spoke, for the smoke seared throats and eyes with savage inflammation.

The contents continued to pile up on the pavement and on the molo. The city guards were responsible for their rescue and surveillance, and they too, worked in shifts, alternately bringing treasures out of the smoke-filled palace and mounting guard on them outside.

The captain of the guards and the palace superintendent managed the whole operation together, routeing the firefighters and directing the salvage teams. Their joint experience of a similar fire a few years before was invaluable and, before long, the clouds of grey smoke had been displaced by clouds of steam.

The links in the chain of buckets were exhausted after a long night of toil. Some collapsed and slept in the piazzetta, some staggered home to rest. None was paid for his exertions or his civic devotion. It was an obligation for every robust, healthy man to serve his city and save her from the perils of fire, and each accepted his responsibility without question, confident that his neighbours would come to his assistance at any time if he should need it.

At daybreak, the smouldering ruins were not as extensive as expected by those who had witnessed the volcanic fury of the previous night. Much was destroyed, but much had been spared. The walls were intact, but the Collegio, the Senate, the Great Council Chamber were gone, and with them, the countless works of art they contained.

At noon, the Doge and the Assembly met in the Chamber of the Council of Ten, which had been saved. The meeting was brief. It was resolved to rebuild as quickly as possible and to make the renovations even more splendid than before. All the best artists, architects and craftsmen were to be commissioned at once to prepare for the enormous task. Letters bearing the great seal of the Republic were penned and dispatched to the architects da Ponte, Palladio and Scamozzi; to the painters Titian, Tintoretto and Veronese, and to the craftsmen Bello and Sorte of Verona. Next day, a dozen more were sent.

Jacopo smiled when he discovered that his old maestro, Titian, had received a similar letter as a gesture of courtesy. He was over ninety and too frail to undertake work on this scale, and, furthermore, his few remaining assistants were a poor lot. The rivalry that had existed between them for years had waned with the old man's advancing fragility. Jacopo knew that all the best work would be shared between himself and Paolo Veronese, but he had one enormous advantage over Paolo, and that was the speed of his production. He had demonstrated this more than once in competition with other painters. While they were preoccupied with their sketches, he had completed and installed the finished work, presenting the patrons with an insolent fait accompli. There would be no need for such tricks now. There was enough work for them all.

He called together his assistants and apprentices to announce his plans for the future.

'We shall be very busy for the next few years. The amount of work to be done is frightening, but we shall not change our usual system, it has been designed for just this kind of pressure.' He pulled his collar higher in a characteristic gesture of self-satisfaction. 'I shall do the roughs and these will be distributed according to your particular abilities. You will be responsible for your own work, and I shall interfere as little as possible. In most cases, I shall do them in oil paint, and you will enlarge them to the required size.' He stopped for a moment and thought aloud. 'I gather that the great picture of paradise has been badly damaged, and I am determined that Veronese shall not get that job; Domenico and I will do it together. It will be the most magnificent canvas ever seen, and the largest. As if Michelangelo used oil paint in the Sistine Chapel and used Titian as his assistant.'

He checked his enthusiasm for this grand project and returned to practical matters. 'I want the doves to be fully used on the work, as painters, so we'll need more apprentices.' Marietta and Giovanni exchanged glances, but the Maestro was in full flight. 'I am going to introduce Marietta's younger sister, Ottavia, to the studio under Marco's tutorship, and we'll need at least three others, one each for Tino, Marco and Bruno. Tino, will you see to that?'

'Yes, Father, I'll do it today.'

'Good! Now, the final point. I am going to buy a bigger house with room for two studios. Tino didn't like the idea when I mentioned it to him a month ago, but now things are different. We've got more work to do, and we shall need more space. My mind is made up.'

'You are quite right, Father,' said Domenico, 'the situation has changed. When do you want to move?'

'Today, or if that is not possible, tomorrow morning.'

Four days later, they all moved to the large house near the church of Madonna dell'Orto, and the work began.

Dozens of small canvases were primed and stretched for the Maestro's sketches. He had the ability to compose an elaborate picture in paint at one sitting. It was a gift he enjoyed exercising, in one hour he could prepare a month's work for one assistant. As he grew older and more assured, his finishing pictures were painted at the same speed and with comparable freedom.

Allegories of Venice, scenes from history, and votive pictures of religious subjects were sent to the Palazzo Ducale for the Senate's approval. As soon as the sizes were known, work began on the final canvases, sometimes before the approval was confirmed. When he was not painting, he moved around the huge studio commenting on the translations made by his skilful assistants. They were allowed more freedom to alter the original sketches than was customary, for Jacopo encouraged them to think for themselves within the general framework of the roughs. The activity quickened his mind and his hand; his output was prodigious.

Some of the designs which he specially liked, he kept to do

himself. One such was *The Marriage of Bacchus and Ariadne*; part of a set of pictures representing concord, which made allegorical references to Venetian power and administration. He decided to indulge in a gentle caprice. He wanted the two lovers to display all the natural grace of genuine tenderness rather than orthodox sentimentality.

'Where are the doves?' he asked Marco.

'They are down in the courtyard sizing a new length of canvas. Shall I send them up?'

'When they have finished, tell them I want them.'

Marietta and Giovanni arrived, glued together and reeking like a tannery.

'I've got an idea that might amuse you,' he began. 'Would you like to play the parts of two great lovers in ancient myth?'

The proposal seemed strange, coming at a time when everyone was so busy.

'What do you mean?' asked Marietta.

'Well, I thought I would put you two into the ducal palace as Bacchus and Ariadne.'

'But why us?' she asked again.

'Because I don't know any other pair who deserve to be remembered as much; because I'm fond of you and because I have forgotten how to draw.'

The absurdity of this last point immediately changed their puzzled expressions into laughter.

'All right,' said Marietta, 'what do you want us to do?'

He roughed out an arrangement for the two figures, and he passed the paper to them. 'Just sit like this for a moment.'

They placed themselves on a low dais in the correct poses, and while they sat, he talked. 'I am going to give you a votive picture of Dote Andrea Gritti to do. The original, by Titian, was destroyed in the fire and the Senate wants the replacement to be as close as possible. But we needn't worry too much about that. The composition was very balanced and formal, but it was right, because a doorway cuts into the design at the bottom. There shouldn't be any problems for you, and we don't need any tricks. What do you say?'

They could say nothing. They thought they would only be

allowed to paint backgrounds for remote ceiling paintings, but they had been offered a large and important picture to do between them.

'Do you think we can cope with something as big as that?' asked Giovanni.

'I don't see why not. If you square up the drawings accurately, it's only a mechanical operation, after all.'

'What about the portrait? We can't do that.'

'I'm getting Sebastian to do all the portraits for the whole series, there are three more of them to be done. He's very good; in fact he's nearly as good as I am,' he said with blatant irony.

He held the sketch at arm's length and squinted at it through half-closed eyes.

'When can we start, Father?'

'As soon as you have washed off that dreadful smell, I should think.' He screwed his face into a grimace. 'I'll do a more careful sketch to help you, and that will take a day or two.'

'But what about Bacchus and Ariadne, then?'

'There's plenty of time for that. I went to take care over it, anyway.'

They wanted to discuss the Gritti picture further, but Jacopo had finished the drawing. 'Marietta, you go and help Tino with the ceiling canvasses. I want Giovanni a bit longer.'

She got down off the dais, kissed her father, lifted his cap and whispered something in his ear. She mimed a kiss for Giovanni as she closed the door.

'I want to do a study of your head for Bacchus – if you can get on without the hen pigeon for a moment.'

He reached for a wreath of leaves on the table behind him. 'Here, put this on your head, and try to look like a drunken god.'

Giovanni sat while the Maestro drew and talked on.

'Have you decided when you want to marry?' he asked him suddenly.

Giovanni was not prepared and he felt the sweat pricking under the leaves.

'No, Maestro, not yet.'

'Why's that? Don't you want to marry?'

'It's not that exactly… I don't know…' Giovanni coloured.

'There's something troubling you, isn't there?'

'Well…'

'I can see there is. And I think I know what it is.'

He turned in his chair and opened a cupboard. He took out a folio bulging with papers and drawings. He pulled out an engraving, glanced and handed it to Giovanni.

'It's all there in a nutshell, if I'm not mistaken.'

Giovanni studied the print intently. There were two women, one sumptuously dressed, the other nude, seated each side of antique catafalque. The balance of the composition was almost symmetrical, but there was another balance implied in their mutual disdain. A landscape with trees folded away into the distance. While he was enchanted by the picture, he failed to see any relevance to himself or Marietta, either jointly or separately. Jacopo was not surprised at his bewilderment.

'It's called *Spiritual and Carnal Love*,' he explained. 'That doesn't only mean heavenly or religious love, and worldly love. It represents the two kinds of love which man can know for a woman. If you're lucky, you can have them both together; if you've only got one, you're in trouble.'

'But why are you in trouble if you've only got spiritual love?' asked Giovanni.

'You're not if your partner is like yourself; but if you find one of the other kind, you can expect pain and sorrow and terrible disappointment.'

Giovanni began to see the connection. 'Do you mean that Marietta and I are different?'

'Yes, I do. Marietta is carnal and you are not.'

'Is there pain and sorrow ahead for us, then?'

'Only for you, Giovanni. That's why I wanted you to marry. There was a chance that being a wife might change her nature and that she would settle down and become less headstrong, more mature – like you.'

Giovanni felt a gradual illumination, an understanding of his recurring uncertainty. He looked again at the engraving, and he saw the truth which had eluded him spelled out in simple terms. He saw himself and Marietta personified in the two figures; superficially similar, but profoundly incompatible. Their eyes were focused on different things on opposite horizons.

His emotions shuttled between the relief he felt at resolving his problem and the emptiness at the prospect of inevitable loss. The world without Marietta promised to be incomplete and monochromatic, and at the same time so unreal that he could not envisage its desolation. Only one course offered certainty. He would test the Maestro's analysis of their incongruity tonight. He would reverse the studio incident and take Marietta unawares.

When the house was asleep he left his room and went silently down the stairs to her chamber. The room glowed with the pink light from a lamp which hung in the corner. A Saviour spread on a large crucifix looked down on her. She lay diagonally across the bed in a similar attitude, her head on one side and one hand trailing over the edge. Giovanni lifted the coverlet and exposed her glowing body. She rolled her head from one shoulder to the other and moved her lips, but she did not wake. He crouched beside her, his desire mounting, his pulse quickening. His mouth touched hers and his hands feathered across her body. She stirred again, but did not wake. He forced his tongue between her lips and pressed her thigh. Marietta trembled and stretched her legs taut.

'Giovanni,' she sighed. 'Giovanni.'

Her eyes still closed, her arms enfolded his neck and her head rose from the pillow searching for his mouth. She arched her back, pressing her body upwards towards his, still asleep.

Giovanni's passion thundered in his head, bursting his temples. When she woke, she was halfway towards capitulation, her body heaving feebly under him. She was trained by his weight and the totality of her own surrender. Wild oblivion consumed them both.

Before the night was over, Giovanni returned to his room. He lay on his back and considered his exploration. He was certainly capable of the most sensitive carnal love. It was a sacramental expression of his adoration of Marietta, deeply satisfying and free from defect. Only in such communion could he demonstrate his tenderness, the mystery and purity of his devotion. Yet Marietta's response had been immediate and unconscious. Her hunger for physical gratification had needed no aperitif, no stimulus. His was an expressive fervour; hers suggested prurience. Yet he knew she loved him deeply and sincerely. The vicious claws of his quandary had been blunted, not drawn.

The work on the Gritti canvas progressed quickly. The kneeling doge was presented to the Virgin and Child by St Mark. The two sides of the picture and the two groups of figures were divided by a vertical strip of sky, yet connected by a youth with a martyr's palm forming a rising transition. Pairs of cloud-borne cherubs played at the foot of the steps on which the Virgin sat, encircled by smiling cherubim. The gravity of the flanking architecture and drapery was offset by glowing babes and resonant colour.

Jacopo visited them to watch their development. He advised a change here and there or a simplification which would be more effective in situ in the hall of the Collegio.

'You're having trouble with the Virgin's head, aren't you? It doesn't sit on her shoulders properly.' They stood back to view the effect and agreed. 'Let me show you,' he said. He took the brushes from Marietta and scrubbed out the right-hand side, losing it in the colour of the curtain. With a flowing line, he tilted the head so that it looked down at the doge and not at the child. He dipped his fingers into the dish of spirit and blended the colour into the new position of the profile. A few scratches and dots of paint established the key positions of the nostrils, then the eyes and mouth. He smudged the shadows in with his thumb. He changed brushes and drew the eyebrow and lids with an arching line pivoted from his wrist; the wing of the nose, then the mouth were delineated with the same assured ease. He stood back, his head on one side.

'There,' he said, 'that looks a bit better, I think.'

'A *bit* better!' they chorused.

The spontaneous skill of his brushwork always beguiled them, but this time the magic was totally captivating. A fully rounded head and an expressive face had been fashioned out of three colours in as many minutes.

'Your saint looks rather apprehensive. He looks like St Lawrence just before he was roasted. But he has been martyred, judging by his palm, so I think he ought to look a bit more cheerful. Let's see what we can do.'

He repeated the performance to demonstrate the method once more. 'Don't get carried away with the details,' he said as he painted. 'Always do the masses first and the details last. If the masses are wrong, the details will be wrong too, and you've wasted your time.' He stuck a brush in his mouth, gripping the handle with his teeth. The wood acted as a fipple and his breath whistled softly. Occasionally, he glanced over his shoulder at the doves who watched, transfixed.

Suddenly, Marietta squealed with delight. 'It's Giovanni!' she exclaimed. 'You've painted Giovanni.'

'I thought I would do a trial run for my Bacchus, just for practice.'

'It's not fair,' said Marietta. 'That means Giovanni will be in two pictures.'

Her peevishness was exaggerated, more to encourage her father to paint her than out of genuine spite. Jacopo was not to be persuaded by such an obvious deception, and he ignored her. 'Now, arrange for Sebastiano to paint the doge's head, and then it will be almost finished,' he said, wiping the brush handle on his sleeve.

'Thank you, Maestro. That's made all the difference.'

Sebastiano Casser was a quiet, almost furtive man who had few friends and was somehow isolated from his fellow assistants. He had been encouraged by Jacopo to concentrate on portraiture, and he had risen to being the acknowledged portrait specialist in the studio. He was more servile than any of the others and his lack of imagination had made him an ideal man for this branch of the work. His technique was recognisably that of his master, but less robust and spontaneous.

He had a drawing by the Maestro and an engraving of the doge to work from and he set about his task in a cautious way which contrasted with Jacopo's almost casual performance. He drew in charcoal first to shape the head, then gradually built up the blocks of light and shade in thin paint.

'I shall need some more white and yellow ochre, Giovanni. Go and get them for me.'

Giovanni disappeared. When he was away, the young man engaged Marietta in unctuous conversation. He spiced his remarks and questions with subtle flattery and made innocuous jokes at Giovanni's expense.

'I expect you have a lovely time together when you're alone,' he ventured. 'Tell me, what do you get up to in your room?'

The insidious confidence he had cleverly built up had encouraged Marietta, who began to reveal the secrets of their lovemaking and the platform on the roof where they lay and sunned themselves in complete privacy.

Giovanni returned with the paint and was sent on another errand.

'Do you take off all your clothes up there?' he enquired.

'Of course, we do. There wouldn't be any point if we didn't.'

'And do you like being naked?'

'Oh yes!' she stretched herself seductively. 'I'm really myself then.'

'Aren't you yourself now?'

'Not really.'

'I think you are very beautiful now. I wonder what you must be like on the roof,' he wheedled.

'Giovanni says I'm beautiful, and I feel beautiful.'

'But does he *show* you how beautiful you are?'

Marietta felt her knees weaken.

'Of course.'

'And how does he do that?'

He drew the horn on the doge's cap and looked at her lewdly.

'Well, he kisses and caresses me; he's very gentle.'

'Is that all?'

'How else can he show me?'

'Ah! Now that's *my* secret.'

Marietta's curiosity and the dissolution inside her clothes intensified.

'I don't like secrets; so tell me!'

'No, I couldn't tell you that.'

'I think you are horrible!'

'But I could show you.'

She looked at him with disbelief, but her restlessness was

becoming unbearable.

'How?'

'I could show you how a man loves, and I bet you'd enjoy it more than anything you've ever known before.'

'How do you know?'

'Well, every girl has to become a woman some time. Don't you want to be loved like a woman?'

'Of course, I do.'

'Then I will show you.'

'When?'

'Right now, if you like. Giovanni won't be back for a long time yet.'

'All right. Let's go on the roof.'

He put down his brushes on the table and took his maulstick with him.

She led him up the stairs and through the attic and showed him the hidden door. They stepped out into the blinding sun on to a wooden platform above a valley of tiles. Hot shafts of air grilled up through the boards. As she bent down he cut his stick across her tight breeches.

'That's just to get you in the right mood,' he promised.

Giovanni returned to find the head barely started and the brushes scattered on the table. Only Bruno was there, working in the far corner.

'Have you seen Marietta?' His forehead was furrowed with vague anxiety.

'No, she was here five minutes ago, but I haven't seen her since.'

'I wonder where she has gone.'

'I don't know. What was she doing when you left?'

'She was watching Sebastiano do the doge's portrait.'

'Sebastiano? My God! She hasn't gone with him, has she?' Bruno got up clumsily, scattering debris on the floor. 'We must find them before...'

'Why? What's the matter with Sebastiano?'

Bruno looked at him with candid impatience.

'Because he's a monster with women. That's why.'

'What do you mean?'

'He debauches them, you idiot,' he shouted as he pushed Giovanni through the studio door. 'You see if they are in her room, and I'll look in ours. But hurry!' Their routes diverged at the head of the stairs.

'There's no sign of them here,' called Bruno. 'And you?'

'Nothing.'

'I'll go down to the storeroom. You look up here.'

Giovanni opened every door he came to, but the whole floor was deserted.

'The roof!' he said aloud.

He raced up to the attic and crashed through the maze of beams, choking with terror. He heard Marietta scream. Invigorated with panic, he tore at the bolts. She screamed again.

'That's lovely, Seb...' she caught her breath, 'do it again... please! Please!'

What horror lay beyond the planks that separated him from his ecstatic Marietta was too hideous for him to see. His head dropped on to the door with an empty thud. But the familiar sound of her exaltation paralysed his body, obliterated his will and assassinated his love.

Recompense

The vacuum in Giovanni's existence was filled by work. In close collaboration with Bruno, his capacity and capability proliferated. Painting was his only sustenance; sleep, his only reprieve from effort. He fought to induce a blissful amnesia, and only rarely was he defeated. Marietta's continued presence in the studio weighted the struggle unevenly against him. Her vivacity and appetite for pleasure were the nails of his crucifixion and her nonchalant chatter the mockery of his agony.

She had instantly recognised his pain and indifference towards her, but no explanation was needed. They were too embarrassed to talk at all; he by the shame of rejection, she by her own betrayal of Giovanni. But she was not overburdened with guilt. She had become a woman in submitting to Sebastiano's exquisite sadism, and her new sense of fulfilment made it easy to reject and even despise an adolescent attachment.

Jacopo had noticed the estrangement, but did not enquire into its origin. He did not know how severely Giovanni had been mutilated, or that Marietta had been the executioner. But it was clear to him that it was the injured boy, not his daughter, who needed succour, and this became his main concern.

His compassionate nature and wealth of common sense suggested a solution which would safeguard them both and provide an interval in which their damaged affection might recover. He would send Marietta to stay with his wife's family to give her a taste of gracious living before her marriage. Maria would be her companion and chaperon.

He took Giovanni about with him for recreation and diversion from his suicidal mania for work. Jacopo's conversation about painting, mythology and religion was more than a mere distraction; he infected his charge with his own enthusiasms and sensibilities. He was continually astonished at the talent and receptiveness which he recognised as being just like his own, following the same pattern of his own precocious mastery. His sons had not inherited his abilities. They were competent, but not much more. In Giovanni, he saw his artistic heir, the one who would inherit his success, and his loneliness. Their relationship, with its own kind of understanding and gentleness, ripened into love, which, in some measure, repaired their individual isolation.

'Your apprenticeship has two more years to run,' said Jacopo, 'but it seems to me to be ridiculous that your status and waves should be held down by an absurd legal formality.'

'What are you suggesting?' asked Giovanni.

'I want you to be my assistant right now. Of course, you can't set up on your own till you've served your time, the Guild wouldn't allow it, but I need you to be my right hand.'

'Thank you, Maestro. But what about Tino and Marco, won't they object?'

'No, why should they? Tino is the heir to the studio, and he enjoys the business side as much as the painting, and Marco, well, Marco isn't very able; he's a miniaturist, really. No, you needn't be afraid of their jealousy.'

'What about Marietta, then?' The name sounded unfamiliar on his lips.

'She seems too much absorbed with Sebastiano to notice what is going on. Mind you, I love her dearly and I would never do anything to hurt her, but she's too irresponsible to be my right hand. She'll probably marry soon, anyway.'

Giovanni felt the blow strike below the line of resistance.

'Do you think she will marry Sebastiano?' The words seemed like a malediction.

'God only knows! I hope not. I don't care for him much. He might be a very good portrait painter one day, but he's a poltroon.'

Giovanni had never heard the Maestro express such scorn before, and he approved. He wondered if it had sprung from shrewd observation or from knowledge of his perversion. He could not know that his precious daughter had been desecrated in his own house. There was nothing in his expression or manner which betrayed a hint of appropriate anger or indignation.

'Her mother and I have decided to send her to her grandparents' house for a while,' he went on. 'A girl should discover some of the social graces and learn more about life than she can in a workshop, so it will be good for her to be away from us all. I think she needs a chance, anyway.'

Giovanni was greatly relieved by the news, but the pain of rejection remained.

Jacopo studied the boy, unseen. The calm, refined features were knotted in anguish. He could not leave matters as they were.

'It's a pity about you two, though,' he said at last. 'But I did warn you about the pain, didn't I?'

'You did, Maestro, but I didn't really understand then.'

'How could you? If you had believed me, it would have been a flaw in your loyalty for Marietta.'

'You made me think, though.'

'Well, if it went on any longer, the pain would have been worse, I know.'

'I don't think it could be any worse than this,' confided Giovanni.

'My poor boy! I know how you feel. You see, it happened to me once, and it still hurts.' He put his arm round the boy's shoulder to demonstrate his sympathy and that true affection for others could provide a modest compensation. He changed the subject.

'Tomorrow I have to meet the Senate, and I want you to be there by my side.' Giovanni was amazed at the announcement. 'So you had better have something decent to wear. Come along; I'll take you shopping.'

They left the house by the Maestro's gondola and were rowed to the molo. Their arrival coincided with the disembarkation of the envoys from China, and all the panoply of state was marshalled in the piazzetta for the occasion. A solemn procession headed by musicians playing Gabrieli's new canzone, and accompanied by the officers of the Republican guard and members of the Council, proceeded to the Gate of the Papers. The diminutive ambassadors were fully responsive to the magnificence of the ceremony and the setting, and they paused to register their appreciation from time to time, bowing and sailing to their escort. At the polychromed gateway, they halted to inspect the intricacy of the carving and the splendour of the gilding. Their restrained, yet impeccable courtesy made a deep impression on the assembled crowd, and so did the huge lacquered chests that followed them. It was rumoured that the emperor had filled them with ivory and precious stones valued at ten thousand ducats. These were to be presented to the doge as a token of his friendship and esteem for Venice.

Jacopo and Giovanni watched the majestic parade pass into the courtyard of the palace. 'It reminds me of the picture Gentile Bellini painted of a ducal procession in front of St Mark's,' said Giovanni.

'Yes,' replied Jacopo. 'But it's all a bit empty now.'

'What do you mean?'

'There was a time when Venice was the only power in Europe trading with the East, when she supplied the whole of the continent with treasures from China and the Indies. But now the sea route passes us by and those damned Portuguese are picking all the plums.'

'Isn't Venice rich now, then?'

'She's getting poorer every year, but she won't be bankrupt in my lifetime, or yours, please God!'

'It's sad to think that all this will disappear one day,' Giovanni said, indicating the piazza.

'It won't disappear for one very good reason.'

'What's that, Maestro?'

'Because almost everything that has been made here has always been the best, the most beautiful that man could devise.' He stopped before the glowing façade of St Mark's. 'Just look at that! The columns once graced the buildings of the ancient world; the mosaics were, and still are, the finest in Christendom; the carvings as light as lace, yet indestructible, because they're made of the hardest Istrian stone; the horses also came from an ancient Roman workshop, and are the largest and most beautiful ever made. They're incredible!'

'But Florence and Rome are beautiful too, aren't they?'

'Yes, of course, but there's no joy, no movement there. It's all solemn and static, as if they have been frozen. Art should live and breathe, it must have *energy*.' He emphasised the word with an impassioned shout which drew the attention of passers-by.

Giovanni felt embarrassed.

'Where are we going, Maestro?'

'To the Merceria, my boy.' And he strode off towards the clock tower and disappeared in a flurry of billowing cloak into the dark archway.

He was greeted with deference at the entrance to a shop which displayed silks and brocades.

'Maestro Robusti,' chanted the merchant, 'you have honoured my humble shop again. How gracious of your eminence...' Jacopo cut the preamble short.

'I want to see the doublet and cloak you were going to make me.'

'Certainly, Maestro, come this way.'

He walked backwards through the racks, heavy with great bolts of gorgeous material, coaxing his distinguished customer. 'We have made it according to your eminence's instructions, of course, but I fear it will be too small.'

'How do you know that?' asked Jacopo, smiling.

'Because we have your measurements on record, and they don't tally.'

He went over to a stand in the corner of the workroom and carefully removed a fur-lined cloak. The brocade was deep russet coloured, the lining and collar of a speckled cream fur.

'That looks all right,' said Jacopo. The shopkeeper moved behind him to place it round his shoulders. 'No, it's not for me. It's for that young man.'

The cloak was draped on Giovanni whose confusion was even greater than that of the silk merchant.

'A perfect fit, your eminence,' he said obsequiously.

'Now, let's look at the doublet.'

The rolled pleats, tapering down the front, shone like burnished copper. The huge sleeves stood high above the shoulders and were full to the wrists. The cuffs were finished with a thin band of ruched cream linen.

'But, Maestro...' Giovanni began a stillborn protestation.

'Try it on. It should fit you.'

It did. The plumed cat was equally successful. The cloth and the cut were approved by Jacopo's fastidious eye and he smiled with self-satisfaction and at Giovanni's rapturous appreciation.

'We've got to be irresistible tomorrow if we're going to win this contract.'

'Which contract?'

They left the shop and Giovanni started for home. 'Not so fast, young man. We haven't finished yet.'

A belt, gloves, shoes and hose were bought. Jacopo indulged in the extravagance of choosing only the best, but his indulgence was not naive, but symbolic. Again, Giovanni started for home. 'There's one more thing you need if you are going to be my assistant.'

'What's that? I've got everything now, surely?'

'No, not yet.' Jacopo turned into the doorway of a goldsmith's shop.

'I want a very delicate gold chain,' he said casually.

'Certainly, your eminence.' The goldsmith produced several, lying in padded leather cases. 'Will one of these be adequate for your eminence?'

'Choose the one you like, Giovanni.'

'But I can't wear such a grant and expensive thing, Maestro. I'm still only an apprentice.'

'No, you're Tintoretto's chief assistant and you're going to paint in paradise!'

Giovanni's eyes filled with tears in silent expression of his gratitude and affection. He took the thinnest chain from its case and held it up for his master's approval.

'If that's the one you like, it's yours.'

As they were rowed home, Giovanni recalled a cryptic aside of the Maestro's.

'What contract did you mean back there?' he asked.

'Guariento's painting of paradise was destroyed in the fire, and it will have to be replaced,' he explained. 'And I want to do it.' He sat back into the cushions and looked at the gilded carving of the canopy; his eyes passed through it to the sky beyond. 'It's going to be superb. The best thing I have ever done, or the city has ever seen. It will make all other Venetian paintings look like miniatures. I want to fill the entire wall with my vision of heaven.

Christ set in the centre of waves of figures and cherubim, receiving the faithful and lighting up the whole universe.'

He waved his arms in gestures of abundance.

The numbness of Giovanni's existence had been invaded by genuine emotions again. His sincerity could not be expressed in words, but he knew that his master could also understand what could not be said. Their affinity had no need of conventional phrases or gestures. The bond which joined them carried their reciprocal feelings of regard and affection. Their strange unity transcended the wide disparities of age and experience.

Their progress to the ducal palace caused a sensation on the following morning. There was nothing unusual in spectacles of ostentation on the canals or in the piazza of this most hedonistic, luxurious city. Venice could boast of many families whose personal riches rivalled the courts of Europe; and eminent visitors from those courts were frequently seen by the populace. But this pair of travellers displayed neither affectation nor pomp, but rather the natural dignity of gifted men quietly confident of their merit and attainments. Their modesty in success was more impressive than exhibitions of mere wealth or rank.

They entered the courtyard below the Gate of the Papers and were saluted by the halberdiers who recognised the great Tintoretto. They climbed the Golden Staircase to the anteroom of the Collegio which had just been completed to Palladio's designs. It was Giovanni's first visit to the palace and the splendour of the interior was astounding. It reminded him of the magnificence of St Mark's, but here the coloured marbles and the gilded decoration shone with a pristine glory. He imagined the spaces on the walls filled with his master's pictures; his pride in his own situation expanded instinctively.

They were led to the Senate Chamber where small knots of foppish men were talking in muted voices. Giovanni looked around the room. It was more richly decorated than St Mark's. The golden exuberance of the ceiling was awe-inspiring. Scrolls, volutes, swags of fruit and leaves and intricate grotesques rolled above in well-ordered patterns. It was a cornucopia of imaginative invention before which nature was bound to concede defeat. Set in the bold framework of carving was one of the pictures recently dispatched from the studio. It represented Venice as the Queen of the Seas, whose conception and birth he had witnessed. The shock of recognition was magnified by its incredible beauty. The dominant cool greens and blues sang delicately against the ground bass of the surrounding gold; the red and orange accents created an elaborate counterpoint. The effect was one of intense joy, healthy vigour, of sinuous movement and sophisticated sanity. There was no hysteria, no florid vulgarity, simply the evidence of human intelligence and creativity elevated to the status of religious experience. Giovanni was more moved than he had been in church, more than he had ever been before.

The door opened and a stately column of superbly dressed officials passed down the centre towards the empty dais. The Council of Ten was followed by the doge dressed in scarlet, who walked under a blue and gold umbrella supported by four noblemen. It was a semi-formal occasion.

There were no musicians, no armed guard, just a few attendants, scribes and lawyers carrying bundles of vellum.

The Council divided, and five each side of the central throne stood and waited for the doge to be seated.

A voice intoned the general announcement. 'The Senate of the Most Serene Republic of Venice is convened to receive petitions from its distinguished citizens relating to matters of state. The session shall be recorded as taking place in the forenoon of the tenth day of October in the year of our Redeemer one thousand five hundred and seventy-eight.' The voice paused. In the silence papers were rustled, and then it continued. 'First, the petition of Marcantonio Soldi, senior member of the Confraternity of St George and merchant of the Republic.'

An aged man stepped forwards to the central position bowed and introduced his petition.

'In the fifth month of this year, a portion of my fleet, homeward bound from Alexandria, called at Heraklion in Crete for provisions and water. They lay there for three days before starting on the last stage of their voyage. Two days out, in the first hours of light, they were attacked by Turkish pirates. Three escaped, but two were boarded, plundered, and destroyed. It is my belief that there is a Turkish spy in Heraklion who can alert the pirates to intercept Venetian vessels at exactly the most favourable moment for attack.' His story was interrupted by one of the chief advisers.

'Why do you suspect that intelligence is passed to these pirates? Could it not be sheer coincidence?'

'I think not, my lord. This has happened to my ships before and other merchants have had similar losses in similar circumstances. The latest one was last month and the pattern was the same as I have related.'

A thin murmuring crept from the dais which encouraged voices from the floor of the hall. The doge held up a restraining hand and the noise died.

'State your petition to the Senate.'

'Six merchants for whom I speak and I petition the Senate, first, to send a war fleet to the waters north of Heraklion to intercept the Turks, and second, to discover the spy and dispose of him according to Venetian law.'

'Your petition is recorded and will be considered.'

A crescendo of voices rose all around Giovanni. The scribes scribbled and Jacopo whispered, 'It's our turn next.'

'Do you mean that I have to speak?' asked Giovanni, hoarse with fear.

'No, leave it to me.'

Silence was called for.

'The Senate will consider and give its answer one week from today.' The voice cleared its throat. 'Second, the petition of Maestro Jacopo Robusti, member of the Confraternity of San Rocco, painter and honoured servant of the Republic.'

Jacopo and Giovanni planted themselves on the spot which the merchant had just vacated and bowed. The doge smiled and returned the mute salutation.

'The Doge and Senate of the Republic will know that the great *Paradiso* in the hall of the Council was irreparably damaged by the fire. It seems to me and my assistant here that the hall should have, not just a replacement for this fine painting, but one which will be modern in style and feeling, rich in colour and full of God's gracious light. We, therefore, petition the Senate to grant to your servants the commission to paint a new *Paradiso*, worthy of its setting, worthy of the Republic and of the Senate which governs it so justly and effectively.'

The doge leaned forward and said, 'Maestro Jacopo, you have graced this palace with your work for many years now and the Senate has been fully appreciative of your gifts and grateful for your unfailing promptitude in delivering your paintings. While I personally feel it would be for the Senate to grant your petition, I am bound to tell you that a decision has already been made regarding the *Paradiso*.'

Jacopo was thunderstruck by this gently administered death blow. He gripped Giovanni's arm to steady himself. He held his breath, prepared to hear the name of Veronese. The doge continued. 'It will be announced that the contract will be awarded to the design adjudged the best from those submitted in open competition. All the master painters will be invited to participate. Thus the justice of the Senate, which you so eloquently referred to, will be demonstrated once more.'

Jacopo was infinitely relieved to know that the contract had not escaped him. The doge added, 'The Senate hopes that you, Maestro Tintoretto, will favour the Republic by submitting your proposed design in the regular manner and not according to the practice in San Rocco.'

The reference to Jacopo's stealth in placing the completed painting in situ was enjoyed by all the Senate and the rest of the assembly, and not least by the Maestro himself, and the use of his nickname in such a formal situation alleviated his tension. He smiled and bowed and left the chamber.

Giovanni was aware that all his tact would be required to soothe the disappointment. He grasped the Maestro's arm. 'I am sorry it didn't work out in the way you hoped, especially after all the expense…'

'Don't worry about a thing. We'll get the job. It's the delay which makes me angry. It might be years before we can start on it.' A steward had followed and begged to speak.

'The doge requests that you visit him in the Ducal Apartments in half an hour, Maestro.'

'Very well, we shall be there.'

'Can we go to the Hall of the Great Council?' asked Giovanni.

'That's a good idea. You ought to see it.'

As they walked, he talked about his vision and the problems there would be in realising it. He pushed open a large door and motioned Giovanni in. The gigantic space was overwhelming. The ceiling was ready to receive its paintings, but in spite of the bare spaces, the carved, gilded design blazed above them. In less than eight months, Christoforo Sorte had completed supervising its construction and carving; the gilders' trestles were still in position in one corner.

'How does it stay up there, Maestro? There are no pillars to support it.'

'Sorte has been very clever. He's hung the ceiling from chains hidden in the roof, so there is no need to hold it up from below. There will be a clear view for everyone.'

'I've never seen anything like it.'

'Nor has anyone else, it has never been done before on this scale. When it's ready to receive visitors from other countries, it will knock them sideways, and so will our *Paradiso*.'

'Where will it be, Maestro?'

'Along that end wall.'

'All along it, do you mean, or just between the doors?'

'No, it has to cover the whole wall.'

'But it must be twenty-five yards long!' exclaimed Giovanni incredulously.

'It's more than that. It's a big job, but it's going to be marvellous.'

Jacopo's plan for the removal of his wayward daughter was approved by everyone, not least by Marietta, whose enthusiasm for new experiences was as keen as a rutting animal's for the scent of a mate. She left with her usual ebullience, kissing all those she was to leave behind, including Giovanni, with casual jauntiness. It was as if she had been given a new pair of shoes, and had simply thrown the old ones away.

Dubious Heritage

Doge Nicolo da Ponte was a small man who appeared to be wearing someone else's head. His frail body and effeminate hands were perfectly matched, but the slitted eyes, the long features and beard were unequivocally masculine, hard and brutal.

He was passionate about two things: power and justice. The former, he had known all his life in every activity which had exercised his enormous energy. Now, in his old age, he was the titular head of the Republic; his personal power was restricted by law, but his octopine influence was formidable. His passion for justice was a reflection of his lack of imagination. He regarded the law as infallible as the Scriptures. What was written was sacrosanct, and he was never to be found guilty of the heresy of modifying one or questioning the other. In legal matters and in public life, extenuating circumstances were irrelevant, and to give them a moment's consideration was a sign of humiliating weakness. Compromise was acceptable only when he was the sole beneficiary.

Like all unimaginative men, he had no real taste for art. Art was a commodity and an investment, and it was meritorious when the return could be measured in terms of advancement or enhanced prestige. Titian was admired, so he acquired Titians, without any thought of the personal pleasure they were capable of providing. His recent elevation created an opportunity for him to exercise his talents as a manipulator of men and affairs. His admiration for Jacopo was founded upon the stories, most of them apocryphal, of the Maestro's ability to bend the system to his own advantage rather than on any aesthetic considerations. In this, he believed that they had more than a little in common.

He floated into the room, peeling off his scarlet gloves, which he gave to an attendant.

'Maestro Jacopo,' he said warmly, 'it was good of you to accept my invitation. May I offer you some wine?'

'Thank you, Master Doge.'

'...And the young man?'

'Please, my lord.'

The wine was poured with eucharistic solemnity and the goblets distributed.

'I hope this is to your taste. It comes from one of my vineyards near Verona.'

Jacopo and Giovanni sipped and savoured.

'It is very good, my lord.' It wasn't, but this was no time for contention.

'Do you have vineyards on the mainland, Maestro?'

'No, Master Doge.'

'What a shame. Now, if you are interested, there's a small estate next to mine which is being sold very shortly. It has been offered to me, but I don't know if I really need it. If you want enough vines to supply all your own needs, I am sure I could divert the sale to you on very favourable terms.' He sipped again, looking at Jacopo over the edge on his goblet.

Jacopo was immediately impressed by such consideration, although he had no ambitions for viticulture, even to supply his own table. 'I would like to think about your offer, my lord.'

'Please do, but I think you would be very surprised how little it would cost you.'

'I'm not a wealthy man, Master Doge.'

'You have a mint in your fingers, Maestro,' said Doge Nicolo tendentiously.

Jacopo's instincts signalled caution. He decided to feign gullibility. 'It is generous of you, my lord, to recognise the ability of a poor craftsman like myself.'

'You, Maestro Tintoretto...' the familiarity had a different ring which Jacopo noted, '...need never be short of anything you may need that is in my power to provide, and my power is quite extensive.'

'You are more than generous, Master Doge.'

'We could quite easily come to a mutually beneficial arrangement, I'm sure.'

The veil of cordiality was parted and the underlying colours revealed. Generosity had been transformed into bargaining.

Jacopo was aware that he could be easily outflanked by the skill of the doge's persuasion and superior position. But he was also aware that devious men were disconcerted by honesty, so he brought the prelude to an abrupt end. 'What exactly can I do for you, my lord?'

There was a pause while the pursuer adjusted to being pursued. 'I have been thinking about the four votive pictures you are doing for the Collegio,' he began rather uncertainly. 'I believe you have finished one of them already. The Gritti one, isn't it?' He digressed to recover his composure. 'Which are those you have yet to do?'

'Donato, Mocenigo and Venier,' answered Jacopo. 'The designs are all done and the Donato is well under way.'

'Venier, my predecessor, only held office for a year, and it seems rather extravagant that such a short tenure should be marked in this way. And, furthermore, the Venier family is already honoured in other pictures.'

'That is true, my lord.'

'I think that our close association and mutual regard might be suitably recorded in a votive picture, you as the artist and I as the subject.'

'But what will the Venier family think of that?' Jacopo played his trump card.

'Oh! There's no need to worry about it, I have already sounded them out and they will be quite agreeable.'

There was a sinister note of triumph imbedded in the assurance. The ace was out.

'Will I receive official instructions of the change?'

'Of course. You have my word for it.'

'Are there all other changes that will be needed?'

'I don't think so, except that I would like my family coat of arms placed in the picture somewhere. Noticeable, but not too prominent.'

'Very well, that will give us no problem.' Jacopo had a bright idea. He would place it right in the front where it could not be missed and he would make sure that it was the only one of the four to include the arms. It would be his public announcement of his private submission.

'I would like to know your assistant better, Maestro.'

'This is Giovanni, my right-hand man, my lord.'

'I thought your son was your chief assistant.'

'Domenico is in charge of the workshop. Giovanni is a painter of outstanding talent for his age and soon he will be recognised as one of the great painters of our time. Of that, I have no doubt.'

'You value him very highly, Maestro.'

'I do, Master Doge.'

Nicolo da Ponte saw an opportunity to enlarge his patronage with a safe investment. 'I wonder if I could persuade you to allow him to paint something for me.'

'I am sure that could be arranged, but he is very much occupied with the contract for the palace at the moment, my lord. I will inform you when his services are available.'

The audience was ended, with the doge smiling like a satiated snake. Giovanni had been silenced by awe during the conversation, but the polite duel between the two men had not escaped him. As they walked across the courtyard, he could be silent no longer. 'You didn't like him, Maestro, did you?'

'No, he's a Philistine, a bumptious, vainglorious villain, and a very clever one. He could have trussed, carved and eaten me for lunch without even trying.'

'But he didn't, did he?'

'No, not quite. But you will have to be very careful if you have any dealings with him. I didn't like the way he looked at you, I didn't like it at all.'

Giovanni went to Luca's house that evening, wearing his new clothes and gold chain. His father was there, and he was greeted heartily.

'Great God! There's a peacock at the door.' Luca's ridicule lightly camouflaged his admiration and kindness.

'You'll give the neighbours something to marvel at,' crowed Sophenisba, wobbling with jubilation. 'My words! Have you been to see the doge?'

'Yes, I was there this morning...'

'You're teasing!'

'No. I went to the palace with Tintoretto and we had a private audience with the Doge da Ponte after meeting the Senate.'

He related the incidents in order, animating his account with descriptions of what he had seen.

'We are all very pleased for you, lad,' said Luca, and we are all proud of your success.' He broke off to embrace the boy again. 'And how is the buoyant Marietta? We haven't seen her for some time.' Giovanni had hoped that his good news would divert attention from his solo appearance. 'That's all over and done with. She's found someone else.'

He thought a jocular dismissal would close the enquiries, but the extent of their concern for him would not allow them to be satisfied with half-truths. Giovanni invented an innocuous explanation and his face burned with the burden of his lies.

'Tell us more,' begged Sophenisba.

Giovanni despised her insensitive curiosity.

'Can't you see that the boy's embarrassed? Leave him alone, woman, and get the supper.'

Mercifully, the subject died. Luca's compassion prompted waves of silent gratitude and affection.

The meal was enlivened by their customary banter. Sophenisba's irrepressible crudity was punctuated by the familiar bombardment at her stern, and each assault was reciprocated by an indiscriminate volley of profanities. She continued to bait Giovanni.

'I suppose you will soon be too grand to visit us.'

'No, of course not. I will come as long as I am welcome.'

'You'll always be welcome here.' Luca put his hand across the table and covered Giovanni's. 'And I hope you will always feel at home here, in spite of that shrieking monster.'

'Thank you, Luca.'

He glanced at Sophenisba whose rage was about to explode on her husband's ears again.

'You feeble bastard! Giovanni knows I love him as much as you do,' she screamed. 'To hear you butter him up, anyone would think he was as crazy as his poor mother.'

Her words reverberated in the stillness. Luca looked at the table; his father scratched his ear. Giovanni looked from one downcast face to the other; Sophenisba's glowed with guilt.

'What does she mean, Luca?'

He tried to withdraw his hand, but the grip was irresistible. The two men looked at each other with weariness and mute resignation. Sophenisba tried to cover her face with podgy fingers, but their inadequacy irritated her and she crossed herself, muttering to the ceiling. His father stared sadly and apprehensively at Giovanni.

'Your mother had two children before you were born. The first came into this world horribly deformed and, mercifully, quite dead. She was terribly upset and she blamed herself for it; she believed that somehow God had punished the child for her sins.'

He pushed a few small crumbs into a heap with his fingers, concentrating on the difficulty of making the heap regular. He wetted a finger, pressed it into the crumbs and placed them on his tongue.

'We all thought she needed to have another child to take her mind off her guilt. Well, she did have another, a girl this time. It was a beautiful child, and your mother clung to her desperately, as if she was afraid she would be taken from her. She prayed all day to be worthy of this little one; that her sin might be washed away. She washed her hands, twenty, thirty times a day to keep herself clean. It was a kind of self-baptism, and she wouldn't let anyone touch the baby, not even me.'

He paused, pushing crumbs, but his eyes were too wet for him to see.

'When the child was one year old, it died, but your mother didn't cry or show any sign of loss. She wrapped the baby in a shawl and carried the poor dead thing around with her, petting it and talking to it all the time. The child had taken her mother's wits with her.'

Luca's hand trembled and tightened on Giovanni's. His father's voice continued a monotone. 'At last, we managed to get the pathetic bundle away from her when she was asleep, and we buried it. She made another with a cushion and walked around the house with it. She would talk to no one, except her old friend, Maddelena, who gave her some comfort. When Maddelena went to the convent, your mother went with her to be a nun as well, but they wouldn't have her; they brought her home to me. When you were born, we were all afraid that you would die too, but you didn't. She was happy and very calm until the day God called her away to join her babies…' His voice stopped short, arrested by a choking sound. No one moved.

Giovanni remembered the warmth of her embraces, her quiet voice and large, dark eyes. He remembered the care with which she sewed and baked morsels for his plate, the caressing hands, and how he had caressed her hair, and he remembered that forlorn strand of hair that hung from her bier. He wiped his eyes roughly with his knuckles.

Sophenisba bent over him clumsily and placed her cheek against his. 'Forgive me,' she pleaded. 'But perhaps it's better that you know.'

Giovanni walked back, unconscious of the route he took, or of his surroundings. He strained every effort to recall everything he could about his mother, but his memories were elusive and refused to come into focus. An anonymous face hovered in front of him, cloudy and unrecognisable; it was disembodied, there was no height, no carriage, no substance. Instead, a grimacing, salacious Marietta materialised, jaunty and arrogant. He doubled his concentration to erase the blasphemous image, but succeeded only in defacing that of his mother. Anger grew from his inepti-tude; frustration turned to guilt. He had betrayed this gentle woman by displacing her image with his own miserable preoccu-pations, his own venal sin. Yet in his self-reproach, he became conscious that a part of himself was reunited with her virtue, a virtue that was incorruptible.

He shared a room and his confidences with Bruno. He had even revealed the secret of his alienation from Marietta, with the result that Bruno insisted that Sebastiano changed places with Giovanni. It was a rewarding arrangement for them all, and especially for Giovanni when his wounds were festering. He was able to draw on an inexhaustible supply of comfort and good cheer that was offered with all the liberality of friendship.

The disclosures about his mother and the new light which illuminated his father's personality had affected him deeply, but his enlightenment produced not distress so much as self-effacement and intense sympathy. His own personality had shrunk perceptibly and he felt dislocated from the present.

It had also occurred to him that he might be germinating the seeds of his mother's madness, but this did not dismay him either; on the contrary, he welcomed the possibility of such an atonement. The enigma his father had always presented was becoming comprehensible and he felt that a deeper understanding had grown between them. He had a great compassion for this taciturn man and the tragedy which had scarred him with continual sadness and reticence.

'What's that?'

'You ought to go about more and enjoy yourself. There's always something happening here, but you never join in; you just stand on the edge looking lost and glum.' Giovanni recognised the truth of the remark.

'Why don't you come out with us one evening?'

'But I don't feel exactly jovial at the moment.'

'You could if you let yourself go.'

'Do you think so?'

'Of course. We have a marvellous time. There's a party on Saturday on the Giudecca – you come with me.' Bruno had some of the strong masculinity of Luca, and Giovanni felt a great sense of security in their presence. The invitation was accepted with only the smallest misgivings.

The sun was melting in an orange crucible as they rowed across to the island with a group of voluble young people. Bruno was persuaded to play his mandolin and accompany the singing which raped an innocent madrigal. Their raucous voices echoed across the water. They passed close by the Redentore, its walls hardly high enough to warrant the forest of scaffolding poles which rose in black, untidy clusters against the sky. The boat slid under a rude wooden bridge into a side-channel which cut the island. Voices and music poured out of the open doorway and windows of a brick house. They clambered ashore and ran indoors. The house was cool, a breeze moved down the passage from a garden lit with festoons of coloured lamps. Giovanni glimpsed whirling dancers on the patio, their shouts and laughter amplified by the narrow walls. Bruno's arrival fanned the excitement.

'Hi, Bruno! Who's your friend?'

'It's Giovanni, the painter.' He was introduced to an anonymous bunch of seething faces.

'Come into the garden and join the dancing.'

There was nothing elegant about the merriment; no one was restrained by etiquette or finesse. It was jostle and be jostled. The boisterous jiggling and singing approximately matched the rhythm of a harsh drum and the tuneless efforts of three wind players who were more intent on volume than pitch.

'Will you dance with me, Giovanni?' said a short wide-eyed girl, who stood close to him, trembling with expectation.

Without waiting for an answer, she grabbed his hand and dragged him into the group of wild couples. He remembered Bruno's injunction to 'let himself go' and he offered no resistance. She whooped and screamed with joy as her bosom tried to bounce its way out of her bodice.

'There's a couple of scrapping cats down there,' she said, breathlessly, 'and they'll be out before the night is over.' Giovanni was amused by her high spirits and self-ridicule. 'Do you want to separate them?' she panted. 'They're giving me hell!'

Giovanni shook his head, embarrassed by the frankness of the invitation. She pulled her neckline down even lower as an extra inducement. Giovanni collided with another dancer and used his apology as a pretext to ignore the offer, which seemed to be not only misplaced, but quite resistible.

Large earthenware pitchers of crude wine waited on a table; they drank and danced again till their legs resigned.

The wide-eyed girl disappeared and was replaced by two others who were distinctly unsteady, full of wine and giggle. They were in a coquettish mood, though incapable of being more than mildly ludicrous. They brashly competed with each other for Giovanni's favours; each begged for a tumble, but Giovanni was neither impressed nor flattered by their attentions. They compensated for their lack of success by fondling each other before they expired into a pool of wine, blotting up the spillage.

Giovanni explored the food and was joined by Bruno, who was hoarse with an hour's singing.

'Are you enjoying yourself?'

'Yes, but I'm a bit tipsy.'

'Good! Let yourself go, for tomorrow we don't have to die.' They were interrupted by an older woman who was better dressed, more sober and more voluptuous than the girls.

'Who's your handsome friend, Bruno?'

'This is Giovanni; we work together. Giovanni, this is Bianca. She's a good sort, she can make you forget anything.'

'Is there something you want to forget, Giovanni?' The warm friendliness of her voice and her natural ease were like a soothing bath.

'No, not really, but I'm a bit depressed.' He was also a bit unsteady.

'You must tell me about it.'

'No, it's very boring and I don't want to spoil your evening.'

'You won't spoil it; I'm fed up with this party, anyway. It's too noisy for me.'

'And me,' said Giovanni. Their eyes confirmed their agreement with peevish expressions.

'Why don't we find somewhere quiet?'

'You mean somewhere a mile away.'

They laughed.

'No, I live next door. We could go there if you like.'

She did not need to be more persuasive. She led him to a low door in the garden wall, almost covered with trailing vines. She stooped and went through. Giovanni followed in a cloud of her perfume.

The inside of Bianca's house was ornate in a rather pretentious way. The walls were hung with Eastern embroideries and inferior pictures in heavy gold frames. Animal pelts covered most of the floors and the couches were strewn with Persian cushions. Small plants stood in blue and white majolica pots. But for all its doubtful taste, there was an air of comfortable friendliness that complemented Bianca's nature. The room which overlooked the canal was cool and silent. 'There, I told you it would be quiet in here.'

She lit lamps with a taper and poured two large glasses of white wine. The bouquet and flavour were delicate and temperate to a stomach marinated in vinegar. She sat on a huge bed and beckoned to Giovanni. 'Come and sit near me. I feel a bit swimmy.' She patted a cushion. 'Now what has made you depressed?'

Giovanni outlined the story about Marietta and his discovery about his mother.

'I expect you feel all alone and unwanted.' Her sympathy was in no way patronising.

'Well, I've got Bruno. He's a good friend; then there's Luca and my work. So it could be worse.' He tried to smile.

'But it could be better, I'm sure.' She drank again and lay into the cushions. 'Do you know, I feel lonely too.'

'You?'

'Yes, does that surprise you?'

'I would have thought you had dozens of friends.'

'Well, you'd be wrong. I've got plenty of acquaintances, but no one I can talk to like this.' She put her hand on the back of his head and moved it up through his hair. 'Would you like some more wine?'

'I don't know if…'

'Oh! Come on, you don't have to work tomorrow. I would like some more.' She passed her glass to him. 'Please.'

Her childlike naivety was compelling, in spite of being well rehearsed. They drank and lay together, their hands almost touching. Music from the garden drifted into the room, muted and magical. Bianca's perfume rioted in his head; he felt himself levitate and hang above the bed in a cloud of musk.

'I think we could give each other the contentment we both want,' she whispered.

Without waiting for assent, she rolled towards him; her mouth covered his and her hands explored with devastating experience.

Giovanni laid, a vanquished victim of her initiative. She loosened her hair in a cascade which imprisoned him in a cavern of blackness. All connections with his body were severed. Like a bisected worm, he felt his extremities wriggle away from him, anaesthetised and uncontrollable. He wrestled vainly to retain a hold on the flotsam which drifted out of reach on the tide of Bianca's passion.

Kneeling astride him, she uncovered and revealed herself. The efficiency of her lust was terrifying. She had a missionary zeal to convert young men to the worship of her body, and their latent virility was an irresistible challenge to her own sexual athleticism and versatility. She was infected by the same demon which drives men across uncharted seas, but it was not only an ardour for conquest; it also satisfied a compulsion for self-advertisement. That such vanity was dangerous in a well-manhandled, middle-aged woman had not occurred to her, but she still pursued the ultimate satisfaction in every opportunity, no matter how tenuous.

She was never more confident than she was at this moment.

He remained inert, pinioned by her perfume, the wine, his fatigue and self-consciousness. The soft parts of her body were pitted with deep depressions, her thighs reticulated with fine, livid veins. The pendulous paps swung above him, threatening suffocation; the creased skin was scarred with teeth marks, clearly not of her own making. Unclothed, she was a hideous travesty of woman; obsessed by her appetites, she was moronic. She raised her arms above her head and dropped on to him, shuddering with the triumph of supremacy.

He closed his eyes to dismiss the obscenity of her nipples, urgent and purple, her dark, wet armpits and her terrible grin. Cruciformed, his muscles paralysed, he concentrated on recalling the face and form of Marietta, but the image refused to clarify, ever repelled by the thrusting weight above. He tried to call her name, but all the breath was expelled. His whole being vomited in revulsion at the contact with her flaccid flesh. The perfume turned to feline acidity. The heaving, grinding form paused, trembled and swung like a compass needle finding north. His eyelids tightened against the horror beyond all imagining. Breath returned in poisonous gasps, cauterising his throat and lungs; his ears screamed between her knees; a flare exploded in his head and effort died.

The ceiling over the bed became animated with fluid reflections from the canal below. Giovanni lay spreadeagled among the skins and scented cushions, ravaged and plundered. A nerve twitched at the corner of his mouth and a foot reciprocated. As his eyes opened to a silent liquefaction above, his body trembled with returning consciousness and insane images kaleidoscoped his mind. A pressure in his temples and a suction behind his eyes increased alarmingly. He sat up and scanned the room. The furniture, the hangings and the objects were unfamiliar; the bed reeked of debauchery, and at once he felt despoiled. The edge of a fringed shawl was slowly lifted to reveal the face of Bianca. Her hair stuck to her skin and her blurred mouth leered derisively. 'Are you feeling better now? I am.' She cleared a tendril of hair from her eye.

Between the fringes of black silk, she looked like a caged animal; caged but venomous, Giovanni remembered. He shrank away from her as from a rotting corpse, his disgust more potent than before. His dry mouth and the totality of his humiliation obliterated his words of anger and contempt. His mouth opened and closed silently. His face sank into his hands; his fingers dug into his eyes. The pain relieved the torment and nausea within; the crimson of his own blood, a relief from the reality around him. The compulsion to cleanse himself washed over him. Bianca stretched out a hand, the fringes fell from her arm like black worms. She touched his thigh and dug her nails into his flesh. He recoiled as from a branding iron, his skin scarified.

'You are a silly boy! Now look what you have done. Let me kiss it better for you.'

She slid out of the shawl towards him, her lips pursed, as evil as the serpent of Eden.

An anguished cry set the goblets ringing on the table by the bed. Giovanni fell to the floor, the tray and glass crashed beside him. Half-crawling and half-blinded, he tore at the curtains.

Poles and brocades glissaded around him. With a long pole in both hands, he scythed his way across the room, smashing everything within its sweep. Lamps, urns, glass, plants echoed the explosions in his head. His feet slipped in his own blood and he fell sideways on to the bed. The pause in his indiscriminate destruction was assaulted by shrieks of laughter from the serpent beside him in a deafening crescendo.

'You poor bloody fool!' she screamed. 'Smash it all up! I don't care.'

Her last words were smothered by breathless hysteria.

White-hot rage and humiliation cancelled all reason and self-restraint. He threw down the pole and reached for the broken decanter. He fastened his fist around the neck and with all his strength, drove the jagged bell into her face. The heaving laughter continued. She looked foul with one eyelid slit open and her mouth distorted by a spear of glass. Her breath clouded the inside. He raised and plunged it into her face again; the spear cut through her cheek. With both hands, he twisted it, completing a deep circular incision, leaving only the nose intact and bloodless. The laughter had stopped, but the heaving continued. As he knelt over her, he noticed the incongruity of the brilliant red face and the unmarked body. With renewed determination, the glass axed again and again into her thorax and belly with the steady rhythm of a pile driver. The heaving faded as the body changed form and colour.

He felt elated.

A beast had been sacrificed, a poison neutralised, a memory expunged by blood. Atonement had restored purity to the world, to Venice, to Giovanni. He was cleansed. A shame had been expiated, for ever.

He went home wearing Bianca's blood and his own beneath his clothes.

Part Two
Maturity

The Fox and the Pullet

The Palazzo of the da Ponte family was built at a time when Gothic design, so nobly used in the Palazzo Ducale, had become over-ornate. Decoration was applied promiscuously and its quality had declined into sterile stereotypes. The façade and the interior displayed crude ostentation rather than good craftsmanship. It was neither large nor well appointed because the family fortune had for many years been dissipated by reckless speculation and unsuccessful gaming. Doge Nicolo had been elected to the position of titular head of the Republic more for his personal authority and prudence than to honour his family name. He was a political schemer of Machiavellian competence and his isolation as head of state, with prescribed and limited powers, made the other members of the Council and Senate feel relatively secure.

Doge Nicolo had ideas for promoting his fortune and prestige by carefully laid intrigues. His official dealings with foreign powers offered an opportunity for social and financial advancement which a more honourable man might have resisted. Avarice, however, was not regarded as reprehensible in Venice, especially when it was successful. The laws of the Republic, severe though they were for crime and treason, allowed plenty of scope for personal gain, so long as it did not prejudice the fortunes of the state.

Part of Nicolo's plan was to refurbish his palace as an alternative venue to the state apartments in the ducal palace. There, he was always observed, never alone. At home, he could freely instigate the schemes he had so diligently prepared. He knew that the building was openly regarded as third rate, old-fashioned and tasteless. In an age of artistic refinement, he himself was known as a barbarian, unpolished and uncouth. He was feared and ridiculed with equal vigour.

It was his intention to commission Maestro Jacopo or Maestro Paolo Veronese, both of whom had been engaged on the restoration of the ducal palace, to paint murals for his saloon and staircase. But his enquiries had suggested that their services would be very costly. He knew that Tintoretto had worked for the Scuola di San Rocco for nothing, and for a time, he was encouraged to think that he might persuade the artist to offer him favourable terms. That is, until they had met. The prospect of a set of Tintorettos excited him, but the price of the kudos would be too high. Consequently, it was of some comfort to him that the exploratory and unsatisfactory interview had provided an acceptable alternative in the master's favourite pupil, and, furthermore, if Tintoretto was right in his assessment, Nicolo could only gain prestige as the patron of a brilliant new painter. Such a bonus appealed enormously to the old man. He had arranged an audience with the assistant alone, which he was certain would achieve the maximum return for the minimum outlay. With attention to every detail, he might even find a way to relieve himself of the cost altogether. The anticipation warmed his thin blood.

Jacopo inspected Giovanni. His eyes moved up from the green leather shoes. He checked that the hose fitted well, that the doublet was the right length, the belt not too tight, the cap at the correct angle, neither too rakish, nor too symmetrical. He returned to the belt and adjusted the position of the purse. His movements were punctuated by grunts of approval. He placed the gold chain around Giovanni's neck and stood back to review the whole effect.

'That will do very well, my boy,' he said. 'You won't need a cloak today; it's going to be hot.'

'Thank you, Maestro.'

'Before you go, I want to talk to you.' He led Giovanni to the window and sat on a bench. 'Sit down, and try to remember this.' He leaned an elbow on the sill and fingered his beard thoughtfully. 'Da Ponte is a cunning fox; cunning and deadly. With his years and his rank working for him, you'll have to be very careful, or he'll twist your neck when you think he's patting your cheek. So don't let him pat your cheek – keep your distance.'

He paused, still looking across the canal, and his great eyebrows joined over his nose. He picked his words carefully to warn rather than to alarm the boy, whose expressions became more fearful. 'Don't let him be familiar,' he went on.

'But how do I…'

'Keep in the middle of the room and don't for God's sake sit down, even if he insists. Tell him you've got a boil on your rump. Tell him anything.' The eyebrows enmeshed again. 'He's a fox and you're a pullet. Remember that.'

Giovanni fidgeted on the leather cushion. A pigeon dropped off the cornice above the window and floated in a steep arc across the water.

'A pullet without wings,' added the Maestro. 'But above all, don't agree to anything. Whatever he wants, whatever he suggests, tell him that you will have to get my approval. Don't commit yourself to anything. That way you'll always be one jump ahead. If he sees half a chance, he'll use it.'

He disengaged the eyebrows and put a hand on Giovanni's shoulder. 'It's not that I don't trust you, my boy. I don't trust *him*.' His voice became a shout which attracted a gondolier who passed quietly below. He knew the Maestro, smiled and waved a hand. Tintoretto returned the greeting automatically and bent forward, his voice whispering urgently, 'And you mustn't trust him either.'

Giovanni noticed that his eyes were moist. Then they disappeared behind the eyebrows. The hand tightened on his shoulder. 'You had better go now, and God go with you'.

As he reached the door, Giovanni turned to say what he had been unable to say before, but the hunched figure in the window, supporting his head with his fist, seemed old and frail and pathetic. The words would not come.

He was still there when Giovanni returned two hours later.

'Maestro, I'm back.'

The creases in the old man's forehead dissolved. He rose and came towards Giovanni with open arms. They embraced.

'Pour some wine and tell me how it went.'

His voice was agitated by impatience and concern. He sat in his great chair and fitted his head into its contemplative niche.

'Well,' began Giovanni, 'I did exactly as you said. I told him that I was not a free man and that you would have to approve the arrangements, the subject and the contract. He didn't like that and he tried to persuade me to accept a private arrangement between him and me, but I was firm.' Jacopo nodded approvingly and sipped his glass, smiling. 'He said I was old enough to leave you and enter into his household. He would pay me wages.'

'Bastard!' grunted Jacopo.

'But I refused. I told him that I could not be disloyal to my master, that you had been so kind to me, more like a father and that I owed everything to you and that I wanted to repay you, not betray you.'

Jacopo wiped the corner of his eye with the back of his hand. 'But what does he want you to paint?' he asked quietly.

'Well, on the staircase, he wants scenes from the life of St Mark, finishing with the burial in San Marco, with a great procession going over a bridge...'

'A bridge, indeed,' growled Jacopo, 'with himself at the head, no doubt.'

'Yes, he did suggest that.'

'Da Ponte on a *ponte*, sounds like incest to me! The Apotheosis of a Ponte,' he roared. 'Christ in heaven! What else?'

'In the saloon he wants a great panorama of the Venetian fleet engaging the Genoese, with pennants of all the noble families streaming above the smoke...'

'Say no more. I get the picture; his arms in the foreground, I suppose.' His sarcasm was so vitriolic that even Giovanni felt abashed. 'What else did he say?'

'Well, he wanted me to work in the Palazzo. He said he would set aside rooms for me to work in, that I would be looked after like a guest, not an employee. He said that he could supply girls for my bed.' His voice faded as his cheeks flamed.

'I bet he did. The devil in a whorehouse! But you didn't agree, did you?'

'No, Maestro,' protested Giovanni. 'I remembered what you said. I told him I should have to work here and that the contract would have to be drawn up between him and you.'

'Good, you did well, my son.' He extended his arms and embraced the boy again. The Maestro's paternal love and concern flooded Giovanni's spirit. He had never been so addressed before, except by his own father, and the bond of trust and admiration that had grown over the years of apprenticeship had been cemented in deep, mutual affection.

They finished the jug of wine in eloquent silence.

The next day Jacopo rose earlier than usual and surprised his assistants by appearing in the studio before work had started. The sun streamed horizontally through the windows, raking the wet canvases with dramatic light.

'Clear all this stuff away and bring me a couple of easels and a strip of canvas about a yard and a half wide.'

The Maestro was rarely in such a dictatorial mood and his urgency was greeted by the disciplined compliance of everyone there. Unaccustomed to menial work, Domenico and Bruno moved stretchers and stools with the others; Giovanni gathered up a handful of brushes and flicked dust from tables with a paint rag. Marco's pupil, Ottavia, the most recent arrival in the studio, stood helplessly by her father as he paced in the centre of the room rolling his sleeves. Marco brought a long offcut of primed canvas. 'What do you want this for, Maestro?'

'Tack it to a plank and I'll show you.'

He was enjoying the confusion and mystery he had created. Above all, he was a man of action, yet he had an appetite for drama, for underlying currents of irrationality, which he revealed more in his work than in his daily life.

Today had everything. Today he would exercise his mastery over materials, situations and people, and he thrilled at the prospect. He knew that the challenge, the anticipation was sweeter than the achievement; experience had taught him this. Adulation was a hollow reward for the labour he loved. It never compensated for the disappointment that the finished work almost always fell far short of his vision.

Marco tacked the canvas to a long plank of cypress wood, each end of which was placed on an easel.

'I want golden ochre, burnt umber, black and white', Jacopo announced. 'Give me some of those brushes, Giovanni.'

He walked between the easels, drawing in the air with a dry brush, his hand describing long, flowing curves. The preparations complete, the assistants perched on stools and tables in an arc around the canvas. The stage was cleared for the solo performer, who stood mute and still before an audience riveted with expectancy.

'*Benedic nos, Domine*,' he muttered, crossing himself. He raised his head, and with a dripping brush, drew an ellipse in the top centre of the long rectangle. He pulled two tangential curves up to each corner and with rapid movements, undulated wave lines beneath them. He blocked in the ellipse with ochre and scrubbed more into some of the spaces below. Paint dripped off the palette on to the floor. He changed brush and colour to umber and flicked a series of comma-shaped marks roughly into the remaining spaces.

There was, as yet, no hint of what the subject was to be, but his audience was mesmerised by the rhythmical ease and assurance of the master's strokes. Area flowed into area; lines, at first apparently broken, began to join across voids and masses like woven patterns, over and under, until a huge tracery of orchestrated movement swung in complementary and contrasting rhythms around the central space.

Only the Maestro moved, choreographing the canvas. The ring of faces, awed and motionless, concentrated on the growing image which absorbed them completely. Changing brush and colour again, he drew a central figure with astonishing speed, and dipping a finger into white, he pulled a shining nimbus away from the head in crisp impasto. The Saviour materialised high above the storm waves; the Virgin appeared by his side, looking towards her son. Two balancing groups of Apostles reclined on clouds to left and right. With the butt end of the brush, he scratched sharp incisions into the wet nimbus; lines of radiant glory shone from the Saviour's head, a crown of stars settled around the Virgin's. In a few minutes of concentrated effort and prodigious skill, the Maestro had vitalised the figures at the heart of the design.

'It's the *Paradiso*!'

The words rippled through the spectators. As the tensions of the mystery were relieved, they moved on their perches like roosting birds and settled again.

'Yes, you have it,' said Jacopo, who, for the first time, stepped back to view what he had done.

He squinted through his lashes, his head tilted to one side. He returned to the canvas, dipping his finger in the white once more. Delicately, he pushed Christ's head down half an inch, so that it returned the Virgin's gaze. The rhythm of his fluent brush hardly paused. Saints and angels, prophets and princes, popes and bishops emerged from formless chrysalides, filling the elliptical spaces below the holy pair. Between each dark row of figures, he washed a river of golden light.

The sun now slanted down on to the floorboards where the paint had dripped in oily discs. The Maestro's feet had pressed some into irregular patches of colour, white, ochre, brown and black, like lichen on an aged roof. The colours mirrored those in the canvas above. The Maestro noticed the mess he had made and he turned to his pupils, smiling. 'Here, the order and harmony of heaven; down there, the disorder and discord of hell. The choice is yours.'

Between the two stood the magisterial figure of Jacopo Robusti.

In the ensuing days, the sketch was reworked on a larger scale by Domenico, Bruno and the master himself. The colours were extended to greens, blues and reds; some rich, some restrained. He altered only the details, regrouping them into more coherent masses; he modified their scale, adding accents of tone and colour. Never before had a painter created such a vast impression of space or such a richness of heavenly light.

Over and over he repeated, 'The colour of Titian and the form of Michelangelo; then we shall have paradise.'

At least twice each day, the painter left his house, without a word, to visit the church of the Madonna dell'Orto, there, in a secluded corner, he prayed for guidance.

'Permit me, O Lord, a glimpse of Thy paradise.

Grant, O Mother of God, a vision of the eternal light.

Not for myself do I ask, but for the greater Glory of Father, Son and Holy Spirit. Amen.'

But illumination was denied. His prayers always ended in the same darkness as they begun, but the sketch was completed, and the huge canvas was delivered to the ducal palace in accordance with the rules of the competition. Paolo Veronese, Francesco Bassano and Palma the Younger had each produced his best work for this prestigious commission.

The Senate would decide which would receive it.

No more could be done.

He was exhausted.

He advised Giovanni on the sketches for the Palazzo da Ponte, but the whole project seemed unworthy of his, or Giovanni's time. He walked about the city trying to lose himself in the crowds, but he was constantly recognised by citizens and visitors, so that the privacy he wanted was denied him. He went to the Arsenal and talked to shipbuilders and to the quay to talk to the fishermen. The accounts he heard of exotic places, of tempests and sea creatures, and ribald tales which sailors told, satisfied him very little. He wanted to work, but his cup was drained.

The situation was saved for him by a message from Mantua. Duke Guglielmo Gonzaga required a series of eight pictures about the life of his illustrious family. The terms he offered were very favourable, but Jacopo accepted the invitation only because it was an escape from his indolence. The prospect invigorated him and the preliminary sketches which had been demanded and the preparation for the journey abounded with his usual enthusiasm and optimism.

He would take Domenico. No, he was needed to run the studio in his absence.

He would take Giovanni. No, he would be 'up to his ears immortalising that Devil da Ponte'.

Bruno, he would take Bruno – and Ottavia would become Giovanni's assistant. It was settled.

Giovanni had acquired an assistant.

Acquisition and Deprivation

Ottavia was totally unlike her sister. Quiet and diffident by nature, she had grown up overshadowed by an ebullient individual who had allowed her character very little scope for normal expansion. Consequently, she was unsure of herself and preferred self-effacement to involvement, but beneath the reticence there was a deeply sensitive personality, which, in spite of her youth, responded to every nuance of human feeling.

Physically, she was less engaging than Marietta. She was plump and gave the impression of being lethargic. A childlike face under a low forehead was framed by a confusion of curls of an indeterminate brown, which seemed to compress the features into doll-like proportions. Her eyes were large and moist, quiet and passive.

Her upbringing and the repressive influence of her sister had made her demure and complaisant to the point of dullness, so that her virtues passed largely unnoticed in the limited circle in which she was known. Yet her virtues were considerable. She was valued by her father alone, who continued to treat her like a small child, for all her sixteen years. There was no intellectual contact between them, but a mutual devotion existed, even though the father's remained much the same as it had been when she came into his life in his forty-fifth year.

She had been further swamped by the relentless activity and the exercise of skills quite beyond her grasp which were taken for granted in the studio. She had, by necessity, been excluded from the real work of the place. She played no part in the production of the pictures for the Palazzo Ducale which had occupied most of the time since the fire. Her tasks were those required of and accepted by every junior apprentice in every studio; the grinding of colours, priming of canvas, cleaning of brushes and palettes, the fetching and carrying. In all these, she was unfailingly conscientious and unobtrusive.

Her joy and satisfaction in her promotion were tempered by anxiety, for although she admired Giovanni and found in him characteristics which were immediately attractive, the responsibilities which lay before her had been amply illustrated by Giovanni himself as an assistant. Her lack of participation had provided plenty of opportunity to learn from observation and example, his example. His method and integrity were derived from and matched those of his master, and his skill was rapidly approaching that for which the studio was justly famed. She saw herself as a link in a chain which stretched back to Giovanni Bellini, and beyond.

Her natural timidity diminished in the first few days of their partnership. Each discovered common experiences, common attitudes in the other; they shared responses and objectives to a remarkable extent. Ottavia became less inhibited as she became less servile, and the confidence Giovanni had in her ability to participate fully encouraged her to assume a total commitment to the success of the project and their relationship. As the work grew, their interdependence strengthened.

'Come and tell me what you think of this,' said Giovanni, pointing to a portion of a sketch depicting St Mark, Paul and Barnabas preaching.

She put down the palette knife carefully and, wiping her hands on her apron, stood by Giovanni. Instinctively, she placed herself slightly behind him, away from the window, so that no part of her shadow fell upon the work or the palette. She studied the area, but her concentration was deflected by gratification at being consulted as a more or less equal partner.

'Do you think that the architecture is too heavy for the figures?' he went on.

She screwed up her eyelids to drain away the detail, as her father often did. Her independent judgement was sought and she was determined to be as objective and truthful as possible.

It was a subtle point.

'No, not exactly. The figures are very strong, but do you think the shadows here are a bit dark?'

She pointed to an arcade stretching away into the Forum of ancient Rome. The deep perspective gave a spacious magnificence to the city which, to a Venetian eye, appeared massive and extravagant.

'Let's reduce them then,' said Giovanni, blotting the wet paint with a rag. They both squinted at the effect and, stepping back, collided. A fully charged brush scored Ottavia's arm and a pot of thick varnish medium exploded at their feet. Ottavia was mortified by her clumsiness. She had wrecked a situation which, only seconds ago, had given her such satisfaction. Her cheeks reddened and her eyes became moister. She recalled Marietta's performance and fully expected to earn a similar response and a similar penalty. Either would be painful; both would be unbearable.

Before Giovanni noticed her embarrassment, he was laughing at his own awkwardness, a grotesque, balletic attempt to avoid the falling oil. Ottavia's bespattered skirt and his own stockings seemed equally absurd. But looking into her face, he could see that she was crying.

'Oh, come on! It doesn't matter. Don't cry over spilt varnish.'

She cried more.

'It was my fault, not yours,' he said.

His gentleness and his laughter seemed misplaced to Ottavia, who felt she deserved a reprimand rather than conciliation.

'No! I'm stupid. I'm sorry.'

Giovanni laid the palette on the floor and stuck the brushes into the thumb hole. Still on his knees, he wiped her skirt with his rag.

'But I'm so useless,' she sobbed, agonised by the confession.

Giovanni realised that she could not be persuaded by reason or soothed by simple assurance, but whether to leave her to her grief or to stay and comfort her, he was not sure.

'Come and sit down over here, Tavi.' The abbreviation of her name spontaneously expressed the protectiveness and the tenderness he felt for her. 'Come on.'

He put an arm around her neck and led her to the settle by the window. The crying abated.

He felt mature and dependable. Except for minor convulsions, she became quiet and contained, but her chin covered her throat and her swollen eyes remained lowered in humiliation.

'That's better,' he said quietly. 'It's all over now.'

She made no reply and sat motionless. Puzzled by this sudden passivity, he placed his hand below her chin to lift her face.

'Don't look at me,' she said, jerking her head away. 'I'm ugly.'

'No you're not. You are...' the right word eluded him. She was neither pretty, nor beautiful. He had never thought of her as attractive. In fact, until this moment, he had hardly thought of her appearance at all.

'...Upset,' he added lamely.

'Aren't you angry with me, then?' she asked.

'Of course not! Why should I be? It was not your fault.'

'It wasn't yours either,' she said, wiping her eyes impatiently. She laid her cheek against the hand that gripped her shoulder. 'But thank you, anyway. I feel better now.'

She looked up at him and fabricated a smile. A trivial incident had germinated an affinity, a sympathy between them which she had not been aware of before. Giovanni also recognised a transition from a working relationship to a personal one. For him, however, it lacked the significance it had for Ottavia. 'Come,' he said. 'That's enough for today. Let's go for a walk.'

She dried her eyes and took the helping hand he offered with brotherly politeness.

The city was stirring after siesta.

It had been very hot and the paving of the parched squares was warm beneath their feet and still convected an arid drift of air around their legs. The alleys which had been shaded all day were chilled and damp. They passed from extremes of light and dark, of humidity and temperature every few yards.

Shopkeepers banged open their shutters and swept their doorsteps. Voices alternated shrill and gruff assertions and responses. Cats stretched their legs and spread their claws, mutely resentful of the disturbance of their shaded peace. Baskets, sausages, stockings and poultry were raised on poles to sway suspended from hooks by doorways. Women carried splashing buckets and ewers from the well heads, scuffing, and chattering against the counterpoint of tenon saw and planishing hammer.

'Where are we going?' Ottavia asked, half running to keep pace with Giovanni.

'Not far now. You'll see.'

She knew they would soon reach the Grand Canal. They went through the fish market where baskets of molluscs, shrimps and squids and trays of fish, arranged in close order, gave off a clean, marine smell, more sea-like than the sea. She gathered her skirt in a twisted handful, raising the hem clear of the wet cobbles. She was still holding it so when they reached the Rialto.

Giovanni paused. A boatman waved.

'Come on, Tavi!'

He grabbed her hand and weaved his way through the crowd to the boat station. She followed unsteadily, her indoor slippers being unsuited to rapid changes of direction.

'Hello, Luca!' Luca stood in the prow of his boat in a classic pose of masculine ease, his brown arms folded in front of him. 'This is Ottavia; Tavi, this is my friend Luca.'

The man smiled in greeting and at his thoughts simultaneously. Ottavia read his thoughts and went pink.

'Can we come to supper?' Giovanni asked ingenuously.

'I think we can manage two small ones. Come aboard! I was going home anyway!'

He swung the boat about with a couple of strokes and a trailing oar. He mused back to a similar situation when he had ferried Giovanni and Marietta to his house. While his eyes scanned the water, he noticed the girl placidly sitting, arranging her skirt, adjusting her slippers. *A woman of quality, in miniature*, he thought. He avoided any reference to Marietta or any question of the relationship which existed between his two passengers. He would be patient, but in the meantime, he was satisfied by the answers he drew from observation.

Sophenisba hugged Giovanni with ursine ferocity.

'We haven't seen anything of you for months. What have you been up to? Flirting, I suppose!' She leered at Ottavia and winked.

'This is Ottavia,' said Giovanni, ignoring her taunt. 'She's the Maestro's daughter,' he added.

The ample devil in Sophenisba blurted, 'So you are Marietta's sister. She came here with Giovanni often. What's she doing now? We always had a good laugh. How is she? We haven't seen her for ages.'

The coda of her torrent was not interrogative, so neither of them felt the need to reply. The flow persisted while she prepared the meal.

She poured olive oil into a skillet, and when it was hot, she dropped small-floured fish and sliced octopus into the rumbling pot, where they puffed into golden mouthfuls of indefinable shape. She chopped lemons into chunks with fearful inaccuracy. Squalls of laughter rang the pans above her head.

Giovanni studied his discomforted pupil; Luca studied them both.

'What are you working on at the moment?' he asked.

'We are doing some pictures for da Ponte's palazzo,' said Giovanni.

Ottavia noted the plural with surprise and some satisfaction.

'We are still on the roughs, mind you,' he continued, 'so there's a lot to do. We want to get the job done by the time the Maestro gets back from Mantua, but I don't expect we'll manage it, do you, Ottavia?'

'I don't think so,' she said diffidently. 'In any case, we don't know how long he will be away.'

'Wait a moment. You're not telling me that you are doing this alone, are you?' Luca's feigned surprise was exaggerated, for he knew the reply even before he had asked the question.

'Yes, we are,' said Giovanni. 'The doge wanted me to do the work for him. He must have thought I would be cheap, but the contract is really with the Maestro, so it won't be all that cheap, after all.'

Luca ignored the financial detail. 'Well, this is good news! So now you are a master painter. Did you hear that, woman?'

His wife nodded abstractedly, without comprehension.

'Not exactly, I'm still part of the team, of course.'

'But you must have done well to be trusted with such an important job,' said Luca seriously. 'And what about Ottavia, what does she do?'

'She's my assistant. We're doing the work together.'

Luca sailed approvingly at her.

'And do you like it?' he asked.

'Oh yes!' she replied. 'Giovanni is very good to me and very kind.'

She looked towards him to find that he was more discomposed by receiving her compliments than she was by bestowing them.

'He's not a galley master with a whip, then?'

'She has been in the studio for two years now,' interrupted Giovanni, 'so she knows what has to be done and how to do it. I don't have to tell her anything. Her ground pigments are as smooth as silk and she can prime canvas better than I can.'

Luca sensed that behind the reciprocal praise lay a deeper understanding than either of them would admit to at present. He decided to change the subject, and would have done, given the chance.

'And what do you do when you're not working?' trumpeted Sophenisba. 'I bet you get up to all sorts…'

Luca cuffed her rump with the back of his hand.

'Shut up, you serpent!' he growled.

'I will not! I want to know everything. What do you do when you're not working?' she repeated, glaring defiantly at Giovanni.

'We come to see you to enjoy a peaceful supper,' said Giovanni, mocking her defiance.

Luca enjoyed the deft riposte and leaned forward towards Ottavia.

'Take no notice of her. She's impossible. She's a good woman really, but she has a mouthful of guile. She's quite a handful, as you may have gathered.'

Ottavia laughed for the first time since her accident in the studio.

'Can I call you "Tavi" too?' he asked.

'Of course you can. Only Giovanni calls me that, but you can too.'

The tension slackened and the rest of the meal, the pastries filled with ripe figs and the cheese, was demolished in relaxed approval.

After they had parted with embraces which included the newcomer, Luca said, 'They're well suited.' He blew out he candles. 'Well suited.'

Jacopo returned home for Christmas full of dazzling accounts of the Gonzaga court, the lavish entertainments and the palace itself. The paintings, especially the frescoes by Mantegna, excited his admiration most of all.

'Mantua is a ghastly place in winter, though. Nothing but a curtain of mist can be seen from the windows. It hangs there day after day. You feel imprisoned. They have to provide all sorts of entertainment to prevent the inmates from going mad. But the cold and the damp have got into my bones, so I have come home for the Blessed Incarnation, and to get warm. God in heaven, what a place!'

He sipped a liqueur and felt the glow of aniseed and alcohol spreading into his limbs. He settled himself by the fire and asked for a report on the work he had left behind, in Domenico's charge.

'Things are going very smoothly, Father. Three pictures are ready for you to retouch; three more are well on their way. We've followed your sketches exactly, so I think you will be pleased.'

'Any news of the *Paradiso*?' Jacopo asked.

'Not yet,' replied Domenico, 'but I ran into one of Maestro Paolo's assistants the other day, and he said that the Senate would announce their decision in the new year.'

'Oh good! Then I shall be here when the news breaks.' He sipped again, glowing with warmth and contentment. He turned to Giovanni. 'And how is your job going, my boy?'

'Rather slowly, I'm afraid, Maestro,' said Giovanni. 'The sketches for the St Mark series are all done and we've got one canvas roughed-in in monochrome.'

'Has Ottavia been useful? Now, be honest.'

'Oh yes, Maestro. I couldn't have managed without her. In fact, she has done most of the monochrome as well.'

Jacopo was astonished to hear that she had been painting. It was unusual for an apprentice to reach this stage in two years, but he was confident of Giovanni's judgement and gratified that his own talent had shown up in another of his children. 'Come over here, my child,' he said to Ottavia. He took her hand and directed her to the footstool. Content with the praise of Giovanni and the affection of her father, she sat down and rested her head on his knee. His hand fondled her curls. 'I am delighted, my dear. You have made me very happy.'

His fingertips explored the form under the scalp. He found that it was the same as his own. They detached themselves from the others, who felt excluded and remote from this display of unaffected tenderness.

It was Domenico who invaded their silent pleasure. 'Father, when do you want to view the work?'

'Later, Tino. I want to rest now and enjoy my homecoming. Leave us now.' He closed his eyes. They turned to go. Ottavia rose slightly, but the fingertips restrained her.

'I want you to stay, Giovanni,' he added. 'Come and sit by me.'

He placed his glass on a side table and motioned towards the stool on his right. Giovanni sat down, completing the pyramid.

'This journey has made me feel old, and now that I am home, I don't want to leave it again. It's not that Venice draws me, you understand; Venice can go to hell, and will go, whether I like it or not. No, I mean, to be here in this house, with those I love. I am like a dying tree whose roots have found a new watercourse.' He placed his hand on Giovanni's shoulder. Ottavia looked at her father with eyes full of anxiety.

'You are not ill, are you, Father?' she asked.

'No, no, just tired and sated with the wealth and luxury of others. When you get old, material things lose their importance and their value; they become tawdry. Duke Gonzaga has a treasury as big as this house, but I am richer than him.' He drew them closer to him. 'In my two hands are all the riches of Mantua, China and India, and more. More than I deserve, more than any man could measure or desire. You are my treasury, and I thank God for His great bounty.'

Giovanni felt a slight tremor transmitted through his Maestro's knees. Ottavia could not control her feelings. Giovanni struggled to control his, but without success.

They remained there, a perfect pyramid of joy, radiating and absorbing affections.

'Now let me see your pictures.' Jacopo had fractured the silence, but not the joy. Still interlocked, they went to Giovanni's workroom. The master studied the sketches, arranged in sequence along one wall. He tugged his beard and frowned. Giovanni looked fearfully at Ottavia, certain of a disparaging verdict.

The silence seemed interminable.

'These are too good for that polecat, da Ponte,' he said at last. 'They're too good for the ducal palace; too good for Venice.'

The visible relief on the two young faces dissolved into smiles of amazement.

'Are they as good as that, Father?' asked Ottavia.

'I wouldn't say it if they weren't.' There was no anger or impatience in his voice, just a carefully measured assurance.

'They ought to be placed where the whole world can see them and be...' he paused, '...inspired. The new basilica in Rome ought to have them, not that decaying ruin on the canal. They are superb.'

He held out his arms to Giovanni, the corners of his eyes sparkling.

'My son, you have made me very humble. You can learn no more from me. You are a master!' They embraced. 'I never thought I should live to see the equal of Titian, in science, in skill, in feeling.'

Giovanni was stunned by this reception. Had the old man's judgement been warped by the euphoria of Christmas and his homecoming, he wondered.

After supper, Tintoretto had a travelling chest brought into the room. He gave his gifts to everyone in the household; calf-bound volumes of verses and histories for the men with their initials tooled in gold on the front boards; jewellery for the women; cloaks, hose and boots for the servants. For Giovanni, there was an inlaid wooden box containing a selection of lenses, concave and convex, perspective glasses, prisms and mirrors of the finest quality. There was a slim book, recently translated from the English, describing the properties and uses of lenses. But the cover displayed the greatest surprise. In a cartouche, it was inscribed:

GIOVANNI ROBUSTI AD MDLXXIX

Giovanni drew breath in astonishment. His finger ran over the tooling to confirm by touch what he could no longer see for tears.

'This Christmas, I give Giovanni, my adopted son, my own name. Receive him into the family as I do, with warmth and benevolence. I know you will do this for his own sake as much as mine, for we all love him.'

Domenico stepped forward first, smiling, his hand held out.

'Welcome to the "dyers", Giovanni! You have put up with us long enough to know our faults. We are glad to have you.'

His cordial words and relaxed manner eased Giovanni's intense feelings. Their long embrace provided a sanctuary in which he framed a few words of reply. The others crowded in with their own expressions of pleasure and an enthusiastic bombardment of his back. Jacopo was overjoyed by their response to his idea. 'Let us drink to the new Robusti.' He raised a carafe to replenish empty glasses, slopping wine carelessly into and around those proffered by jostling hands. Giovanni gained more time.

'Giovanni, saluté!' they shouted and drank.

Hot with self-consciousness and emotion, Giovanni cleared his throat.

'I will never forget today,' he began, 'for today I have been given a family I have always admired, and a generous, loving father whom I honour and respect above all men. When we are all dead and forgotten, our father will be remembered. He will be honoured and respected for his goodness as a man and his greatness as an artist.' He turned towards the Maestro, who was clearly moved by the boy's sincerity. 'My father, I thank you and I will love you always.' He reached for the nearest goblet and held it towards the old man. 'My father, saluté!'

The cheers and applause were deafening, but barely audible to the pair at the centre of the uproar. They were transfixed in a private communion of understanding and admiration beyond words. Of the others, only Ottavia understood.

In the new year, Jacopo was summoned to the ducal palace to hear the result of the competition, but he found himself unexpectedly alone.

The Senate had been divided, and no single artist had received a clear majority of the votes. Out of the substrata of prejudice and intrigue, a compromise had emerged, and it had been agreed to consult Tintoretto before a public announcement was made. He was asked if he was prepared to modify his sketch by making the figures larger and the areas of space smaller. They argued that his paradise was too sparse, giving an impression of an elite rather than showing the promise of salvation for all the faithful. The arguments presented arose from a turmoil of theological, social and quasi-artistic factors which impressed the painter very little. He reviewed his bold, luminous sketch as complaints were advanced by various members of the church and the Senate. By nature and from long experience, Tintoretto was unwilling to compromise on artistic matters, and a closer examination of the sketch confirmed his reluctance to change it at all.

'The Senate feels that your design, for all its merits, lacks an element of majesty and grandeur,' was a recurring theme among the reasons given.

'But larger figures will not necessarily create a more majestic effect,' explained the master. 'There is a real danger of achieving confusion if the spaces are reduced. Grandeur demands *space* in which to breathe.'

They were not to be deflected. The discussion continued.

Tintoretto chose his words carefully and suppressed a mounting impatience. Experience had convinced him that stupid patrons could be guided from folly by applying gentle reason and the adoption of a suitably deferential attitude. But it would soon become clear to him that the well-tried formula would not succeed in the present situation. Political factions, undercurrents of bias and self-interest had already corroded their judgements, No one supported the compromise with any enthusiasm or sincerity. He identified those who held preferences for Veronese and Bassano, those who were in favour of himself and those who had no preference, but were aligned to the view of some other senator, whatever that might be. He assessed the strength of his own support and became despondent. He would not waste his reason, his deference or his time on attacking the compromise. He was tempted to withdraw and leave them floundering in the stalemate, but prudence was not to be squandered by irritation. There was too much at stake.

'My lords,' he said at last, 'will you allow me a week to consider your proposal and to work on a revised sketch?'

His request was granted immediately and with visible relief.

In two days, Tintoretto had painted another, enlivened by anger and contempt. He had decided to give them what they wanted; no more, no less. If it looked closer to hell than to heaven, their wretched taste would be vindicated; *they* would bear the responsibility. Driven by an impulse to create a design which could destroy itself with its own internal dynamism, he barely guided it on with the light rein of his artistry. It teetered on the edge of confusion and anarchy. Except round the figure of Christ, he eliminated every inch of luminous space; between the swathes of writhing figures, hundreds of cherubim crowded the golden rivulets like toad spawn. He gave to paradise some of the terribilità of Michelangelo's *Last Judgement*.

The mastery was his, the irony was his, the destruction of his own concept was his, the contract was his, but he vowed not to paint a single brush stroke on the final canvas. He would negotiate the highest fee ever known for the largest oil painting ever known, but the Senate would receive a studio job, and they would never know the difference.

He returned to Mantua savouring the triple victory of wisdom over folly, of ridicule over pomposity, of high art over philistinism. He had won the most prestigious contract the Republic had ever offered a painter, and he would leave its execution in other hands.

Giovanni and Ottavia had worked methodically into the St Mark series. Two finished canvases representing the *Healing of the Cobbler Anianus* and the *Miracle of the Venetian Fisherman* stood each side of the *Burial of St Mark's Body in Venice*. This last one was to fill the landing wall, the other two, and three similar sized canvases were for the staircase of the Palazzo da Ponte. The effect common to them all was a dramatic relationship of the figures to the background. The powerful human forms were richly coloured and alive with suspended movement. Their gestures were not rhetorical or contrived, but naturally expressive of individual personalities and emotions; their faces glowed with unselfconscious conviction. The saint himself was ennobled by faith and charity. The backgrounds, however, were spacious and atmospheric, each successive plane softened almost imperceptibly into an iridescent infinity. Superficially, the effect was similar to that achieved by Veronese with diluted monochromes, but here the distance was painted in opaque colour, each surface fractured into a scintillating area of broken brushwork. The particular hues were indivisibly blended, yet were paler mixtures of those present in the foreground draperies.

Giovanni had created a subtle unity in his painting which was magical and unique. He had combined his master's skill in handling paint with a sensitive observation of reality and his own experiments with the prisms which Tintoretto had given him for Christmas. The pictures retained the essence of grand decoration and, at the same time, presented a wholly convincing naturalism. Real people in real settings were transubstantiated into jewels set among pearls.

Ottavia worked delicately into the spaces, placing touches of pale, prismatic colour into Giovanni's under painting, matching the tones exactly, blending edges according to a predetermined progression he had indicated for each picture. In practice, they had reversed the conventional procedure in which the assistant laid the monochrome and the master superimposed the final colours. She recognised the importance of the role she had been given and worked with absolute dedication. Only occasionally did Giovanni intervene and modify what she had done, but when he did, it was in a spirit of cooperation rather than of criticism.

Their closeness and division of labour generated a harmony which each understood and cherished. Each put the other's interests second only to the project in hand. Working together and relaxing together, their lives were inextricably entwined and the outward result of that harmony could be seen in their paintings and their mutual affection.

It was, therefore, a cruel shock when a boatman, whom Giovanni knew slightly called at the house with a message from Sophenisba. 'Luca is ill and is asking for you,' he said simply.

'What is the matter with him?' asked Giovanni, who was unable to grasp the idea of Luca being anything else but strong and healthy.

'No one knows, but it's serious. Can you come now?'

'Of course,' said Giovanni. He raced upstairs to tell Ottavia.

'I'm coming with you, then.'

The boatman rowed them along the familiar canals to Luca's house with long, firm strokes, unhurried but powerful. The bow cut through the water deeply, disturbing the boats moored behind them, bobbing at their posts. No word was spoken during the journey; each was imprisoned by fear and bewilderment. Ottavia sat close to Giovanni, holding his arm tightly.

Sophenisba met them at the door, mute and tearful. She pointed upstairs and sank on a stool. 'Hurry...' she murmured. Her mouth was paralysed and further words were strangled by a high-pitched moan. Ottavia put both arms round her neck and kissed her taut cheek.

Luca lay on his back, his face furrowed with pain. His breathing was rapid and shallow, his hands clutched the bedclothes covering his stomach. The bandages on his arms showed that he had been bled; his pallor confirmed it. Giovanni was filled with horror by Luca's appearance. He placed his hands over his friend's knotted fingers and called his name.

The face uncreased slightly and the rocking head paused, resting towards Giovanni. 'My dear boy, I'm glad you could come.'

Another spasm screwed his nerves together, tightening his lips and teeth.

Giovanni recalled the gentle, handsome face of his friend, now distorted, drawn and skeletal, and wet with sweat. He sponged the forehead, cheeks and mouth, crying out in silent protest.

'I wanted to say farewell to you, Giovanni, and to thank you for all the happiness you have given.' Luca's voice was barely audible and the cost of every word was excessive. 'I could not go without seeing you once more.' He winced again. He raised a feeble hand to Giovanni's face.

'Luca, you mustn't die. Not you, Luca, not you. Please God...'

Giovanni held the hand and his tears ran between the brown fingers. As he spoke, the grimace gradually dispersed, the swollen veins drained and the fissures of pain were repaired.

'You rest, Luca; try to sleep. I will stay with you.'

Giovanni was relieved and delighted by the peace which had settled over his friend. The pain had subsided, the tensions had been released and a smile of profound contentment had displaced the facial contortions. He sponged the face again, the forehead, cheeks and eyes. As the sponge passed over the left eye, the lid, pulled slightly upwards, remained open, staring at Giovanni. It was the eye of death. He closed the lid to shut in the awful revelation. Oblivion had stared him in the face.

Numb and dumb, Sophenisba swayed backwards and forwards on her stool, each muscle and tendon as tight as a lute string. Involuntary moans escaped rhythmically from within her, expressing nothing. Shock and grief had eliminated every trace of her personality. Ottavia knelt besides her, smoothing her like a cat.

Giovanni brought the news to them. 'He's gone,' he said, bereft of emotion. His own composure surprised him.

'On no!' wailed Ottavia softly. 'Poor Luca.'

Sophenisba swayed on heedlessly.

'What are we going to do, Giovanni? What about Sophenisba? We cannot leave her.'

'We shall have to fetch a priest.'

'You go. I'll stay here, if you like,' offered Ottavia.

Giovanni found the priest and returned immediately. Prayers were said, the body washed and laid out, the bed remade. They were alone again.

Sophenisba sat up all night, swaying and moaning, uncomforted by the words or gestures of her two loyal companions. Pathetically helpless, weakened by lack of sleep and the harrowing day before, they had to respond to the demands of a new day. Decisions could be postponed no longer.

'We cannot go on like this, can we'?' asked Ottavia.

'No, but what can we do'? We cannot leave Sophenisba; that much is obvious. She doesn't seem to know what has happened.'

An assessment of the situation was easy; an appropriate solution to their predicament was not.

Sophenisba's swaying continued uninterrupted.

'We must get help,' suggested Ottavia.

'But where from? She hasn't any friends and I don't think the neighbours are going to help.'

'Why ever not?' asked Ottavia, ignorant of the conflicts which Sophenisba had caused in the district. 'At times like this, everyone helps, surely.'

'If they do, it will be for Luca's sake, not hers.'

Their exchanges merely circumvented the real problem, and they fell silent. Their mounting despondency was arrested by a noise on the stairway. The porcine grunting became louder. The door opened and was filled by an enormous woman with a basket. She looked startled by the pale, wide-eyed pair.

'Who are you?' she asked, easing herself in sideways. She kicked the door closed with her heel.

'We are friends of Luca,' began Giovanni, 'and Sophenisba.'

He felt uncomfortable and gauche. She surveyed him peremptorily.

'You must be Giovanni. I heard there were visitors.' She placed the basket on the table. 'I'm Sophenisba's sister,' she explained, 'and I've come to stay until after the funeral.'

There was no trace of sorrow or compassion in her voice. She knew what had to be done and how to do it. She exuded efficiency and experience.

'What's this, then?' she said, noticing the swaying heap. 'Come on, Sophi, pull yourself together.' The command had no effect. 'Sophi!' she screamed.

No response.

She swung her massive arm back and directed her hand in an accelerating arc at Sophenisba's face. The impact sounded like a snapping oar. The swaying stopped.

The two women confronted each other, as watchful and cautious as angry lionesses. Ottavia was terrified. Sophenisba slowly raised a hand to her cheek and fell upon her sister in an awkward embrace.

'Tina, Tina!' She repeated the incongruous name over and over, prefacing nothing. The two clung to each other, inseparably.

'You can leave her to me now,' said Tina gently. 'We shall bury him tomorrow. Come again then, if you like.'

They thanked her, kissed Sophenisba and left. They went

home in silence, Ottavia clutching Giovanni's arm as she had done the day before, evincing her support of him and surrender of herself.

Alone in his room, he wept uncontrollably with anger, grief and deep desolation.

Luca's boat bore Luca's body to the cemetery across the water. A hundred boats rowed by Luca's friends followed the coffin. Black ribbons fluttered from their hats and oars as they left the city behind. Women scattered flowers on the water, marking Luca's last journey.

The burial was brief and bleak and formal, a stark antithesis of Luca's life.

Giovanni and Ottavia travelled back in Sophenisba's boat. The pathos of returning through the route of sodden flowers agonised their emptiness; an agony which tears could not relieve.

As they parted, Sophenisba confided, 'You are all I have got, now. Come and see me when you can. Please!'

They kept their promise. They called on her often, passing quiet evenings and Sundays with her. She expressed her affection and gratitude with mountainous meals.

She adjusted to loneliness quickly.

She found a young man to run the boat which was Luca's legacy. She was independent and strangely integrated.

Luca's death had extirpated the raucous, belligerent, insensitive part of her nature. It was as if he had taken that with him, and left behind a gentle, kindly soul. A slip of his own good nature had rooted and flourished in his widow.

Giovanni and Ottavia felt his spirit become stronger with every visit, and what might have been a morbid duty was stimulating and rewarding. But they missed his presence bitterly; his conversation, his humour and the warmth of his genial welcome had gone for ever.

They were impoverished by their loss, yet richer for having known him.

In Concert

Tintoretto returned from Mantua drained, but triumphant. He had worked well, with a sense of occasion, glorifying the Gonzaga Court. The frescoes by Mantegna were a source of great pride to the duke, and they had incited Jacopo to supreme efforts of his own in oil paint. Mantegna's cycle was magnificent, statuesque and solemn; Tintoretto's was magnificent, but radiant and dynamic. Each series complemented the other; each represented not simply a distinguished family, but the distinctive values and aesthetic principles of two successive centuries. Each crowned the artistic endeavour of two generations of painters and, at the same time, displayed the individual artist at the zenith of his achievement, both as an initiator and as a consolidator. It was a conjunction of giants and genius.

Jacopo's luggage contained gifts for his family, his assistants and his servants. In this way, he shared his payment with his household. It was characteristic of his generosity and indicative of his financial ineptitude.

Pairing Ottavia and Giovanni in his mind, he had bought a pair of instruments, superbly made in Bologna by a master craftsman. It consisted of a lute and chitarrone, with parquetry embellished with ivory, the fingerboards decorated with inlaid arabesques. It was his dual intention to stimulate what he believed to be their musical potential and, at the same time, to symbolise their harmonious association with objects which were visually and tonally compatible. It seemed perfectly natural, and in no way extravagant, to provide the finest tuition from the finest virtuoso to realise the former and to reinforce the latter. To do less would be unworthy of his love and the objects of that love.

He was pleased with his choice and exhilarated by its reception. But their enthusiasm surpassed mere gratitude. They were determined to learn to play sufficiently well to divert their father's leisure and to delight his fastidious musical taste.

'Now, let me see your pictures,' he said.

The blaze of colour which greeted him radiated an exotic splendour. He stopped in the doorway, fixed in wonderment. 'My God!' he breathed. 'These are astonishing.'

He went in.

He could find no words to match his feelings. He paraded up and down the room, first standing back and then advancing to examine the brushwork. The whole surface scintillated. The backgrounds, as he had seen them in the sketches, were delicately monochromed in cool greys. These had now been vitalised with shimmering iridescence. The effect absorbed his attention, provoking the highest admiration. 'My God!' he murmured incredulously.

Giovanni and Ottavia stood together by the door in silence. The old man's response was so full of respect, and so enraptured was he by the spectacle that words were superfluous, almost blasphemous. The scrutiny continued. At last he spoke. 'I have never seen anything like this before. It's new! It's magnificent!' He pulled a stool into the middle of the room and sat down. 'Tell me, how did you think of painting air with colours?'

'Well, you know when the sun breaks through the mist over the lagoon,' began Giovanni. Jacopo nodded. 'It seems to have no colour, yet it must have. It's not just pale, it is light. I wanted to show the breaking up of light by the moisture in the air, but I didn't know how to do it. Then your Christmas present solved the problem.'

Jacopo looked puzzled.

'How did it help?' he asked.

'We will show you. Close the shutters, Tavi.'

As she went over to the window, Giovanni collected the box of lenses from a cupboard. The room darkened.

'Now watch the wall, Father.'

He suspended a prism from a thread and opened a shutter, allowing a chink of sunlight to cut through the glass. The wall became striped with rainbow colours, moving in slow procession as the prism turned.

'There it is. The glass creaks up the light, just as the rain does on a sunny day, and just as the mist does in the morning.'

'So light is really coloured, you mean,' suggested Jacopo tentatively.

'Not exactly. The rain or the glass seem to give it colour, but how, we don't know. But we took the colours of the rainbow, mixed them with white and painted broken areas to represent the refraction of raindrops,' Giovanni explained as he opened the shutters. 'It's a scrambled rainbow, really.'

'So why doesn't it look as if it's raining?' asked Jacopo.

'Because we blend the colours into each other while they are still wet. They have no form, no direction, so they don't look like falling drops, but more like a haze.'

'That's incredible. You know, this is a very important discovery, and it's all yours. I don't know what to say.' He surveyed the pictures again more thoughtfully than before. 'You've hardly used any earth colours in the figures, have you?'

'No, we didn't want to lose the unity of the whole, so we used the rainbow colours for the draperies as well, as far as possible.'

'It's incredible,' repeated Jacopo. 'Quite incredible.'

'Ottavia painted all the backgrounds,' volunteered Giovanni.

'So it really has been a joint effort, then? If you can paint in concert like this, you should be able to make sweet music on your lutes.'

He held them in his arms. He felt elated, but his feelings were inexpressible.

Three weeks later the canvases were delivered and marouflayed to the staircase wall in the Palazzo da Ponte. Tintoretto supervised the operation. He insisted that they were handled with the reverence due to them and although he knew the workmen, who had done similar jobs for him in the Palazzo Ducale, he felt they might not accord the same care and consideration to Giovanni as they would to him.

The plaster was rubbed down with pumice and sized, the canvas gently rolled, glued evenly in strips and stuck to the wall. It was a skilled job, perfected by Venetian workmen using an adhesive paste made from white lead and linseed oil. It required speed and accuracy, for every air pocket had to be forced cut by firm pressure applied systematically from the centre to the edges of the picture, without damaging the paint surface. Sometimes damage had to be retouched by the artist in situ. Tintoretto was there to make sure this would not be necessary.

He studied the final effect from above, below and in passage. It was even more splendid than it was in Giovanni's room. The height of the hallway and the diffused light made the figures and the atmospheric perspective dramatically convincing, without sacrificing the decorative, planar quality of the design. The subtle paradox was perfectly balanced.

Jacopo's admiration deepened. It was while he was congratulating Giovanni again that Doge Nicolo arrived to inspect his acquisition. He was impatient to relish the completion of the first stage of his great scheme.

'So the work is finished, Maestro Tintoretto,' he began.

'As you see, Master Doge.'

'Let me see, that is St Mark with St Paul and Barnabas preaching in Rome.' He raised a thin, quivering claw in the direction of the second picture. 'That is the miracle with the fishermen of Venice.' He started up the staircase. 'This must be the curing of the cobbler, St Anianus.' He moved higher. Jacopo and Giovanni followed. 'This is the martyrdom in Alexandria, and this shows the Venetian merchants exhuming the body.' He reached the landing where the Palazzo San Marco was filled with gorgeously attired figures moving in solemn procession. The pageantry of heraldic banners, silver trumpets and a golden-fringed umbrella was sumptuously arrayed above their heads. 'And this,' he said, with magnificent banality, 'must be the reburial in our sacred Church in 1094, if I remember correctly.' Jacopo groaned softly. 'Yes, it's all as I planned it,' he went on. 'It's a bit modern for my taste, but I am quite satisfied.'

Giovanni looked anxiously at the Maestro. He expected him to explode, but Jacopo laid a hand on his arm to assuage his fears. 'Philistine!' he hissed out of the side of his mouth. 'Your eminence will permit an observation?' he asked coldly.

'Certainly,' replied the doge.

'My partner, Maestro Giovanni, has produced for you what is, without a doubt, the noblest cycle of pictures in Venice. Your eminence will be the centre of admiration and envy of every discerning patron, not only in the Republic, but in all the states of Europe, including the Vatican. I venture to suggest that although you may consider it to be too modern at the moment, you will revise your opinion when you receive the praise of those who are qualified to judge your acquisition on its artistic merit.'

The doge extracted from this what nourished his vanity, and was well pleased. Giovanni's admiration for the diplomatically concealed rebuke was partly displaced by astonishment at being referred to as 'partner' and 'Maestro'. But this point had not escaped the commercial and legalistic instincts of da Ponte.

'Maestro Tintoretto,' he began sententiously, 'I am certain that our contract explicitly names your "assistant" Giovanni as the executant of my pictures, yet you now call him your partner. I trust you will not be seeking additional payment on that basis, because if you did, I must warn you that we would find ourselves in opposition.' His lips formed a line of self-congratulation.

'Indeed no, Master Doge. I shall honour our contract exactly as it stands, as I always do. But may I remind you that it specifically applies to the six canvases you now have, and that any further work shall be determined under a separate contract? Since my assistant has become my partner, the terms of remuneration for any additional work will, of course, have to be revised.'

The self-congratulation curled into a snarl. 'There might not be any further work,' he said acidly.

'As your eminence pleases. But I am bound to say that you will find no one who is capable of providing comparable pictures for your saloon. I feel sure that your eminence would not wish to furnish your piano mobile with an anticlimax.'

Having played his trump card, Jacopo tipped the workmen generously and left, holding Giovanni by the arm.

Once aboard their boat, they started to laugh, enjoying both the relief of their escape from formalities and the sweetness of Jacopo's verbal victory. He caught sight of the sour face of da Ponte peering furtively from a window, but his decorum was too exhausted to spoil his merriment.

Nicolo's fury did not curtail the pleasures of acquisition for long. The next day he invited every connoisseur and discerning collector to his palace. Unanimously, they confirmed Tintoretto's extravagant claims. Some wanted to know the artist's name; others, the price demanded for works of such distinction; a few expressed their covetousness quite openly; some were so grudging in their praise that Doge Nicolo clearly felt the undertow of envy. There were a few who could remember the emergence of Titian as a mature artist and who compared the new master with him.

Nicolo sought out Jacopo Contarini and asked him for his opinion. His pronouncements carried considerable weight with the nobility and he had advised the Senate over the decoration of the ducal palace after both fires. He had been a patron of every important Venetian painter in turn and his private collection was outstanding. His assessment, therefore, was awaited with respectful silence.

'There is no doubt that we have among us one of the finest artists in the history of La Serenissima,' he began. His audience nodded in agreement. 'These paintings, while reminiscent of our beloved Tintoretto, surpass his work in their subtlety of colour and delicacy of brushwork. In composition and draughtsmanship, they are his equal. It is only in their vitality and gravità that they fall short of the Maestro's finest work.' He paused and looked about him, as if inviting disagreement. 'I thought I had seen the greatest art that man is capable of, but today I find myself a witness to the birth of a new excellence beyond my expectations. Pope Julius will be remembered as the patron of Michelangelo and Raphael; you, Doge Nicolo, will be honoured as the first patron of Maestro Giovanni, who has already taken the lead of a new generation of masters.'

The applause which followed signified the consent of the company, not respect for da Ponte, but Nicolo interpreted it otherwise. Contarini held up his hand and added, 'But I shall be the second!'

And so it was. From that day, the name of Giovanni Robusti was linked with those of Veronese, Bassano, Palma as well as with Tintoretto, the contemporary masters of Venice and with Titian, Giorgione and Bellini, now dead, but immortal in paint and civic pride.

The canal door of the Palazzo da Ponte remained open for visitors to inspect the amazing St Mark cycle, which was discussed and lauded in the Scuoli and saloons, in the markets, the shipyards and in the lanes and squares of the city.

Giovanni was lionised.

But his greatest pleasure stemmed from the music that he and Ottavia pursued with such dedication. The duo had studied and practised the complex tablature with their tutor, until they became fairly competent in two gentle pieces, one a melancholy air, the other a simple dance. Tintoretto had employed the finest virtuoso in Venice, at enormous expense, to ensure that their tuition should be as accomplished as possible.

The harmonies they produced from their instruments delighted them and perfectly expressed their deep affinity. Their spare time was enriched by a common dedication and a common objective, which was to share their delight with Jacopo. They wanted to return what he had given them, augmented by their own efforts and affection. It had to be as near perfection as possible; anything less would be unworthy. Jacopo had taught them this, not by precept, but by example. The time they consumed was symbolic of their sincerity.

They waited for the right moment for their first recital, and several days passed after they felt ready to perform. It arrived when Jacopo was resting after he had completed his Battle of Zara for the ducal palace.

It was customary for him to be restless after finishing a major picture. The creative effort exhausted his spirit and this, combined with his hatred of inactivity, made him tetchy. He was not a man of great intellect and books held only a transitory appeal for him.

He sat in his richly carved chair after supper, reading *Orlando Furioso*, but his concentration constantly sidled away from him, leading nowhere. He fidgeted and tapped his fingers. Giovanni and Ottavia left the room unnoticed to collect their instruments.

They returned as quietly, sat down and started to play. Jacopo had dozed off, and in his semi-conscious drift he became aware that the air was imbued with a mysterious sweetness. It was neither intoxication nor hallucination, but something substantive yet delicate. As he wakened, he defined a melody. Its plaintive line rose and fell, but could not settle or find resolution. Now, two threads of sound were braided together in a strand which had an unrequited yearning; striving, yet not achieving. The timbre he recognised as the lute and chitarrone. He identified the musicians, but was afraid to turn lest the magic should slip away and be lost for ever.

The melody found rest, like a perching bird. His head was enraptured by fragile fancies. At last, he faced the smiling pair. 'That was so beautiful,' he said. 'Do play it again.'

The tentative nature of their first performance gained assurance on repetition. The expression was more confident, more controlled and more affecting. Jacopo was transported by the simplicity, the innocence of the melodic line, which was half-lament, half-cradle song, and by the tenderness of the accompaniment.

'It's for you, Father, with our love,' explained Ottavia. They registered the old man's incapacity for reply.

'Let's do the other piece,' suggested Giovanni.

They played a stately dance, each phrase of which alternated with a flourished motif in strict tempo. Jacopo beat time with his hands, flickering his fingers at the appropriate intervals.

'I know that one,' he said. 'I haven't heard it for years.' They repeated the flourish skittishly. 'I'll get my spinet, and we shall play it together.'

In his youth, Tintoretto had been an accomplished player of the viol, the spinet and the organ, but his position as the premier painter in Venice since the death of Titian, had given him little time to exercise his youthful passion. Yet music was an instinctive part of his nature and he had expressed it unwittingly in his paintings, in linear rhythms and coloured harmonies, all through his maturity.

He returned with the spinet under his arm. He blew the dust off the parquetry, opened the lid and fingered a scale.

'It's out of tune, but that doesn't matter.'

They played the dance in consort. Jacopo struggled to embroider the continuo part and was amused by the lapses inflicted by his inflexible fingers.

'We'll do it again, and *this* time I'll get it right!'

The effort was invigorating; the result creditable enough to foster mutual congratulations. Jacopo felt rejuvenated.

'Now I will play you one of my favourite pieces, if I can remember it. There's a basso continuo like this…' His left hand measured a phrase, paused and repeated it. 'Once you've got that, the right hand works variations over it until you get tired.' He played a few bars of a solemn passacaglia. 'Now, Giovanni, you try the ostinato.' They picked out the phrase together. 'Ottavia, you do the theme at the top.' He guided her towards its realisation. 'Now, we'll all do it together. One, two…' His foot indicated the tempo.

Each of them drew confidence from the others and from the richness of the combined sound which uncannily filled themselves and the space around them. Initial hesitations were dispelled by familiarity with the interlocking parts and soon they achieved a string ensemble of modest precision and lavish enthusiasm.

They played on in concert till the candles extinguished themselves one by one.

Conquest of Venice

In order to stem the flood of commissions which inundated the studio for Giovanni's work, an apprentice was taken on to relieve Ottavia from the mundane tasks. He was a conscientious and reliable worker who rapidly learned the supporting role required of him. Giovanni and Ottavia were fully occupied fulfilling orders for the new, clamorous clientele.

The demand for mythological and religious subjects was fairly evenly balanced and it became possible to alternate them and retain the order in which contracts were drawn up. Tintoretto kept an experienced eye on the terms of agreements, but he had relinquished his prerogative of being a party to contracts, in favour of Giovanni, who was, in effect, running an independent studio within the household. There was no resentment from the others, who generously acknowledged Giovanni's success as the just reward for talent and industry.

For Contarini, they produced a *Birth of Venus* in which the trembling, nude figure appeared to materialise before the spectator, born out of spray and air. For Morosini, they painted a pair showing the miraculous draught of fishes and Christ walking on the water. In each, the light shimmered above and into the water in crystalline refraction. Christ hovered, almost insubstantial, yet miraculously alive.

The discerning patrons had suggested subjects which would display Giovanni's peculiar atmospheric innovation. The results astounded them, transcending their expectations. Their pride of ownership became notorious, and the envy which promotes emulation ensured that the workshop was fully extended. Giovanni could not accept all the demands made on him. Some selection was inevitable, or life would wither into servitude.

He invariably referred portrait and history commissions to Domenico. He felt most effective in transcribing literary subjects, and whether they originated in myth or scripture was of no consequence. It was in this field that his lyrical imagination flourished, delicately poised between reality and fantasy. The demand for such pictures seemed inexhaustible; the physical stamina of the two painters, however, was not.

Their proficiency as instrumentalists increased as they devoted all their spare time to practice and to playing with Jacopo. In their working lives and their recreation, the harmony accrued, but emotionally, the relationship stagnated. While Giovanni simply accepted this as inevitable, if he thought of it at all, Ottavia was both puzzled and hurt by such inertia and Giovanni's placid resignation. Their only physical contact was merely functional or accidental and she yearned for more.

'Do you realise,' she said, broaching the subject at last, 'that after two years of partnership, of being together every day and all day, you still treat me like a sister?'

'Of course. You are my sister, aren't you?'

'Yes, in one sense, but that doesn't make us blood relations.'

He looked perplexed. 'What's the matter? Don't I treat you well?'

'Yes, you do… as well as any brother could.'

'You know I am very fond of you and that I couldn't do without you.'

'You don't show it very much then,' she said sadly.

'How can I? How can I treat you better?'

His naivety made her impatient. 'You really don't know, do you? You have no idea what I need from you. You don't even notice how unhappy I am.'

'But you're not unhappy. We have every thing we need…'

She cut in abruptly. '…You have every thing *you* need, but inside, I am dying.'

'Of what, in God's name?' Giovanni was utterly perplexed.

'Of love,' she said gently. 'You poor blind fool, I love till it hurts.'

The tears flooded her eyes. Giovanni took her hands in his.

'Oh, my poor Tavi! What can I do?'

'Nothing, I suppose. You don't love me.'

'But I do… not in the same way, perhaps, but I love you.'

'You don't show it then,' she repeated, wiping her eyes.

'How could I treat you differently without betraying Father's trust and kindness to me? I couldn't hurt him. You know that.'

'Do you really think he would be hurt if you loved me more than a brother would?'

'Yes, I do.'

'Well, you don't know him any better than you know me. He *wants* us to be a part of each other in every way.'

Giovanni remembered Marietta and how her father had been sympathetic to the situation, and the concern he had shown for Giovanni's welfare and happiness. He looked into Ottavia's face and saw there more tenderness and adoration than he had ever seen before.

'Poor little Tavi,' he said. 'Please forgive me for being blind and stupid. I didn't know.'

She kissed his mouth as a token of absolution.

'I want you, Gianni,' she murmured.

Pleasurable though it was, his response was confused. Ottavia's softness was attractive, but it did not inflame his desire. She offered herself without reservation, but he could not be sure if he could accept her on those terms, nor was he sure about what his own terms were. He admired and respected her, loved her for her gentleness, her consideration, her childlike simplicity and her innocence, but not with the passion he once had for her sister.

'I want you, Gianni,' she repeated. She lightly kissed his mouth again, his eyes and forehead. Her warm breath fanned his cheeks; her hands clutched him and stroked his hair. Her excitement was contagious and he felt his restraint weaken.

He held her face between his hands. Her expression was pacified by contentment and total submission. He placed kisses on the corresponding parts of her face, returning them with added firmness. She closed her eyes, savouring the brief attachment of his lips, capitulating to the sensation of being desired.

They lay in a voyage of reciprocal discovery, aware that their sensuous pleasure was almost sacramental, but the last vestige of their separateness remained intact.

Giovanni awoke with watery reflections coruscating the ceiling, swaying the plaster garlands and the dancing cherubs. In the stillness of her room, he reflected upon the sequence and implications of the events which had brought him there.

Was it love or lust that had been requited?

Was it his, or hers… or theirs?

Had they stained themselves with incest?

Had they murdered something precious and durable with a transient self-indulgence?

The speculation disturbed him. Probed with spears of guilt and veiled with clouds of uncertainty, his thoughts refused to be ordered into any rational progression. The spectres of Marietta and Bianca careered before him like demented moths.

The reek of debauchery.

Black worms.

Sweat.

Blood.

The eddies of recollected horror swirled round the gentle face of Ottavia, the soft body of Ottavia, the innocence of Ottavia.

It was she that he had defiled. It was she that he had bruised. It was she who would be scarred by lasciviousness and bestiality. Her innocence had been ravaged. He was culpable; he was damned.

Demons wrestled to possess him.

His torment was arrested by Ottavia's waking. She smiled at him and placed her arm across his body. It was the same smile of tenderness he had seen the previous evening. It gave all, demanded nothing.

'Good morning, Gianni,' she said.

'Good morning, Tavi.'

'What's the matter? You look very solemn.'

'I've been thinking…'

'…About us,' she continued. 'I know. You are worried, aren't you?'

'Yes. I think I have done wrong. I have wronged you.'

'No, you haven't. You returned my love. It was freely given and freely received. No conditions, no coercions. Just a gift exchanged.'

'Is that how you see it?' he asked. 'You don't think I behaved badly?'

'Of course not. For once, you behaved perfectly,' she said with a non-malicious irony.

'I think I have spoilt things.'

'That's rubbish! *We* have improved on something that was nearly perfect, and now it is. It is we, *us*, you should think about, not yourself. You didn't even take my virginity. If you had wanted it, you could have had it as a gift, gladly.'

'I did want it, but I couldn't take it, or even accept it.'

'Why not? It belongs to us, not to me alone.' she said.

'I don't see it as you do, obviously.'

'That's only because you haven't got used to the idea yet. I've lived with this for nearly three years.'

He became thoughtful. Her simple explanation made him enquire into his own insensitivity and ignorance during the same period. Two intangible factors became illuminated; the first was his fear of consanguinity and their father's disapproval; the second was a reluctance to become sexually involved again after the pain and degradation he had suffered before. Both stemmed from a radical fear, but recognition did not banish them altogether as feeble or unworthy. He was not as certain as she was about her father's reaction, but this was a simple matter to put to the test. The rest hovered restlessly in his mind, generating an uncertainty which distorted his reason and his emotions.

'You look so worried and I am so happy. It just doesn't seem fair,' she said, moving closer to him. 'I wish you wouldn't worry, then we could be happy together.'

She stroked his face very gently. He was tempted to surrender to her endearments. It would be very easy and delightful, but fear or conscience intervened. He kissed her summarily and left the bed.

'We must talk about this more,' he said. 'I still cannot rid myself of the idea that something is wrong.'

'Very well, if that's what you want, but I don't think talking will do the slightest good.'

They dressed and went down to breakfast separately, as Giovanni insisted.

The following days brought a slow completion to their current work. Each was aware that the progress was cumbersome and the results curiously taut and stilted, though neither acknowledged the fact.

The subtle perfume of Ottavia's skin and hair filled his nostrils, the fleeting view of her arm inside her sleeve, the curve of her breast, briefly revealed as she bent forward, distracted and delighted him. She was there with him, available and desirable, yet barricaded by a taboo which he could neither understand nor justify. Their music making was tempered more by effort than spontaneous pleasure of the kind to which they had become accustomed.

Ottavia waited patiently for the promised discussion, which she now regarded as essential, but Giovanni was unable or unwilling to reopen the subject until the pictures were finished.

When the last was delivered, they went to the mainland by way of the Brenta River for a day of relaxation. Ottavia carried a basket of food and a wicker carafe of wine. She tried to display a carefree mood by singing and swinging her load. They walked in open fields of spring flowers and by streams bustling with April rain, but only the birds joined her in her song; Giovanni was too preoccupied to notice the *concert champêtre* around him.

Just before noon, they rested under a green canopy of spreading leaves; a place fashioned, it seemed, for contemplation and love. It was here that Giovanni at last revealed his thoughts.

'I have been thinking about us,' he began. Much as Ottavia expected him to revive the subject on this day, his opening caught her unprepared, her mouth filled with spiced and honeyed pastry. 'We cannot work together as we used to any more,' he continued. 'We were lucky not to ruin the last picture, so we have got to make a decision.'

Ottavia was stunned by the brutality of his preamble. She knew that he was right and feared the inevitable corollary. She was equally unprepared for the directness and cold logic he had adopted. It was so unlike him.

'What do you suggest then?' she asked timidly.

'Well, it seems we cannot go back to where we were before, do you agree?' She nodded, licking her fingers to occupy her tongue. 'So we either stop working together at all, or we separate for the time being and see how we get on.'

The choice was barren. Both demanded separation and both were unacceptable to Ottavia, who had only briefly considered such extreme action and had immediately rejected it because it created more problems than it solved.

'If we stop working together, will we still see each other and make music in the evenings?' she asked.

'I don't know. I expect so, but our music hasn't been much good lately, has it?'

'That's true.'

Despair was beginning to close in on her. She wished that she was not so deeply involved. She envied the painless, unemotional clarity which Giovanni possessed but she hated the inescapable conclusions which were clarified. She was angry with herself for not keeping quiet about her feelings in the first place; she had practised acquiescence all her life and the first time she had abandoned it everything she desired was about to be snatched from her.

There was one slender shaft of hope in the second alternative and she decided to pursue it before it was overlooked, or gave way to something worse.

'Suppose we separate for a time, how do we do it?'

'I could go away. I would like to see Florence and Rome. I've never been further from Venice than we are now.'

'Nor have I,' she said. 'And I would like to travel too.'

'Well, you could. I've got plenty of money, so that's no problem. Where would you like to go?'

'To Florence and Rome.' She could not resist a smile at the irony of their identical choice.

'We both want to travel, we both want to go to the same places and we both want to separate.'

'No, *you* want to separate,' she declared with some vehemence. 'I just want you.

'But it's not practicable, is it? You must see that.'

Ottavia sensed the futility of argument which could so easily exacerbate the situation, and her patience, though strained, was by no means exhausted. She would have to exercise it further.

The sun beat down almost vertically from a cloudless, windless sky. The birds fell silent, the air shimmered over the lush grass. Nature decreed a siesta.

She pulled off her heavy brocade dress and rolled down her stockings. The air felt kind to her skin. She peeled the stockings from her feet and exercised her liberated toes. She unfastened the bodice of her shift and fanned herself. There was no hint or intention of seduction. She behaved exactly as if she were alone, seeking unrestricted comfort and ease. She lay back with her head pillowed in her linked hands.

Giovanni did not see her undress; he was concerned with other things. But now his attention was drawn towards her feet. Her toes reminded him of shrimps, pink and curled; her ankles of polished ivory. She had a rarefied beauty which he had hardly noticed, but she rewarded careful study. His eyes moved up her body which modelled the folds of the shift like classical Greek sculpture. Her face had the form and serenity of a Raphael Madonna. In repose, she seemed to possess a refinement which aroused his most delicate feelings and protective instincts. He lay prone, his chin in the palm of his left hand, pondering on the mystery of Ottavia. She personified all that was rare and pure, and much that was transient and vulnerable. She had the ineffable quality of clouds and mists, of flowers and butterflies; exquisite, but ephemeral, susceptible to injury or derogation. She personified innocence and virginity which, once sullied, would destroy them both. He adored her, and yet was restrained by a profound superstition; his adoration was almost idolatry, full of fear for her dissolution.

His finger traced the line from her cheekbone to chin. Her eyelashes and the corners of her mouth stirred. She turned her head in his direction. She said nothing, but Giovanni understood.

He kissed her reverently, as if she were an icon. She understood.

'You do love me – a little, don't you?' she said.

No answer was needed or given.

They found Jacopo tuning his spinet.

'I have been waiting for you two to return from Cythera,' he said, with a sly smile. 'I've got a surprise for you.'

'What's that?' asked Ottavia.

They were slightly disconcerted by his initiative and his playfulness. 'Today, I collected some trio sonatas from Maestro Gabrieli, and I thought we might try them this evening.'

'You mean you commissioned them?'

'Of course. Six months ago I told him I wanted some pieces for our ensemble, and today they were ready.'

It was obvious that they could not discuss the matter they had prepared. His excitement could not be thwarted by their personal problems.

'Give us a few minutes to change and we'll be ready.'

He continued to adjust the temperament of his instrument.

Once alone, they replanned their intentions. Postponement was necessary, but a signal had to be arranged, so that they both agreed when the time was right. The smallest nod, given and returned, would suffice. Dressed more for comfort than for neatness, they rejoined Tintoretto with their lutes.

He detected a hint of resignation in their expressions and demeanour.

'Would you like to eat first?'

'No, thank you, Father.'

'I expect you are thirsty. Would you like a chilled drink? It has been very warm today.'

'Yes, that would be perfect. Thank you,' said Ottavia.

He removed the damp cloth which clung to an ewer of dry white wine and poured three glasses. He handed one to each of them and carried the other to his chair, closing the lid of the spinet as he passed.

'You must be tired after your long day.'

Giovanni nodded in agreement as he sipped his wine.

'Not really, Father, but we would like to talk to you before we play. Do you mind?'

'Of course not. Let's drink and talk, then.'

Giovanni marvelled at how quickly Ottavia had forgotten their prearranged signal.

'Giovanni and I are in love,' she began simply, adopting the directness she had learned earlier that day.

'Yes, I had noticed that,' said Jacopo with equal simplicity. 'Go on.'

'Well, we find that we cannot work together as we used to, and we are worried. Giovanni thinks we ought to have a break for a while.'

'That's a very good idea. You have been far too busy lately and you need a complete change of routine. You have certainly earned it.'

'Giovanni thinks he ought to go away. He wants to see Florence and Rome...' She stopped abruptly, conscious that she had blundered into Giovanni's territory. He took over where she had left off.

'You see, Father, I am so important of the world outside Venice and this seems to be a good opportunity to travel.' Jacopo listened, nodded, but made no comment. 'It will also give us time to sort ourselves out,' continued Giovanni. 'We cannot go on as we are.'

Jacopo's suspicions were confirmed. 'So it's not just your work you are worried about.'

'Not entirely,' replied Ottavia.

'Now, let me understand you. You have fallen in love, but it has affected your work. Giovanni wants to travel and you both have something else to sort out. Am I right?' They agreed. 'What I am not sure about is why Giovanni has to leave to sort out a shared problem.' They felt they had been inept in trying to conceal anything from their father. They looked at each other with expressions of helplessness. Giovanni nodded the signal.

'It's a bit complicated,' said Ottavia. 'I have been in love with Giovanni since before you went to Mantua, but he didn't love me until much later, so it's all new to him.'

'I see,' said Jacopo. 'So you think he will catch up with you if he goes away. Is that it?'

'No, Father, not quite. To start with, I didn't think you would approve if I loved Ottavia as a man should love a woman, completely. After all, you made me your son.'

'Well, you can put that out of your minds. Nothing would give me greater happiness. It's what I have prayed for since I came home the Christmas before last. I thought you understood that. Of course, I didn't say so specifically, because I didn't want your own feelings or judgement to be affected in any way.'

'I was wrong about that then,' said Giovanni. 'But it seems we love each other in different ways.'

'How long have you known this?'

'About three weeks.'

'Well, give yourselves more time. Don't try to solve everything at once. True affection needs time and room to grow to fruition. You wouldn't expect to pick grapes three weeks after planting the vines, would you?'

'But we cannot work properly until all this becomes clear, and that is wasting time, not using it,' insisted Ottavia.

'I am not suggesting that you just hang about until you feel you can work again, nor am I suggesting that a separation will solve anything either.'

'What do you suggest then?' asked Giovanni.

'I think you ought to forget work for at least a month. Take yourselves off, wherever you want to go, be together, enjoy each other. Don't come back until you are certain about money, you can have as much as you want.'

The wisdom and simplicity of his counsel impressed them both. Giovanni knew that it was eminently sensible and, at first, he could not understand why it had eluded him. Then he knew. Ottavia was overjoyed. It had not occurred to her either, but it offered the perfect resolution to the tangle of fears and desires that had enmeshed her. Now, all her fears were dispelled and most of her desires fulfilled simultaneously.

She hurled herself into her father's arms, expressing relief and gratitude in tears and kisses. Jacopo gently extricated himself from the effusion which showered upon him. 'Shall we play a sonata now?' he asked.

The Pilgrimage to Perfection

For a Venetian, Tintoretto was a considerable horseman. He admired the nobility of the animal, its strength and its capacity for obedience with dignity. The impact made upon him, when he was still a boy, by the great equestrian statue of Colleoni had never waned and he had drawn on this unfolding enthusiasm in his paintings at Mantua. It was natural, therefore, that he should insist on, and typical that he should supervise, the riding lessons which would equip his two children for their long journey south.

He was deeply pleased by their progress, by the elegance of their seat and the striking picture they presented when mounted. He also insisted on buying them a pair of superb animals and elaborate matching harness and panniers, more suited, perhaps, to royalty than painters. Into the saddles he had pouches cunningly concealed to accommodate a secret reserve of gold coins against emergency. A copy of Vasari's *Lives of the Painters* was presented as their guide to their grand tour of Renaissance art and as a reference to the men and the circumstances which fashioned it.

They set off with the zeal of knights of the crusades, but their goal was not conquest, but learning. The architectural books of Vitruvius and Palladio and Serlio were well known to them through their professional study, and the engravings of paintings and sculpture which Tintoretto avidly collected had stimulated their excitement for an itinerary of discovery and inspection at first hand.

They made their way first to Padua. The streets clattered with the seat of iron-shod hooves and rumbled with the roar of wheels. The noise was frightening to young Venetian ears, accustomed to the slap of waves beneath a boat and the creak of oar and spar. It seemed a poor place after the visual splendours and sophistication of La Serenissima, but they rested here for a few days.

The Arena Chapel, built by the guilt-ridden usurer, Scrovegni, as a passport to paradise, contained the great cycle of Giotto frescoes, and this they visited several times. Vasari insisted that Giotto had brought art out of its antique darkness into light, and prepared for the masters who were to give painting its true excellence. In his solemn, rigid figures and shallow backgrounds, they found little to admire, but they rejoiced in his colours, subtle and muted. They discovered relationships of warm and cool which delighted the eye and their imagination. To them, colour was a property of light and specific materials, here they found the ancient master had manipulated it separately from either as an abstract element in the composition. Their appetites were whetted, but they had no regrets in leaving the rackety street arcades and the rowdy students from the university who hailed them facetiously as 'gondoliers'.

They passed through quiet villages to Ferarra, where they rested before the climb over the mountains, through Bologna to Florence. The clarity of the mountain air was astonishing and they had to revise their estimates of visible distance. The pearly moisture of their lagoon often reduced the mainland or neighbouring islands to flat silhouettes, dissolving form and detail into a blue haze. Here, they could see every rock, every tree, every campanile for twenty miles without the familiar dilution.

From such a hilltop, they first sighted the towers and domes of Florence, picked out with the sharpness of an etching needle. It was late afternoon and they agreed to lodge overnight in Fiesole and drop down into the city in the cool of the morning. They read over Vasari on Masaccio, Uccello, Fra Angelico, Leonardo and part of the chapter on Michelangelo before fatigue drained all effort and sleep bore them towards another day.

Their progress into the City of Flowers matched a crusader's entry into Jerusalem. It was a land of promise, a return to their artistic roots, a land of illumination and cultural fulfilment, which they had reached by their own diligence. It was a culmination and a reward for all their striving.

In the Palazzo Signoria, they stopped before Michelangelo's David, who gazed down at them with monumental disdain; fourteen feet of marble magnificence and masculine grace which offered confirmation of Giovanni's suspicion that art could transcend nature, and sometimes did.

'Have you ever seen anything like that?' he whispered.

'I had no idea it was so big. He looks more like a giant than a boy.'

'It is quite superb. No man ever looked like that, nor ever will.'

'I wonder why he made the hands so big,' she mused aloud.

'I don't know, but I have heard that he wanted to suggest a young, immature figure rather than an older man.'

'Well, you are a young man, but you haven't got huge hands, so I don't think that can be right.'

'Perhaps he wanted to show David was a complete man, a man of action and a man of spirit, so the hands symbolise the action, just as the face symbolises determination and faith. That's exaggerated too.'

They had not unlocked the mystery, but they intended to return until they did. They walked down to the Arno and on to the Ponte Vecchio.

'It's very splendid, isn't it?' said Ottavia. 'It's a pity that our Rialto is so old and rickety. A new stone bridge would look so much better.'

'Well, they say that they are going to replace it fairly soon, and when they do, I hope they put little shops on it, like these, and I like the way all those wooden workshops stick out over the water. Don't you?'

'I am afraid I don't,' said Ottavia. 'They look a bit squalid to me. I prefer clean lines and uncluttered design in buildings; these are too busy.'

'That's what I like about them – it *is* busy with trade and people, and in that sense, it's honest.'

But she was fascinated by one particular goldsmith's shop. This craftsman specialised in chains and he displayed every kind, from the most delicate to the heaviest and most portentous chains of office. His workmanship was superlative in design and finish, especially where he had used enamels to embellish the decoration.

'Which one do you like most?' asked Giovanni.

She pointed to a very line one where the tripled links produced a plaited effect. 'That one is very attractive, isn't it?'

'Would you like it?'

'Yes, of course, but it's far too expensive.'

'Let's find out.'

Inside the shop, the goldsmith eyed the young couple with thinly disguised suspicion. They were hardly typical of his usual clientele. As Giovanni spoke, he recognised the Venetian dialect, and his suspicion subsided.

'And how was Venice when you were last there?' he asked politely.

'How did you know we were from Venice?' said Ottavia with a disbelief she might have reserved for a necromancer.

'Signorina, in Rome, the accent is broad and round, but monotonous; in Florence, we speak with the most musical and refined intonation; in Venice, it is quite different and unmistakably Venetian.'

'Have you travelled a lot then?' asked Giovanni.

'Oh yes. I was in Venice last year. I often go there to buy gold and gems from my brother, who is a member of the Guild of Goldsmiths. He has a shop in the Merceria. Perhaps...'

'His name isn't Francesco Bardelli, is it?' Giovanni interrupted.

'Indeed it is,' replied the goldsmith.

Giovanni unfastened his doublet to reveal the chain given to him by Tintoretto. 'He made this, then.'

'He most certainly did, I can recognise his work quite clearly.'

'That is extraordinary! We came into your shop by chance to buy a chain for my sister, and your brother made mine about five years ago. It was a present from our father, Jacopo Robusti.'

'Tintoretto!' exclaimed Bardelli.

'Yes, do you know him?'

'I know his work, of course. A very great man, and a worthy successor to our own Michelangelo, if I may say so.' The two were impressed. 'When I was in your city last year, my brother took me to see some remarkable pictures by one of his sons, I believe. Would he be your brother, young sir?'

'Not exactly...' began Giovanni.

'No, *this* is Giovanni Robusti. He painted those pictures,' interrupted Ottavia with ill-concealed pride.

'My dear sir! I am honoured that you should come to my

shop, of all the shops in Florence... and wearing a chain made by my brother, too. It is, as you say, extraordinary.' They negotiated a price, the chain was placed around Ottavia's neck, the business settled and they were about to leave. 'I must ask where you are staying in our city,' enquired Bardelli.

'We arrived only this morning and we haven't yet found an inn.'

'Allow me to suggest a place where you will be comfortable and quiet and well fed.'

'Oh! Please do,' said Ottavia. 'We have stayed in some horrid places on our way here, where even the bugs were starving. We want nothing to spoil our visit to Florence.'

'Go to this address and tell them that Bardelli sent you. It's near Santa Croce and very convenient. It's a small inn, clean and well run by my wife's sister and her husband. I know you will be happy there. And if there's any way in which I can be of service to you, don't hesitate to ask. You know where you can find me.'

They thanked him warmly and continued to the ancient church of the Carmine to see the frescoes by Masolino and Masaccio in the Brancacci Chapel. Vasari maintained that Masaccio had been the great successor of Giotto and had mastered space by his understanding of the science of perspective and had given his figures weight and individual characteristics.

The art of fresco painting had not flourished in Venice because of its susceptibility to damp. Consequently, those which remained were faded and unrepresentative of the medium. But here, although the cycle was over a hundred and fifty years old, the colours were firm and bright, the gradations clean and subtle. To Giovanni, they were a revelation, but Ottavia was somewhat disappointed. 'They are certainly fine decorations,' she said, 'but I'm not sure I like the static figures. They have no feeling of life.'

'I know what you mean, but what they lack in liveliness, they make up for in dignity.'

'Yes, but they are so remote from us.'

'Surely, you can feel the shame and distress of Adam and Eve as they are driven out of the garden?' he asked.

'Not really. They seem to be acting the part rather than actually feeling as you or I would.'

'Would you say they showed more emotion than the Giottos at Padua?' enquired Giovanni, trying the Socratic method.

'Oh yes! Much more; all his faces were the same.'

'Why do you think that is?'

'I suppose because Masaccio lived a century after Giotto, and ideas had changed quite a lot.'

'And how long is it since Masaccio died?'

'Over a hundred and fifty years.'

'So it's not surprising that we don't think as he did…'

'Or paint as he did,' continued Ottavia, her voice animated with enlightenment.

'Or perhaps even see as he did,' concluded Giovanni.

They made their way back across the Arno to Santa Croce to find the inn. The stabling for their horses and their own accommodation were excellent and invited a prolonged stay.

For four weeks, they breakfasted on Donatello, lunched on Fra Angelico and dined on Michelangelo, and in between they nibbled at every other Florentine artist they could find. They planned their time so that every third day they rode out into the Tuscan countryside for recreation or to visit a church or a monastery. Giovanni was concerned lest Ottavia's appetite for works of art should become sated, but he found that he himself returned to study refreshed after their excursions and al fresco meals. The peasants of Tuscany were quite accustomed to the passage of royal and noble persons on their way to Florence, but they were captivated by the sight of the imposing young couple who rode by laughing and singing. They seemed more like a pair from ancient legend than living beings. Consequently, the attention they received when they stopped at a tavern was often overwhelming. While they ate or drank, children came and stood by them, gazing in wonderment. At first, Giovanni resented their intrusion slightly, but Ottavia's easy manner and gentle conversation with them soon reduced his irritation and he joined in with questions of his own. He left them a few coins when they resumed their journey, emulating Ottavia, who had brought a bag of coloured beads for just this purpose; these she gave to children who danced or sang for them, or to those she especially liked or seemed especially pitiful.

It was early summer and Giovanni wanted to be in Rome before the heat became too oppressive. 'I think we should be on our way very soon,' he announced.

'But it's lovely here. There's so much to see and do, and I adore the countryside. Tuscany is so green and well cared for. It looks so fresh, as if it had just been made, and yet the castles and towers are obviously very old. Somehow, it seems... different from the other places we've seen.'

'It does. I love it too. These gently rolling hills, spiked with cypresses and bell towers make natural pictures wherever you look. It's surprising that the Florentines didn't invent landscape painting with all this around them!'

'The people are so wonderful, too,' continued Ottavia. 'The Bardellis have been kind and helpful all the time, and it seems almost ungrateful to ride away and leave them because we don't need them any more.'

'I feel that too, but I also want to be in Rome. Don't forget that it gets very hot there later in the year.'

'Could we stay here this summer and go on to Rome in the autumn, spend the winter there and come back here in a year's time?'

It was an attractive idea, but Giovanni was impatient to see the city of the Caesars and the popes. It was an irresistible magnet drawing him further south. At last, Ottavia agreed, but only after she had secured a promise of their return on the way home.

Tearfully, she said farewell to their new friends and assured them of a longer stay when they passed through Florence on their northward journey in a few months' time.

Rome exploded their senses. After the tranquillity of the journey, the city was tumultuous. There were carriages everywhere. As a symbol of quality and status, they were paraded incessantly by their owners in pursuit of self-advertisement and contentious rivalry. The nobility was emulated by merchants and the enormous army of bureaucrats, who in turn were emulated by courtesans and charlatans. It was said in Rome that success came to those who loved God and owned a carriage. Giovanni reflected that he would love the Romans more if they adopted the former and sacrificed the latter.

The noise on the main thoroughfares was insupportable. The city was constipated with traffic; it teemed like an anthill with whores and beggars who were equally importunate. The squalor, the gaudiness, the tempo of life and travel seemed quite demented to natives of Venice.

Ottavia was subdued by the activity and the vastness of the spectacle. She clung to Giovanni for reassurance. For a while, they adopted the practice of leaving the city on alternate days. The campagna was a gentle salve for their lacerated spirits, and it was here, among the trees and ruins that they felt naturally in tune with their surroundings and each other.

The rebuilding of St Peter's was the focus of all attention in the city. Since the sacking, some fifty years before, the air had rung with the sound of the mason's chisel; the Forum was cleared, streets had been replanned and widened, new buildings graced the Via Giulia and Via della Lungara, which provided dramatic access to the Vatican and a worthy approach to the new basilica.

Michelangelo's design had survived his death, but the work had proceeded erratically under successive popes and architects. Behind the ancient façade stood the drum of Michelangelo's dome, which although still open to the sky, dwarfed every other building, apart from the Castel San Angelo and the Imperial Colosseum. Della Porta had completed a pair of cupolas with the ovoid profiles he intended using for the great dome. Inside, the western arm and transepts were finished, and the Gregorian Chapel, with its rich, polychromed marbles and brilliant mosaics, gave an indication of the final appearance of the whole.

As they stood before the altar of St Gregory, which contained the relics of the saint recently confiscated by the Pope who bore his name, Giovanni and Ottavia were less impressed than most visitors seemed to be. It was generally regarded as the apogee of luxury and good taste, but to Venetian eyes, accustomed to richness subservient to quality, the effect was meretricious.

'If they could have found a hundred more coloured marbles, they would have used them,' remarked Giovanni.

Ottavia recollected the mosaics of St Mark's and the

refurbishing of the ducal palace at home and concluded that there was no excuse for such vulgarity.

'It's so hard and cheap looking, isn't it?' she said.

Giovanni agreed. 'Vulgarity is all right as long as it's not permanent,' he observed, 'but this will last for ever.'

'I wonder what Michelangelo would have thought of it.'

'I think he would be appalled,' said Giovanni.

All around them was the evidence of a grander conception. The solemn magnificence of the massive arches and piers, relieved by the lightness of the vast spaces he had created, impressed them deeply. Void and mass, light and shade complemented each other perfectly; the tensions and counter-tensions were sufficiently unresolved to generate a feeling of spiritual power and aspiration which pervaded the worshipper and spectator alike. A wooden model was on exhibition which gave a hint of its finished splendour.

'I wish we could come back in a hundred years from now to see it completed,' said Ottavia.

'I am afraid I cannot arrange that,' said Giovanni, 'but we can go to the new Jesuit church. That is almost finished.'

Il Gesu, the mother church of the order, was founded by St Ignatius Loyola in the most populous part of Rome, below the Capitol. The building was begun by Vignola and finished by Della Porta, but the internal decorations still remained to be done. Its design was a development of the simple classicism of Palladio, the Venetian, and it was destined to become the prototype of almost every church in the Old and New Worlds for two centuries.

Ottavia had to admit that the facade was as fine as Palladio's San Giorgio across the water from the Palazzo Ducale, but she missed the crystalline sparkle of reflected light on Istrian marble.

'It's very beautiful, but it's not as *happy* as San Giorgio, is it?'

'No, everything is very well mannered, confined to its proper place and proportion. Every niche and every window fits into a box of just the right size, happiness is like freedom, I suppose, it needs no harness; it needs room to spill over, but here, nothing can.'

'I just don't understand that. It doesn't make sense, does it?'

'Well, the architect or the painter has a choice. He can design with vitality like Michelangelo, but measured proportion is the way of Masaccio and the ancient Romans, and even Palladio, but he was clever enough to use both.'

'I don't think I would want to have everything measured exactly, and I would get bored if I had to do it all the time!'

'Some people would get bored doing what you do; filling in all those spaces with tiny brush marks.'

'That's quite different, though,' protested Ottavia, 'that is building up something very subtle and beautiful, making it come alive.'

'Ah! The designer who uses geometry would probably say the same thing. You both want subtlety and beauty, but you get there by different routes.'

'I don't see that at all. Beauty comes from living things, from movement and rhythms, not squares and triangles.'

He found a piece of paper in his purse and leaned against a post in the piazza. 'Let's draw it and I'll show you.' He drew a square and divided it horizontally and vertically, making four equal quarters. 'Now, that's balanced and boring, isn't it?' She agreed. 'If I put one square on top of two, it's more interesting. It makes part of a triangle, and now I put a complete triangle at the top. One is implied, the other actual.' He ran a horizontal line through the lower pair of squares. 'This line gives the top of the main door and the bottom of the two niches each side; one hanging, the other standing on it. It starts to move now, doesn't it?'

She was dubious. He drew a circle with its centre at the top of the door, and where it cut the base line he added the two side doors. He placed smaller circles above, which, when halved, became the heads of the niches and the central window, and four more which formed the scrolls on the side brackets.

Ottavia watched, fascinated by the way the orderly lines fitted together, some as recognisable features of the façade, some lines of construction or continuity.

'You know when you play a chord on your lute, I can echo it lower down. Well, that's the beginning of the rhythm; repeat it and it becomes movement. This is just the same. The cornices echo the horizontal, the pilasters echo the vertical; they beat time and the detail puts the melody on the top. The busyness is kept in the middle; the plainness at the sides, so the eye keeps moving, but it always comes back to the centre.'

'Yes, but you cannot be sure how people will look at a thing', said Ottavia.

'You can, if you know how. They might not realise it, but you can make their eyes travel up or down or sideways, fast or slowly, according to the rhythms in your design.'

'I really cannot believe that.'

'Try it then. You keep your eye fixed on the left-hand edge of the building. Try to keep it there, and I'll see how long you can hold it.'

He shifted his position and looked into her eyes. She tried, and managed about ten seconds before her gaze strayed. 'Aha! I saw you move across.'

'Yes, I know I did, but that wasn't a proper try.'

'Do it again, and look at the third step up, in the centre this time.' After a few seconds, her eyes moved upwards. 'You see, you cannot do it, even when you're trying. So when you're not trying, your eye is being led from one thing to another all the time.'

'You are right, I give up!'

'They call that composition, you know,' he said with casual sarcasm. She slapped him playfully. He took her hand and kissed it.

On the following day they went into the campagna. It was hot in the city and the malodorous assault of rancid food, bodies, horse manure and rudimentary sanitation had become too aggressive. They longed for the fair smell of the Grand Canal, but, instead, fresh country air would serve.

They rode along the Appian Way, the horses eagerly trotting towards the scented lure of lush grass. Away from the road, on the edge of a vineyard, they found a few standing columns and a low wall of a ruined villa. They tethered the horses to a tree and lay in the cool shade. A breeze ruffled Ottavia's hair, which bubbled from beneath a bandana. The peace was flawed only by the sound of birdsong and the occasional stamp of a hoof.

'I wonder what it would be like to be an ancient Roman,' said

Giovanni.

'It was probably good if you had plenty of money and could live in a house like this, but I wouldn't want to be a slave or a soldier.'

'I don't suppose it was much different, then. We are lucky, we have plenty of money, we have a good life, we can read and write and travel. But most people cannot do that even today.'

'Suppose you were a Roman senator, then. What would you do?'

'To amuse myself, you mean? Because I wouldn't be a painter, would I?'

'No, you come from a wealthy family, you have a business which provides money, but you don't have to work at it – other people do that for you. So you are an educated man of leisure.'

'I would eat well. I would have a library and collect Greek sculpture. I would make music – and I would have lots of beautiful brown slave girls to dance for me and fulfil every desire before I knew I had it myself.'

'Why would you want *brown* girls?' asked Ottavia peevishly.

'Because they are warm-blooded and sinuous; because they know how to make a man happy.'

'And light-skinned girls don't, I suppose.'

'Oh no! It's a well-known fact…'

'That's rubbish,' she interrupted. 'If I were our slave, there is nothing I couldn't do for you. I can make music; I can dance and I could fulfil your every desire, as you put it.'

She knelt up to emphasise her claims, but Giovanni remained on his back with eyes closed, feigning patrician hauteur.

'Well, get me some food then, slave,' he said.

She fetched the basket, spread out a cloth and arranged pies and fruit on wooden platters. She had chosen the wine herself, a white spumante with the raffia well soaked to keep it cool. Quite content with her self-imposed servitude, she unwired the cork. There was a loud report, the cork shot into the leaves above and a fountain, worthy of Rome itself, cascaded over them both. Ottavia knelt, paralysed by shock and chilly foam, which ran down her face, arms and her dress in an effervescing torrent. Giovanni catapulted up, similarly drenched.

'You are a rotten slave! You ought to be whipped for that. You've ruined our clothes, our meal and wasted half a bottle of wine.' He wiped the bubbles from his face and saw Ottavia gazing down at herself in rigid incredulity. 'In fact, you *shall* be whipped for that.'

He reached for a switch which lay nearby. His action brought an immediate response. Ottavia sprang to her feet and took off in a curving, screaming run, with Giovanni in pursuit. Around the trees and walls she went, dodging the hissing switch as it flailed near her legs. The chase continued round pillars and pedestals with Ottavia squealing with childish delight and spurious panic. She caught sight of a covert of thick ilex bushes and headed for an opening. She parted company with a shoe and limped on through the gap. It was dark and cool inside, the ground slippery with moss. The green shade enveloped her like a thick cloak and she picked her way deeper into the dark. She could hear Giovanni crashing through the stiff leaves behind her. The foot wearing the shoe skidded and she slid into a hidden culvert. The icy water reached her knees; the second shock made her cry out.

When Giovanni caught up with her, he found her lying on her back, clutching at the moss, with her feet and the hem of her skirt below the water. He dropped the switch and put his hands under her arms and hauled her up the slope. 'That serves you right,' he panted unsympathetically.

Her breath spent and she wriggled awkwardly to the flat ground with legs akimbo, trying vainly to avoid contact with her dripping skirt. 'I am soaked,' she said with genuine petulance.

'Well, at least we can wash off this wine before it gets sticky,' comforted Giovanni. 'So you have done some good, finding this spring.'

They unfastened their clothes. Ottavia stepped out of her dress, pulled off her stockings and her shift, and went cautiously down the slope into the water. Giovanni followed.

'It's freezing!' she said, holding her elbows in her hands.

'Mother of God! So it is.'

He squatted down; the chill speared his crotch with icy savagery. Ottavia copied him tentatively, but courage fled.

'I can't do it,' she whispered, drawing breath.

'Yes, you can. Once you get over the first cringe, it's fine.'

She lowered herself again, but the panic was authentic. 'Help me! Gianni,' she pleaded. 'Hold me, and we'll go down together.'

He put his arms around her shoulders and pressed her gently lower into the water. She gripped at him like a drowning woman. Their knees collided as they stooped. They tried again and they submerged until their bodies were covered. Ottavia shivered and clutched her shoulders, when, suddenly, she realised that they were naked and together. Terror left her. In the half-light she reached out a hand to Giovanni's face.

'I am sorry I have been so stupid and spoiled things for you, Gianni.'

'We wouldn't have found this place if you hadn't made such a mess, would we?'

He touched her face with a reciprocal gesture of tenderness, and cupped her cheek in his palm. Her body was tinted with pale emerald.

'You are beautiful, Tavi,' he said expressing his thoughts out loud.

'No, I'm not! I wish I were like your Venus being born from the waves.'

She stood up slowly, the water streaming from her shoulders, her breasts and her hips, following the contours of her skin like molten silver. She raised her arms to lift her hair; diamonds dropped from her arms into annulets by her thighs. She tilted her hips and turned her torso into a classical contrapposto.

She was Aphrodite indeed, thought Giovanni. All the beauty of the world, the art of antiquity and the Florentine Renaissance was concentrated in the flowing form before him. He was dross, and the awareness of his hopeless inferiority and unworthiness obliterated all desire. To touch her would be a sacrilege.

'You look as if you have seen a ghost,' said Ottavia.

'Perhaps I have.'

She scooped water over her arms and shoulders, occupied in the serious business of washing; Giovanni was submerged in profound idolatry.

They ate their sodden pies with their clothes draped over a fallen column; a pair of woodland sprites in an Arcadia of their own making.

Rome became intolerable in the ensuing weeks, so their visits in the city were made in the early morning. It was while they were admiring Michelangelo's Moses in San Pietro in Vincoli, which formed the centrepiece of the abortive monument to Pope Julius II, that they were engaged in conversation by a nobleman who had come to say his rosary.

He was fascinated by the absorption of the couple as they discussed the figure, and he had observed them for some time before he approached them.

'It's very fine, isn't it?' he said, startling them. 'I especially admire the way those strong, angular fingers play with the curls of the beard, yet it isn't at all trivial, it seems as if it has some symbolical meaning, but I don't know what it could be.'

'Nor do I,' said Giovanni. 'We were impressed by the noble expression on his face. It seems to be strong and yet gentle at the same time.'

'We were also saying that he reminded us of someone we know,' added Ottavia.

'And who is that, might I ask?'

'A painter called Jacopo Robusti in Venice,' she said.

'You know Tintoretto!' he exclaimed.

'Yes, very well,' emphasised Ottavia impishly.

'I am a great admirer of the Venetians. I have a picture by Titan, and I would love to have a Tintoretto too, but he's always so busy working for the state and San Rocco.'

'He never stops working, and his pictures seem to get larger all the time,' said Giovanni.

'I wonder if you would like to see my Titian.'

'Yes, please,' said Ottavia readily; *too readily*, Giovanni thought.

'I am going home now, so why not come with me, if you are not too busy.'

His manner was courteous and urbane, but there was little warmth in his courtesy. As they left the church, he told them about his conversations with Michelangelo when he was designing St Peter's. 'I have some of his drawings. Perhaps you would like to see them as well.'

His leg was lame and they reached the door at his pace. No sooner had they emerged than a carriage drew up at the steps and a liveried servant ran towards his master, offering obsequious assistance.

The journey was a short one, but an exciting novelty for the young ones. From their high position, they could look down on the scurrying pedestrians with magnificent complacence and they understood exactly the social prestige that carriages conferred. Below them, the wheels alternately rattled over the cobbles and were muffled by the dried mats of horse droppings.

They swung into a pedimented gateway in the tympanum of which was a perilously large coat of arms. The courtyard was planted with trees which met overhead in a green vault.

'My house was designed by Sangallo. Perhaps you have heard of him,' enquired the nobleman.

'Indeed we have,' said Giovanni. 'The Palazzo Farnese was one of his works, I believe.'

Inside, the cool marble and exquisite proportions of the hall proclaimed a refinement rare in this grandiose city. Pink columns of the Tuscan order supported an arcade on three sides of the square, the fourth was occupied by a staircase which divided at the landing into two opposing flights. Between each arch was a circular niche, containing a terracotta bust of a Roman emperor. The walls were quite plain. Only the stuccoed ceiling and the floor were decorated. The effect was one of dignified restraint and tranquillity. Upstairs, in a beautifully appointed saloon, hung the Titian.

Giovanni was mesmerised. It was the original painting of which he had seen an engraving years before in the Maestro's studio, the *Sacred and Profane Love*.

'I bought this some years ago from the heirs of the Venetian Grand Chancellor, who commissioned it when Titian was a young man,' explained their host.

'I didn't think I would ever see this,' said Giovanni, his voice hushed with reverence and astonishment.

'You intrigue me, young sir.'

'Many years ago, I studied an engraving of this picture with Tintoretto. I admired it then, but now I see its colour and its brushwork, I am simply amazed.'

'You talk like a connoisseur, but you are too young. Could it be that you are a painter?'

'I am,' said Giovanni. 'I was trained by Tintoretto, and now I am his partner.

'You seem too young for that too, but to be the partner of such a master, you must be very talented.' There was a hint of scepticism in his intonation.

'He is,' blurted Ottavia defensively. 'He has painted for the doge and many important people at home. He's very well known there…'

'This is Ottavia, Maestro Jacopo's daughter,' said Giovanni, to cover his embarrassment rather than to observe civilities.

'Are you a painter too, might I ask?'

'I am Giovanni's assistant, so I only do as I am told.'

'Let me introduce myself, then. I am Piero Farnese.' He bowed his head slightly in a gesture of stylised modesty. 'I would be delighted if you would stay and have luncheon with me. I am alone, except for the servants and I would enjoy your company.'

His illustrious name silenced Giovanni, whose knowledge of the family history was sketchy. He recalled reading about the beautiful Giulia Farnese, who had captivated the Borgia Pope, Alexander. He had heard of the Farnese Pope, Paul III, patron of Michelangelo, and the Dukes of Parma. Fragmentary though that knowledge was, it inspired respect and a certain apprehension. Ottavia was altogether ignorant of such things. 'Thank you, we would like that,' she said in a tone of casual friendliness.

He showed them some of his treasures during the morning. They marvelled at pictures by Fra Angelico and Ghirlandaio, whose work Ottavia especially admired from their stay in Florence. He had antique cameos, bronzes by Ghiberti and Benvenuto Cellini, drawings by Raphael and Michelangelo and engravings by every conceivable master, including Mantegna. 'My father thought the Mantegna frescoes at Mantua were superb,' she said.

'I had heard that he had been there to do some pictures for the duke, but I haven't seen them yet. I don't travel much these days. I am locked up in this godless city most of the time.'

He took them into his library, where his collections of coins and illuminated manuscripts were housed. 'I think you will feel at home here. I have many volumes printed in Venice.'

He took down a book and opened it. It was printed by Nicholas Jenson with the type he had designed himself. 'These are a great joy to me. Fine printing can be as much a work of art as anything else. That will seem a heresy to you, perhaps.'

'Well, it's more mechanical than painting, surely?' suggested Ottavia.

'The technique may be, but to design a beautiful alphabet and arrange it on a page as perfectly as this is much the same in my opinion.'

He illustrated the point with an analysis of the letter forms; he explained the proportion of the page based on the Golden Section and the relationship of type size to the page.

'You Venetians made the craft of printing into an art. Left to the Germans, it would have been merely functional and efficient, but look at this!' He opened a slim book printed by Aldus Manutius in graceful italics. He paused for a while in silent homage, then turned to the printer's mark: a dolphin twisted around an anchor. *Make haste slowly*, he reflected to himself, quoting the motto of Emperor Octavian who had used the same symbol. The paradox of the words intrigued him and his thoughts set out on a voyage of history and philosophical speculation, but the woodcut on the page was a beacon, redirecting his attention towards reality and the obligations of hospitality. He addressed his guests. 'Please forgive me,' he said. 'I am too accustomed to my own company. I must remember to show you a coin of the Emperor Titus, who completed the Colosseum. It has the same mark stamped upon it, a bit crude perhaps, but impressive for its antiquity.' The motto seemed apposite and he turned again to the page. 'That is so simple, yet so beautiful – a perfect balance of curves and straight lines in just a few inches. So many people today underrate or even ignore a design because it's simple.'

'Even though I cannot share all your enthusiasm for printing, I have to agree with you there,' said Giovanni.

'You must go and see the inscription at the base of Trajan's Column. There you will find the paradigm of all lettering;

everything aspires to it, but nothing, carved or printed, has ever surpassed it.'

He turned more pages, immersed in his own reverie. A steward appeared briefly and withdrew silently.

'After luncheon, I will show you my garden and you can rest there, if you would like to.'

The meal was a revelation. Small chickens had been boned and stuffed with smaller boned birds, which themselves had been stuffed with an aromatic pate and roasted. Eaten cold, with artichoke hearts, they were ambrosial. Next, a bunch of black grapes was served to each person in a silver dish of sugared rose water.

The garden was a formal arrangement of hedges and potted shrubs interspersed with statuary, some antique, some modern. At the end of a paved walk was a shallow, semicircular basin into which water poured from a huge scallop shell. Rising from the shell, her feet submerged, stood Aphrodite. The figure was slightly mannered in the Roman fashion, but she was regal and delectable.

Giovanni was speechless. It was Ottavia!

'The sculptor was a namesake of yours,' said Farnese, disturbing the young man's enchantment. 'Giovanni da Bologna cut this for me when I designed the garden. It was one of his first great sculptures. He has developed into the finest sculptor of our day, and it has not been easy for anyone to follow the divine Michelangelo.'

Giovanni barely heard the explanation and Farnese's assessment of a great contemporary. He was mesmerised by the image which so closely corresponded to his recent fantasies about Ottavia in the campagna.

'Let me show you where you can rest,' he continued to Ottavia. 'Ladies usually find it agreeable.' He moved off towards a sheltered corner of the garden, leaving Giovanni to his preoccupation.

The grotto was covered in shells and terracotta reliefs. Marble statuettes of nymphs and tritons were set in niches which were festooned in ferns. In the centre was a circular basin of water lilies, out of which crawled green sea horses and mermaids. It was backed by a crescent-shaped sarcophagus filled with ferns and trailing flowers. The floor was patterned with green and blue veined marbles, reminiscent of crested waves.

It was Ottavia's turn to marvel in unspoken delight.

'Please stay as long as you like. I must go in and rest now.'

Left alone, she explored the grotto, touching the statues and the ferns, drifting her fingers through the water. On every side, there was some feature or colour or texture to excite the senses. The scent of flowers hung above the mossy dankness; the sound of water spilling from a dolphin's mouth in a soft gurgle and the chilled air on her arms and throat enveloped her. She felt like an interloper in an alien, but not inimical, world.

Giovanni arrived, still half-distracted. 'What a gorgeous place,' he said.

'Gianni, it's the most beautiful thing I have ever seen. It's like being at the bottom of the sea. Listen!'

He noticed that the air was not silent. Behind the gentle sound of trickling water, he was aware of an aerial activity, hardly a sound, more like the feeling in a hand caressing silk. The whole grotto collected currents and amplified them, as a large shell would do.

He looked about him, full of admiration for the inventiveness of the designer who had realised a delicate vision with such subtlety and skill. He had created a submarine paradise.

'Could we stay here for a while? Piero Farnese said we might.' She settled herself on a low marble bench, leaving room for Giovanni. She patted the space beside her. Giovanni occupied it and put an arm round her shoulder. 'He is very kind, isn't he?' she began. 'And so knowledgeable about so many things.'

'He is, and he certainly has a magnificent collection, but I'm not sure you should trust him, Tavi,' he began cautiously.

'Why ever not? He is most correct, the first real courtier I have ever me—'

'I know that, but sometimes good manners can conceal a deeper menace, even wickedness.'

'You surely don't think he is evil or wicked, do you?' She laughed derisively.

'No, I am not saying that he is, but there might be something lurking there which we cannot see...' Ottavia scoffed, but Giovanni continued without showing impatience. 'His family has known enormous wealth and power, and I don't suppose they achieved that by being gentle and honest.'

'You cannot judge a man by his family. But Piero is a Christian, a gentleman. He is cultured and very intelligent. He couldn't possibly wish any harm to anyone.'

'You may be right. I hope you are, but I think you should be more careful.'

He did not wish to be specific, but he had heard of the strange passions indulged by the nobility and he was fearful of his responsibility. Ottavia was offended by his scepticism and vagueness.

They talked at length about all they had seen, and Giovanni explained the meaning of Titian's painting. He hoped that it would serve as a prologue to his understanding of their relationship, but Ottavia's mercurial excitement led them away from love to the palazzina, its contents and garden.

As the sun angled through the trees into the grotto, flickering the shells and statuary with broken light, they returned to the house to thank their host and take their leave.

'I have enjoyed your company enormously. It has been most rewarding to show you the things I love. Most people are not sympathetic any more. They are too concerned with the cost, and not the value.'

'We have enjoyed our visit very much. It has been a privilege to see your collection and we thank you for your great kindness to us,' said Giovanni.

Ottavia concurred.

'I have been wondering if you would both like to stay here while you are in Rome There is plenty of room, and it will give me pleasure to do what I can to make your pilgrimage as rich and full as possible. It will be delightful for me to have young people about.'

Giovanni's suspicions increased, Ottavia was uncontrollable. 'Oh yes! We would love to, wouldn't we, Giovanni?'

He reflected on the cautionary advice he had given her. Acceptance was dangerous and he needed time to consider, but he did not wish to appear discourteous in case he had misjudged Farnese. His dilemma had made him acutely uncomfortable. Ottavia tugged his sleeve, prompting agreement.

'Yes, thank you. That is very kind of you. Are you sure we won't be in the way...' he stammered absurdly.

Piero was reassuring. 'You will be most welcome. Stay as long as you like, come and go as you please. I will make no demands on you and I hope you will consider me as a friend; there if needed, invisible if not.'

His courtesy bore the clearest imprint of sincerity; mere manners had given way to kindness. Ottavia kissed his cheek impulsively. Giovanni was mortified by her familiarity to a kinsman of His Holiness, Paul III.

'Thank you, my dear. That's the first time I have been kissed by a lady for twenty-five years.' He smiled graciously. 'Welcome to my house.'

They moved their baggage and their horses to the palazzina that evening and embarked on the most deeply satisfying and unpremeditated part of their travels. Giovanni came to admit that his caution had been misplaced and that Ottavia's intuition was vindicated. Piero Farnese was a man of cultivated taste and refinement. His conversation and his interests were stimulating, and his instruction, though never didactic, enlarged their awareness of the arts, of poetry and philosophy.

As their mutual regard grew deeper, it was natural for them to exchange confidences. He told them of his marriage, which had been arranged by two families whose concerns were financial, political and territorial. He and his wife lived as strangers for half a year, each suspicious of the other, neither having any real attachment for the other beyond the golden band. The families exerted pressure on them to have children to cement the alliance and to preclude any move towards an annulment which either might seek. But the very idea of consummation was repulsive to them both; on this they agreed, without malice or without reservation. The pressures, however, became more intolerable than their repugnance, and at last, they consented, only to placate family demands. To their astonishment, the physical act of union, committed in benign consideration for each other's feelings, was the apotheosis of their lives. Their relationship coalesced in mutual respect and devotion.

The child was stillborn.

A year later, while carrying their second child, she had died of plague. Piero was wild with grief and anger. He cursed God, the Blessed Virgin and the Church for his deprivation. He was inconsolable.

He became a soldier and fought with demonic zeal and savage self-immolation in the hope of winning death and reunion with his beloved wife. But death was elusive. He was gravely wounded at the Battle of Lepanto, and, as he lay near to death, a vision of his wife appeared. She told him that the time had not yet come for him to join her, but in his remaining life of pain, she would meet him daily in his prayers.

The zealot, killer and atheist became a devout Christian, interceding with St Catherine, communing with his wife in his daily office.

Ottavia found the story deeply moving, and, furthermore, it supported the conviction she had about her love for Giovanni.

'Will you tell me something, Piero?'

'I will, if I am able.'

'Do you think that physical union always completes a loving relationship?'

'I do. In my own experience, this was true and the experience of many others seems to confirm it. But who can be certain that it is always true for all people?' She had received the answer she hoped for, in spite of its final reservation. 'Mind you,' he went on, 'there are records of those whose love excludes the physical. There was Dante and Beatrice, for instance, and Titian's picture refers to a love more sublime than most people ever know. I can vouch for that, because I love my wife more deeply now than when she was alive. Spiritual love, in isolation, is very rare indeed, but it occurs from time to time. Plato invented platonic love to explain something else, but I'm sure it does exist; we have it on better authority than his.'

Giovanni had received the answer he had hoped for. It explained exactly what he knew was true of himself.

'But spiritual love, as you call it, seems so remote from life to me,' said Ottavia. 'Forgive me, but you only found this kind of love after your wife died, didn't you?'

'That is partly true, but looking back to the last year of her life, I can recognise that we knew spiritual love then.'

'So you have known both?'

'Yes, and in this, we were more fortunate than we deserved, and more fortunate than most people who love each other.'

She was perplexed and was becoming impatient with herself.

'Think of the most sacred place you know,' he said.

Her forehead puckered in thought and then cleared. 'I suppose it must be St Mark's tomb at home.'

'Very well. Could you fornicate there?' he asked gently. Ottavia coloured. 'Well, that is a measure of the difference between carnal and spiritual loves,' he went on before she could reply.

'But St Mark was a holy man and is buried in a church,' she protested. 'No one fornicates in church, or anywhere in public for that matter.'

'No, no, my dear, you have missed my point. I agree that it is unthinkable in real terms, but it illustrates the separation between the two. The Church, in its infinite folly, teaches us that fornication is a sin, so the separation goes even deeper and gets more complicated. All I am saying is that this plane of love is incomprehensible to those who do not experience it, and that it is independent of the appetites of our bodies.' He observed Ottavia closely and read signs of dawning comprehension. 'My wife is with me in church, and when I think of her, I think of her body too. Kneeling before St Catherine, I feel her presence, I caress her body, I feel her breath and the softness of her loins. It's a sacrament; we are complete, united in every way. Does that shock you?'

'I suppose it does, but I don't really understand it. I want to, but I don't see how she can be there, and yet not there.'

Giovanni had remained quiet during the exchange, but he had undergone an enlightenment which had clarified a deep mystery. He understood exactly what Piero meant. 'Piero, this subject is very important to us, because we have just the difficulty you describe, but we haven't been able to discuss this with anyone else. May I explain?'

'Please do.'

He outlined their predicament and the problems they faced. 'The truth is,' he continued, 'that I love Tavi so completely, so beautifully that to treat her like a rutting animal is not just irrelevant, it's sacrilege. And yet, that is what Tavi really wants. In other words, she wants the only thing I cannot give, but all I want to do is to make her happy.'

'I understand that perfectly,' said Piero, 'but I want to say two things. The first might sound like advice, and I hate advising anyone. It seems so arrogant to me. Giovanni, you mustn't assume that just because my wife and I found bliss in each other when we had coition the same will happen to you. People and circumstances never duplicate exactly, even when they seem to be similar, and the greatest mistakes they can make, and do make, arise from adopting others' solutions and actions for their own problems and situations.' Giovanni nodded. It was an extension of an idea he was formulating about the arts, so it seemed totally acceptable in terms of human behaviour. 'So I respect your position exactly as you stated it, and I would not want to interfere in it in any way.'

'Now, Tavi,' he said, taking her hands. 'I want to tell you something. You may not realise it, but you are one of the most privileged of women. I can understand your disappointment and unhappiness, but try to think of it like this. You begged for a pretty glass bead and were given a pearl beyond price. We do not always know what is best for us, and sometimes, quite unwittingly, we desire the second best. Fragile beads, you can get by the handful; a pearl like yours is inimitable and indestructible.' He lowered his head and kissed the palms of her hands. 'Do you see what I mean?'

'I think so,' she said wistfully. 'But why does it hurt so much?'

'It hurts just because you love him.'

She remembered her father's enigmatic words about *his* riches, and she understood. But as they lay together that night in each other's arms, she yearned for the glass bead.

Their tour of Rome flowed slowly through the summer. In addition to the churches and public places, they were granted access to the whole of the Vatican and many important private collections through Farnese's introduction. The doors of the palaces of every member of Rome's nobility were graciously opened to them. Their thirst was unquenchable.

They visited their ruined villa and bathed in the culvert; they took al fresco meals quite naked, unencumbered by guilt or modesty. Giovanni joked about himself as a satyr, tamed by the beauty of a woodland nymph. They made chalk studies of each other, concentrating on muscular anatomy and proportion. Her drawing, always delicate and diffident, was an exact reflection of her personality, and her anatomical knowledge was never applied to secure a sound, rational structure. Giovanni's, on the other hand, was positive and sculptural, as if Michelangelo had adopted a lithe, feline quality in place of the weight and mass so characteristic of his draughtsmanship.

Bologna's Aphrodite was a constant source of wonder to him. Here, the combination of nature and artifice was in perfect accord, and his daily visits to the basin enhanced his veneration. Here, he found Ottavia's beauty elevated to a consummation achieved only by a few idolaters of genius. Michelangelo's youthful *Pieta*, Titian's *Sacred and Profane Love*, Giorgione's *Sleeping Venus* and Raphael's *Madonna with the Goldfinch* all had this ethereal loveliness which transcends mere excellence. It was something he responded to with reverential humility when it confronted him and he was determined to try to realise it himself. He believed that a subtle synthesis of rationality and intuition, in some unknown, unknowable proportion, was the key to that realisation. It was in the campagna that he conceived the perfect theme, the perfect setting and the perfect subject for their own attempt to scale the lonely heights of perfection. Tentatively, he introduced the plan to Ottavia.

'Tavi, do you think we might paint a picture for Piero as a thank you for all his kindness?'

'What a marvellous idea! I am sure it would mean a lot to him if we did.'

'What sort of subject do you think we should choose?'

'I don't know.' She paused. 'His portrait, perhaps, or better still, a religious picture. What about St Catherine?'

'Yes,' he said thoughtfully, 'you could be right, but there's one thing that worries me about that.'

'Tell me.'

'His religious experience is so very personal that it might be impossible for us to give it any form which would mean anything to him.'

'Yes, you are right,' she conceded. 'Have you any ideas?'

'I am thinking that a pastoral would be suitable, something like Giorgione's poetic landscapes, but with our atmosphere. We need a goddess or a nymph in a setting fit for a deity, rich with autumn gold.'

'You had that in mind all the time, didn't you?' she said impatiently. 'But that does sound exactly what he would like, and we could do.'

'I also think we must use you as the model,' added Giovanni cautiously.

'Why not both of us? You have said before that we are like a nymph and satyr, so that would make a very personal gift, wouldn't it?'

'We shall have to rent or borrow a studio to work in, because we cannot paint in the palazzina, can we?'

'That's true, but we can start the sketches now.'

They discussed the composition and Giovanni drew, in chalk, the preliminary rough, structuring the design around a series of catenary curves, then running horizontals and verticals over them to interlock at crucial points. Lines of limbs and trees, shoulders and hills, hair and rivers were related in simple harmonies.

Ottavia approved the result and couldn't wait to begin.

'I want this picture to be the very best we have ever done. Piero knows about painting and he will appreciate every subtlety we can include,' said Giovanni. 'And he will know if it is inferior, or just a pastiche. It must be very, very good.'

They hired a studio and set to work on the canvas, Ottavia priming and grinding colours while Giovanni made a working sketch. They prepared small studies of the landscape and the separate figures in paint and, when they were satisfied that they had found the best solution to each design problem, they made the cartoon. Once transferred to the canvas, they estimated that in about a month the picture would be finished. The canvas was large enough for them to work on simultaneously, without obstructing each other.

While they painted, a framer was making and gilding a frame, which he believed to be quaintly old-fashioned, but they had designed it themselves to conform with the refined simplicity of Sangallo's architecture. The only carved decoration was an oval cartouche which was to be incised in Roman letters.

TO PIERO FARNESE
MENTOR AND DEAREST FRIEND OF
GIOVANNI AND OTTAVIA ROBUSTI
WITH AFFECTION, ESTEEM AND GRATITUDE
MDLXXXIII

It became a votive picture and their pledge to achieve the highest possible standards absorbed them completely. They were working in concert again, undistracted and unhampered.

They were dedicated and methodical, trusting that the whole would be greater than the sum of the parts, First, they established the rhythms and the distribution of the tones, then the modelling of the forms in light and shade, then the mantle of colours spread over the forms, and finally, the calligraphic details of grass, hair, flowers and foliage. Giovanni contributed the finite qualities of drawing and design, Ottavia the amorphous, atmospheric colour, but all the time, the growth of the concept and the controls they applied were corporate.

The whole surface glowed in warm gold, copper and bronze, interspersed with cool pools of aquamarine. The figures of the seductive nymph and the adoring satyr faced each other in complementary poses, epitomising feminine grace and voluptuousness, and masculine strength and protection. They were real, yet not of the corporeal world; a lyrical summation, not just of the elusive perfection of antiquity, but of the utmost delicacy of human emotion. Between them stretched a distant Arcadian landscape, fulgent with the golden rays of a dying sun. It brought into focus those dimly apprehended visions of harmony and perfection which seem to recede according to the effort made in grasping them. It was a requiem for the end of a day, the end of an era, a lost golden age. It poignantly expressed the end of a relationship which had given them joy, spiritual enlightenment and a fulfilment which could only be affirmed in metaphors and allusive images.

There was no ceremony in the presentation. They unwrapped their gift from its cloth cover and said simply, 'This is for you.'

Piero recognised its merit and the two figures immediately. Its distinction communicated instantly to one of his long and deep experience. His surprise registered equally spontaneously. He moved forwards to examine the detail and to read the inscription. 'Have you painted this for me?' he asked incredulously.

'Yes, just for you, with our love,' explained Ottavia.

'And our thanks for all you have done for us,' added Giovanni.

Piero was intoxicated by the beauty of the colour and the design, deeply moved by the poetic evocations of the subject and astounded by the brilliance of the technique.

'What can I say? What could anyone say to such a masterpiece?' He paused. 'If it were anything less than that, I would have plenty to say, but this, this is a painted miracle...'

He turned to Ottavia and kissed her hand. She kissed his cheek. He shook Giovanni by the hand and embraced him with the other. 'Thank you both so very much,' he said with unconcealed emotion. 'Thank you. I cannot say more for the present, please forgive me.'

The transcendental beauty of the picture provoked contemplation of an almost mystical nature, and his disciplined responses to works of art permitted him to progress to an aesthetic ecstasy comparable with that experienced by certain religious mystics. It was neither an exercise of reason nor of intuition, but a process of empathy in which he identified with the deepest spiritual forces inherent in the work. In physical terms, he ceased to exist; time had no meaning and sensations were nullified. The aftermath of this experience produced more than a sense of well-being. It was a spiritual cleansing, a rebirth into a state of intensified awareness and purity.

At last, he returned, reborn and revitalised, into a human situation which he had not encountered before. It was as if he had received, not simply a gift, but a benediction. Such an expression of devotion he had not known since he was bereaved; such a force of pure sentiment he could not equate with his previous experience of human relationships, immediate or vicarious. For all his intellectual and emotional maturity, he was quite unable to express the effusion of his spirit. He reached out his hands to them both and held theirs in silent thanksgiving.

'This is our parting gift,' said Giovanni. 'We have been here a long time and we couldn't think of any way of thanking you for your kindness and friendship.'

'I have given you nothing; you have given me everything. I am grieved that you have to leave. When you go, I shall be desolate.'

Nymph and satyr exchanged glances.

'We can stay a little longer if you would like us to,' offered Ottavia, who found the idea of separation pointless and distressing once again.

'If we are going to visit Florence on our way home, the winter will be upon us before we cross the mountains,' warned Giovanni.

'Could you spend the winter here?' asked Piero. 'You could go to Florence in the spring and be home early next summer.'

'Could we?' pleaded Ottavia. 'Please, Gianni.'

'We should love to spend the winter here with you,' said Giovanni.

Piero shuffled his feet in an uncharacteristically frivolous gesture of joy. His lame leg did not cooperate; he stumbled and had to be supported by four willing hands which came to his rescue. He was highly amused. 'Next week, we shall hold a grand reception and banquet. I shall invite everyone who values the arts to come and see your picture. It will be an occasion Rome will never forget.'

The palazzina was scoured by dozens of imported helpers; the regular servants dusted, cleaned and polished every surface that was visible and a few that were not. Ceremonial decorators wove foliage, fruit and flowers into huge swags which were draped from the cornices of hall, staircase and saloon. Marble urns were filled with blooms of pink and red and magenta. Piero decreed that no yellows should be used and that golden and silver gilt objects should be hidden; he wanted nothing to detract from the predominant hues of his picture.

The guests, however, knew no such restraint. Their costumes and jewellery testified to every material extravagance, devised to proclaim the self and outshine all others. The result would have eclipsed the court of the Byzantine emperors. Rome abounded with wealth unearned, and it was a social duty, sanctified by the Church, to display it as lavishly as possible.

By Roman standards, the banquet was modest. Forty dishes of poulet à la Catalane were followed by eight dishes of roast meats and six each of pheasant and pigeon, all served to the music of harps, psalteries and viols. Fruits, nuts and sweetmeats, wines from Frascati, Montefiascone and Piglio were there for the asking in inexhaustible quantities. The formal magnificence of the scene and the participants isolated Giovanni and Ottavia as if they were the subjects of hypnosis.

The major domo called for attention and invited the company to Farnese's study. There assembled, Piero introduced the climax of the afternoon and the reason for his celebration. The mystery hung behind a curtain.

'My friends, I have recently had the good fortune to become the custodian of one of the finest examples of creative ingenuity and subtlety I have ever seen. In these days of excess and hyperbole, it has become a commonplace to call every successful artist a genius. I do not use that word lightly; I reserve it for that exclusive company of Praxiteles, Giotto, da Vinci, Michelangelo and Titian. They are divine, and beside these giants, we are but grasshoppers. Last week, I added another name to the immortal elect, and I am privileged to be entrusted with one of his works, a work which will outlive us all, a work which will be revered as long as men remain sentient beings. You are here so that I may share my pleasure and my privilege with you all.'

He released the curtain which fell to the floor. The picture radiated its golden benison, subduing everyone present. They stood, spellbound by its benign sorcery. At first, the only movement was a ripple of heads, shifting so that no part of the miracle should be obscured. Polite whispers passed among them, expressing wonder and voicing the inevitable question, 'Who was the artist?'

Piero enlightened them. 'I have shared my house for the last three months with two young people from Venice, Ottavia and Giovanni Robusti, daughter and adopted son of the great Tintoretto. He taught them his skill and his secrets, he made them painters. But no one can make an artist, God alone can do that, and only He can do it with special human material. Skill, sensitivity and humility combine to form that material. These two young friends of mine have it in abundance and God has richly blessed them. This is the result.'

Ottavia and Giovanni had discreetly left the study before the end of the eulogy. Their embarrassment at being praised and gazed at somehow seemed inappropriate to their private token of friendship and gratitude, and the further praise of the guests could only make matters worse. They were temperamentally and socially unequipped to be the centre of such an august gathering, which included three cardinals, one of them Piero's cousin, five dukes, one of them Piero's nephew, seven duchesses and innumerable counts and scholars. They retired, unseen, to their room.

Ottavia was excited by the spectacle and by the appreciation Piero had proclaimed so publicly and so sincerely. 'He put you in the same class as Michelangelo and Titian,' she said.

'He put *us* in the same class, you mean.'

'Well, he meant you, it's your picture really.'

'It was a joint effort, and the best thing we have ever done.'

'Do you think he was right, then? That it is a work of genius, I mean?'

'I don't know whether it is or not, but if Piero says so, I expect he is right.' His flat tone of voice lacked conviction and enthusiasm.

'Isn't it exciting!' she said. 'I am so proud of you.'

She looked into his face with undisguised adulation, and noticed that he was neither excited nor proud. He looked almost dejected. 'What is the matter?' she said, kneeling beside him. 'You look sad.'

'It's the best thing we have ever done, and for that I am glad, but I am afraid we shall never do as well again.' He paused and placed his hand among her curls. 'If you think about it, we painted ourselves as a gift for him. It expressed everything we felt for him, for each other, for nature and for art. Just suppose we put all that we had into that one picture… and there was nothing left for the future…'

Palestrina

Among those present was Giovanni Pierluigi who, after a long association with the music of the Vatican, had been appointed Master of the Music at St Peter's. The erratic progress of his career in Rome, where he had been subjected to the vagaries of papal favour, was in no way reflected in his music which had displayed a consistent excellence and beauty for over twenty years, He instantly recognised in *Nymph and Satyr* qualities similar to those he exercised in his compositions, and he was determined to meet the creators of this gorgeous visual music. Their sudden departure from the company was a disappointment to him, but he arranged with Piero an introduction in circumstances more congenial to conversation and intellectual enquiry.

Ottavia and Giovanni were apprehensive about their meeting with this titan from Palestrina whose unrivalled mastery had earned him the title of 'The Raphael of Music'. They had heard several of his masses in the Julian Chapel and in San Maria Maggiore, where he had been Maestro for about seven years, and they had always marvelled at his celestial harmonies which seemed to hang in the air like a fragrant oblation, nourishing the spirit.

His reputation and ascetic appearance, however, concealed a warmth of personality and a genuine simplicity which were soon recognised by the young ones with relief and gratitude.

'Forgive me for being a nuisance,' he began, 'but I felt I had to congratulate you on your picture. I don't know very much about the technical side of your art, but I was intrigued and deeply impressed by the finished result, and I would like to know more.'

'Thank you, Maestro,' said Giovanni. 'We don't know anything about the technical side of your art, but we greatly admire your music, and we are honoured by your interest.'

'Well, it seems we have two things in common; ignorance and appreciation of each other's achievements.'

Ottavia returned the smile which had enlivened his cadaverous face, but she remained too diffident to contribute to the conversation. Observing this, and directing his next question to her, he said, 'Tell me, my dear, where would you rather live, in Rome or in Venice?'

'I am afraid I have to say Venice,' she admitted cautiously.

'Don't you like our Eternal City, then?'

'I like it very much as a place to visit,' she said, 'but I would rather live in Venice.'

'I wonder why you prefer a place where the streets are always flooded. Surely, it must be very damp. Don't you all suffer from rheumatism?'

'Oh no! It's not damp at all,' she replied ingenuously, 'except perhaps in winter. We may live on the water, but we don't get wet.' She was conscious that her reply was a trivial defence of her native city, and returned to the comparison. 'And a boat is so much quieter than a horse and carriage.'

'Now, I have to admit you have a strong point there. I have always found the racket here quite impossible. So what else would make me pack up and follow you to Venice?'

'Well, first of all, it's not so big, so overwhelming as Rome. You feel it was made for people, not giants, and the people are more friendly, more relaxed.'

'Perhaps they are friendly to you because you are one of them. Do you think they would be friendly to an ill-favoured alien like me?'

'I am sure they would be…'

'Right! That's all I need to know. They want me to go to Vienna to work, but I shall leave this Gomorrah as soon as I can and try to be a Venetian. If you'll have me, that is.' He affected a courtly bow.

Ottavia was fully aware that she was being teased, but she was pleased to indulge his playfulness. His humour and gentle chaffing were altogether unexpected and she submitted with naive delight.

'Maestro Giovanni, I would dearly like to know where your delicate vision of Arcadia comes from. Of course, I don't want you to give away your professional secrets, but do you think you can give me some idea?'

'I'm not sure if I can explain it, not that it's a secret, but it's complicated, you see. I will try, though.'

Conscious of his responsibility as an ambassador of his art and the compliment he had received, he folded his arms across his chest and lowered his head thoughtfully. 'To start with, you have to understand that Venetian painters were the first to appreciate the beauty rather than the utility of nature. They found something in the landscape of the mainland which fulfilled one of man's deepest needs; for security and peace.'

'It doesn't surprise me that those who had no landscape of their own should be responsive to its mysteries. The familiar, we take for granted. We Romans, for instance, have less respect for our ancient ruins than our visitors seem to have. But please go on.'

'Giovanni Bellini and Giorgione first revealed the poetry in nature. Their landscapes are not just descriptive or accurate, they evoke a range of delicate feelings in the spectator which are equivalent to the artist's original sentiments.' Palestrina nodded encouragingly. 'They communicated their own feelings for the benefit of those less perceptive than themselves,' he continued. 'It's difficult to define and impossible to convey in words, because their language was form and colour, line and tone, but I am sure you would feel it if you could see their pictures.'

'I have felt it, imperfectly perhaps, in Piero's Titian, so I know what you mean. As a musician, I know that form and harmony have a direct communication which transcends the intellect, speaking to the soul itself. So in effect, then, our languages are similar.' His smile registered a growing insight. 'I am sorry, I interrupted again – but I find this fascinating.'

'So first, there is an artistic tradition which we inherited and which we try to keep alive by exercising it as well as we can.' He paused. 'Then there is another, much older tradition, in literature that goes back further than our paintings or your ruins. The Greeks believed that certain places had a presiding deity—'

'The genius loci—'

'Exactly! They acknowledged that, apart from the material elements – the rocks, the water, the vegetation – there was something invisible, intangible which was actually more important and more permanent. When we read the ancients, we come closer to the original spirit of Arcadia than we can in the modern world. It's something elemental, a deep yearning for perfection, which we all have, I suppose.'

'…Which we all *need* if we are at all civilised. But most of our fellow beings seem to find those material elements quite sufficient; all they look for is what you called "utility". At best, they compensate by using the Church as an easy contact with the mysteries; easy because no effort, no commitment is required. It's all made digestible, stirred and pulped like an infant's gruel, until the true flavour, the true nourishment has gone. Consequently, the liturgy becomes an end in itself, not a means to an end, as it was meant to be.'

'But, Maestro Palestrina, you yourself are a part of this process, surely? Yet you seem to despise it. How can you reconcile what you do with what you believe? Surely, they must be in conflict nearly all the time.'

'I try to do what you said Bellini and Giorgione did, to convey my own feelings, my own faith through my music. The sounds I produce are a bridge over which my beliefs pass to others and, I hope, to God, who gave me my beliefs in the first place. I am an instrument, a messenger, that's all.'

'You say your beliefs come from God, but does your technique come from God too?'

'Ultimately, yes. But it comes more immediately from a tradition, just as yours does, and from long and serious study, just as yours does.'

They faced each other, aware that the years which separated them were no barrier to their mutual understanding. Each had his own creative resources confirmed by the other. Each felt the comfort, the confidence of brotherhood. Each acknowledged the authority of the other, but Giovanni was aware of a discrepancy in the strength of their religious convictions. This alone divided them.

Ottavia had joined Piero in the garden, where, against the sound of birdsong and the scent of oleanders, they talked sadly of the future and the time of parting.

They were interrupted by the two Giovannis.

'Tavi, Maestro Palestrina has invited us to visit him in the Vatican to hear his music.'

'I shall be delighted if you will honour me with a visit.'

'*We* shall be honoured, Maestro,' she replied, hastily adjusting to the present. 'Thank you. We can come whenever it is convenient for you. We realise how busy you must be.'

He kissed her hand.

Appropriately dressed in their most sober clothes, they were taken to the Vatican in Piero's carriage and were conducted to Palestrina's apartment. He chose to live outside the walls in the house owned by his second wife, but, as Maestro di Cappella, a small suite of rooms was allocated to him in the Choir School. It consisted of a study, two living rooms and a rehearsal room adjacent to a vast music library. They found him alone in the practice room, seated at a small organ between two smoking candles. He was amending a manuscript. 'Welcome, my friends! How good of you to come.' He shook their hands warmly. His face was rejuvenated with pleasure. 'I'm afraid this is a dismal place. Let's go to my study.'

He picked his way through a forest of music desks and led them to a small room next door. Its white walls and sparse furnishings were almost concealed by littered books and papers, caps and cassocks. A spinet was submerged under more papers, ink pots, dried leaves and feathers. He pushed open the window which looked over the Vatican garden.

'There, that's better! Ottavia, come and see my view.'

They all leaned over the sill and peered down on the contrasting orderliness of shrubs, paths and statuary which lay below. Black umbrella pines cast deep shadows in the brilliant sunshine.

'Isn't it peaceful here,' ventured Ottavia. 'I think the best parts of Rome are the gardens, but this one is huge.' She did not admit to having visited it before with Cardinal Farnese.

'I remember your aversion to our traffic, but this is not so bad, is it? Let me give you some wine.' He poured three glasses from a simple ewer. 'I have a practice shortly, but it won't take very long. Would you like to stay and listen, or would you prefer to explore the garden?'

'We should like to stay, please,' said Giovanni.

They chatted about inconsequential matters as they drank. The Maestro was relaxed and he seasoned his conversation with a sprinkling of witticisms. As she listened, Ottavia reflected that so many of the great men she had known seemed quite indifferent to their own prestige. They were never as dignified as their achievements or their office might have suggested. This man, whose music had won the approval of popes and cardinals, had caused the Council of Trent to revoke its musical dictates and had been compared with the music heard by St John in his vision of the New Jerusalem, was, by nature, kind, gentle and unassuming.

The Sistine Choir had silently taken their places in the room beyond and were exercising their voices with disorganised, discordant scales and runs.

'Forgive me, I must leave you. If you would like to wander round, please do. Your presence will not disturb us.'

The chaos dissolved as he entered. Each head was deferentially bowed and the Maestro reciprocated.

'I want to run through the motet *Veni Sponsa Christi* and the hymn for this evening. First, we'll do the plainchant. Men only...'

He raised his arms, looked around and waited for composure. The arms dropped decisively. Voices rose obediently from the silence.

'No! No! You are not together. Once more.'

The action was repeated and precision gained on the third attempt. Four simple phrases were delivered in simple lines in which tenors and basses were blended into a single voice. The Maestro was not pleased.

'Let's separate the phrases with a little more determination. They are four links in a chain; your chain is like a slimy rope. Now, *articulate*! Again!'

The difference in the repetition gave a pleading, tentative inflexion to the words 'Come Bride of Christ, Receive the Crown...'

'Better! Better!' he coaxed, waving them on. After the Alleluia, he declared himself satisfied. 'Good! Now, the motet...'

He raised his arms. The boys' voices responded to the

downward beat with clarity and precision. At the second syllable, the altos joined; at the fourth, the tenors strengthened the line; finally, the basses added their foundation. The polyphony soared and wheeled into the high vault, weaving a continuous, yet ever varied thread into an almost tangible canopy of sound. The effect of combining and distinguishing the voices was opulent and yet devotional too. Ottavia and Giovanni moved from the study, magnetised by the music.

'That was dreadful!' said the Maestro with bored petulance. 'You were all over the place, sliding over the notes. I couldn't hear a single word after Veni. We'll do it again.'

They did. The Maestro smiled, frowned, smiled again. The singers responded to each signal willingly and with obvious pleasure.

'That's better, but still not right. You are singing too fast. Remember, the acoustic of the chapel is not as intimate as this. If you lose the words in this space, what would it be like in a bigger one? Come now, articulate! More dignity! More control!'

He enunciated each syllable of his instructions with emphasis. He sounded like a sergeant-at-arms drilling recruits.

The near perfection of the first attempt was honed to faultless purity before he was satisfied. The rehearsal of the hymn followed the same progress, each nuance of expression was clarified until the meaning of the words was complemented by their delivery.

He dismissed the choir politely, thanking them for their efforts, and joined his two guests. Their eyes were filled with tears, broached by the sumptuous beauty which had enveloped them.

'It wasn't as bad as that, was it?' he said gently. The incisive, authoritative voice had vanished.

'Don't tease,' said Ottavia, wiping her face. 'It was beautiful.'

'Oh good! For a moment, I thought you were displeased. Come and have some more wine.'

'Tell me,' said Giovanni, 'how do you manage to hold together all those strands of sound and blend them with such variety? It seems terribly complicated.'

'Well, it isn't really. There are rules; some notes harmonise, others don't. Once you have learned the principles, they become instinctive, and you don't think about them consciously.'

'That's all very well, but we have heard hundreds of combinations and there cannot be hundreds of rules, surely?'

'No, but the rules govern groups, so we don't have a single rule for each possible combination.'

'I'm sorry, but I don't see how that can be the whole explanation. If it were, the whole thing would become mechanical.'

'You are quite right. I use another guide, which is my own experience. I do some things my predecessors never dreamed of, and having studied the Flemish masters, I can see where their limitations lay and I have merely extended them.'

'I noticed that the four phrases in the plainchant reappeared in the motet in ways which transformed the simplicity into a kind of depth and richness.'

'Quite right. I confess I owe a huge debt to the old chants, and I use them a lot, but remember, they were sung in buildings quite different from ours today. High, narrow Gothic buildings are full of reflecting angles and sound traps, so they needed a direct line which could penetrate the forest of pillars and niches. Our buildings are more open, spacious, so we can flood the space with many layers of sound at the same time, without loss. But that doesn't mean that plainchant is obsolete or ineffectual. Quite the opposite, *our* complex textures cannot carry in an old building. Our way has the limitations, not the old way.'

'I can see that the architecture affects music in much the same way as it affects the pictures we paint for it. An oil painting by Tintoretto would look wrong on the Sistine Chapel ceiling. Michelangelo hated fresco painting, but the building demanded it.'

'Exactly,' said Palestrina. 'Frankly, I hadn't thought of that, but it's an exact parallel.'

'Well, how do you decide whether the sound goes up or down, swells out or pulls in? I'm expressing myself crudely, I know, but how do you decide?'

'The words… and nature,' he said casually.

'What do you mean by nature?' asked Ottavia.

'Let me show you.'

They followed him to the window. The garden was still and silent except for the plash of a fountain and the bubbling of the pigeons.

He clapped his hands.

A flock of them erupted into the air simultaneously. At a certain height, they levelled out on planning wings, turned and split into three groups. One drifted towards the pavement, one proceeded with wings beating in unison, another rose in a steep arc over the dark pines, hung there momentarily and swooped through the level group, joining those who had settled on the ground. The second group wheeled and disappeared behind a tree; it emerged divided, some perched on the roof of a loggia, the others floated to rest beside a marble basin.

'The movement, the rhythm of that flight is like a vine climbing up a pergola,' he said, making sinuous turns with his wrists. 'Or like the branching of a tree, the flow of water, the swimming of a fish or the rise and fall of hills. They are nature's rhythms, and because we are part of nature, we respond to them with pleasure, and when we dance or sing, we repeat them ourselves, quite naturally. Or at least, our ancestors did. We have lost the ability to move and behave naturally, that's the price we pay for being civilised, but you and I can do it in our art. *You* most certainly do it; that is what attracted me to your picture in the first place.'

His explanation brought some enlightenment to them both.

'I see exactly what you mean,' began Giovanni, 'but I cannot believe that is the whole explanation. There are rules in your art, and in ours; and we are perhaps, more sensitive to natural rhythms than others are, but that's not all, surely? It's too simple.'

'No, that's not all. But the rest, I cannot explain, because I don't understand it myself. The rest is a mystery, and only God has the key. Give thanks to Him that He has favoured you with a precious gift, even if it doesn't include understanding.'

As he accompanied them to his house, he talked about his life, his friends and the death of his wife and three sons in a plague a few years before.

'When they died,' he said, 'I seriously considered entering the priesthood, and but for a chance meeting – or so I thought – with a woman who had also been bereaved, I should be a priest now.

But God convinced me that I would be more use to her as a sole partner than I would be to the Church as just another cleric.'

It was clear from his face that he still felt the pain of his loss, in spite of his faith. But it was also clear that it was no marriage of convenience that he had contracted with the wealthy widow, Virginia Dormuli. His eyes betrayed genuine feelings of affection and pride as he talked about her.

'Some of my *friends*,' he stressed the word with bitterness, 'expressed their enmity or jealousy by insisting that I married her for her fortune, but security of that kind didn't enter into it at all. I had always been poor, but I had always had enough for my needs. I have never been, nor will I ever be, an extravagant man. I need very little to enable me to work, and that is all I want to do.' He paused for a moment and smiled. 'That's not quite true! The fact is that I adore women. Not all women, you understand, but I do seem to have an enormous capacity for the tenderness which most women enjoy.'

Ottavia stopped suddenly and faced him to return a little of his banter. 'You would have been miserable in the priesthood, then, wouldn't you?' Her timing was not propitious and he did not rise to her lure.

'Well, let me say – not completely fulfilled. But at the time when I had lost everything, it seemed to be the best course.'

'Do you regret it?' she asked, returning to seriousness.

'Not for one moment, and when you have met my wife, you will see why.'

Virginia was an intelligent, capable woman who, in widowhood had successfully continued her first husband's business as a fur and skin merchant. In the exclusively masculine world of trade, she had competed as an equal, and had won the confidence of her employees and the admiration of her competitors. The fact that she had been successful without jeopardising her femininity was remarked by all those who knew her and this gave enormous pleasure to Palestrina. He adored her, not with the exuberant passion of youth, but with the leisured temperance of respect and friendship. They rejoiced as much in each other's independence as they did in their conjugality, so that each meeting continued the excitement of discovery.

She welcomed her visitors warmly and her husband with unaffected devotion, balancing the duality of her greeting with ease and graciousness. The refinement of her manner and voice impressed Ottavia and Giovanni immediately as expressions of her character rather than of shallow etiquette. Her conversation was centred around the interests, the achievements and the aspirations of her guests, without sounding inquisitive. As they talked, she nodded with assent or encouragement, and stimulated their narrative in the natural pauses by further enquiries or the inclusion of her husband, who for the most part, sat in mute admiration of her social finesse.

'Gian tells me that you have painted a wonderful picture for Piero Farnese. It must have given him enormous satisfaction. He is such a good man, such a sad man. Gian and he have been friends for many years, and when poor Gian lost his wife and his boys, Piero was a great comfort to him. He introduced us, you know, so we have a special affection for him.' She reached out her hand and placed it over her husband's, restoring the moment of union in the marriage sacrament. 'So we owe him a great deal, don't we, Gian?'

He returned her smile. 'Everything,' he said. 'Without him, *we* would not exist; only you and I.'

She did not indulge in private sentiment a second longer than it took for her gesture to be understood. She turned again to Ottavia and Giovanni who were sharing a similar mutual attentiveness.

'I wonder if you would paint a picture for us, when your time permits. Gian lives most of his life among Raphaels and Michelangelos, but to be quite honest with you, I find them rather forbidding, and certainly not suitable for a house like this,' she said, seeking their approval. 'But from Gian's account of your work, I am sure you would produce something more approachable.'

They looked at each other to confirm their separate enthusiasm for the commission, found it and answered in unison, 'We shall be pleased to do so.'

'What sort of subject have you in mind?' continued Giovanni.

'I haven't given any thought to that, have you, Gian?'

'Not really, but what I would like is something analogous to my *Song of Songs*. Then we would have the same theme expressed in words, music and painting.'

Virginia nodded with approval.

'We know the Song of Solomon in the Scriptures, of course, but what is the theme you refer to, exactly?' asked Ottavia.

'Love,' said Palestrina tentatively. 'The love which can only be expressed in allusions, in metaphors. Love which is both erotic and sacramental at the same time.'

He looked at them quizzically.

'Like Piero's Titian, you mean?' said Giovanni.

'And like your *Nymph and Satyr*,' replied the Maestro, smiling.

The two glanced at each other again. Each had unexpressed doubts. Could they succeed once more? A repetition was unthinkable in such different circumstances. Each understood the other's misgivings.

'Can we think about it a little more? asked Giovanni. 'We will paint you a picture with pleasure, but what you suggest is not going to be easy...'

He broke off, hoping it would not be necessary for him to explain fully.

'There's no hurry. Please, please, take your time, and if it cannot be, we shall understand, won't we, Virginia?'

She leaned forward to stress her concern and sincerity. 'We do not expect you to produce work of your quality to order, and if you prefer to do something else, we shall accept whatever interests you.'

A slight trace of disappointment shaded Palestrina's agreement.

'Thank you. We must give it more thought,' repeated Giovanni. 'But in the meantime, can you tell us more about your setting of the *Song of Songs*?'

'I can do better than that. I can show you, and even play you some of it, if you like.' Their appreciation and anticipation were evident. 'Do you read music?'

'A little,' said Ottavia. 'We are better with lute notation, but we can manage the stave, slowly.'

'You play lutes, do you? Splendid! Virginia plays the viol and I can manage a keyboard, we must see what we can do together. But I forget, it's the *Song* you are interested in.'

He left the room quickly, humming nothing in particular, improvising on happiness.

'He's a very sweet man and you mustn't mind if he gets carried away with enthusiasm for music,' explained Virginia.

'He *is* a sweet man, and we love his enthusiasm, don't we, Giovanni?'

'He may be a master of music to the world, but what the world doesn't know is that he is a slave of music and a slave of the Vatican. They expect music to flow from him as it does from a fountain.'

'I must say, he seems to be like a fountain; inexhaustible.'

'But he's a reservoir, and reservoirs dry up some day. He pours his entire soul into endless settings of the Mass, motets, anthems and hymns. Once, he set himself a task which no one had thought possible. He solved it with such grace and apparent ease that it set standards by which all Masses are now judged, but it wasn't written in the white heat of inspiration; he worked at it, fashioning every syllable; revised it and revised the revisions, destroying more than he retained. When he finished, it was sublime. A jewelled crown beyond imagining. And now they expect him to write one such every week. It's absurdly insensitive and greedy of them, and they pay him as if he were a porter.'

There was pride and compassion in her voice, but no anger, no bitterness. She smiled sadly and added, 'What the world doesn't know…'

Ottavia broke the ensuing silence. 'Which was the Mass you were referring to?'

'The one he dedicated to Pope Marcellus. Now, he was *not* a greedy man; he knew Gian's true worth, but he was pope for just a few days, and then he died. But his Mass was specially performed for the cardinals of the Council of Trent to prove to them that the words need not be obscured by complicated music. Even they were convinced, and they changed their ideas about polyphony. That was long ago now, but it hasn't been forgotten.'

'Do you mean that he doesn't have the chance to work as well as he can any more?' asked Giovanni.

'He always works as well as he can, but the circumstances vary. He cannot control the limitations within which he works. He does not compose for the Church, the College of Cardinals or even the Pope; he composes for God first, and then for himself. His *Song of Songs*, he wrote for himself first, though. It was his understanding of that human love which aspires to heavenly love…'

She stopped as Palestrina bustled into the room clutching an unruly bundle of papers. He was buoyant and eager to begin. He shuffled through the pages perfunctorily and sat at the spinet. The others joined him and stood where they could see the score.

The manuscript was neatly written, but scarred with alterations.

'Gian, do you expect us to sight-read *that*?' Virginia laughed and ruffled his hair.

'Of course you can,' he said impatiently.

Ottavia noticed again how readily his usual considerate manner changed into an abrupt, dictatorial one when he was concerned with music making. She was slightly fearful that their performance would irritate him and mar the occasion.

'Come on now, there are four of us, so we can sing some of it. Ottavia, you sing the soprano line; Giovanni, you take the tenor; Virginia and I will sing alto and bass.'

'Am I to sing bass, then?' she asked mischievously.

She had guessed that the result would be unsatisfactory, even if the soprano and tenor could read music and sing in tune, and her flippancy was contrived to forestall her husband's disappointment.

He coaxed and rehearsed them with boundless fervour and limited forbearance for about an hour, and they occasionally achieved a harmonious ensemble for a few bars, but he refused to concede defeat or consider compromise. 'It's getting better – once more now!' he kept repeating.

But Virginia was aware that satisfactory part-singing is not won easily or quickly, and that their guests were being subjected to demands which good hospitality should not allow.

'Gian, I am tired,' she announced, detaching herself from the group. 'And furthermore, I don't think the results are worth the effort.'

His manner changed instantly. 'I am sorry, my dear. I have been inattentive to you and our friends.' He closed the spinet and led Ottavia and Giovanni by the hand to the settee they had previously occupied.

'Forgive me, please,' he said. 'I'm a boorish old fool! I should know better than to treat you so churlishly. I am sorry.'

He poured and distributed penitential goblets of wine. His genuine contrition was so pathetic that each of his victims was ready to begin again to ease his distress, but none of them expressed it aloud.

'Why don't we have a musical supper party next week with a group of singers from the choir to perform it for us?' he suggested. 'We could invite Piero and Philip Neri and a few more friends.'

'Now, that's a much better idea,' said Virginia with obvious relief. 'But I'm not sure that Ottavia and Giovanni will come after their experience today.'

Palestrina caricatured his own remorse in a grimace.

'We should love to come,' said Ottavia for both of them, and Giovanni readily agreed.

'I must go back to the chapel for vespers,' he said. 'I'm glad you can come. Goodbye!'

And he was gone.

The party and the performance were equally successful. In the relaxed atmosphere of friendship and refreshment, the whole company was profoundly moved by the music, which was poised between the secular madrigal and the liturgical motet. The ecstatic melodic line and sumptuous sonorities floated and wheeled like flocks of divine birds, enriching each listener with rapture and wonder at Palestrina's lyrical invention. But to Ottavia and Giovanni, it had an additional relevance, reflecting much of their personal relationship and artistic achievement.

Piero was sensitive to the affinities between his picture and the motets. The clarity, the purity and the splendour of each was a perfect marriage of nature and art. With characteristic economy and percipience, he epitomised it as 'joy perfected by discipline'.

The subject matter of the picture they painted for their friends gave them more difficulty than its execution. Eventually, after much deliberation, they agreed on a new interpretation of the story of Solomon and the Queen of Sheba. Instead of the familiar Presentation of Gifts, or the Enthronement, they portrayed the king and queen in private, in a garden, simply dressed and surrounded by the tokens of their mutual esteem. Their delicately joined hands recalled that eloquent gesture of Virginia's; their eyes transmitted serene confidence and devotion; their faces embodied the wisdom of Solomon and Palestrina and the sensibility of the queen and Virginia as complementary, but equally significant qualities. Their masculinity and femininity were conveyed by colours and by the rhythms of draperies, and their sovereignty by the innate dignity of their poses rather than by regalia or pageantry. It seemed appropriate that nature should be the arbiter of every judgement, not artifice.

Palestrina immediately recognised the syntax of his own language transcribed into paint. The rhythmical pulse of the whole design, the linear flow, the varied textures from thick impasto, through velaturas to transparent glazes, the accented transitions of warm and cool colour uncannily mirrored much of his own experience in counterpoint and harmony.

Virginia immediately recognised the tenderness which suffused the whole picture and which was condensed in the two figures. She was astonished that such subtlety of feeling could be entrapped and held in coloured pigment, and more astonished that it should emanate from the talents and experience of two young people.

They both recognised the very personal treatment of the subject and the intimate references to themselves. As their initial amazement subsided, they unconsciously submitted to the pervading spirit of the picture, which invited their contemplation and, at the same time, induced their communion.

Giovanni was aware that they had not – in spite of their dedication – approached their accomplishment in Piero's picture, but he was not discouraged. It was good, but not sublime; partly, he hoped, because *Nymph and Satyr* was not a commission, but an act of love.

They agreed to stay on in Rome for an additional year. They pursued their quest for enlightenment, and by studying excellence and mediocrity with equal attention, their judgements matured and their standards of craftsmanship and creative integrity appreciated.

They executed commissions for noble patrons to meet a demand which was initiated by Piero's reception and they were received in audience by the Holy Father. Giovanni became known as *Il Leone di Venezia*, but for all their superficial success, it became clear to him that the fears he had confided to Ottavia were a presage of the truth.

The Lion

Tintoretto greeted his children with all the cordiality and affection his passionate nature could convey. His spirit rejoiced as much with relief for their safe return as for the personal gratification of having a deprivation restored. In their absence, he had laboured like Hercules. Absorbed as he was by work, his spare time seemed empty and, in spite of the presence of the rest of his family, he felt anxious and lonely. He had played his spinet fitfully, but without pleasure or the benefits of recreation.

He spent the next days listening to the accounts of their journey, the descriptions of what they had seen and done and their assessments of the great works which he knew only by reputation or through copies or engravings. In imagination, he travelled with them, sharing their enthusiasm, their disappointments and their fulfilment.

'Tell me about Michelangelo's Sistine frescoes and Raphael's in the Stanze,' he said. 'By all accounts, they are magnificent, but totally different.'

'The chapel ceiling,' began Giovanni, 'is crammed with power on a superhuman scale and the movement twists and floats over your head, making you feel quite giddy. The architecture and painted framework hold it together in a solemn grid which can only just contain the design. Some of the figures seem about to burst out in protest at being confined and not just physically, they are spiritual giants who refuse to be restrained by human limitations. The section where Adam reaches out his finger to touch the finger of God is...' he searched for the right word, '...unforgettable. Adam is limp and feeble, in spite of his huge physique; but God is so full of energy that what He imparts to Adam will not deplete His power at all. It is one of the most wonderful things we saw. As I said, it's unforgettable.'

'The colour is very beautiful too,' added Ottavia. 'We had not thought of Michelangelo as a colourist, but we were wrong; the way he used warm and cool is all part of his contrasts and tensions. It's not just decorative.'

'And when you see his *Last Judgement* on the end wall, it becomes clearer that he knew a great deal about colour as an expressive language,' continued Giovanni.

'What a pity he hated oil paint then,' observed Jacopo. 'He might have made colour even more important. Fresco is a miserable medium; pale, thin and wishy-washy.'

'Much of it is here, Father, but in Florence and Rome it can be splendid, in a way that oil paint could not be.'

'But you were going to tell me about the *Last Judgement*.'

'It's terrifying,' said Giovanni. 'The figures seem to fracture the wall; it disintegrates above the altar, and just hangs there menacingly, as if it will collapse and engulf you at any second, And the colour – brown, slate grey and cold blue – has the quality of decay. It's not a picture anyone could *like*, but everyone must be affected by it. It's human and superhuman at the same time, so it's very disturbing.'

Jacopo remembered the second version of his own *Paradiso* with a measure of gratification. 'Now, what about Raphael's frescoes?' he said.

'We were given special permission to visit the Vatican by Cardinal Farnese, so we saw much more than most people could,' began Ottavia, 'and we spent two whole days in the Stanze without being hurried. So we had time to make lots of drawings.'

'It sounds as if your friend Farnese was very useful to you,' observed Tintoretto.

'He was, and we'll tell you more about him later,' said Ottavia. 'But the Raphaels were simply marvellous. I am sure that if you had seen those frescoes you would change your mind about it being a miserable medium. It's absolutely right for a simple, classical architecture, the two fit together perfectly. Yet in one picture called *The School of Athens*, he has painted architecture in the background which is as huge and majestic as Michelangelo was to design for St Peter's. It's like a prophecy. And in the foreground, he painted Michelangelo's portrait as Pythagoras.'

Jacopo knew all this quite well from his reading, but he did not interrupt the flow of received ideas and opinions from his daughter.

Giovanni continued where she left off. 'This is the most superb picture in the Stanze. Most of the figures are like ancient statues which have come to life. The design is taut and formal – like the architecture – but the figures ripple across it in coloured, moving waves.' Jacopo nodded, grasping the implications of the simile. 'But in the same room is the first picture he painted here. Vasari wrongly calls it *The Disputation on the Sacrament*, but Cardinal Farnese told us that it was really *The Church Triumphant*. It has a group of earthly figures on each side of an altar; popes, bishops and theologians towards the centre and ordinary people at the edge. Above, the sky opens to reveal the Trinity, flanked by apostles and prophets. We found the design impressively simple – balanced, but not symmetrical.'

'Did it remind you of anything you had seen before?' asked Jacopo with a smile.

'Not particularly. It was much like a number of very old pictures in its arrangement, but apart from that, no, I don't think so,' said Giovanni thoughtfully.

'Now that you mention it,' said Ottavia, 'it did remind me of something more recent, but I cannot think what.'

'Well, it doesn't matter,' said Jacopo. 'It's not important.'

'Yes, it does matter,' replied Ottavia. 'If I cannot think of it now, I shall get no rest until I do.'

'I am surprised Giovanni doesn't remember.'

He looked puzzled and mildly ashamed at the same time.

'I know!' cried Ottavia. 'It was like your first *Paradiso* sketch!'

'You're quite right! I decided to adapt the same ancient formula that Raphael used, but to lose the old symbols of the Glory and the Rely Spirit. In essence, though, we both updated a convention which is as old as Christian art.'

'Why didn't I see that?' asked Giovanni, recalling Palestrina's use of plainchant. He was irritated with himself.

'Perhaps because you looked at them with the eyes of an artist rather than a theologian or iconographer,' answered Jacopo.

'Well, I am certainly neither of those, but I am still surprised at being so stupid.'

'Let's get back to the Stanze, though. Tell me about some of the others.'

'*The Parnassus* is very fine,' continued Giovanni. 'As you know, it represents the idea of beauty in the arts. Apollo is the central figure and around him are arranged the muses and poets in two processions, curving up the hill on either side. All the figures are wonderful, full of rhythm which you can almost hear. The sounds of Apollo's viol and the gurgle of water from the spring seem to decorate the silence and mystery which surround beauty. It is beauty celebrating beauty.'

'Piero Farnese believed that simple design was often most effective, and this is certainly true of Raphael's pictures. Most of them were symmetrical, echoing the design of the rooms, but his colour and his drawing were extremely sensitive, so there is no monotony,' said Ottavia.

'That is a very profound statement to come from my little girl,' said Jacopo. 'I can see that you learned a great deal on your travels.'

'I have. I know about things I had not dreamed of before, and I have seen things more beautiful than I thought possible. Giovanni taught me most, of course, but Piero helped me to understand things too.'

'Before you tell me about him, I would like to know more about Raphael. As you know, Michelangelo has been a divine hero of mine, and still is, but Raphael somehow puzzles me. His refinement seems just a bit too perfect. The world he created is not a world I can enter freely; there is a barrier. I'm not sure if that barrier is in his work or in me, and I would dearly like to know.'

'Giovanni can explain that,' she said. 'He showed me how classicism works in architecture, and he made me understand that the barrier was in me.'

'That was different,' said Giovanni, 'because we had a building in front of us then.' It was little more than an excuse to cover his reluctance to instruct his old master. But Jacopo looked at him with encouragement, so he continued. 'As I understand it, there are two approaches to design; the first was discovered by the ancient Greeks, who believed that beauty came from harmony, that harmony could be achieved by measurement and proportion, and that it was the artist's mission to idealise nature by refining it with the subtleties of geometry. It was the rebirth of that rational art that we call the Renaissance and Raphael represents the most complete expression of it since Phidias. Theirs was an art of serene vitality.'

'To me,' said Jacopo, 'that vitality lacks one crucial ingredient – *energy*. It's serene, granted, but it has the guts refined out of it, and that is why Michelangelo is greater. His vitality has a superhuman energy, not imitated, not borrowed, but inherent in every line, every form, every space even.'

'But energy, physical energy, is only a part of human activity, surely, Father,' argued Giovanni. 'You wouldn't deny that there is mental energy and spiritual energy too, would you?'

'Of course not, but I believe that spirituality can only be conveyed through material things and light. Light most of all.'

'That is your way, you are a master of light, but it's not the only way.'

'Michelangelo conveyed mental and spiritual energy through bodies. The human form was his vehicle, and what a superb one it was.'

'Raphael had a vehicle too. It's difficult to describe it, but I think the best word for it is *grace*.'

Tintoretto was inclined to accept the theory which Giovanni had proposed, but he could not reconcile it with his own conviction that painting energised ideas by heightening reality as it could be observed.

'Tell me, did you see a single picture of his which conveyed conflict?'

'Oh yes! In the Stanze there are several. *The Expulsion of Heliodorus* is full of it. Most of the figures are in conflict with each other, and most of the design is turbulent. Then there's *The Deliverance of St Peter from Prison*, I know you would admire that. It's full of light and shade, and amazingly lifelike. The brilliant light around the angel glitters on the guards' armour; Peter is sleeping in chains, but is just about to waken. The whole prison is seen through a black grille of iron bars. The tension is as dramatic as you could possibly wish for. Raphael *could* do it when he wanted to.'

'You do surprise me,' said Jacopo. 'How I wish I could see it, but I don't suppose I shall ever go to Rome.'

'We made a study of it, because we thought you would be interested.'

Ottavia went through a bulging portfolio and found the drawing. 'Here it is, Father.'

'You thought of everything, didn't you?' He took the sheet and looked at it attentively. 'This is by Raphael?' he said incredulously. 'If you had said Giorgione or Titian, I should not have been surprised, but this...'

'You mustn't forget that he also admired Michelangelo, and borrowed from him, but his vision was different. It was a vision of purity and grace.'

'It seems to me that you, Giovanni, share that vision. Your exemplar is Raphael rather than Michelangelo. Am I right?'

'I think you are. I have a great respect for them both, of course, but I have come to realise that we live in an imperfect world. Men are imperfect creatures, yet in rare moments they can aspire to, and glimpse, perfection. The artist is the man who can reveal that perfection to others who cannot grasp it unaided. That is his purpose and his responsibility. Anything less than that is mere craftsmanship. Or mediocrity.'

'You are too severe! I grant you that the artist should always do his best, he owes that to his patron, to his teachers and his calling, but most of all, to *himself*. But I always fall short of what you call "perfection". It's an impossible, unrealistic goal.' He sat back and waited for Giovanni's reply.

'I know, and I don't think I can justify it rationally, but I believe it to be true all the same. We cannot give up the effort because something we want is beyond our reach; we find or make a hook to lengthen our arm.'

Jacopo tugged his beard, thoughtfully reviewing his own position in the face of this dogged idealism. 'You believe that painting is a sacred vocation don't you? One that can be profaned very easily, even by men of integrity.'

'Yes, I do.'

'Well, let me tell you something I have told no one. Until the first fire in the ducal palace, I spent time and care on everything I did. Each picture was conceived and then modified for its proposed setting; each was carefully considered so that it would reveal something new, and thus broaden the spectator's experience. Now, except for the pictures I do for San Rocco, that is no longer possible, but I still do the best I can within the limitations which are imposed, whether I like them or not.'

His words might have been spoken by Palestrina, thought Giovanni.

'Doesn't that make you unhappy?'

'In some ways, yes, it does, but it seems to me better to give people what they want rather than nothing at all. In San Rocco, though, I paint for myself first of all, and I charge them nothing...'

Giovanni became reflective. Although there was something tragic in what Jacopo had admitted, there was also a stubborn heroism which had to be admired. But he knew that he could never accept this form of compromise.

'Do you remember, many years ago, you showed me an engraving of Titian's *Sacred and Profane Love*?' asked Giovanni.

'I do. I have it still.'

'Well, we saw the painting in Piero Farnese's palazzina in Rome...'

'And what did you think of it as a painting?'

'It's not so much what I thought of it. It's a superb picture, one of the finest I have ever seen, but that isn't the point. When we talked about it long ago, it was the first time I realised that a picture was much more than paint on canvas, drawing and design. There was a layer underneath and although I didn't appreciate it fully then it helped me to understand something of myself. Looking back, it was a landmark in my life; it was as if Titian had spoken to me alone in the language of metaphors. It was a window looking into a world of unreal realities, and at the same time, a window into myself. That is what great art can do, and that is what mediocre art can *never* do.'

'I am sure you are right, but God help us poor painters! We cannot always deliver great art, even if we have it within us. Titian didn't; he did some pretty wretched things sometimes.' He leaned forwards to stress his sincerity. 'We have to live, you know; we have to earn a crust.'

'But if we don't try, we shall never succeed. It's easy to satisfy most patrons; they don't want our best, and even when they get it, they don't appreciate it.' He paused. 'Take your *Paradiso*, for instance.'

'True, true.'

'So, it's the patronage system itself which encourages mediocrity—'

'Raphael and Michelangelo gave Pope Julius more than he could ever have envisaged for himself,' interrupted Jacopo. 'So it doesn't always work that way, does it?'

'No, it doesn't always happen, I agree, but it happens too often, so I'm not going to change my mind because of a few exceptions.'

'I don't see how we can change the system, Giovanni. As long as we are aware of its limitations, as long as we don't merely satisfy the needs of the patron alone, we are all right. As I said, the artist owes something to himself.'

'Yes, but I cannot reconcile success and being busy with high standards. Too often, the pressure of the contract makes an artist careless, or take short cuts. He is forced to do less than his best. You should have seen some of the rubbish we saw in Rome, squalid vulgarity masquerading as art!'

Giovanni reinforced his contempt with a sweeping gesture which reminded Jacopo of Christ in the *Last Judgement*. It confirmed what he had already realised, that this was no intellectual posture, but a conviction as sincere and as consuming as that which drove the saints to their martyrdom. The inevitable consequences of such commitment disturbed Jacopo deeply, as the concept of martyrdom ceased to be figurative and became a tragic portent.

Ottavia had followed the discussion closely, with quiet respect for an exchange of opposing ideas which led, not to confrontation, but to mutual understanding. She found she agreed with both points of view equally, but at this outburst, she intervened. 'We had a taste of success both here and in Rome. We were very busy all day and sometimes we didn't stop for meals or siesta, but the best thing we ever did was not a commission; there was no hurry, no pressure and no payment at the end of it. You could say that we did it for love.'

'What was this then?' inquired Jacopo.

'We wanted to say thank you to Piero in a practical way. He had been so very good to us by giving us lodging, giving us his time and his guidance,' she began. 'But what was more important, we had become fond of him; he was such a gentle, understanding man with a life centred around religion and art. He believed in both; they gave him all he needed and it seemed as if he drew enormous strength from faith in one and knowledge of the other. He passed on so much of that knowledge to us that we felt that, although we could never repay him, we could give back a little of what we had received by painting him a picture. It was Giovanni's idea, of course, but we painted better than we had ever painted before; we were more involved with it than we had ever been before. It was like putting ourselves into the picture for him alone. We thought he would understand that.'

'And he did,' added Giovanni. 'He was never at a loss for words about pictures, sculpture, architecture and books, and what he had to say always seemed to throw the subject into clear relief. We saw things differently after listening to him. He wasn't just intelligent, though, he was very sensitive to the mood or the spirit, to what was *implied* in a piece.'

Jacopo nodded in complete understanding and fitted his head into its familiar niche. He was impatient to hear more, so he resisted the temptation to comment lest it should impede the narrative. 'So you painted him a picture. Go on.'

'When we gave it to him, he was speechless. Not because we had given him a present, but because he felt what we felt. The picture was like a bridge between him and us, and what passed over it could not be said in words. You see, it was more than a painting. It was a symbol of love, and the love was more important to us than the painting, and to him too. We painted for ourselves and for him, as Tavi said. And it was marvellous!'

'How I wish I could see it! I think I would rather see that than all the pictures in the Vatican put together.'

'Father, it was so good that we really couldn't believe that we had done it, could we, Giovanni? There was a huge reception which Piero held for all the important people in Rome, and he said that it was a work of genius, equal to Raphael, Michelangelo and Titian, and he didn't say things like that if he didn't mean them.'

'What wouldn't I give to see it?' His eyes focused on infinity.

'We have brought back the sketches which you can see soon,' said Ottavia.

'Ah! But I remember well the difference between your sketches and your finished work. What subject did you choose?'

'It wasn't so much a subject as a theme,' explained Giovanni. 'We chose a nymph and a satyr – not the usual lewd, evil type but a gentle one – set in a classical landscape. But what it all implied was far, far more important than what it showed. It was the autumn and twilight of the Golden Age, a kind of epilogue for all the beauty and harmony that ever was. It was a tragic picture, really, but it was full of contrasts; male and female, youth and age, light and shade, strength and delicacy, warm and cool, which we poised in such a way that the feminine, the light, the delicacy and warmth slightly outweighed its opposite. So it was a very difficult thing to control, but a stimulating challenge all the same.'

'You say it was your best picture, so you must have succeeded in what you attempted. I have known that feeling twice, and I found it disturbing because it makes one wonder if it can be achieved again.'

'Exactly! We stayed on in Rome to do five more pictures, including one for Gian and Virginia Palestrina which turned out quite well, but we came nowhere near the quality of Piero's picture, no matter how hard we tried. Theirs was the nearest, but perhaps that was because we were fond of them, too. We made a lot of money, but had no real satisfaction. But in Rome, success is counted in coins. The more people spend, the more they are admired. And it's not only people, it's the same with the Church, and this is what leads to terrifying vulgarity.'

'It's the sickness of our society,' said Jacopo. 'It's just the same here, of course. God knows where it will all lead!' His frown relaxed into gentleness. 'Christ, in the Gospels, St Benedict in his Rule and St Francis anticipated this when they insisted that poverty was a virtue. If wealth is a virtue, people will think that it's virtuous to acquire it, no matter how. Robbery and fraud would be sanctified, and then where would we be? Or rather, where would *you* be? Because, thank God, I shall be dead!'

Giovanni pondered on Tintoretto's words. His vivid imagination conjured hideous pictures of a world of licence, greed and self-aggrandizement. The ideas and ideals he had formulated with such painful sincerity would be irrelevant; there would be no place for subtlety or grace or sensibility.

Life would be dehumanised, desensitised; living would be intolerable. Was he already a misfit in contemporary society, miscast or mistimed for the vocation which had chosen him? Was his master's advice born of experience and accurate analysis? Could he afford to ignore it? Was he an anachronism, left high and dry on the tide of progress?

Questions abounded, but not answers.

Jacopo broke the web of his gloom with another question. 'Will you tell me more about Piero Farnese?'

'To start with,' said Ottavia, 'he was related to Pope Paul III, patron of Michelangelo and Titian, and he was a cousin of Cardinal Alessandro, who took us over to the Vatican and his own home, the Farnese Palace. It was still unfinished when we were there, but it's very fine, isn't it, Gianni?'

Giovanni agreed, but he could not rid himself of the uncertainties that crowded in on him. Ottavia, however, was excited by reminiscence.

'Piero had been a soldier, but he lived peacefully on his own in a small palace which Sangallo designed for his grandfather's mistress. It was very beautiful, cool and rather sparse, but extremely dignified. After the noise and heat of the city, it was like returning to a green and white oasis.'

'Everything was of superb quality, but nothing was ostentatious,' continued Giovanni with Ottavia's enthusiasm. 'His collection was selected with the greatest care so that everything invited contemplation. His Titian, for instance, had a wall to itself, so that nothing detracted from it. Many of his treasures were not on display at all, but kept in chests or cupboards to be inspected when the time was right. And in a way, he was like that himself, very modest, yet full of wisdom; very serene, yet full of genuine qualities and feelings.'

'At first, Giovanni didn't trust him, did you, Gianni?'

'No, I thought his friendliness and cool manner might be just a thin veneer covering something sinister. But I was wrong.'

'You were right to be cautious, though, my boy. You could have found yourselves the victims of—'

'Father!' protested Ottavia, 'what possible harm could have come to us? He was so obviously a good man.'

'You are too innocent, my child, but Giovanni was quite right to be suspicious and not to take him at face value.'

Ottavia felt unnerved by this exclusively male perspicacity, and she decided to change the subject. 'His garden was beautiful, too,' she began uneasily, 'and the grotto was a perfect underwater fantasy. Shells, statues and plants were all combined with such… The word eluded her.

'Felicity,' supplied Giovanni.

'That's it,' she said, 'but you tell Father about the garden. You are so much better than me.'

She settled herself by her father's knee, resigned to listening with him.

'The palazzina had a courtyard, as most Roman houses do, but this one was planted with trees, which shaded the flags and the windows, keeping the air cool. A doorway from the house led into a walled garden, not very large, but away from the noise of the street. Two paths crossed it at right angles, and there were statues and terms breaking the lines of low hedges. Some were early Greek and Roman pieces, others were more modern. In the centre was a bronze well head with complicated decorations, rather like a smaller version of those in the courtyard of the Palazzo Ducale here. But one's attention was directed to the far end, where there was a large, fluted shell, brimming over with water, which cascaded in separate falls like splayed fingers…'

Jacopo followed the account with interest, picturing in his mind every detail of the description. He became infected by Giovanni's mounting enthusiasm, and wriggled on his cushion.

'In the shell was an amazing sculpture of Venus. In some ways, she was like Botticelli's Venus, but in other ways, it was clearly a stone shape, worked with full, firm curves, not as Michelangelo would have done it, but with astonishingly apt simplifications.'

Jacopo's interest was stimulated further. 'Do you know who carved it?' he asked.

'Yes, it was one of Giambologna's early pieces. But there was nothing at all tentative or immature about it. It was full of assurance and mastery.'

'He's a Frenchman, isn't he? I have seen some of his relief's and bronzes, mostly small ones, it's true, but they do have a pent-up energy which I like. The only major work of his I know is the Neptune Fountain in Bologna. I made several drawings of it. Quite wonderful. I seem to remember Vasari being enthusiastic about it, and for once, he was right about a living artist. Yes,' he nodded, savouring the retrospection, 'it was quite wonderful…'

His voice faded.

'So was this Venus,' said Giovanni. 'No other sculpture, apart from those by Michelangelo, could approach it. It was absolutely compelling. You couldn't see where nature left off and art began, it was a perfect synthesis. It had a hint of sorcery about it.'

'You mean, you couldn't be certain whether nature manipulated art, or art nature?'

'That's exactly it,' said Giovanni. 'Exactly!'

'That ambivalence is puzzling, yet emotionally very satisfying, too. It exercises both parts of our being simultaneously, and yet it reminds us that they are different. You are quite right to call it sorcery. That is what I call what you call great art.'

'Palestrina knew about it too. He called it the mysteries. So we do agree after all!'

'So we do,' said Jacopo, patting Ottavia's shoulder.

It was late and she had lost the struggle to remain awake and follow the discussion. The comfort of home and the warmth of her father's affection had brought her a peace which pervaded her body and her spirit, and to this she had surrendered voluntarily and completely.

On the following day, they showed him the sketches for their *Nymph and Satyr*. The response was immediate and rapturous.

'When you said you had painted yourselves into this picture, I didn't realise that you meant it literally.'

'We didn't,' said Giovanni, 'but that wasn't really important.

We are symbols for something else, not just portraits.'

'So the ambivalence begins...'

He studied the work more closely. The complexity of the composition was foreign to his method. The underlying rhythmical lines which he would have rendered as bodies, draperies or background features were here half-concealed with a different, more severe discipline of linear and spatial proportion. There was a masculine and feminine duality in the design as well as in the subject. Natural forms and intervals were modified by a subtle, contrived geometry. The result was almost musical; he felt, first, a two-part harmony, then four-part, then six, eight... it multiplied beyond counting, carrying him into an infinity of barely resolved tensions.

'This is most extraordinary, but it seems to me that you have taken painting into the realms of religious ecstasy. It's wonderful, but I am not sure if that is where it ought to be.'

'I don't know what you mean,' said Giovanni, fastening on the afterthought.

'The painter has always been a special kind of craftsman. He is an image-maker, and I suppose he has always been a bit of a magician, but his magic was meant for the people. In churches, he brings life to the Scriptures, the saints and the prophets of old; he clothes the mysteries of the Nativity and the Resurrection with the light of reality. He conjures images and dramas out of the written word. He communicates *his* understanding to those who have little or none of their own; he speaks to the people. But this! This is too fine for the people; it's beyond their comprehension. Instead of clarifying a mystery, this creates one. I doubt if there are more than five people in the whole of Venice who could appreciate what is here.'

'We didn't paint it for them,' protested Ottavia. 'It was for Piero, and he *did* understand it, just as you do.'

'That is what I mean. Your picture can only speak to an elite, the initiated. You might as well go out into the piazzetta, set up a stage and harangue the crowd in Japanese.'

He did not intend to wound with words. He had tried to explain the facts about the artist's role in the community, but they interpreted his criticism as condemnation, and were hurt and despondent. He was irritated by his clumsiness.

'Now, you mustn't be miserable about it. If I had said that your work wasn't good enough, I could understand. I said it was *too* good, and I am suggesting that you could lower your sights a little. You will never have any problem in earning your living. There's a fortune waiting for you out there.' He waved his hand contemptuously towards the window. 'You'll never have to struggle as long as the world is as it is.'

'But money is not what we want, any more than you want it,' said Giovanni. 'We want to make good pictures, that's all.'

'My God!' exclaimed Jacopo. 'You can certainly do that. I only wish I could do as well.' He paused, considered for a moment and added, 'Going to paint for – the Pieros of this world?'

They went out to walk the familiar lanes and squares of their own city to rediscover its glories and 'the world as it is'. They crossed the Grand Canal to visit the Gothic brick church of the Frari and see the altarpieces by Bellini and Titian. For there, in the span of two generations, lay the origins of Venetian painting and their own artistic roots.

As experienced observers, they first absorbed each picture from a distance, soaking up the atmosphere, the spirit of the work. Then they peeled it back, one layer at a time, till they reached the heart, and finally put it together again, allowing it to reiterate its individual message. Analysis and synthesis revealed that each picture had its own character, its own unique tone of voice, and they responded accordingly, drawing aesthetic satisfaction and spiritual sustenance from it. Gradually, a comfortable feeling of confirmation and vindication of their artistic convictions settled on them like a gentle rain after a drought.

'I was afraid we were wrong in our ideas,' began Giovanni, 'that somehow we had taken a wrong turning and got lost, but here are Titian and Bellini clearly pointing in the direction we have taken.'

'I'm glad you think that, and relieved too, because I've been worried.'

'So have I. But we can only do what we think is right. It's no good trying to do something we don't believe in, so everything depends on finding patrons who think as we do.'

'That won't be easy. Piero said that in Rome most people knew the cost of everything and the value of nothing, and Father doesn't think much of Venetian patrons either.'

'They both seem certain that society as a whole – not just the patrons – is heading towards perdition. I cannot see that there would be a place for our pictures in a world hopelessly damned.'

'He was pretty depressing about the future, I must say.'

'And yet he's optimistic by nature; full of faith, hope and charity.'

'I wonder what things will be like in ten or twenty years' time.'

'Perhaps it's a good thing we don't know,' he said sadly, 'but it's difficult to be optimistic when the two men whose judgements we respect most take the same gloomy view.'

'It frightens me,' confessed Ottavia. 'Destruction seems such an evil thing, like plague or mortal injury. Have you noticed that most evil things are strong, too strong for us to do anything about? Goodness seems weak and helpless.'

They took a boat across the wide entrance of the Grand Canal to the molo, where the doge's state barge was moored. Men were unfurling the banners of scarlet and gold from gilded poles fore and aft; others brushed and polished the ornate carving which encrusted the bow and stern. It was the ark of the Republic, the Bucentaur.

In the Piazza San Marco the stalls of sellers of miraculous medicines, charms, trinkets and fripperies were crammed together almost to the entrance of St Mark's itself. Mountebanks, tumblers and tricksters performed on rickety platforms; trumpets screamed and cymbals clashed in contention with raucous ballad singers who contended with each other for the bawdiest songs; chained bears danced pathetically to the grinding of a hurdy-gurdy and the wail of bagpipes. They were accosted by beggars and vagabonds who smelled as evil as they looked. Fortune-tellers, gypsies and whores importuned in strident competition, ignoring the patriarchal procession which moved in dilatory vestments to the entrance of the ducal palace. Except for the sounds of hooves and wheels, they might have been in the Piazza Navona in Rome.

The splendour of the architectural setting and the crude turmoil of the human activity could not have been more incongruous. It was the eve of Ascension Day, when, in celebration of the marriage of the Republic to the sea, the doge was rowed out to cast a golden ring into the Adriatic. The central ceremony still preserved its ancient solemnity, but the surrounding carnival had become tarnished by rowdy and lewd entertainment and every form of dishonesty and fraud. Originally, the religious feast had been embellished with a civil ceremony of similar dignity, yet these now provided an arena for the seven deadly sins to make mockery of both with impunity. Venice was infested with every unscrupulous and worthless villain who could make the crossing from the mainland. The stench of vice was as heavy as incense in a shrine.

Between the Frari and the piazza, they had witnessed the roots of their past and an omen of the future. Their instinct and temperament insisted that they should cleave to the one and repudiate the other. They turned their backs on the piazza and hurried home.

There Giovanni found awaiting him a formal invitation from the doge to be present as his guest on the Bucentaur. Such a distinction was reserved for visiting diplomats, ambassadors and senators of the Republic. Giovanni was mystified. There seemed to be no reason for that honour to be granted to him, so he consulted Jacopo.

Immediately, the old man suspected some devious gambit which lay behind the invitation, because it would be characteristic of da Ponte, but he refrained from verbal speculation, lest his cynicism should damage Giovanni's innocent pride and pleasure. He admitted that he was equally mystified, and so he was.

Wearing a suit in the Roman fashion, consisting of doublet, short cape and breeches in plum-coloured velvet edged with passementerie, Giovanni presented himself at the entrance to the Palazzo Ducale. His invitation was scrutinised by the guards, endorsed and returned with official deference. He passed through the dark passage behind the Gate of the Papers and into the sunlit courtyard. A lowly palace attendant holding a sheaf of documents hurried towards him.

'Are you Maestro Giovanni, the painter?'

'I am.'

'Will you follow me, sir.'

They made their way through loose and round tight knots of splendidly dressed dignitaries and entered the palace by the Golden Staircase. They passed through the antechamber where the paintings of Tintoretto glowed from the walls. Not without secret embarrassment, Giovanni noticed himself, representing Bacchus and Marietta as Ariadne in a picture the master had painted seven years before. Haughty ambassadors and their haughtier retinues relieved their boredom by studying the unknown young man whose dress and bearing invited conjecture and respect.

'Will you wait here a moment, please, sir', requested the aide. He approached the magisterial figure of Jacopo Contarini. 'Maestro Giovanni is here, my lord.'

Contarini nodded perfunctorily and detached himself from a group of senior senators. He advanced, smiling. 'Maestro Giovanni, permit me to introduce myself. I am Contarini.'

'Yes, Cavaliere, I know you by sight.'

He wore across his right shoulder the stole of knighthood, embroidered in high relief with thinly drawn gold wire, so the mode of address was correct. They shook hands.

'Welcome back to Venice. I have heard reports of your spectacular success in Rome. Please accept my congratulations.'

'I had no idea...'

'Ah! Good news travels fast. We know what is going on everywhere, even in the Vatican.' He made a grimace which mocked omniscience.' I understand that you were hailed as "The Lion of Venice" by the nobility of Rome. Quite a distinction!'

'Is that why I am here, Cavaliere?'

'You are here to receive the Order of the Golden Stole from the doge.'

Giovanni was so staggered by the information that he had not recovered his composure when he was summoned into the adjoining hall of the Collegio for the investiture. Here, Palladio's immaculate architecture was complemented by Tintoretto's workshop paintings, including the recently completed one for da Ponte, which was appropriately garish and almost crude. Giovanni was overwhelmed by the avalanche of colour and splendour.

With Contarini by his side, he stood trembling like a sick dog while the citation was read, trying to focus on the enthroned figure of the doge. His corna, robes and shoes were made of cloth of gold, so that with each small movement or gesture, he shimmered insubstantially.

'Most Serene Prince,' began the herald. 'By the order of the Senate of the Most Serene Republic, I am required to declare their unanimous decision that Maestro Giovanni, known as Robusti, citizen of the Republic, should this day, in the year of our Holy Redeemer fifteen hundred and eighty-five, be received into the Most Noble Order of the Knights of San Marco, in recognition of his talents in the arts and a mark of esteem for his services in promoting the name and honour of the Most Serene Republic abroad.'

Contarini guided Giovanni by the arm to the foot of the throne where a fall of cloth of gold covered the top three steps.

'Who is it that presents Maestro Giovanni for knighthood?' called the herald. His voice rang in the ceiling.

'I, Jacopo Contarini, knight and senator of the Republic, sponsor and guarantor, present Giovanni Robusti to you, Master Doge, to my fellow knights and to the Senate.'

Giovanni knelt before the gilded figure of da Ponte whose emaciated, sallow face bore the smile of reptilian satisfaction he knew so well. The doge placed the Golden Stole across his shoulder and presented the rolled parchment bearing the grant. Contarini helped him to his feet, they bowed and left the hall to a ripple of genteel applause.

'I don't understand this at all,' said Giovanni ingenuously.

'There is no doubt that you deserve this honour and title, and I welcome you most cordially to the Order.'

Giovanni felt the warmth of brotherhood as they shook hands again.

'What do I have to do?' he asked.

'Nothing really. You are entitled to attend all state functions, you may claim precedence over everyone in the Republic except the doge, the Patriarch and the Senate, and of course, your fellow knights, for we are all of equal status.'

'Are there any duties required of me?'

'We mount a guard on important occasions as equerries of the doge, but only our legs are required, not our arms!'

The witticism, though rather puerile, relieved Giovanni of the nervous tension and doubts which had made him feel so insecure.

'So it's only a ceremonial office, then?'

'You could say that. But there are prerequisites too. You don't have to pay any dues to the state, apart from import duty on commercial operations. In fact, they pay you an annuity for life, or until you are bored to death, and that might not be very long.' He laughed quietly to himself. 'The only thing you cannot do is to resign. No one has thought of the machinery for that yet; but you can be expelled, for treason, or something like that. You will have to surrender your stole before they cut your head off, because bloody stoles cannot be used again, I suppose.'

His impious humour was quite unexpected and Giovanni found himself on the brink of uncontrollable laughter, but a stirring behind them restored a more formal attitude to Contarini.

'It is almost time for the procession of the marionettes. We will talk of this later,' he said. Giovanni moved to leave. 'And we are part of the show,' he added with a smile. 'If you care to accompany me, I would be very pleased.'

The six musicians with long silver trumpets and the eight standard bearers had already assembled in the courtyard below. The woodwind players waited in an anteroom, nervously sucking their reeds. The bell of the campanile boomed over the city, inviting its inferiors in every other campanile to join its plangent sound. The Grand Chancellor marshalled the rest of the procession in the Council Chamber, where they were joined by the doge and the Patriarch and the bearers of the Sword and Cap of State and the Chair and Cushion.

Giovanni was greeted fraternally by his fellow knights, most of whom were twice or thrice his age. There was nothing submissive or deferential in their attitude to the occasion; they spoke and joked among themselves as if they were at a party, exercising, but not abusing, their privilege.

The band of flutes and oboes started uncertainly, dropping a few cracked and overblown notes before they attained unison, and the procession moved off slowly down the Staircase of the Giants to the waiting lines of dignitaries, retinues and trumpeters below. The inordinate length of their instruments and the corresponding weight required the additional support of six young pages, who walked before, each with a trumpet bell on his shoulder.

The processional, written by the ageing Andrea Gabrieli, swelled in sonority as the trumpets and sackbuts added their forte. The dark vault of the passageway to the Gate of the Papers rang in deafening reverberation. In the sunshine of the piazzetta, the air vibrated with the clang and jangle of the city's bells. The crowds, organised with savage efficiency by Venetian halberdiers, heaped shouts and cheers to the tumult. Guns fired a salute from the Arsenal. The doge and the Patriarch mounted the carpeted gangway to the poop of the Bucentaur, where they sat on golden thrones in a golden tabernacle. Below decks, visible through square oar ports, the rowers of the gilded galley who had been drawn from the fleet for the occasion gripped the scarlet sweeps. The scarlet and gold banners of the Republic stirred in the breeze above.

Contarini, Giovanni and the knights took their allotted places by the standards, while other magnates, nobles and less distinguished guests boarded smaller and less magnificent vessels, each of which bore the flag emblazoned with the winged lion of St Mark.

The state barges and a thousand gondolas, rolling perilously in the wash of the Bucentaur's oars, pulled away from the molo on their passage to the open sea. The forts by the Lido thundered in full salvo.

The throng of waterborne citizens suggested that the city must be quite deserted, and Giovanni searched the motley flotilla, hoping to glimpse Jacopo's gondola, but the profusion and confusion made recognition impossible. The carillon faded as the city fell behind them and the sea breeze intervened. Looking back into the wide entrance of the Grand Canal, flanked by the ducal palace and San Giorgio, Giovanni was flooded with pride and patriotism for what he believed to be the most glorious and beautiful place fashioned by human skill and conceived by human ingenuity. As the sun flashed from the turbulent water and was returned, transformed by brick and marble, mosaic and glass, he knew that for all their splendours, no other city could offer anything comparable with what La Serenissima lavished in such abundance. She and he were totally integrated; his roots and his life, like her foundations, were consolidated in the sandbanks of the lagoon.

During the journey, Contarini detailed the history and traditions of the Order to Giovanni, who was anxious to know why he had been singled out for so rare an honour.

'Venice has always been governed and administered by the aristocracy, as you well know. Every young man, born into a patrician family, must present himself when he comes of age to the Council, and there begins his life of service to the state. The poor devil has no choice; he's born to bear responsibility, whether he likes it or not, whether he's capable of it or not. If he's an idiot, the state will find a part for him to play, just lately, they seem to have made him the doge!' He jerked his head back towards the gilded tabernacle. 'We have resisted conferring honours for service on men of less than noble birth, as many states do, because such a system might threaten the hegemony of the aristocrats, and the last thing they want is a *meritocracy*. God forbid! But the Order of San Marco is an exception, but it gives no powers to the recipient, it merely decorates him.'

'But my service to Venice was so unimportant and incidental,' said Giovanni.

'The days when knighthood was conferred solely for merit have passed long since. But it's true that in your case, your talent and your reputation were largely responsible for your election, as the citation accurately stated.'

'Do you mean there was something else, then?'

'Of course. There was a political motive too.'

'Can you tell me what it was?'

'I can tell you, but I wouldn't want you to be disillusioned, especially today. But it's better that you hear it from me than from someone with a mouth full of malice, and there are a few of those about, believe me.'

Giovanni wanted to have the mystery revealed, whatever it might be, and he had complete faith in Contarini's honesty and integrity.

He turned in his seat towards his noble friend and fortified himself against disappointment and humiliation. He studied the generous face and imposing bearing of his companion. His lineage and his statesmanship had conveyed a dignity which could not be assumed merely as an act of will, still less as an act of deception. His authority, however, was lightly borne, as natural as his handsome features. He turned to Giovanni.

'Before you left for Rome, da Ponte tried to persuade certain senators to propose your election in exchange for unknown favours. I don't know what he had in mind, but I suspect it suited some personal advantage he was contriving. Perhaps he simply wanted to humiliate Tintoretto, I don't know. Then about a year ago, he proposed yet another action against the Turks to regain Cyprus, and he generated some support for this, but many of us were opposed to it on the grounds of strategy and timing. To divert his reckless ambitions and to unite the Senate, which was bitterly divided at the time, subtle tactics had to be used; one of which was the remodelling of part of the ducal palace, which we knew would appeal to him, and another was your election.' He looked at his boots to conceal his discomfort. 'But I want you to know that I supported you from the beginning, but *not* if it suited da Ponte's devious purposes.'

In spite of this last assurance, Giovanni expressed the conclusion that he had been used as a pawn in a political game. Contarini's reply surprised him.

'I was afraid you would think that and be disillusioned, but sometimes, the right things are done for ignoble reasons. Political life is full of compromises stratagems, subterfuge and intrigue, that's why we Venetians keep it in the family, so to speak. It's second nature to us, and the ordinary citizens remain in blissful ignorance. They would have nothing but contempt for us if they knew just how they were governed, and rightly so.' He leaned closer to ensure that his confidence should not be overheard. 'In one way or another, we are all pawns manipulated by people and circumstances. If we are aware of it, we can be fairly secure; if we are not, we become impotent victims of forces which may do us great damage, not the least of which is self-delusion. Make no mistake, I am more of a pawn than you are; that is my destiny, and da Ponte is the biggest of us all. The difference is that we know we are, but he does not. He believes that he is the great chess master, and it's a delusion.'

As Giovanni pondered the implications of this admission, his despondency diminished. It all made very good sense.

They had arrived at the spot where the marriage ceremony would take place.

'Now, watch this! Da Ponte believes he is a divinity, but he's totally controlled by custom and protocol. He's only a small part of a continuing tradition. In fact, everyone here is a freer agent than he is. We chose to be here, after all. He is a cipher; his presence, his persona and his role are symbolic, as is the whole of his life. He is the most important man in the Republic. He has neither power nor volition. We, on the other hand, have freedoms which he has sacrificed to pride and prestige. Ironical, isn't it?'

The Patriarch blessed the ring, a priest poured a libation of holy water into the sea; Doge Nicolo, fatuously emulating the display of a farmyard cockerel, dropped the ring into the dilating ripples with the words, 'Sea, we espouse thee in sign of true and everlasting dominion.'

The brittle sound of distant bells fluctuated with the breeze during the silence which followed the ceremony. The peace was smashed by a fanfare of silver trumpets proclaiming the remarriage of the Queen of the Adriatic with the waves which bore her prosperity and power. The flotilla turned and bent its oars back to the city, to feasting and drinking and merriment.

Such frivolities held no attraction for Giovanni, nor did he wish to exhibit his newly acquired rank after having witnessed da Ponte's absurd self-deception.

He said farewell to Contarini and thanked him for his support and his confidences. He went directly home to share his honour with his family, who would welcome his good news without dubiety or cynicism.

The Golden Stole was inspected and admired. Giovanni was embraced and gently chaffed. 'Cavaliere,' said Jacopo, bowing and sweeping his cap before him, 'have I your permission to embrace your honour?'

'Cavaliere,' whispered Ottavia from the depth of a coy curtsey. 'Will your honour grant his humble servant permission to kiss his hand?'

He disdainfully held his hand above her head, and as she rose, it moved beyond her reach. She stamped her foot peevishly. The family crowed in chorus.

'I am very pleased for you, Giovanni,' said Jacopo earnestly. 'It really does seem as if talent is being properly recognised at last. They usually wait until after death. We must celebrate!'

Quite early in the evening, Giovanni and Ottavia added to the excitement by announcing that they were to marry in six months' time. The warm congratulations and affection which were showered on them strengthened their own happiness and confirmed their certainty. Jacopo expressed his acclaim and satisfaction through every facet of his nature. He laughed and sang, jigged and cheered quite openly, and privately, he gave thanks to God, wept a little and planned Ottavia's dowry with true Venetian extravagance.

The private feasting, drinking and music which continued into the night were enlivened by spontaneous family pleasure. Each contributed a song, a poem or an instrumental piece. The dancing and the madrigals were unruly and interrupted by paralysing laughter. As fatigue and plenitude at last displaced their high spirits, Giovanni reflected that the joys of home and family completely supplanted those of financial and social success.

As each oarsman of the Bucentaur left the ducal palace carrying the traditional gift of the cup and plate he had used at the feast, the Robustis retired to their rooms, aware that there would never be another Ascension Day to rival this one.

Separation

Commissions for Cavaliere Giovanni's work occupied them totally for the next year. Nicolo da Ponte, most Serene Prince of the Republic for seven years, had died and the pictures for his saloon were never completed. His successor, Pasquale Cicogna, was an unexpected choice, being the first in his family to wear the Corna. It was widely expected that Jacopo Contarini would be the fourth doge bearing that name, but Giovanni suspected that he had managed the election to ensure that he should retain what political freedom, influence and personal independence he could. It was not consonant with his nature or his intelligence to allow himself to be hobbled like a refractory horse. Neither his wisdom nor his dignity would condone that.

Giovanni received many invitations from his sponsor for conversation, and gradually they became deeply involved with the refurbishing of the Palazzo Contarini, one of the noblest on the Grand Canal. Their plans reflected their common taste for simple proportion rather than the bizarre and extravagant decoration which had been fashionable in some parts of Italy for several decades. Together, they believed they could arrest the decline in architectural and decorative taste by a return to the purity of the ancient Greeks.

Each was acutely conscious of his responsibility in adding to the panorama of the Grand Canal, and excellence was of the essence, not speed. They were prepared to digest every treatise they could find, from Vitruvius, through Serlio and Vignola to Palladio. The drawings which Palladio had bequeathed to his friend Contarini became frequent references as each authority was tested against the other's in search of a moderate consensus.

As they became imbued with the rationality of the classical spirit, each sensed a stability, peace and humility which strengthened their relationship. Predilections matured into convictions; acquaintance into friendship.

Contarini discovered in his young companion a mind capable of the absorption of ancient principles, of sound analysis and of a creative application of abstract concepts to finite materials and structures. He became familiar with an almost organic progression of activities; first, the diligent study, then cautious consideration, and finally, imaginative conclusions which flew upwards with amazing audacity and power. Here was a rare intellect which he prized and nurtured; here was an individual of rare grace and sensitivity, in utter contrast with those he knew in political life. His contempt for, and alienation from, that life accumulated as their work progressed.

It was while they were immersed in such research that a letter for Giovanni arrived at Tintoretto's house, bearing the Farnese arms. Ottavia could hardly restrain her impatience to open it. It was brief and informal.

To my dear friends, Ottavia and Giovanni,

During the time taken for this letter to reach you, I shall have been relieved of my sins, my pain and the intolerable loneliness of life.

I know that you will rejoice with me that I depart as a bridegroom, impatient to meet his bride.

I hope you will accept a small legacy as a token of my everlasting affection and happy remembrance of your stay with me, and not as a futile attempt to repay what I owe you.

I shall not be permitted to take with me my most sublime treasure, your picture, nor can I countenance its disposal to others who know not the tenderness and devotion it symbolises. I am, therefore, returning it to you, the only possible custodians of our exclusive and precious enigma.

I send you all my earthly love and I shall pray for you in the next world, where, with God's grace, we shall be reunited. Make haste slowly.

May Christ protect, sustain and guide you, always.

Piero Farnese

They both wept, more with joy for him than in grief for themselves. But their feelings, like their picture, were an interfusion which could not be disjoined.

Before the arrival of the orated picture, they received confirmation of the handsome endowment payable on each anniversary of Piero's death. It ensured financial security for life.

Jacopo walked about in restless excitement as the picture was unpacked. He had become reconciled to not seeing the work, which above all others, he yearned and prayed for.

His reaction duplicated Piero's at the time of its presentation. He was annihilated.

After a long silence, he spoke, slowly constructing an honest evaluation.

'This is the most astonishing painting I have ever seen. It is a compendium of every artistic subtlety and achievement of the Renaissance. I don't mean it's a dry catalogue, but a living embodiment of all the poetry and music, design and colour which man has aspired to, but realised only separately and, very, very occasionally. It is the picture of all pictures, and it justifies absolutely your notions about perfection and the artist's vocation, Giovanni. It makes me feel very humble and ham-fisted.' He tugged his beard thoughtfully. 'Thank God I have been spared to witness this. *Nunc dimittis*.'

He crossed himself.

Ottavia and Giovanni became involved in the picture again, not as active executants but as passive participants. It enveloped them with a spell which carried them beyond time and place, into an apotheosis of bliss. They remained suspended by a magical magnetism, victims of their own creation.

'I think your friend Contarini should see this,' suggested Jacopo. 'He would appreciate it, I'm sure.'

'No, that is not possible,' said Giovanni, adjusting to the here and now with some difficulty.

'Why ever not?'

'Much as I admire and respect him, I don't want to share this with him. It's not just another picture, you see. It is our personal message of love to Piero, and it is too private.'

'But you let me see it, it isn't too private for me.'

'That's different, because we love you too and we owe you everything that made it possible for us to paint it in the first place.

There's some of you in it as well.'

Self-evident though this was, Jacopo was moved by the simple acknowledgement of his contribution to this unique achievement. But his modesty prevented him from accepting any of the responsibility.

'If I had painted nothing, I would die a happy man if I knew I had played some part in this single picture.'

'If you had painted nothing, Father, this picture could not exist,' said Giovanni. 'So if you want me to show it to Contarini, or anyone else, I will. For your sake.'

'That is magnanimous, but it is your picture and it must be your decision. I will say no more, except that I do congratulate you for a stupendous achievement. It's just... overwhelming.'

'I think Piero felt about it just as we do,' said Ottavia. 'He sent it back to us because he knew it belonged to the three of us, and anyone else must be an intruder who could not understand all it said.'

'But he invited his friends to see it, didn't he?' ventured Jacopo.

'He did,' replied Giovanni, 'but I think he regretted it afterwards. He saw that they only regarded it as a good painting, but to him, it was more than that. He used to sit for hours just looking at it, oblivious of everything else. It was as if he had stepped into it, into another world where he was not old or lonely or crippled.'

'He even said that he loved it more than anything he possessed...' added Ottavia.

The intimate remembrance of their noble friend suddenly saddened her and she could not continue. She walked over to the window and looked out on to the familiar canal, which shimmered now with blurred iridescence.

Cavaliere Giovanni received a continual stream of visitors, some making social calls, others professional ones. The work on their canvases was constantly interrupted and the creative flow was distorted into an erratic and protracted process. Furthermore, the activity hampered the progress of work in Tintoretto's studio, and Domenico, as chief assistant, was growing irritable. Ottavia and Giovanni felt obliged to find another studio, conveniently placed so that they could continue to live at home, yet work and receive elsewhere. Not far from the Fondamenta dei Mori, and still in the parish of the Madonna dell'Orto, a small house of modest distinction was empty and for sale. They visited it several times before making a decision.

Situated on a corner where two canals intersected, it had windows on two sides, allowing light to flood the saloon on the first floor from early morning to late afternoon. The painted stucco front was peeling, but the stone tracery over the windows and on the balconies was in crisp condition, and the timbers were sound.

The staircase was not wide, but an ample landing permitted the passage of large canvases. The bedchambers were small but airy, neglected but promising comfort when they no longer served as dormitories for pigeons. Servants' quarters in the roof, a minute kitchen and courtyard completed the premises. It seemed ideal for their purposes. Tintoretto approved, and the house was purchased.

Ottavia insisted that the whole be repainted inside and out before they took possession. She was anxious to repeat, as far as possible, the restful atmosphere of Piero's house, and this provided a challenge which she delighted in. The deep Venetian red and umber of the walls was replaced by ivory and cool green within and golden ochre outside. Timbers were stripped of heavy varnish and waxed, terrazzo floors were re-ground and polished, the pigeons evicted and the house grew larger in gratitude. She added small, potted trees to the balconies and the old house rejoiced in its rejuvenation.

Giovanni did not interfere. He was too preoccupied with the classical orders and proportion to be stimulated by the modest domesticity of a merchant's house, so he was more than pleased that Ottavia assumed total responsibility and undertook all the necessary organisation. Privately, he believed that she was being more fussy than their need for a studio could justify, but he allowed no hint of his misgivings to detract from her enormous pleasure and satisfaction. He had reason to congratulate himself for his discretion when it became clear that it was her intention to make it a home rather than a workshop.

They chose a middle-aged couple, Giulia and Franco, to be

housekeeper and boatman, who would live in the house and be caretakers in their absence. As servants, they bore the sullen scars of a hard and unprivileged life; they were not just miserable and dejected, but blackened by the gloom of envy and resentment which enveloped them. It was their pathos not their skill or willing disposition which had won them their new position and new home.

Furnishing the renovated rooms was an even greater delight for Ottavia, who pestered local craftsmen for their finest workmanship and simplest designs. The furniture was sparse, but solid; the hangings, plain but heavy; the crockery and glass, restrained but elegant. Everything she acquired was subjected to a critical examination and nothing was admitted which would have been unworthy of the Palazzina Farnese.

The result of her efforts in nest building pleased them both. It invited unimpaired concentration on work and relaxation when work was over. The saloon was transformed into a spacious studio, and its anteroom provided adequate space for reading and the reception of visitors.

The first picture they completed there was a variant of a subject they had painted in Rome, a Bacchanale. The dancing figures, crowned with vine leaves in the foreground, were less abandoned than was customary. The celebration of Bacchus was here depicted as a ceremony which proclaimed human suppleness and grace, not indulgence and vice. The classic proportions of the dancers' bodies elevated them to a natural dignity which matched that of the incidental creatures which punctuated the design. Nature was invested with a religious significance, and the picture was the invocation and the eulogy. Landscape, figures and animals were united by a silvery light as fragile as the poetry of the whole concept.

They were not discontented with the finished work, but they were aware that the movement and presentation did not synchronise as naturally with the inherent spirit as was the case in Piero's picture. In their judgement, it was second rate, but more consistent than some of their recent work.

The patron, Vincenzo Morosini, senator, procurator and Knight of the Golden Stole, was delighted. His taste for art and literature was refined by lifelong experience and study, and he was one of the first noblemen to acquire a painting by Giovanni after the success of the da Ponte series. He had recently commissioned a Resurrection from Tintoretto, which he had donated to the Church of San Giorgio Maggiore. He was anxious to add another of Giovanni's pictures to his private collection before he died. At the time of its completion, he was too old and infirm to leave his bed, so he had the painting hung on the facing wall to illuminate his last days with a vision of the sweetness of antiquity.

Giovanni visited him several times at his earnest request. He sat by the bed listening to the secrets of state intrigue and individual improprieties. It was as if Morosini needed to purge his mind of guilt and disgrace in a secular confessional before he could approach the heavenly throne. He was a man more feared by superstition than comforted by faith, and on the threshold of death, he wished to make his entry into paradise as easy and unencumbered as possible. The Resurrection picture was, in essence, an insurance premium, paid at the eleventh hour; but paid it was, and he felt more secure.

His confidences, however, were both valuable and disturbing for Giovanni. They confirmed that the radical weaknesses of the Venetian state and society were more perilous than he had believed. An economic decline, which had been in progress since the Portuguese opened a sea route to the East, could not be arrested, and with the loss of important territories and maritime supremacy, the Republic faced financial ruin which it dared not admit. Her enemies and friends knew her plight, but not the extent of it, or the time left to her before disaster closed its hungry jaws.

Morosini claimed that the Republic was wilfully hastening her inevitable downfall by maintaining a hollow display of affluence and extravagance. Venice was drowning in the remnants of her own reputation. Stringent economies and ascetic resolve might save her, but these would be beacons which would signal her dreadful secret to her rivals and enemies. Gold had given life and power to Venice; gold was now destroying her.

'What can be done about it?' asked Giovanni.

'Nothing. Absolutely nothing! You might as well ask, how can we keep the winter floods out of St Mark's Square. If you block up one low point, another will spill over, and another, and so on.'

'Is it too late to economise and produce more things ourselves?'

'Far too late. Fifty years ago *might* have been in time, but no one took any notice; twenty-five years ago was already too late. So now we have to keep our secret, because as soon as we are seen to be ailing, the rest of the world will abandon us as they would a leper.' He dragged a limp hand across his pate, leaving his hair absurdly awry. 'Who would rescue a drowning leper? It might be kinder to let him go.'

The old man's breathing was shallow. Giovanni drew him higher up the pillow.

'I cannot believe that Venice is dying,' he said. 'How can a city die? There will always be people, won't there?'

'Some will stay, I suppose, but the wise ones will leave, taking their wisdom and their riches with them. Already, a large number of patrician families prefer to live on the mainland, almost as if they expect the end tomorrow. Some give absolutely nothing to the city; they only grab what they can while the going is good.' He shook his head with indignation. He returned to the matter in hand, prompted by the urgency of the situation. 'No state can survive without wisdom to guide it. No state can survive without the wealth of its people. No state can survive if it earns less than it spends.' He seemed to find some reserve of energy and his voice became clearer. 'Consider what happened to the Roman Empire. It conquered the world, but not human nature. We are repeating its downfall by duplicating its weaknesses. The process will be slow, of course, but every year it will get shabbier, more dissolute, more greedy, more frivolous, until the rats finally take over…'

Giovanni shuddered at the image of a decaying city, swarming with rats. He had a pathological disgust of the animal and a fear which was as intrinsic as original sin.

The image proliferated.

Scurrying rats.

Swimming rats.

Multiplying rats.

Rats whose bellies split open, discharging bigger, more

voracious rats.

Rats gnawing human flesh down to the bone and cackling obscenities at their victims' screams.

Rats that raped and ravaged.

Rats blocking the canals with their own bodies, and splitting the walls of churches and palaces with their own excrement.

He swayed with waves of nausea at the spectacle and the stench. He gripped the arms of the chair for support. The room revolved drunkenly.

He recovered to find that he was alone.

Morosini was dead.

He went back home, adrift from reality. He sat in his new gondola, tense and fearful of what might lurk in the water which sped past him. He dared not look at the green, mossy edges of the canals, fearful that a pair of bright, hungry eyes might return his gaze. He kept his hands off the gunwale, fearful lest rodent teeth might amputate a finger.

He was relieved when the boat pulled alongside his steps and he was able to enjoy the spotless security of the house. His head reeled vinously as he climbed the stairs. By the time he had reached his room, he was shaking uncontrollably.

From the studio, Ottavia heard his arrival and was surprised that he did not join her there, as he always did. Following a premonition upstairs, she found him lying on the bed in a foetal position, convulsed with what she took to be pain. She sat beside him. 'Gianni, what's the matter?' Her voice was softened with concern and apprehension.

There was no reply.

His mouth was clenched like a vice, his eyes screwed tight, his hands stuffed in his armpits.

The rats returned, seething in through the doorway, the windows and on to the bed. They brushed his legs and his cheeks. The smell of evil fillet his bursting head. A huge rat hung over his face. He felt its breath and its whiskers.

In an involuntary, panic-stricken gesture, his arm swept it away. The dull thud of impact was followed by a scream, and it was gone. The intense relief he felt suppressed the convulsions, but he dared not open his eyes. His temples still pounded.

Gradually, the panic and the terrible ague subsided. He was at home, on his bed. The familiar coverlet had a familiar smell; the white walls and timber ceiling were reassuring. He felt the warmth of the sun on his legs.

He swung his feet to the floor.

There, lying in an insensible heap, was Ottavia. A great weal disfigured her face from chin to eyebrow; her mouth was full of blood and her eye was puffed into an ungainly swelling. The other side of her face was blank.

He called her name, but there was no reply.

He tried to lift her shoulders, but her head dropped awkwardly and hit the floor.

He felt instinctively that he was once again in the presence of death, Tavi's death. The realisation hit him like a cannonball.

'Oh, my God! My God!'

He placed his ear to her breast to confirm what he feared most. He felt her stir and heard her shallow breathing. Her pulse fluttered feebly.

'Giulia!' he screamed. 'Come quickly!'

He pulled her on to the bed.

'Giulia!' he called again.

He raised her head and drew a pillow beneath it. Giulia came into the room wearing a disagreeable expression. She sighed impatiently.

'Now what's the matter, Cavaliere?'

'Ottavia has fainted.'

'Is that all? I expect she's pregnant,' she said unsympathetically.

She walked over to the bed with dilatory insolence and saw the red weal on the other side of Ottavia's face.

'God preserve us! What's that?'

Giovanni hesitated. He could think of no explanation.

'I think she must have hit her head as she fell…'

'Is she breathing?'

'Yes.'

'I'll get some cold water.'

Left alone again, he straightened her hair and clothes, whimpering like a lost child. He noticed something very strange at the side of her throat. It was not like a swelling, but resembled a sharp finger, poking the skin from inside into a low cone. The clavicle was broken. He touched the peak and found it to be hard and unyielding. He understood.

Giulia shuffled in with bowl and towel. She sponged the blood away impassively, but the swellings remained; moistened, they looked angrier than before.

'What's this, then?' she said.

'I think her collarbone is broken.'

'I should think it is!' She poked it roughly. 'This could be very nasty. We must get help.' Her icy heart seemed to thaw very slightly.

'Will you ask Franco to fetch a nun from the hospital, please.'

'I will, if I can find him,' she said.

Giovanni placed another coverlet over Ottavia and knelt by the bed, praying hysterically.

Two hours later, a very young nun, hardly more than a novice and bland as a lamb, appeared at the door. She smiled modestly at Giovanni and withdrew her white hands from her white sleeves. She put a hand on Ottavia's brow and bent over her to detect signs of life. She smiled again. She examined the bone end with delicate pressure of her second and third fingers. Giovanni thought he saw the placid smile falter momentarily.

'Will she be all right?' he asked.

'With God's help,' she replied enigmatically. 'How did it happen?'

'I am not sure, I think she must have fainted and fallen.'

'That wouldn't explain the marks made by knuckles on her face, would it?' she said with cool assurance.

Giovanni was stunned.

'Where?'

She showed him. He remembered the threatening rat and nausea gripped his entrails again.

'Oh my God!' he exclaimed, burying his face in the coverlet.

The nun made no sign of disapproval.

'We have to undress her and bandage her shoulder. Perhaps you would wait downstairs.'

Giovanni was rejected by her undiminished kindness and

consideration. He was rejected by Ottavia's insensibility and by his own self-immolation. He had committed the vilest crime against the object of his tenderest emotions. Abject misery closed over him like storm waves over a drowning man. His inclination was to go to Jacopo, to confess and beg for absolution, but he could not leave Ottavia as she was. He wrote a note for Franco to deliver.

Jacopo arrived, panting, in his painting clothes, his face and hands grotesquely daubed. Giovanni explained what he knew had happened and what he suspected had happened.

'Father, can you forgive me?'

Jacopo's face was grave; his eyes burned; his chin was like stone beneath his beard. His voice was calm.

'Of course, my boy. Did you think I could believe that you could hurt Tavi intentionally? I know you better than that. There is nothing more we can do, except pray that God will restore her to us, quickly and completely.'

Giovanni's humiliation was doubled by Jacopo's immediate forgiveness.

They knelt together in the studio, each praying fervently for the same blessing, the same deliverance. But Jacopo prayed for Giovanni with equal fervour.

The nun appeared silently.

'You may go up now. She is awake.'

They found her lying flat and motionless, staring at the ceiling through one half-closed eye. The other had disappeared altogether beneath a ball, bulging with blood. They knelt each side of the bed. Giovanni placed himself on the side he had brutalised. Recognising their presence, she smiled on her father's side; the other was immobile.

'Tavi, how do you feel?' asked Jacopo.

'I feel,' she began uncertainly, 'as if I am only half here...' Her words were delivered to her father; not to exclude Giovanni, nor in confidence, but only half of her mouth could articulate.

Giovanni gazed at the hideous contusion before him. His gorge and his guilt rose at the transformation and his own violent perpetration. It was ironical that all his attentive efforts to protect her from physical and mental damage had been revoked in one stupefied moment.

'Is Giovanni there?' she asked.

'Yes, Tavi, I'm here.' He touched her hair.

'I cannot see you. Are you all right?'

'Yes. I am.'

'Oh good,' she sighed. Her continued unselfishness and solicitude were too much for him to bear.

Tears filled his eyes and he sobbed frantically.

During the next four days, Giovanni left the bedside only when the visiting nun required it. He tended her constantly, sponging her face, brushing her hair, giving her drink and what comfort he could. Goaded to unconscious self-sacrifice by devotion and terrible guilt, he thought of nothing but Ottavia's recovery. In the brief moments when she slept, he prayed for God's punishment to visit and cripple him, that he should bear her suffering into the depths of hell.

His own, and the nun's, attentions produced a steady improvement. The swelling subsided, the eye changed from red to purple and her lips began to resume a measure of symmetry. With one arm strapped to her body and tight bandages around her upper ribs, she was incapable of any but the smallest of movements. She held Giovanni's hand and stroked his unshaven face in gestures of tenderness and concern. His weariness troubled her deeply and she tried desperately to resist or minimise the need to cough which also troubled her, lest it should add to his pain.

On the fourth evening, she insisted that he should go into the adjoining room and sleep. He protested that he could not leave her until she could do everything for herself, but his sunken cheeks and dark, hollow eyes contradicted his resolution to maintain a constant watch.

'I am quite comfortable now, and I shall feel better if you go and sleep.'

'I cannot leave you, Tavi.'

'Please, Gianni, it will make me happy to know that you are resting…' He shook his head. 'I am much better now. I shall be all right.'

Her anxiety for his welfare was plainly distressing her, and at last, he agreed. He instructed Giulia to take his place, but to wake him if he was needed.

He retired to the empty bed, leaving the door open. Once there, he was asleep.

He awoke suddenly as the first light flared through the gap in the shutters. He felt refreshed, his face taut and youthful again, his mind relaxed and untroubled. He stretched and punched the pillow. Then he remembered Ottavia, and he raced into the room next door.

She lay, very pale and still, except for her tortured breathing. Her hair clung to the sweat which covered her face and stained the pillow.

Giulia was asleep, full of peace and contentment.

Giovanni shook her violently.

'Wake up, you hag!' he shouted. 'Wake up.'

She stirred sullenly and yawned with maddening lack of urgency.

'Wake up!' he shouted again. 'What have you done?'

She opened her eyes and looked about her with slothful indifference.

'Look at her! She's ill, don't you see?'

Giulia got out of her chair like a buffalo heaving itself from a mud wallow.

'Christ! She does look bad.'

'Go and get the sister. Quickly!'

He knelt by the bed and wiped the dripping face, the despoiled face of Aphrodite. Her breathing was short and painful, more like gasps of exhaustion, but there had been no exertion. Giovanni felt the pain in his own lungs as the air was rapidly inhaled and exhaled. He placed his hand inside the bed; the wet heat was intense and a drift of steam rose from the space and from his hand. She simmered insensibly in her own perspiration.

She coughed, rattling her throat ineffectually. A thin stream of frothy blood crept down her cheek, threatening her ear. He wiped away the awful obscenity. The panting continued.

The nun arrived, serenely confident and efficient. She placed her hand on the patient's brow.

'I am afraid pneumonia has set in,' she said. 'It was a possibility from the start, but I thought we had passed the prime threat two days ago. Has she coughed blood?'

'Yes, a few minutes ago,' Giovanni said, opening the stained kerchief.

'Then I expect the broken bone has punctured the lung.'

The words crashed like a heap of stones upon Giovanni.

'That sounds...' he paused, unable to grasp the inevitable, '...very serious.'

'Yes, it is.'

'How serious?'

'Well, if it were one or the other, there might be a chance of her survival, but together, I am afraid, there is not much hope.'

'Do you mean...'

'Yes, there is nothing we can do, except to be with her and make her as comfortable as possible for the journey which lies before her.' Giovanni was crushed again by the stark implications of her words. He looked at the racked, gasping remnant of the lovely Ottavia.

'Will she be in pain?' he asked.

'She might, but she will certainly be distressed, and that is why she needs our comfort and our presence.'

The words seemed remote, as if they applied to someone else, unknown and unloved. But very gradually, the impossible became conceivable.

With hope extinguished, he felt more capable of coping with the agony ahead. He would not leave her again in this life, of that he was determined.

But determination was temporarily displaced by frantic images which crowded his mind. Morosini's expressionless face swayed before him like a luminous death mask. It tried to speak to him, but rigor mortis had frozen the lips in dumb desperation. Luca's disembodied head writhed and grimaced at him, more horrible in death than it was in suffering. It screamed inaudible words at him, until the unsupported jaw hung loose, swinging, mutely repulsive. It dissolved, leaving a dark void in which the only sound was that of his own heartbeat. The rhythm generated the footfall of the pallbearers carrying his mother's corpse. The strand of hair bobbed below the hem of the sheet, ludicrously mimicking the life which was no longer there. The hemline trembled and rose, forming a dark cavern from which the gory face of Bianca peered and leered. A white nose bloomed in a sea of blood, twitching silent importunities. A green blowfly settled on the tip, turned half a pirouette and dipped its tongue into the blood. As it drank, it grew, obliterating the nose, the blood, the whole ghastly head. It grew fatter, more viscous and taut, until it burst in a crimson explosion.

He opened his eyes.

He had imagined the explosion, but not the taut ball of blood. It filled his cone of vision with its hideous presence. Actuality was more disgusting, more humiliating than his hallucinations. He closed his eyes again to recall the spectres, but for all his efforts, they refused to return. He remembered Piero's agony and anger at the death of his wife. He, too, cursed God for His cruelty, for His deception and His worthlessness. If Tavi died, he promised himself, he would never pray again, never worship, never enter a church as long as he would live. But how long would that be? How could he live, having killed life in Tavi? He could not and he would not try.

The gentle, aristocratic voice of the sister disturbed his resolve.

'I think you might send for your priest and any close relations she may have.'

Her words were a blasphemy.

Tintoretto came first, his face deeply furrowed with grief and despair. They knelt together once more by the bed while the priest celebrated the last rites. His rapid recitation was almost smothered by the quickening gasps from Ottavia's throat.

Domenico and Marco came and wept. Bruno brought the young apprentice, but both were speechless. Sebastiano came, muttering unctuous platitudes. Sophenisba came and stayed, offering copious support and a solid stoicism which carried the suffering Giovanni through the long two days in which Ottavia languished.

Death was a gentle liberator, restoring peace and beauty to her tormented body. Giovanni and Tintoretto witnessed her departure together, bereft of grief and confident of her arrival in paradise. They joined hands across her body in token of their shared loss and mutual sustenance.

They sat on each side of her coffin as it was borne in Luca's boat to the cemetery where he too lay at rest.

On the lonely way home, they wept silently together, conscious that, henceforward, the world would be a darker place.

Giovanni went to collect a few of his things for his period of mourning in Tintoretto's house. There was a chill in the empty bedroom. The coverlet lay flat and uncreased over the bed. On the white walls hung a crucifix and the *Nymph and Satyr*. It halted his preparations and he sat down on the bed and gazed.

He found himself drawn into the frame, beyond the picture plane, where a golden Ottavia sat glowing and full of life. He was transported into a timeless world of beauty, where she was the presiding and pervading deity.

The poignancy of his voyage was unbearable when he returned from Arcadia to the edge of the bed. With firm resolve, he went down to the store for the crate. He lifted the picture into its coffin and nailed down the lid with decisive strokes.

When it was secure, he murmured the words, 'Goodbye, Tavi...' and left the house.

Isolation

The will to work blunted Tintoretto's jagged bereavement, but a comparable will deserted Giovanni. His art, though his in spirit and direction, had been a joint achievement in execution; the result was a cooperation of two absolutely synchronised minds and processes. In life, he and Ottavia were products of each other's influence and interdependence; in work, their individuality may have appeared, to a casual observer, to be divisible, but in fact, each was incapable of making a constructive contribution without the support and participation of the other. With that fragile duality broken, it was not just the will to work which was absent, the ability to work had gone with Ottavia.

In the months which followed that desolate return from the cemetery, Giovanni had shut himself away from everyone who had known and loved Ottavia. The lanes and camps had known her footfall; their gondola had borne her as its cargo; her old home had been her nursery and had witnessed her laughter and her labour; the church had heard her prayers. Each was tainted with memories too painful to be endured; each was ostracised.

Their house, however, saturated with memories of their last days, was tolerable as a hair shirt is to a penitent. Here, he could not forget or forgive himself; here, his private guilt for a private act was privately expiated. In detachment and isolation, he mortified himself daily with recollections of everything she had said or one since their relationship began. He relived each joy and grief, each pleasure and disappointment, each place and person they had known. He was determined that he would not repeat his dismal forgetfulness of his mother. His life, such as it might be, was dedicated to the commemoration and extension of Ottavia's life. No other existence would be viable. The present had no significance, except as a slipway to the past. The pain of reminiscence he welcomed as a memorial of the pain he had given Ottavia. The deteriorating face, the matted hair and beard, the sunken eyes which stared back at him from her hand mirror showed the unmistakable signs of the terrible retribution he deserved. He observed the havoc with some satisfaction.

His days were spent in a shuttered cell, where he was oblivious of the sunlight, the clouds, the showers and the activity of the teeming city. Franco and Giulia came and went unnoticed, she leaving food and drink in the anteroom from time to time to replace a half-empty bowl or pitcher, but they rarely met their master, nor did they notice his condition. With all the devious skill of practised incompetents, they avoided anything which might disturb their luxurious indolence, anything which might threaten their sinecure. They enjoyed security of tenure without responsibility, and they displayed their satisfaction in contempt rather than gratitude.

When he reached the margin of debility and degradation, Giulia approached him with a complaint and a proposal.

'I find I can't manage this house any more, let alone look after you,' she said acidly. 'I need help. Now, there's a young niece of mine who needs a job, and she would do very well.'

Domestic details held no interest for Giovanni. He could not understand her complaint, nor her proposal to increase his staff. Such matters were tiresome and irrelevant. 'Do as you please,' he said indifferently.

He wished only to be left alone. He felt insulted and he could not look at her. He was alarmed by his intense hatred for her.

'Is that all you have to say? What about her wages, then? She can't be expected to work here and wait on you for nothing.'

There seemed no justification for either duty as far as he could see, but his overriding impulse was to separate himself from the woman who had failed Ottavia in her night of desperate need. The sullen face and graceless manner were offensive to him.

'She will be paid, don't worry.'

'But how much? She's not just a skivvy, you know. She's an experienced servant.'

It was a lie which required declamation as camouflage. Giovanni quoted a figure far beyond her expectation to encourage her departure. It had the desired effect, and as a bonus, almost silenced her.

'That's all right, then. I'll tell her to come straight away.'

Even in shock, her facility for lying did not desert her, for the girl was already in the house and had been a party to the plot which, they hoped, would install her as the Cavaliere's concubine. An experienced whore, she had traded with visiting sailors since she was twelve, and ten years of industry had added twenty to her appearance. Her face seemed permanently buckled.

Giulia hurried downstairs; the news was too good to be delayed.

'Lisa, it's all arranged, and you'll never guess what he's going to pay you.' Lisa's face distorted further with avarice and astonishment at the promise of riches beyond the grasp of a common whore, even in a port as bountiful as Venice.

'What else did he say?' she asked, picking her nose.

'Not much. He couldn't really be bothered.'

'We'll soon change all that, won't we?' she giggled.

Franco agreed loudly and poured another brimming goblet of wine for each of them.

'We'll take him out to sea,' he said, using a figure of speech familiar among Venetian villains. 'Saluté!'

'Saluté!'

They drained the goblets lustily.

Lisa explored the rest of the house with feelings bordering on awe, and chose a room for herself which she decorated with souvenirs, gaudy trinkets and potions she had collected during her former employment. She glowed expansively at the prospect of a new life of comfort and luxury, and her advancement from strumpet to courtesan, and perhaps, mistress of a fine house.

She decked herself garishly to take a supper tray to Giovanni. She knocked on the door and slid into the darkened room.

'I've brought you some lovely broth,' she said, placing the tray on the table. She was not aware that the dark heap in the chair was her new master. 'Christ! It stinks in here! I'll open the shutters so you can see.'

She stumbled towards the vertical slits of light, groping nervously. When she reached the window, she could not unfasten the shutters.

'Don't do that! Leave them alone,' growled Giovanni.

She could only guess his location from the direction of his voice, but she continued to fumble with the unfamiliar catches.

'Leave them alone,' I said.

'But you need some light in here…'

'I don't! Now get out!' he said imperiously. He became rigid with rage.

She paused, surprised by his tone of voice. Discretion seemed prudent, but her wiles were not yet exhausted, nor was her patience.

'All right,' she said, 'but I'll be back later when you have finished.'

She was not accustomed to being deferential; her trade had given her little experience in courtesy, but she could not understand why her best manners provoked such a hostile response. She left him alone, prepared to try again.

'He's a queer one, isn't he?' she announced when she returned to the kitchen. 'Why doesn't he like daylight?'

'There's no telling,' said Giulia. 'He's half off his head, but he's not violent, so don't worry.'

'I'm not worried, but he got quite angry when I wanted to open a window. Very queer!'

'I'm surprised he spoke to you at all. He never says anything to me.'

An hour later, she returned for the tray, resolved to make better progress. The fish soup was untouched and coated with floes of grease.

'You haven't eaten a thing,' she wheedled. 'That's very naughty of you!'

Giovanni heard nothing. He was in Piero's garden with Aphrodite.

'You must eat something, you know. You have to keep your strength up, or you'll be ill. Shall I pour you some wine?'

Her prattle had rudely ejected him from Rome.

'No! I have all I want. Just leave me.'

Until now, he had not looked at her, but to emphasise his words, her turned in her direction.

She stood like a rustic dancer, hands on hips, her skirt hitched up to her knees and one shoulder bared. Her mouth and cheeks were stained scarlet and her bleached hair was frizzled and be-ribboned.

'God in heaven!' moaned Giovanni. 'Are you Giulia's niece?'

'Yes, Cavaliere. I've come to look after you.'

She undulated her hips, signalling inducements. Her tongue lolled in the corner of her open mouth.

As if scalded by hot water, he leapt from his chair and flung open the door.

'Giulia!' he roared. 'Giulia!'

He paced the room furiously.

She appeared with a broom and a scowl.

'Giulia, will you keep this woman out of my sight. I never want to see her again; do you understand? If I do, I may do her an injury.'

'If you do, you'll be in trouble, I can tell you,' she crowed. 'You'll be had up for assault and go to prison, I shouldn't wonder. And that would look well in a Cavaliere, wouldn't it?'

'Just keep her out of my way, that's all.'

'I can't do that. I'm too busy looking after the house, most of the time. She'll have to bring you your food, or do you prefer to starve?'

He felt impotent; trapped between Lisa's blatant seduction and Giulia's insolent authority. He could not escape their determination, nor penetrate their secret. As the spring tightened, frustration and disgust rose like vomit. 'G–get out! – Both of you!' he stammered.

He tried to marshal his thoughts to evade their trap, but he knew he was helpless. He suspected that their plan, whatever it might be, was well prepared, and he knew he must either outwit them or be reconciled to having his solitude despoiled by domestic trivia and strife; perhaps to having his house infested by more of Giulia's kin. The only solution was to rid himself of all three of them, then he could be left alone in uninterrupted penance. He would dismiss them in the morning.

He sat in his chair through the night of blessed silence, reliving their second visit to Florence. He walked the quiet cloisters of the Ognissanti with Ottavia – placid, fastidious Ottavia – and stood before Ghirlandaio's *Last Supper* with her in wrapt devotion. They dined with the Bardellis, and learned Tuscan songs of chivalry and love, which Ottavia accompanied on a borrowed lute with haunting delicacy. They examined the angel which the young apprentice, Leonardo, had painted in the corner of his master's picture of the Baptism. The fragile grace of the angel sapped the masculine power of Christ and St John till they became mere furniture. They read Vasari's account of Verrocchio's anger at being outstripped by the mastery of the boy's drawing. It was the first flowering of da Vinci's genius; that precious quality which the apprentice had, and, for all his experience, the master did not, Genius could be recognised, but not fabricated or explained. It was, Palestrina insisted, God's gift to a chosen few, which isolated them from their fellow workers, gave them immortality – and pain.

He composed some lines in his head which hinted at the distinction between the gift and mere talent. By candlelight, he wrote them on a piece of paper. He altered a few words, cut a quill and rewrote them carefully on a scrap of vellum in a laborious Chancery script.

Verrocchio sits in his studio
Modelling a putto
With partridge's wings
And buttocks like plums
For a Medici's pleasure.

Before him hangs a Saviour
With blood like Chianti
And calm eyes against
A luminous Tuscan sky
For the monks of San Donato.
Behind him with swinging fish
Tobias and celestial guide
Stride in arabesques
Of elegant drapery
For a Florentine notary.

In the corner his pupil
Leonardo from Vinci
Ellipses a nimbus
Over his angel
And dreams of flying
Of ships under water
And mechanised war…

While Verrocchio dreams
Of fish in the Arno
Of partridges, plums
And Chianti.

At the head, in capital letters, he wrote the word *Genius*, and underlined it.

It was the first task of any kind he had attempted for over a year, and his hands had become intractable with inactivity. It was also his first attempt to compose words, and he was not displeased. At first light, he opened a shutter and peered out on to a deserted canal, scumbled with wisps of morning mist. The world he had deserted was indifferent to his presence; he was merely an inertial witness of its forms and colours. He had caught it unawares, and he felt a certain pleasure in being unnoticed and uninvolved.

Giulia came into the studio carrying a tray, banged it on the table and turned to leave. Her silence rang with contempt.

'Just a moment, Giulia. I'm sorry I was angry last night. I shouldn't have lost my temper.' She had not expected an apology. She grunted a semblance of acceptance or acknowledgement and made to leave once more. 'But will you tell Lisa to have a wash and smarten herself up. She really does look a mess.'

Giulia took refuge behind a barrage of indignation.

'My God! Look who's talking. *You* are the biggest mess I have seen for years. Just look at yourself before you criticise others.'

'That's not the point. In my own house, I can do as I please. She's a servant in my house, and *she* will do as I please.'

'Oh! So that's it! I see. We're only servants, at your beck and call. We've got no rights or feelings at all, I suppose.' Her voice rose in a piercing crescendo.

'I didn't mean you had no rights or feelings. All I meant was that I wanted Lisa to look wholesome and behave properly. That isn't asking very much, surely.'

Giulia realised that her stratagem was not seriously threatened and she quelled her fury. She went down to the kitchen where the other two were eating quantities of fried liver.

'It's going to be all right,' she said. 'He's in a better mood this morning, so you can go and get his tray later.' She filled her mouth. 'But he says he wants you to smarten yourself up. So humour him, will you?' She sucked at the fat which ran down her chin.

'All right,' said Lisa, 'but he scares me. There's a wild look in his eye when he's angry.'

'He's quiet enough now. I think he fancies you, really,' Giulia added.

Lisa grinned. 'What was his wife like?'

'Wife!' snorted Giulia. 'That's a good one, they weren't married. They were half-brother and sister.'

The scarlet gash spread across Lisa's face again. 'So he was screwing his sister, was he? He won't be difficult, then.'

A scheme began to form in her mind which would advance her cause and hasten the conclusion. She went upstairs.

Giovanni had brushed his matted hair and washed his face in cold water. His beard was too barbarous to respond to any but drastic treatment, but combed, it resembled that of Christ.

The sunlight crept across the studio floor, suspending the dust raised by his movements in a dry mist. His eyes smarted at the brightness. He sat down and, with some difficulty, read over his verses. He felt the stirring of modest pleasure and he felt that Ottavia shared it with him. He looked up as the door opened.

In the half-shadow stood Ottavia! She had come back to him. She was not dead, but here with him again. His eyes moved incredulously up the familiar brocade. Ottavia's hips, her waist, her breast, her shoulders – were crowned by Lisa's leering face. The travesty was loathsome, repellent. His gut contracted and paralysed his throat. His eyes burned with disbelief and fury.

The hideous grin advanced.

His hand was guided to the scrivener's knife on the table; his fingers fastened around it. With a cry of an enraged animal, he hurled himself through the crimson curtain, flailing the blade in wild sweeps before him. The door slammed in front of him and he heard the clatter of Lisa's feet fleeing to the kitchen.

'He went for me with a knife,' she panted.

'Serves you right, you stupid bitch! Fancy dressing in her clothes. Haven't you got any sense?'

'I thought he would like me in one of her dresses…'

'You've got no idea, have you? You'll get us all kicked out, you will.'

They could hear the pacing above and the spasmodic cries of agony from the torturer's victim. Giulia was worried; Franco, who had said nothing, was furious. They both expected expulsion before the day was out.

'How was I to know?' protested Lisa, sobbing.

'Take it off now and I'll put it back in a minute.'

Lisa undid the fastenings, edged her shoulders out and let the brocade fall around her feet. Giulia picked it up.

'On second thoughts,' she said, 'we might get a good price for this. He'll never miss it.'

Giovanni had latched the shutters and reclaimed his darkness. He sat in his chair, stupefied by the grotesque impersonation which had assaulted his brief excursion into daylight. He could not decide if it was an apparition, a demon from a nightmare or something monstrously substantial. His memory and his perception would not disentangle the truth. He shook his head to rid it of the clouds of dry mist which hung there, shimmering like the motes in the sunbeam, but instead of clarity, there was deeper confusion. Helpless and desolate, he sobbed in awful frustration, vainly calling Tavi's name. The masquerade was over, but its consequence was terrible.

Tintoretto's patience and anxiety finally burst into action. He had seen nothing of Giovanni for several months, but his paternal thoughts were never far from the young man's anguish; his concern constantly distracted his concentration.

He appeared at the house and demanded to see the Cavaliere.

Giulia resented his intrusion and was foolish enough to show it.

'Woman, tell your master that I am here, and be quick about it.'

She pared her nails with a fork, chewing noisily. 'And who shall I say wishes to see him?' she asked, shamming ignorance.

'Maestro Jacopo Robusti, you impudent harridan!' he roared.

'Wait here, then and I'll see if the Cavaliere is at home.'

'No, I won't!' He pushed past her. 'I will show myself up.' Even in old age, he was still a striking figure, with a formidable strength of purpose to match his physical strength.

'All right, please yourself,' she said, acknowledging defeat with her usual gracelessness.

He was appalled by what he found in the studio. The dark, the dirt and the fetid air revolted him. The floor was littered with scraps of paper and indeterminate rubbish; greasy plates with mouldering remnants of food covered the table, and a crock of urine in the corner brimmed malevolently.

'In Christ's name! What has happened here?' he said. He crossed to the window to open the shutters.

'Please, Father, don't open them. Please!'

'Don't be such a fool!' he said cogently. 'I need some light, even if you don't.'

He flung open the shutters and windows and inhaled deeply. Light and fresh air poured in, disturbing Giovanni profoundly. He covered his face to conceal his eyes and his shame.

Tintoretto looked at his son and was shocked by his appearance. His natural affection could not be expressed in terms of the concern and compassion he felt. This tragedy of degradation demanded sterner treatment, but he did not know exactly how to employ it, or what effect – if any – it might have.

'Get your things together, my boy. You are coming home with me.'

'No, Father, please leave me alone. I only want to be left alone.'

'Rubbish! You are coming with me!' he repeated more firmly.

'Please, Father,' he begged. 'This is my home.'

'Damn you, Giovanni! I *need* you!'

Tears flooded the old man's eyes. His cruelty and his lie were alien to his true feelings and he felt ashamed. Giovanni uncovered his trembling face and looked at Jacopo. He saw the tears.

'Did you say you needed me?'

'Yes, I did. I cannot wait any longer. I need your help.' He sat down and took Giovanni's hand in his. 'I have never asked you for anything before, so don't reject me when I do.'

'Father, I am sorry. What can I do?'

'First, you must come with me. I cannot explain it here.'

'I must change and put a few things into a bag, but it won't take me long. Would you like to wait here a moment?'

'No, I will come with you.'

They went up the stairs together. Giovanni opened the cassone where his clothes were kept. It was empty.

'I don't understand,' he said, quite bewildered.

He opened Ottavia's cassone. That was empty too.

'Where has everything gone?'

He opened a cupboard and pulled out the drawers. They were empty. Tintoretto realised what had happened. 'Those damned servants of yours have stolen everything. Get them!'

Giovanni called down the stairs, but there was no reply. The house was deserted.

'Where's your money, Gianni?' asked Jacopo with an expression of grave anxiety.

'Some of it was here, but most of it is in the studio.'

'Go and see, quickly!'

The leather bags of coins were still in the cupboard below. They had not found it all. Giovanni inhaled sharply with relief.

'Thank God you stayed in here,' said Jacopo, 'or they would have got it all. I will tell the city guards; they cannot have gone very far.'

'Don't bother, Father, I am glad to see their backs. It's good riddance to the three of them. They have saved me the trouble of sacking them!'

Jacopo could not understand why he had not dismissed them before, but decided not to enquire. To him, they were voracious parasites, and that offended his regard for the host and his sense of justice.

There was nothing for Giovanni to carry but his bags of gold, so he locked the house and left with little regret, holding on to his father for support. The muscles in his legs had atrophied, and he staggered with weakness. Jacopo tried to invent some plausible need he had of Giovanni. The first part of his mission was accomplished; the second demanded more ingenuity. The short walk was long enough for one of his fertile imagination.

Once at home, he explained.

'I am getting old and near the end, but I have one big commission to do before I die, and I want it to be well done, so that I can go to God without shame,' he began. 'I have two large canvases to do for San Giorgio Maggiore, to be set on each side of the altar. An Old Testament subject – The Gathering of the Manna, and a New Testament one – The Last Supper. The boys are too busy on other pictures, but in any case, I would like to finish my labours on this earth with you painting by my side. What do you say?'

'Of course I will help if I can, but I haven't painted for a long time, and I won't be up to your standard by a long way. But I will certainly do the rough work for you.'

'We'll see how it goes. You will soon get into the way of swinging a paintbrush again. So don't worry about that.'

'Have you done any sketches yet?'

'Only a few drawings. Mind you, I have done the Last Supper many times before, so I want this one to include all the improvements I can manage.'

He produced some chalk drawings of the two compositions and studies for some of the individual figures.

'I like them,' said Giovanni. 'They are very strong and full of movement. How big will they be?'

'About twenty feet long, twelve high.'

'And about twenty major figures in each. It's a big job.'

'Yes, it is, but working together will reduce the tedium, and I do want them to be the crowning works of my life. Together, we can do it, I know.'

Giovanni was very uncertain of his own ability, but Jacopo had made it clear that he needed his help and he was determined to do all he could. He was awed and daunted by the vitality of the designs. They were so typical of Tintoretto and so unlike the style he and Ottavia had developed, but that had gone, beyond his reach, beyond recall. Could he meet the tremendous responsibility which had been laid upon him? He was not sure.

The canvases were stretched, primed and set up each side of the studio. For Giovanni, the area was daunting too, for he had not worked on such a scale for years. Jacopo handed him a drawing of the Old Testament subject.

'Would you like to rough in the main lines of this?' he said, 'and I'll make a start on the Last Supper.'

The great project had begun.

Giovanni measured an initial triangle, based on the bottom of the canvas, with its apex inside the top edge. This would contain all the important figures from foreground to distance. Tentatively, he marked the positions of individual figures and landscape features. The sides of the design were enclosed in parenthetical curves, which also linked front and back. Upon these lines, he calculated and marked the positions of subsidiary lines and major figures. With the geography of the design accurately constructed, he climbed off the trestle to view the whole from a distance.

To his astonishment, he found that Jacopo had completed his network of lines and was already drawing figures into the spaces he had created. The perspective was firmly established in a great diagonal, thrusting across the picture. In half a morning, an intelligible, coherent space was animated with human activity.

When they broke off at midday, Giovanni felt the need for a sound and agreed working arrangement.

'Father, do you want to put your own figures into my framework, or do you want me to carry on further?'

'I don't really know,' he replied thoughtfully. His creative rhythm had become synchronised with those in the Upper Room, and he was reluctant to adjust to another. 'You carry on at your own speed and in your own way and we'll see how things shape up later. You are perfectly capable, you know, of doing the whole thing yourself. If I'd wanted a mere apprentice, I would have got one.'

'But you will have finished yours long before I am halfway through.'

'That doesn't matter. If I am idle, I can help you; if you get bored with a diet of Manna, you can help me. I prefer flexible arrangements, don't you?'

'Well, not as a rule. I like to know in advance what the limitations are, how much room there is for manoeuvre; then I can adjust from the start and work towards a clearly defined objective.'

'That's not my way! I like to keep as many options open as possible, then if a good idea presents itself, at any stage, I can incorporate it on an impulse.'

Giovanni smiled. He had seen him add ships, camels, buildings and still life groups to pictures where no provision had been made for them in the sketches. The excitement of creation and the rhythmical execution became identical and were visible in the finished work, and, for this, Tintoretto was widely and justly celebrated. But he knew that such a loose, casual approach would not work for him; his success was born of discipline and methodical application.

During the ensuing weeks, Jacopo injected more and still more vitality into his picture. With reckless surgery, he cut away things which seemed perfectly suitable, opening up spaces for even more energetic, more effective additions. Figures swung this way and that; front views became back views; shadows were brightened with pools of light; lights were extinguished in whirling gestures of his arm. The whole picture was modelled as if the material was moist, coloured wax.

Giovanni could neither compete nor keep abreast with this feverish spontaneity, and he did not attempt it. But with cautious imitation, he achieved something which complemented the vitality and tension of the Last Supper. Jacopo was pleased with the progress of both canvases and he was an agreeably surprised at the successful pastiche which Giovanni achieved. Furthermore, he was delighted that he had contrived to restore Giovanni's interest in living and working. His perjury was vindicated.

When the canvases were nearing completion, Jacopo threw down his brush and palette without warning.

'That's enough for now. Let us go away from here and take stock.'

'But for you, the end is in sight...'

'That's exactly why we need a break. It's the final touches which go on top, remember, so they have to be good, the best. We don't want to do those when we're jaded or less alert.'

They walked the lanes and squares which were damp and dull with winter mist. The city contrasted with the sparkling light in the pictures they had locked away; here, everything was a pale monochrome. The swollen waters had crept in at many a doorway; gondolas rode high alt their mooring posts. Work had been suspended on the new Rialto Bridge and boats moved silently beneath its huge arch. The city had been washed over in grey, obliterating height and distance. Campaniles rose into the sodden air and were suddenly truncated; the Grand Canal had lost its majestic sweep and ended abruptly a few yards away where boats mysteriously materialised or vanished.

'This always reminds me of Mantua, you know. A terrible place in winter; it's like this for months on end.'

He pulled his fur-lined cloak around his body, his hands concealed inside.

'I don't mind this as much as you do,' said Giovanni. 'I find that this shortening of distance concentrates my attention on things which are near, and I see them differently, more acutely than I do in full sunlight. And then, I like to focus on the edge of visibility. Curious things happen there, magical things which hover between being and not being. Reality becomes strangely insubstantial and I can perceive its essence.'

'That seems almost morbid to me. I like to feel the sun warming my back. I like the richness of full light shining on surfaces and textures. I like the flash of light against a depth of shadow. I like the fanfare of bright colours against a neutral background, that's reality for me! Everything expands in warmth and light; in this, everything contracts, becomes lean and mean, and so do I.'

They had reached the Piazza San Marco. The domes of the basilica had evaporated; the campanile was a squat stump; the clock tower had no clock face, and the gilded Virgin enthroned above it had retired from earthly veneration.

Water covered the paving, making the piazzetta a sullen tributary of the Grand Canal, and the bases of the pillars of the Palazzo

Ducale were submerged, reducing the columns to an absurd proportion. The boarded footways regimented pedestrian freedom to a shuffling, grey procession, accentuating the chill misery which hung over the place. Giovanni shivered.

'Today, I agree with you,' he said. 'Let's go home.'

They sat on each side of a massive fire, piled high with ancient timber which once had formed the spars and planks of Venetian war galleys, perhaps from ships which triumphed at Lepanto. They watched the flames curl round the baulks and through the holes bored long ago by shipwrights of the Arsenal. There was a pathos in their final, ignoble destruction which both men felt, but neither spoke of. Here was a stark reminder of the ephemeral nature of pride and power, an intimation of mortality.

Jacopo felt saddened by his impending departure from this life; a life he had enjoyed, a life of service, a life of extraordinary intensity and achievement. He was not a wealthy man, but he had been richly blessed. God had been good to him and he had no doubt that He would be merciful and grant him forgiveness and peace. He looked towards Giovanni, the son he loved most of all, and though not of his issue, then surely his artistic progeny. God had, in his wisdom, been harsh to the boy, taking first his mother and then his loved one. That reflective face was scarred, not with age, but with hellish sorrow. The gentle expression and fine features had been remodelled by the hand of tragedy into an empty mask of melancholy which faith or love could not restore. Youth had been annihilated by a fire which burned within, like the timbers in the hearth which flamed no more, but glowed hotter beneath a covering of dead ash.

The desolation of the victim's future was as inevitable as the proximity of his own death, and his helplessness in mitigating it distressed Jacopo profoundly. He grieved, not for himself or his passing, but that his death would remove the only buttress which supported the leaning tower. Collapse seemed as inescapable as destiny.

The timbers settled in the hearth. An inverted Pentecost streamed up the chimney.

Giovanni pondered on the transitoriness of happiness. The house which had been his home and the scene of his adoption and early success was his home no longer. He was a guest of his father's, sharing his fire, accepting his hospitality, without belonging. He saw in the fire, not the blessing of warmth, but the consuming power of elemental forces, reducing solid matter to feeble ash. All physical strength was subject to an irresistible destruction, not from the superior strength of other matter, but from forces which thrived upon it, having no power of their own. The inherent weakness of matter was that it carried potential obliteration in its very structure. Decay was the dissolution of structure by a slow, but inexorable process; fire effected destruction by a rapid, inexorable process. He recognised in Jacopo the fire; in himself decay.

Could this phenomenon apply equally to abstractions like peace and love and happiness? Did spiritual strength also contain its own potential destruction? He thought of Piero and Palestrina, their impressive faith and confidence, but he could not answer his questions.

He looked across to the old man opposite. The tentacles of death were closing around him, restricting his movement and his breathing. The old stamina was fading fast, and although the eye burned brightly, it was the last, brave glow before extinction. But the prodigious energy, physical and spiritual, had been fixed in paint, and that would remain when the body which transmitted it became as feeble as ash. But the physical nature of paint and canvas implied its own mortality, and that too would suffer corruption – and then? Oblivion?

The spectre of death inhabited them both, but in his master, father and friend it was actively fanning the fire of extinction; in himself, it lay like a malevolent foetus, which stirred to remind him of its tenure and its fecundity.

Weary with exertion and the heaviness of their thoughts, they left the dying hearth and went to bed.

It was a combination of faith and industry which had kept Jacopo's spirits resilient all his life. Like all sensitive individuals, he was moody and responsive to external circumstances, but the sheet anchor of his talent prevented him from drifting into moroseness. The worlds he created in paint were to him more stable, more dependable than the external world; the control was his alone. His Last Supper was a compelling master, demanding his labour and his concentration, and refusing to condone slackness or tardiness.

The canvases sanctified the studio with anthems of gorgeous colour and the incense of resinous varnish. He studied Giovanni's work with the pleasure he always felt for a well-wrought chair or boat. The craftsmanship was impeccable, but where was the vital spark? The figures seemed to be trapped in a quagmire; their gestures were merely rhetorical, lacking credible purpose. However, it was far from finished and he reserved his judgement. His own picture had exactly the drama, the mystery and the involvement of real people that he had envisaged. It was the distillation of the excellences of many versions of the subject, stretching back over his career, and false modesty would not restrain his jubilant satisfaction. He was within a few days of realising his final ideas on the subject, and he was thrilled at the prospect.

Giovanni joined him.

'Well, Father, are you pleased so far?'

'Yes, I am. Things have gone very well, but I am concerned about the top right-hand corner.' He pointed to the area where the shadowed end wall joined the coffered ceiling.

'What's the problem then?'

'I don't want to make it brighter, or it will steal some of the light from Our Lord, but the space as it is dwarfs the figures at the far end of the table.'

'I thought you were going to hang a light there,' said Giovanni, referring to the sketch.

'So did I, but it will have to be very small or very dim. I'll think about it...'

They turned away, each to his own task, Giovanni to reducing distant figures with cool glazes; Jacopo to adding clear glass carafes of water to the table. With a white brush in one hand and a blue-grey in the other, he swung his wrist effortlessly round the pear-shaped fullness and drew slender necks up into elliptical rims. He drew in paint, outlining the shape only, creating a crystalline transparency. He placed decisive highlights inside the contours and the carafes sprang into relief; the form, the texture and the shadows were defined simultaneously with sleight of hand.

An idea came to him like a visitation of the Holy Spirit which was immanent in his painting. He mixed a generous heap of yellow ochre and white, diluted it to a creamy consistency and climbed on to the trestle. Unnoticed, he crossed himself, and attacked the canvas with bold sweeps of linear colour. His arm flowed freely like water round boulders. Suddenly, he burst out singing the hosanna from the Mass.

Giovanni turned back to witness the arrival of a radiant, floating angel, arms and wings outstretched in adoration and joy. Mesmerised by the speed and vitality of the drawing, he stood, enveloped by the miracle. Divine faces and heavenly bodies were amazingly foreshortened and imbued with weightless, graceful movement. Accompanied by breathless hosannas, another translucent angel appeared, hovering above the head of Christ and illuminated by the light of his halo. A whole choir of lesser angels haloed the hanging lamp, drawing off individual tongues of flame.

Jacopo paused, smiling. 'You see, I couldn't have done that yesterday. There was no fire in my belly!' He looked towards his immobile spectator. 'Well, what do you think?'

Giovanni could not express his reaction. There were no words he knew or phrases he could conjure which had any correlation with his feelings.

Jacopo climbed down to view his work. Giovanni met him in the open space which separated genius from talent and held the old man in his arms.

The paintings were completed within a few days. Tintoretto worked over the Manna picture, distributing the sparks of genius sparingly, partly because he was satisfied with Giovanni's adherence to his sketches and the conscientious emulation of his technique, and partly because *The Last Supper* came so close to his expectations.

It presented a culmination of a lifetime of painting. It summarised his attitudes to design and colour and drawing, epitomised his dazzling craftsmanship and his ability to invigorate a familiar, even hackneyed subject with his experience of life and his personal piety. He knew its merit; he knew it was one of the very best things he had ever done, and he accepted that its companion would have been inferior if he had painted it all himself. He did not feel the usual restlessness and emptiness at the end of this project; on the contrary, he felt elated and gratified. He had crowned his career of over fifty years with a tour de force.

'Giovanni, I am so very grateful to you for helping me through the last few months. I could not have done it all myself, you know.'

'And I am grateful to you for the chance to watch you at work again. Your picture is magnificent... overwhelming,' said Giovanni, who tried to pull adequate words upwards from the depths of his feelings. 'I only wish *The Gathering of the Manna* could have been *half* as good.'

'It *is* good, and you have no need to think otherwise, and certainly no need to feel that you have let me down in any way. I couldn't have done it better myself.'

'I'm sure you could.' Giovanni shook his head to emphasise his heartfelt denial.

'Lightning doesn't strike in the same place twice, you know.' Jacopo shook his head in mimicry. 'Don't forget that I had done at least a dozen Last Suppers before. I knew the subject inside out, and I had made all the possible mistakes, so this one was quite easy. But I had only done the Manna once before, for San Rocco, so there would have been plenty of weaknesses there, even if I had painted it all myself.' He fingered his beard. 'And if I had to start on it now, I don't think I have the strength to finish it.'

'But it just hasn't got your flair, your vitality, has it?'

Jacopo did not answer, though he could easily have agreed. He changed the subject.

'I would like to have a studio party to celebrate, but I am too tired. My joints have stiffened this winter, and what I need most is rest and peace.'

Giovanni was suddenly aware of the Maestro's frailty. He was drained by his devout efforts to confer his own glory on that Upper Room. The flame was flickering now.

'To be honest, I don't feel like a celebration either. I think we deserve a little luxury and a little pampering.'

They went out just once, to see their canvases in position, to the north and south of the high altar of San Giorgio. The intensity of the conception and the brilliance of the performance had added a dramatic crown to Palladio's austere interior. The sumptuous colours and dynamic rhythms contrasted with the pure white stone in a great paean of praise to God Almighty. It was a sacrament in paint.

The old man leaned heavily on Giovanni's arm as they stood silently at the altar steps, and as they left the church, full of gratitude and satisfaction, they both knew that Tintoretto would paint no more.

They read and talked and played a few duets, but Jacopo felt that his last mission on earth was to inspire some optimism, some faith into Giovanni's shattered life, before solitude embraced him again. Conscious of a handicapped race with time, he was sometimes clumsy, sometimes blatant in his attempt, but now, for the first time in his life, he cared more for success than finesse.

On the last day of May, in 1594, he died peacefully in the arms of sleep. His favourite pupil, to whom he had given his knowledge, his name, his daughter and his heart, watched and waited with him until the end. His body was taken to his parish church, the Madonna dell'Orto, and there, beneath the benediction of several of his finest pictures, he was buried in his wife's family vault.

The last luminary of that most luminous Golden Age of painting had gone, and his only possible successor was Giovanni, The Lion of Venice.

Epilogue

The life of Venice continued, heedless of the disappearance of her most illustrious painter, His studio was being run by his heir, Domenico, who as an artist, was an excellent organiser. There was work to be completed, but little promise of further commissions, and he viewed the future with some apprehension. There was money owing as well, and little hope of its remittance. Jacopo had often negotiated for a contractual income rather than a fee, and now that he was gone, an important source of revenue had been removed. So it was not entirely altruistic of Tino to offer Giovanni the position of premier painter in the studio. His invitation, however, was gratefully and graciously declined.

Giovanni had returned to his home after the funeral, tacitly acknowledging the totality of his isolation. The last vestige of human intercourse had vanished and there was nothing he felt inclined or able to do which would alter what fate had decreed. He felt no obligation to paint, and it was no part of his debt to his master to continue where he had left off. He could not follow Jacopo's advice to assume his rightful position as the official artist of the Republic and the position in public life which his rank had conferred on him.

The short journey home was symbolic. His roots had been cut through and since there was neither substance nor sustenance for any future eradication elsewhere, his only course was to resume his solitude in his own house. As he unlocked the door and disturbed the rats, the brutal truth closed in, a solid barricade through which he could not pass and over which he could not see. The future was impenetrable, holding neither expectation nor hope.

Awaiting him was a message from Rome that Palestrina had died a few weeks before, but he was inured to loss and had no capacity for further grief. Even his recollections were clouded, and he found it difficult to recall the face of the man with whom he had spent so many hours of stimulating conversation. He feared that a total amnesia might be stalking him, and that soon he might forget Ottavia. The thought was monstrous, but the fear was real.

He went up to the studio which, apart from cobwebs and rat droppings, was exactly as he had left it nearly a year before. His instinctive disgust of the stench, the filth and the tenantry was strongly physical, and it required as much courage as he had to enter. He crossed the room as if walking on broken glass in bare feet; the stiff turds beneath his soles transmitted to his crutch a sensation like vertigo. He could not understand how he could have been so negligent of Ottavia's sole creation. He had desecrated the home she had made with such love and joy. He was bitterly ashamed that he had betrayed the only remaining manifestation of that love.

He opened the shutters.

In addition to his desire to make restitution, he decided that as this was to be the cell for his solitary confinement, he first must clean it. The task took him four days of nauseating labour, during which he unconsciously packed away the brushes, pigments and palettes of his calling.

His modest collection of books relating to anatomy, perspective and architecture was arranged carefully and conveniently on a shelf, but he did not notice the irrational distinction. His pleasure in their appearance and their tactile qualities reminded him of Piero, whom memory had not expunged. He made a second decision. He would increase the size and scope of his collection into a small, select library. Jacopo's generous bequest could not be better used, and it would have given him satisfaction that his money should be spent on companions for Giovanni's life sentence. There was no rational explanation for this decision, apart from the pleasure of acquisition, but subconsciously, he sought consolation where Piero had found it in his isolation.

He visited a bookseller in the Merceria who was able to supply his needs and give advice. He did not know where to begin in building a library, but he caught sight of some books which had incited Piero's enthusiasm for fine printing and binding, and it was the chance reunion with volumes printed by Jenson and

Aldus Manutius that launched him as a bibliophile. He purchased da Spira's *Cicero*, printed in Venice in 1469, Ratdolt's *Eusebius* of 1483, the sublime Jenson's *Nonius* of 1469 and *The Dream of Poliphilus*, published by the great Aldus in 1499. Each was a superb example of Venetian typography, and the illustrations of the last were a perfect complement to the fine, round Roman letter, and a compulsory acquisition for Giovanni.

The text he found difficult to read, being written in an obscure Italian, but the woodcut initials, decorations and classical compositions were of such artistry and invention that they might have been designed by the same master who cut the printer's mark for Aldus the Elder, the dolphin and anchor, so much admired by Piero. Many of the illustrations evoked the antique world of innocence and simple harmony which Giovanni had exemplified in the *Nymph and Satyr*, so he was naturally attracted to the book and he was impatient to uncover its textual secrets.

The Dream of Poliphilus was a romance written by a Venetian Dominican, Fra Francesco Colunna, a man of extraordinary imaginative fertility. It described the adventures of Polifilo, the lover of Polia. He fell asleep and had visions of wild solitudes and architectural fantasies, and met the fair-haired Polia, with whom he fell in love. Together, they visited the Temple of Venus and the enchanted lovers' island of Cythera, where all is harmony and bliss. The hero at last awakens to the song of the nightingale; Polia has vanished and his dream is over.

The wonders of architecture and the marvels of sculpture they discovered on their journey; the fountains and temples, the verdant grass and pleasure grounds they enjoyed; their lavish entertainment by the queen, the sumptuous feast, the splendid vessels and ornaments of her palace, all of these fascinated Giovanni and stirred his recollections. He became immersed in the lyrical tenderness of the story, identifying himself with the hero and Ottavia with the beloved. Their pilgrimage to Florence and Rome was comparable in everything but detail with the travels of the fictitious couple.

The book, he discovered to be a poetic prophesy of his brief love for Ottavia. He read and reread the text, wrestling with its difficulties in the hope of uncovering more of the mystery which lay buried there. Unsealing the mysteries was not a scholarly quest, but a voyage of self-discovery. In monastic seclusion and discipline, he devoted more of every day to its study. He felt certain that enlightenment was within his reach, if only he had the wit to trace the labyrinth.

He learned that Colunna's hopeless passion for a nun was the inspiration of the book, and that, forbidden by their vows to enjoy and fructify their love, he wrote the allegory as a covert expression of his devotion. Her name, Ippolita, was cryptically preserved in the name of the heroine, Polia, and this, and the author's name were joined in an acrostic made from the initials of the thirty-eight chapters: POLIAM FRATER FRANCISCVS COLVNNA PERAMAVIT.

He discovered that Colunna's second passion, for antiquity and the classical aesthetic, was like his own. In love and art, they were brothers. Gradually, he became persuaded that the similarity of the names Ippolita and Ottavia was no coincidence, and that his own beloved was a reincarnation of the hapless nun. Was he more than a spiritual brother of the author? He could not be sure, but he was inclined to think so, and he did find a reassuring explanation of his own reluctance to consummate his love. It seemed probable that it was neither rational propriety nor emotional taboo which had safeguarded Ottavia's virginity. It was destiny.

The decorative backgrounds of the capital letters excited his interest more than the acrostic. He believed that the corroboration lay concealed here, but his efforts to decipher them were fruitless. He redrew them, with and without the letters; he masked off halves and quarters; he studied them through lenses and mirrors, but in spite of his ingenuity, they withheld their secrets. Undeterred by initial failure, he returned to them again and again, driven on by a lust for certainty.

The discoveries he had made induced a peace and a resignation to his lonely grief. As it became clearer to him that destiny had written the scenario of their brief love and savage parting, his culpability diminished. Was it, as Jacopo had asserted, God's will?

To pursue the answer to this, he added a number of theological works to his collection. He consumed them avidly, making notes and pondering the message and the implications of doctrine and exegesis.

There was no enlightenment in either. More questions arose than were allayed. There was an unbridgeable chasm between logic and faith which tormented his mind. He tried to simplify the concepts as he would have simplified a form or an image. He took paper and wrote, without concern for style or literary structure.

If God is Love
then God loves Love
and could not destroy
the thing He loves –
the thing He is.

If God is Love
then God loved Tavi.
If God so loved her
that He wanted her
for Himself and took her,
then God is selfish
and selfishness is
the antithesis
of Love.

So God is not Love
and must be Hate.
If God made us
in His own image
why not hate God and
reciprocating
be more like
Him?

Death and the Christian view of immortality seemed to be inconsistent, and he treated this theme to a similar scrutiny.

If Death is God's gift
of a better life

with Him in paradise,
and we should not mourn
for those He claims,
will He not rejoice
for those who destroy this life
and search for that better life
with Him in paradise?

If Faith is virtuous
in life on earth
then greater Faith
is shown by those
who sacrifice this
earthly life
as Jesus did.

He read over his argument several times, objectively searching for fallacies in his simplistic logic, but found none. He exposed faith to another radical examination, and concluded:

If Faith is blind
and cannot see,
can it be blamed for
fumbling in the wrong direction?
Is 'I believe in God'
the wrong way,
and 'I believe in Satan'
Right?

He did not seek comfort or resolution in atheism, but the search brought him closer to a rational humanism and strengthened his attachment to pagan antiquity. He bought and devoured the writings of Plato, Horace and Ovid, and found in them a dignity and a consistency which was absent in Christian dogma. Nature and intellectual integrity were vastly superior to man's muddled and emotional attempts to draw his ethics from superstition and fear; of this, he was certain. He was forced to cling to his scepticism.

In Plato, he found a compelling analysis of human love as an ascent from the material to the immaterial; an ascent in which the mind is drawn upwards by the love of beauty, to goodness and ultimately, to Absolute Beauty, or God. This was confirmed and developed by Castiglione in *The Courtier*, who insisted that man overcomes his sensuality when his reason makes him aware that beauty is the more perfect when it is divorced from matter; that human love is more perfect when the union of two spirits and wills deposes physical union. In such platonic love, there was a rational explanation of his chaste love for Ottavia that was more attractive and more credible than his theory of reincarnation. Here was an explanation which originated in a pre-Christian, antique world, and one that he could verify from personal experience. Since it accorded closely with Piero's conclusions, he readily acknowledged its wisdom and authority.

But in a clouded corner of his mind there lurked a doubt that the emotions could be so neatly determined by rational analysis alone. In discussion, he and Piero had agreed that a buried Greek statue did not possess the quality of beauty until it was excavated and perceived. Beauty was neither an abstraction inherent in matter, nor an abstraction independent of matter; it was a relationship that existed between the object and the observer, just as love was a relationship between two people, even if one of them was dead. The concept of an Absolute Beauty tantalised him. As a perfectionist, he wanted to embrace it, but he could not believe that the imperfections of man would allow him to perceive it, and if he could not perceive it, he could neither identify it nor respond to it. He retained a trace of scepticism for this too.

The intellectual exercise absorbed him, not for itself, and not as a means of passing time, but as a pursuit of truth and understanding, and to some extent, he found what he pursued. The black waters of guilt which inundated him began to recede. Despair and self-immolation gave way to progressive activity, which, while not organised to any degree, was an avenue and not a prison.

Apart from his journeys to the bookshop, he did not go out. The life of the city and the lavish succession of the state calendar held no interest for him. He was out of phase with time. Church bells announced the seventh day of rest, but each was like the others, spent in reading, making notes and writing for himself alone. But the visits to the Merceria provided him with an occasional opportunity to observe the citizens and visitors who thronged the Rialto and the piazza. Penetrating observation was an essential part of his training, and even though he no longer used it pictorially, he had not lost the capacity to exercise it, and his seclusion had, if anything, increased his objectivity.

He had always loved his native city and been proud of his Venetian origins. Its light, its atmosphere, its splendour and the traditions of its art had made him a painter, had given him wealth and honour; but it too, was dying, physically and spiritually. The momentum of decay could not be arrested. Everything he had known was dead or dying. The terrible pathos of this fact depressed but no longer obsessed him; and as for Venice, he preferred to remember her alive and beautiful than to observe her as a latent corpse.

He decorated some of his non-reading hours with dreams and recollections of her beauty and glory, but they did not materialise in line or colour. They remained non-figurative; evocations, not realisations. In words, he had found a means of directing and clarifying undisciplined speculations. He wondered if the ephemeral nature of fantasies could be enriched and preserved in some sort of verse. Had he the skill to achieve an ordered, lyrical equivalent for the pride, reverence and the sadness which coloured his feelings? Could he transform the written word into an act of praise as Palestrina had done in sound?

Below the heading, *Epitaph for a City*, he wrote, painfully and with hesitation;

A jewelled jewel casket sails serenely
In the luminous lagoon sedately;
A gilded barge that bore the
Treasures of the world's sanity.

Cornice, Dome and Campanile,
Arcaded Palace, Canale Grande

Are etched in the pellucid glass
Of Adriatic ultramarine.

And cerulean sky in lines
Of matchless elegance
And eloquent proportion.

Venice, that braided West and East
With strings of pearls and amethyst;
Joined man and nature in a unity.

Of eternal harmony;
Plaited joy and life and artistry
Into an indivisible trinity.

The drama epilogued, the cast eclipsed
By stupidity and cupidity conjoined,
Only the stage and scenery remain
Where Byzantine splendour courted Gothic grace
In a golden fanfared interlude,
Where Sansovino, Giorgione,
Tintoretto, Gabrieli –
Virtuosi di Venezia –
Walked and worked serenely for the glory
Of La Serenissima.

The page was littered with emendations. The perfection he sought had eluded him, but satisfaction slightly outweighed his disappointment. But was it pretentious, immature? He did not know; but since it was never to be exposed to the criticism of those qualified to judge, it did not matter. Nevertheless, he was irritated by his ignorance, without realising that it implied the judgment of others and the desire to communicate.

Sometimes, in periods of fatigue or idleness, his mind relapsed into personal reminiscence from his daily remembrance of Ottavia. He recalled their triumphs, the adulation, the wonders they had seen, the pleasures they had known, but pleasure could not be restored in solitude. It had always been shared, and now, bisected, it was remote and nebulous, bearing disappointment and revitalising his sense of loss. As thought proceeded, it foundered in a quicksand of melancholy. He would not sacrifice his communion with Ottavia, however; it was the toll demanded for passing into the past, but the pain of it did not diminish, nor did his penitence. He accepted them as he did his artistic inertia; he was the willing victim of his own inaction.

Study and writing were not substitutes for the exercise of his talents. They were born of loneliness and deprivation; they were solitary, private pursuits, and his dissatisfactions with both were neither a rein nor a spur to continuation. As much as anything, they were symbols of a new life of voluntary austerity. Yet the very process of recording ideas preserved and clarified them. As he pinned them down with his pen, his understanding intensified.

His thoughts frequently returned to Rome. Piero, who seemed very close to him in his seclusion, was the centre around which they revolved. His books, his pictures, his garden became tangential excursions which ended only when regret or sorrow closed in and obscured the images. But Giambologna's Aphrodite became clearer with each revolution. His continual study, his idolatry of this figure was incomprehensible to him when he was in Rome, he merely responded to its magnetism without question, without resistance. But now, it appeared to have a profound importance, not only for his art, but for his emotional life as well. It was a personification of his aspirations, his idealism and his abnormalities. Only Tintoretto had appreciated its subtle significance, its enigma as a work of art, and Piero had recognised its superb quality, but no one could have assessed its relevance to Giovanni as an individual. He came to regard it as his muse, a persistent, yet elusive analogue, a benign ghost which refused to be exorcised.

He took a pen and sketched a few barely connected thoughts. He read them over and the shadows brightened. Words generated more ideas and deeper insight. Thoughts fell into phrases, lines and rhythms; the piece gained lucidity with a few amendments and alterations.

When he read it over, he was surprised and pleased with what he had discovered. He had revealed a mystery which previously he had accepted as beyond revelation. The ghost had become substantial. He entitled it *The Enigma*.

> Aphrodite
> Erect and languid in her brimming shell
> Fluid, stabile, her marble lines more mobile
> Than the watery fall from the scalloped pool,
> Suspended between art and life, neither
> Stone nor flesh, sacred nor profane;
> A deity hovering between earth and heaven
> Yet wholly belonging to neither.
>
> My pen resurrects the moment when
> That moulded breast inspired,
> The moment when her gathered hair
> Stirred with mine in the Roman air;
> The moment when those chiselled lips,
> Mute and sterile, smiled for me and
> Spoke to me, alone.
>
> She spoke not of here or hereafter,
> Not of this world, nor of another;
> She spoke, as she stood,
> Of the space in between
> Where dreams and reality mingle,
> Where senses submit to the spirit,
> And the spirit flies up and floats free.
> She opened that uncharted channel,
> Unsounded, unknown, but for me.

There was no need for further revisions. As it was, it demonstrated truths beyond the reach of conscious efforts of understanding. His thoughts had been directed by an unknown force, or perhaps had been invigorated by their own impetus, he did not know. An almost palpable elation flooded him like a cleansing tide, and as he read again, his critical faculty intervened; he changed words here and there on impulse, and it ebbed with an awful inevitability. It was not just the words, the metre which he subjected to scrutiny; the ideas were examined with similar cold objectivity.

His thoughts rolled on, gathering momentum, and disillusionment. Had he been seduced, duped by that gorgeous figure? Was the beauty spurious after all? Was his naivety the cause of his submission rather than the intrinsic qualities of the sculpture? Had his absurd susceptibility ensured her success and his enslavement... to a falsehood? Was his own sensibility constructive or destructive?

His mind heaved with all the ineffectual motion of a pot of maggots, utterly without advancement. He paced the room and looked out of the window, but the world beyond refused to come into focus. He could not allay the incessant wriggling behind his eyes. The maggots drove deeper, yet he was not insensible. He knew that this was a moment of crisis; that he could do nothing until it was resolved. His pulse and his breathing quickened as he recognised that he must find answers to his questions. He was alone; there was no one who could help him. The onus was on him. His pace quickened as he scanned around for some assistance. His books? Prayer? Piero?

He returned to the paper and dipped his pen. The tension slackened. He added the lines in a shaking, ill-formed script.

Enticingly
She cast her net
With casual grace
Enmeshed the fish
That was enraptured
By the fairest predator –
Too fair by far to
Be denied, too fair
To engender fear
In me – prey to
Aphrodite.

He crossed out the title and wrote instead *The Stratagem*.

His doubts and disillusion dissolved.

The realisation that he had been infatuated with beauty was something of a consolation to him. Painting, after all, was artifice, unreal. He *had* been deluded; sincere, but deluded, and now all that was over, banished. He felt relieved and unburdened. In writing, he had exposed the truth; in painting, he had concealed it.

He bitterly regretted the time and the effort he had consumed in aspiring to artistic excellence. His false muse had guided him towards a mirage. Her irresistible blandishments had brought him nothing but money, fame and misery. He was not a man, but a marionette, but, at last, he had cut the strings, and he was free; he was no longer manipulated by her calumnies, by patrons or by visions of perfection. Mental activity had given him more satisfaction and self-respect than manual activity, and above all, it had given him a freedom he had never known before.

Religious belief, and now the art which had once been the pivot of his existence, had been subjected to the same analysis, had been faulted and rejected. The process of stripping myths of their insidious power was not wilfully iconoclastic; he did not seek scepticism, it found him. Nor did he reject indiscriminately. His isolation had not induced resentment for humanity, and while he censured injustice, intolerance and cruelty, he remained, as he had always been, generous and compassionate.

In spite of his humanist predilection, he reached the conclusion that living without any objective, however dimly perceived, was no life at all. Physical labour alone was a treadmill; routine, a debilitating force which denied that dignity to man, without which he lapsed into injustice, intolerance and cruelty.

He observed that the fishermen of Chioggia came in with their catch and went to sea again when it was sold. The gondoliers moved about the city like insects who appeared to be industrious, but achieved nothing. The glass-blowers exercised their craft to provide what their customers would break and replace. Manual work, even of the noblest kind, was not the honourable thing he once believed it to be, and without intellectual or spiritual aspiration, mankind was degraded and mechanised, He envisaged a time when men and women would become subjugated by the toil which a greedy, materialistic society would demand of them. The lot of the galley slave, chained to his oar, would become universal, not from penal, but from social development.

The societies he had observed in Rome and Venice paid lip service to freedom, but thrived on acquisition. Property and competition bedevilled their people and their institutions. Patronage, which he knew so well, was only a polite synonym for avarice. He had so narrowly avoided becoming a victim of its vicious demands. It could have annihilated him, had he been less unfortunate. He became intoxicated by his independence, an independence gained by chance and secured by suffering.

The principle was one of choice. The man who chose to labour was a free man; the man who was obliged to was a slave; the man who was not obliged to but did so, not from choice but from habit, was a moron. He applied his own ethics to this theme and wrote a dissertation which recommended a radical alteration in the education of the young which would provide options based on their varied abilities, and ultimately, an independence similar to his own. It was a classless extension of the qualifications and disciplines defined for the perfect gentleman in *The Courtier* by Castiglione.

He had no intention of publishing his thesis, but neither was he content for it to be confined to paper. He became so certain of its merits that he considered opening his house as a school for the children of the parish. He had no illusions about his abilities to teach, but he had some experience of the Socratic method, and this he would try to develop. His idealism and sense of responsibility encouraged him to believe that he had much to offer the young which would fortify them against the spurious values of the world they were entering. Although his own enlightenment had come too late, he might at least prevent others from being damaged or destroyed.

There were practical matters to be resolved, but he constructed a tentative syllabus which was designed to ensure intellectual and social freedom for his protégés. He carefully prepared the progression of studies, anticipating the tedium which might arise from too much theory. He therefore planned visits to St Mark's to hear music, to churches and Scuoli to see paintings and journeys by boat to study architecture, and above all, journeys to the mainland to study nature. Architecture, as living geometry, would provide the key to mathematics and the language of structure and proportion; painting would reveal the worlds of poetry and myth; music, the power of the emotions and the value of discipline. Each offered a basis of morality, discernment and sensibility, which were his ultimate objectives.

Observation and first-hand experience were to be common to all studies, and conclusions would be drawn from what was seen and heard. He was determined that each exploration should develop from the particular to the general, from the concrete to the abstract. He saw himself as a guide rather than an instructor; leading the young to maturity, not driving them.

He examined the principle from every angle and sought its happiest solution in every branch of study. In formulating objectives for others, he had, incidentally, discovered one for himself.

It was on his return from the bookshop with an armful of volumes that he was presented with a totally unexpected and premature opportunity to apply his theory. In the Campo San Salvatore, he was accosted by an urchin of about ten years old. Begging children were as common as pigeons, and they usually collected for idle or unscrupulous parents, or were exploited, as were prostitutes, by pimps who made a lucrative living from their pathetic importunities. A sound beating was the usual reward for returning empty-handed, so they became proficiently pitiable. This one was typically ragged and thin, with dark, appealing eyes that showed no malice.

He held out a grubby hand towards Giovanni.

'Can I carry your books for you, sir?' he said.

An offer of assistance in the hope of some small reward was unusual. He looked like a beggar, but hid not beg. Giovanni was impressed and intrigued.

'Thank you, child, you may have half of them; the whole pile would be too heavy for you.'

He took the proffered half.

Giovanni was not at ease in casual encounters with children, but he remembered Ottavia's success in engaging them in conversation. The secret, he believed, was to show interest in them and their world without being patronising.

'Tell me, child, where are your parents?'

'I haven't got any, sir,' the boy replied calmly.

'Are they both dead?'

'My mother is; my father is a sailor and he hasn't been home for years.'

'Where do you live then?'

'Nowhere, sir.'

Giovanni was appalled to know that the boy was as isolated as he was, and in some respects, considerably worse off. 'Nowhere?'

'I used to live with my aunt, but she kicked me out.'

'Kicked you out? Why?'

'She said I was old enough to earn my own living.'

'Well, I suppose you are old enough to beg.'

'But I don't beg, sir. I do jobs and sometimes I get paid.'

'What sort of job do you do?'

'Anything. I carry things for people like you, sir. I go on errands and sweep chimneys.'

Conversation was easier than Giovanni expected, but he was deeply disturbed by what he heard and utterly convinced of the boy's truthfulness. He began to feel a responsibility to help in some way, but he could not think of anything he could do. Then an idea came. 'But what would you like to do, if you had the chance?'

'I'd like to be a boatman, but I'm not old enough.'

'Couldn't you get a job helping on a boat, then you would learn enough about it to run your own when you are older?'

'All the boys who work on boats learn from their fathers or uncles, and it's very hard to get work if you're not in the family.'

He was clearly not old enough or strong enough to manage Giovanni's gondola, which had been laid up in the store since Franco's unexpected departure. But the problem was beginning to simplify, even if a solution was evasive.

'If you haven't got a home or family, where do you sleep?'

'There are plenty of places; under bridges, in warehouses. It's not hard to find somewhere.'

'What do you do in winter?'

'If I can't find a store, I hide in a church and sleep under the altar. I can always find somewhere dry.'

His innocent acceptance of such a life of hardship impressed Giovanni further. There was no trace of self-pity or resentment.

They arrived at Giovanni's house. 'Come in, and I'll find you something to eat. You look as if you could do with a proper meal.'

The boy ate ravenously in silence, accepting and devouring everything he was offered. What would Ottavia do in similar circumstances, he wondered. He gave him some coins in excess of the usual tip for such a small service.

'Thank you, sir. You are very kind.'

'Now, listen to me. You say you don't mind what work you do; would you like to stay here and work for me? I will pay you decent wages, and there's a room upstairs you can have. There's not a lot to be done, so what do you say?'

The boy's eyes widened with surprise. 'Thank you, sir. I would like that.'

'First, we must get you some clothes and get rid of those dreadful rags. Come on!'

The new clothes and boots, the washed face and hands gave the hungry-looking lad a presentable, even likeable appearance. He was keen to prove his willingness and performed the tasks he was given with efficiency and enthusiasm. Giovanni saw something of himself in the boy, although their circumstances were very different. His former kindness and generosity revived and his own nature expanded in selfless concern for the waif.

His name was Paolo.

After a few days, Giovanni suggested that they should talk about the future. 'Do you still want to be a boatman?'

'No, sir, I want to work here.'

'What, for the rest of your life?'

'Oh yes, sir.'

Giovanni was astonished by his lack of ambition. 'Wouldn't you like to learn a trade? You could be a carpenter, or a metal-worker, a glass-blower or a mason. If there was something you wanted, I could help you, you know.' Paolo shook his head, suggesting that the choice was overwhelming. 'I think you ought to look around and find something you would like to do. In the meantime, can you read?'

'No, sir.'

'Then I think you should. You will be able to have a much wider choice if you can. I will teach you.'

'Thank you, sir.'

The lessons began almost at once. Giovanni' sense of vocation was stimulated by the urgency of the situation, and he was as thorough as he was patient. The boy had seemed quite intelligent until this time, but there was a part of his brain which had never been exercised, and progress was painfully slow. He continually confused the letters of the alphabet and needed constant reminders of the simplest rules. He could barely absorb one thing a time, and any addition dismissed that previously learned.

Giovanni punctuated the lessons with outings to relieve Paolo's burden of concentration. They spent relaxed days on the islands in the lagoon and on the mainland, wandering the fields, looking for wildflowers and listening to birdsong. At first, they treated their excursions as recreation, but Giovanni planned to introduce a constructive element of discovery and observation. He took paper and chalk to enable him to illustrate explanations of anything which interested Paolo. Without being didactic, he made diagrams of architectural structures and proportion, while Paolo watched in vague fascination.

He laughed scornfully at the crooked campanile at Burano.

'Why doesn't it fall over?' he asked, when his giggling subsided.

'It can probably get further out of true than it is, and still stay upright!' He drew a series of stones plied one above the other, each slightly staggered. 'There comes a point when it loses stability, but until then, the weight above presses it into the ground and keeps it standing.' He paused in his drawing to find that Paolo was following his explanation. 'There's a bell tower in Tuscany,' he went on, 'which looks like this…' He drew the campanile at Pisa. 'It has been out of vertical for about four hundred years now, and it refuses to fall over. The only way they could straighten it would be to take it down and build it again, and they're not likely to do that!'

By the time he had drawn half of the arcading, Paolo's interest had been transferred to a group of men loading a boat.

In preparation for a visit to the Veneto, Giovanni had placed some of his lenses in chamois leather bags, hoping that Paolo would enjoy magnifying insects and plants. He packed them carefully at the bottom of the food basket, without a word. It would be a surprise when the right moment came.

It was a glorious day in early autumn, and the colours of the grasses and foliage on the mainland were pale and delicate before the rich extravagance of the autumn. The arid heat of summer had passed; the air was as clean as chilled white wine.

Giovanni found himself retracing the route he had taken with Ottavia many years before. A strange peace went with him as he became conscious of her company and her support. He could not confide his feelings to a ten-year-old boy; they were too private, even if he could have understood. But his intuition suggested that this would be no ordinary day. The countryside had been more cultivated since that last visit, a noble villa having been built in the district, but he found the same tree without difficulty, the tree where they had discussed their adolescent love and their separation.

A veil of memories hung round the place, screening it from mundane reality.

'Let's rest here for a while,' he said. 'Are you tired?'

'No, sir.'

Paolo dropped casually to the ground, lay on his back and cradled his head in his linked hands. They both gazed up into the canopy above.

'Have you noticed that the sky seems brighter between the leaves than it is in the open?'

'So it is.'

'Do you know why that is?'

Paolo considered for a moment. 'No, sir. Why is it?'

He seemed almost interested.

'You know what it's like when you come out of a dark house into bright sunshine...'

'Yes.'

'What does it feel like?'

'Well, as if the sun burns your eyes.'

'That's right! But what happens if you stay out in the sun?'

'You get used to it.'

'Exactly! So the contrast of the dark indoors with the light outside makes the sun seem brighter. Yes?'

'Yes, sir.'

'So what's the connection with this foliage?'

'Is it that the dark leaves make the light seem brighter?'

'Quite right! And we are in shadow ourselves, aren't we?'

'So we are half indoors.'

Giovanni felt that he had made some progress and Paolo seemed satisfied with his discovery; he continued to look at the moving patches of sky with more concentration than he had shown before.

'Why is it... why is it that light flashing on water seems so bright... it's blinding sometimes?' he asked shyly.

Giovanni was delighted to find that an initial interest was being applied to another situation, but he was doubtful if he could explain it in simple terms.

'Some light comes directly from the sun and the sky; some of it hits a surface and bounces off. That is called reflection. More light bounces off smooth surfaces than rough ones, so what are the smoothest surfaces we know?'

'Glass, polished stone,' he paused with his effort, wrinkling his brow. 'And... metal,' he added triumphantly. 'Well, some metals...'

'Any more?'

'I don't know, sir.'

'What about water, then?'

Paolo thought for a moment. 'Well, that's not smooth, it's wet.'

'Its wetness makes it shiny, though, doesn't it?'

He picked up a pebble and handed it to Paolo. 'What's that for?' he said, taking it.

'Look at its colour and its surface.' He did so. 'Now lick part of it.'

'Why, sir?'

'Just lick it and you will see!'

He put his tongue cautiously on the stone.

'Now it's shiny, isn't it?' Paolo nodded dubiously. 'Put it in the sun and see what happens.'

'It's brighter.'

'Do you see this...?' He pointed to the highlight with a twig. 'Well, that's your spit reflecting more light than the stone, isn't it?'

'I suppose so... but I still don't see why the canals look so bright in the sunshine.'

Giovanni remembered his lenses. He took a magnifying glass out of its bag and handed it to Paolo.

'That's shiny too,' he said smiling.

'I said glass...'

'Yes, but hold it in a patch of sunlight.'

'Now it's shinier.'

'But look at the ground underneath it.'

'It's brighter!'

'Now change the distance between the glass and the ground.'

The light brightened and dimmed as he moved it. Paolo was fascinated.

'You see, the glass brightens the light by bending it. That's not reflection though. It concentrates it into a smaller area.'

Giovanni drew a diagram to show the principle, but it had no meaning for the boy. He struggled to comprehend it, but soon lost interest, and went back to adjusting the gap between the glass and the ground. Giovanni watched as he played with it. He wondered if he should proceed with the explanation of the reflectiveness of water, but decided to postpone it. When Paolo paused with the smallest and brightest concentration, he intervened.

'Hold it there for a minute, Paolo,' he said.

'Why?'

In a few seconds, a thin drift of smoke crept up from the ground.

'It's burning, sir! It's burning!'

The smoke thickened.

'The glass not only concentrates the light of the sun, but it's heat too. It makes the sun hotter in just one small space.'

Soon Paolo's head was enveloped in a blue haze. He coughed and laughed excitedly.

'This is fun!'

'Now be careful, or you will set us both on fire!'

He placed his hand over the glass, shading it.

'Mind out, sir, you'll burn yourself...'

Giovanni ignored the admonition and tried to guide Paolo to another use of the lens.

'You can have fun with a glass in other ways. Go and pick a flower over there, and bring it here.'

'All right!'

He ran back with a few roughly squashed petals in his hand.

'Are we going to burn this too?' he asked impatiently.

'No, let me show you.'

He placed the flower at the appropriate distance from the lens and invited Paolo to look through it.

'Well, what happens?'

'It gets bigger,' he said flatly.

'So if you want to see something very small, you can use one of these.'

Paolo looked disappointed. Giovanni was perplexed.

'Let's find a spider or an ant,' he suggested, acknowledging that the bruised flower was not exactly magical.

The disappointment was not relieved by the variety of exquisite insects they found and magnified, and Paolo was soon bored. He spent the rest of the afternoon smouldering pieces of bark and dried leaves until his hair and clothes reeked of smoke.

On the way home, Giovanni said, 'Look, Paolo, you don't have to call me sir, you know. We are friends, aren't we?'

'Yes, sir. You are my best friend!' And he took his hand.

The spirit of Ottavia had been there, cementing a closer relationship between this oddly paired couple. Giovanni reflected that, while it had not been an intellectual success, something quite as important had arisen between them; a deeper trust and a more natural affection which had nothing to do with charity, given or received. This had been Ottavia's gift, but only Giovanni knew who was the donor.

If for no other reason than to perpetuate her influence, he was determined to do everything possible for this child; to graft on to this young life all that was worthy and precious to him.

They were both aware that the bond which joined them had been reinforced, and they both returned refreshed to the task of conquering the printed word, but not to any noticeable improvement in Paolo's aptitude.

At the end of two months' tuition, Giovanni was exhausted. 'I get the feeling,' he said, 'that you don't really want to read. Am I right?'

Paolo smiled and shrugged his shoulders.

'I don't know,' he said.

'You must know what you want, surely.' The shoulders shrugged again. 'Look, there's a whole world of information, of wonders and excitement in books, just waiting for you. Isn't there anything you want to know?'

'I don't think so.'

'You mean you are content to go through life just as you are now, just getting older? Do you want to be a servant or a master?'

The boy thought for a moment.

'A servant, sir.'

'Why not a master?'

He thought again.

'Because that would be difficult.'

'But anything worthwhile is difficult to start with, but once you've mastered it, it seems easy.'

Giovanni tried to recall what he was like at that age, and to imagine what his own reaction might have been, but he could only suppose that it would have been different.

'Listen,' he said, almost in desperation, 'and I will read you something.'

He picked out *The Dream of Poliphilus* from the shelf, and selecting a passage which he knew almost by heart, read of pyramids and obelisks, mysterious temples with beautiful gates and columns of porphyry. He paraphrased obscurities spontaneously while Paolo looked at the illustrations.

'Is that a real place?' he asked when Giovanni had finished.

'No, not quite. The writer saw it in his mind and wrote it down.'

'So it's not real, then?' His voice was coloured by disappointment.

'No, but there are places nearly as marvellous, real places. Florence, for example, has a building with gates of gold.'

'Solid gold?' asked Paolo excitedly.

'No, not exactly, the gates are bronze covered with gold leaf. They're beautiful. They've been called "The Doors of Paradise".'

'If you go through them, are you in paradise then?'

'No, you can't go through them. They are kept locked.'

'Why do they keep them locked?'

Giovanni could see that this interrogation would not produce the results he hoped for, so he changed direction.

'Would you like to see other places and other people, to travel far away?'

'I don't think so.'

'Why not?'

'Well, all the sailors I know have been to places across the sea, and it doesn't seem to have done them much good. They only want plenty to drink and plenty of women, that's all, and they can get that here.'

'But once you wanted a boat, didn't you?'

'Yes, but only a canal boat. I didn't want to go to sea like my father.'

'And now, you don't even want to do that…'

'No, I only want to stay here with you, Giovanni.'

The touching confession ameliorated Giovanni's frustration somewhat, but he remained saddened by the lack of progress he had made, and the paucity of Paolo's mind. The only thing which had developed was his appetite; he ate everything as if tomorrow threatened starvation. He continued to run errands and to do small jobs about the house as cheerfully as before, but Giovanni's avuncular and educational ambitions were thwarted. He would be patient, however, and not force the pace. He would adopt the gentlest persuasion in the hope that the motivation would eventually grow from within. His fervent sense of vocation was battered, but intact.

He planned another visit to the Veneto. Here, perhaps, he would find Ottavia's support again; here, perhaps, he could build on the limited success of the previous occasion. On the appointed day, it poured with rain. Everything would be drenched, the ground sodden, the trees dripping and the absence of light and colour depressing. It was bitterly cold.

'Let's build a huge fire and spend a quiet day at home,' suggested Giovanni.

Paolo brought timber from the courtyard and, while Giovanni laid sticks and lit them, Paolo went off to fill a basket with meat pasties and fruit. When he returned, the blaze was roaring up the chimney. The first fire of the season had loosened clods of soot and Giovanni was sweeping the hearth and muttering curses. Paolo giggled melodiously.

They placed a Persian rug and a table loaded with food and wine between them and sprawled each side of the hearth, panting.

'What are we going to do, Giovanni?'

'I don't mind. What would you like to do?'

'I don't know.'

'We could talk, play some music, or you could learn to play chess. How does that strike you?'

'Let's have some music.'

Giovanni brought Ottavia's lute, tuned it and started to play.

'When I was in Florence, I learned a song about the knights of old...'

'You are one of those, aren't you?'

'Yes, but in the old days, they rode horses, went to war and rescued maidens who were having a bad time. They were far more interesting.'

He taught Paolo the words of a ballad of chivalry and they sang together while Giovanni played a simple accompaniment. The boy's voice was clear and firm, like an oboe, and he had to be restrained to suit the words. In the quiet passages, Giovanni fancied it was Ottavia singing with him, and at others, he was aware of her presence.

The rain gusted on to the window like handfuls of rice.

'Would you like to play this?' said Giovanni, offering the instrument.

'I'll try, but I won't be any good.'

'You might surprise yourself. You won't know until you have tried.'

He was awkward and his memory precluded any real progress, but he enjoyed himself strumming in a haphazard fashion, as if intrigued that his fingers could produce a sound, any sound.

'You won't be very good the first time,' warned Giovanni, 'but if you practise, you'll get better each time. It won't take long.'

Paolo's interest died and he turned his attention to the pasties.

'I want to talk to you,' began Giovanni, 'and this seems as good a time as any.' Paolo diverted part of his attention to his friend. 'You are a good boy; you're honest, hardworking and cheerful, and you are good company. Up to now you've had a wretched life, without family or anything to look forward to, so I can understand if you cannot see much in the future. But things are different now. You have got a friend, and you can think of me as your family if you like, but your future could be marvellous, if you wanted it to be.'

'How do you mean?'

'Well, I can help you to find the things which will make you happy when you are grown up. Your life could be much better, much happier than mine.'

'Aren't you happy then?'

'No, I haven't known happiness for long time, that is, until you came to live here. You have made my life better, and I would like to do the same for you.'

'But you have, Giovanni! I'm happy now. You've been very good to me. I've never had a friend like you…' The words spilled out in earnest assurance.

'So we have helped each other. That's fine! But what will happen to you when I die? I won't live for ever. So don't you think we ought to look at the future?'

Paolo shrugged his shoulders. Suddenly, Giovanni realised that the boy had no concept of the future. He had spent all his life for the present, in the harsh struggle for survival and he had no faculty for anticipation.

'I want you to become independent, to have a full life. I don't mean just to have *things* – they don't bring happiness. I will leave you this house, so that you will always have a home when I have gone; but a house can be a prison, believe me. You need more than things…'

'I don't know what you mean.'

'Well, I cannot explain it fully, but you are trying to read, and when you can, that will be part of it. Music might be another part. Pictures and buildings might be another part. Travel can make life very interesting, too; meeting and talking to people can give you new ideas, so you never get bored. You might want to marry and have children of your own, and that will be important. Do you see what I mean now?'

'I think so. But how do I get these things?'

'By working for them. They don't just come and give themselves up – you have to hunt them down.'

'But if I get a job, there won't be time, will there?'

'There could be time, if you start early enough. But you have got to *want* them, and go after them.' Paolo's face was blank with incomprehension. 'Have you thought any more about what you would like to do when you are grown up?'

'No, not really, but I think I might like to be a tumbler or a juggler, like those in the piazza.'

'That's fine!' said Giovanni untruthfully. 'But,' he added, 'try to be the best juggler in the world.'

He had occasion shortly after to go to Paolo's room. He was amazed to find it filled with vases, trinkets, gloves, boots, knives, strings of glass beads, bangles and books. It was more like a jackdaw's nest than a boy's room, for most of it was trash, or in the case of the boots and gloves, useless for being unpaired. Almost half of it was feminine in appeal, and then only to females of Lisa's calling.

He shouted for the boy, who ran upstairs promptly.

'Yes, Giovanni,' he said, beaming servility.

'Paolo, what is all this stuff for, and where did it come from?'

He was prepared for prevarication or hostility, but there was neither.

'It's mine, and it came from… different places.'

'You mean, you stole it from different places.'

'Yes, sir.' He looked quite unabashed and totally guiltless, but his words were cautious.

'Don't you know that it's bad to steal?' Giovanni asked sadly.

'It's bad if you get caught. You get whipped then.'

'No, I mean that it's *wrong* to steal. Haven't you been told that?'

'Oh yes! I've been told, but everyone does it.'

'Not everyone, surely? Your aunt didn't steal, did she?'

'Oh yes! She taught me. She threw me out because I wasn't very good at it.'

'God in heaven!' he moaned inwardly. 'Well, I don't steal, do I?'

'No, but you don't need to. You've got everything.'

The crude logic of his answer silenced Giovanni. Why, he wondered, should there be one set of rules for the rich and poor alike. Survival demands different rules from those designed to protect property and ownership; get without rules where would the common good lie, in stealing from everyone? Justice and morality were often incompatible, but he could not circumvent the law because of a flaw in its premises.

He looked around at the bewildering array of loot.

'But you don't *need* all this, do you?' He picked up an unworn woman's glove. 'What possible need have you of this, or this?' He held up a necklace.

The boy was silent, but Giovanni persisted.

'Tell me, why did you steal this?' He pointed to an apothecary's signboard.

'Because it was easy, I suppose.'

'But you've been in this house for weeks now, and you could have stolen anything, that would have been easy too.'

Paolo flushed with indignation. 'I couldn't steal from you, Giovanni, you are my friend.'

'Was the shopkeeper you stole this from your enemy, then?'

'No, but he wasn't my friend either.'

'You just didn't know him, you mean.'

'I suppose so…'

'I still cannot understand why you wanted a string of beads, or a lady's glove.'

'It was easy,' Paolo repeated.

Giovanni sat on the bed, mystified. Stealing for survival, he could understand, even condone; stealing for pointless acquisition, he couldn't. Yet there were Venetian precedents for theft on a grand scale. Doge Dandolo's sack of Constantinople was an infamous crime. Venetians had stolen the treasures of the ancient world to beautify their city. The bodies of St Mark and St Rocco had been stolen from their graves to satisfy Venetian piety and pride. Patriotic though he was, he regarded such adventures as disgraceful. It was absurd that such thefts should be applauded by the same state which chastised children for trivial pilfering, There was no thought of punishment in his mind, but he wanted to correct the boy to protect him from his own amorality and the savage inconsistency of the law. It was a duty which he could not ignore.

'Now, please listen to me. If you want things, just tell me and I will buy them for you. There is no need for you to steal ever again, do you understand?' Paolo nodded uncomfortably. 'First of all, you must give back everything you have got here. You took it out of the shop unnoticed, so you can get it back unnoticed, can't you? When you've done that, we'll go shopping together and you can have anything you want.'

'I can't give it all back, though.'

'Why ever not?'

'Well, some of the things I took from pockets, and I won't be able to find the right person again.'

'My God!' moaned Giovanni. 'Well, you will have to get rid of it somehow. I simply cannot have a room in my house filled with stolen goods. It will have to go, all of it. I don't mind how you do it, but I'm sure you will think of something.'

He wondered if he had been foolish in promising anything Paolo wanted, but he had said it and there was no turning back. He hoped the boy did not reveal extravagant tastes for genuine jewellery or plate, but he could not blame him or default if he did.

In a few days, Paolo reported that he had taken back what he could and had given or thrown away the rest. Giovanni was delighted and slightly apprehensive at the news.

'Right! Let's go shopping!'

The expedition was futile. Paolo saw nothing he wanted in the dozen or so shops they visited. He was bored and Giovanni was disillusioned. *Perhaps*, he thought, *my presence distracts the boy*; perhaps the taint of charity had soured the flavour.

On the way home, Giovanni took another initiative. He

bought a leather purse, placed three ducats in it, gave it to Paolo and said, 'Here you are, go and buy what you like.'

It was the last time he saw him.

All his searching and enquiries yielded no clue to what had happened to the boy, but Giovanni could not believe that he would have gone off without saying a word of farewell or without an explanation. Finally, in desperation, he went to see the captain of the city guards.

He was received with sickening sycophancy.

'It seems to me, Cavaliere, that we know what happened to your page.'

Giovanni's initial relief was short-lived; it turned to anxiety, generated by the captain's grave expression.

'Just a moment, please, Cavaliere. Let me get the record book.'

Giovanni feared that Paolo had been caught stealing and was in custody, but suppressed the thought as unworthy. The captain returned with the book and opened it with ponderous ceremony.

'Last Tuesday morning, at the jetty by San Sebastiano, the body of a boy answering your very complete description – if I may say so, Cavaliere – was fished out by a stone merchant.'

If he had been struck with a lump hammer, Giovanni would not have been more stunned. His head and the captain's office whirled menacingly.

'Do you… do you know what happened to him?'

'Oh yes, Cavaliere,' said the captain with official complacency. 'His throat was cut. His clothing was untouched, but there was one boot missing, and what might have been purse strings were cut from his belt.'

He looked up from the book, unable to suppress the self-congratulatory smile of bureaucratic efficiency.

Giovanni reeled again at the information and the appalling implications. The boy had been murdered for a few gold coins and pitched into the water like a scrap of household refuse. Compulsive thief he may have been, but he was still a child; lazy he may have been, but he was loyal; deprived he certainly was, but he was courteous and cheerful. Who could have fared better against such a background? And who was responsible for the terror and horrible death of this innocent, but Giovanni himself? The fact was both inescapable and unbearable. He was as guilty as Herod Antipas.

'I am sorry, Cavaliere, I didn't know you would take it so hard. He was only a page, wasn't he? Not a relative.'

'No, he was not a relative.'

'Well, that's good!' He massaged his palms to relieve his nervous tension. 'Just for our record, Cavaliere, what was his name?'

'Paolo.'

'Paolo what?'

'I don't know.' He was scourged by this confession. It was so pitiful that the only permanent memorial to this human being should consist of five letters in an official record. 'I'm sorry, Captain, I don't know.'

The captain wrote the name in the appropriate column, put a decisive dash after it and closed the book and the case.

'Thank you, Cavaliere.' Giovanni rose to leave with some difficulty. 'Oh, before you go, Cavaliere, if I may detain you for a moment.' The unctuous massage began again. 'I was sorry to hear about your paintings. They were very fine, if I may say so.'

'Which paintings?'

'Didn't you know, Cavaliere? The Palazzo da Ponte was burned down last night and everything destroyed, along with your pictures. A great loss. It's tragic, tragic...'

'Oh, those,' said Giovanni with total indifference. 'No, I didn't know.'

'I am so very sorry, Cavaliere. I'm no expert, of course, but they were very beautiful, and it's tragic that they have been lost. Please accept my deepest sympathy; the whole city will miss them grievously.'

Giovanni looked at the captain with contempt, and left.

He found his way home like a sleepwalker, and once there, he climbed the stairs wearily and went to his room to put away his hat and cloak. As he closed his door, he felt drawn to the narrow stairway to the servants' quarters. Without knowing why, he climbed the flight and entered Paolo's room. There was no sign of a human presence at all. The cache of loot had vanished and the bed was immaculate. It was as if it had been unoccupied since he had thrown out the remnants of Lisa's gaudy garbage, yet he knew that a child had been briefly happy here and had left no trace. This knowledge cross-hatched his mind with grief and guilt, obliterating his own brief happiness and composure. The flat bed with its unruffled coverlet had been a terrible token of death in his house once before, and the poignancy of its repetition was unendurable. He fell on his knees and wept.

'Mea culpa,' he sobbed. 'Mea culpa.'

He had killed three times; first, what he had hated most; then, what he had loved most, and now, the child who was almost his own and loved him.

Impenetrable despair closed around him again as it did after Ottavia's death, and although his affections were not ravaged, his bitter sense of failure was almost as destructive.

He locked the doors, closed the shutters and retired to his studio, not to think, not to read or pray, but to wait for death to claim him. He had no hope for this life, or the next. Nullity could not be more painful than living, and he desired that to the exclusion of everything else. He sat in his chair, trying to empty himself of every thought of reality, every connection with humanity. He sought, by discipline, to become as inanimate as the furniture. He did not move, and hardly breathed. He tried to extend the discipline to repress his pulse, to cancel the smallest remaining movements within himself. He almost succeeded in self-suffocation, so strong was his resolve, but being starved of oxygen, his pulse became excited and involuntary inhalation began. He repeated the discipline again and again, but instinct extinguished will.

Convinced at last that self-denial of this kind would not bring release, he adjusted himself to the allurements of starvation. There was food in the kitchen, but if he did not go and fetch it, it would not come and sacrifice itself, so here he would stay, and wait for benign quietus.

The lines recurred in his mind,

> Will He not rejoice
> for those who destroy this life
> and search for that better life

with Him in paradise?

Self-destruction was reputed to be sinful, but he was not convinced. Logically, at least, it was not. Logically, he was not committing the act of suicide; he was passively forestalling the inevitable conclusion of all life.

But paradise?

Jacopo knew it was real; Palestrina asserted his confidence in everything he wrote; Piero based the last years of his life upon the certainty of its existence. Were they right, and he wrong? Did Piero resume his marriage beyond the grave? Was he there now, enjoying blissful restitution? Was Palestrina deafened now by the silent waters of Lethe? Was Jacopo foully mouldering in his coffin, denied resurrection to the paradise of his convictions?

In his agony of nascence, he called out to him for confirmation. But no answer came. He called to Piero, begging him for a sign. But no answer came. He called to Luca, who had been long dead, and who would break the rules, if rules there were, and communicate with him if he could. But Luca was silent too.

In a torment of indecision, he thought of calling Ottavia. She had been closest to him in life and if there were any justice, any wisdom, any compassion, she would be in death.

'Tavi!' he called at last. 'Tavi! Are you there? Please… please, are you there… in paradise?'

There was no answer.

'Tavi, do you still want me? Tavi! I'm here… Tavi!'

For two days and nights of indistinguishable blackness he called to her, imploring an answer.

He strained to hear the smallest sound, but he heard only the splash of water on his steps below the window. Then, at last, a woman's voice… indistinct, but a woman's voice.

It came from the window.

He rushed across to unfasten the shutters.

'Tavi! Wait! I'm coming!'

He threw open the shutters with a bang.

'Tavi!' he screamed.

The women chatting across the canal paused and looked up at the wild face at the window. The hair was dishevelled; the eyes strangely glazed, open, but sightless.

'Tavi!' he screamed again, almost projecting himself over the balcony.

A dead tree in a small pot dropped into the canal.

'Are you all right, Cavaliere?' asked one of them with neighbourly solicitude.

'Tavi!' The voice was hoarse and broken.

The women looked at each other apprehensively and resumed their conversation with embarrassment.

He closed the shutters roughly, attracted by a voice behind him. They swung back, half-open.

This must be Tavi, he thought.

He groped for his chair and fell into it, panting, his eyes smarting. But the voice did not come again. He sat in silence, straining to hear it. Blood pounded in his ears, driving piles into his head, into the voice. He hit his forehead with the heel of his hand. The pounding, drowning blood drove deeper, menacing consciousness.

In the half-light, he saw the dim face of Bianca, drenched in blood, grinning and heaving. It was monstrous, vile.

He saw Lisa, standing there, drawing up her skirt lasciviously. She opened her leak and a bright, shining rat, covered in blood, squeezed itself urgently from between her thighs.

Giovanni retched with revulsion and turned away towards the door for succour. He heard the voice again, beyond the door, but in the house. He unlocked it and placed his ear to the opening.

It came again; faint, but audible.

He went down quietly, so that he would hear it if it came again. He reached the kitchen, but there was no one there. He looked into the courtyard, but there was only a cat, licking the root of her tail. She looked at him contemptuously, blinked and resumed her toilet.

He heard a sound in the store and went stealthily towards the door.

The voice came again.

As he opened it, a pair of enormous rats fled across the flags, trailing cobwebs from their tails, like exhausts of steam.

'Ugh!' he cried aloud, waving his arms in panic. 'Ugh!'

His blood glacified, piercing his scalp and back with icicles.

When he opened his eyes, the rats had gone, but he noticed, behind a pile of boxes, a corner of the crate he had secreted there long ago. He had neither seen it, nor given thought to it for years, but his consciousness vomited at the horror of its contamination by those most loathsome of creatures. The possibility of its defilement was insupportable.

He pulled aside the boxes and half-lifted, half-dragged it free. He hauled it upstairs, sweating and gasping.

He found a knife and prised it into a gap, and levered roughly. The nails had rusted in; the blade broke. Cursing, he searched for something else with frantic emergency. He opened drawers and cleared cupboards, but there was nothing. He snatched a bronze crucifix from the wall and tried to insert the end into a gap, but it was too wide. He chopped at the corner. The wood splintered, but did not split. He hacked at it again with all his demented strength. The Christ broke away and clattered across the floor. He hacked still more furiously until the timber was pulverised. Using the cross as a lever, he leaned on the foot, and the nails screamed in protest as they were torn away.

He ripped off the plank which edged the crate, his hands cut and bleeding from splinters and nails. He grabbed the frame and drew out the painting.

It was covered in heavy cobwebs, wood dust and mould. None of the original colour was visible; none of the design could be traced. The image was submerged under a shroud of corruption.

He knelt in front of the canvas, contemplating the wreckage. In his unruly, tormented mind, he remembered his conclusion that matter carried potential destruction in its very structure, and he proceeded to answer the unanswered question about abstractions like love and happiness. If not properties of matter, they were related to material things and could not exist independently. Beauty, too, was dependent, perishable and ultimately mortal.

He cared nothing for the loss of his first successful paintings, but this, this was the crowning achievement of his career, his conquest of Parnassus, and the culmination of his partnership with Ottavia. Shut away and forgotten, it had succumbed to inexorable, inevitable decay. He knelt in a crumpled heap, isolated, bereft of comfort, love or hopes, mechanically hammering the floorboards with his head. The quicksands of desolation sucked him down to the very edge of insensibility.

Everyone, everything he had loved, respected and admired had vanished; everything he believed in, everything he had striven for and everything he had accomplished was no more. All that remained was himself, and he, too, was nothing. Pain and shame engulfed him. There was nothing but vacuous blackness.

When he stirred, cramped by his folded legs, he looked once more at the mouldering canvas. He reached out a timid hand for tactile confirmation of the hideous reality. His fingertips, still sticky with blood, penetrated through to the varnish, revealing small ovals of sky and foliage.

The filth was friable.

He found a cloth and carefully wiped away the veneer. With an excitement mounting to ecstasy, he uncovered golden clouds, coppery trees and silvered mountains, speckled with inky spores. With a sacramental reverence, he revealed first the satyr and then the nymph, which, though dulled by time and neglect, were still intact, exhumed from dirt and degradation.

This was the Day of Redemption.

He found another cloth and a jar of linseed oil. The cleansing chrism resurrected the body and the spirit of the picture. It glowed again as if freshly varnished; revivified, its colour, harmony and perfection radiated as it had done in Rome.

His excitement had dissolved into peace and veneration. Then assurance and serenity of the painting enveloped his troubled spirit, dismissing his scepticism, his grief. Freed from his bodily prison, he felt complete again, as if he had been miraculously regenerated by the same sacrament that had revived the painting.

He was no longer isolated. He was integrated with the ethos of the picture; insubstantial, yet infinitely real and aware.

Love, happiness and beauty were not as fragile as he had supposed.

Here was Ottavia, surrounded by and embodying eternal beauty and eternal love; living, breathing, indestructible.

His solitude, his search, his uncertainties were over.

As he gazed in silent adoration, entranced by her beauty, restored by her gentleness, she drew him into their Arcadian tranquillity.

Giovanni felt the power of springtime, of resurrection recharging him. The concept of a renaissance was no longer an abstraction or an event in history; he felt his blood surge again in his feet and hands and flood his whole body. Physical strength returned as he stretched his arms and flexed his thighs, and with it, a new sense of connection with the life and reality he had so recently renounced. Inspired by his last minute reprieve from madness and death, he crossed the room, flung open the shutters and stood on the balcony.

He breathed deeply. The turning tide had scoured the canal below him and the scent of sea water filled his lungs.

How many times had that cleansing occurred since he had incarcerated himself? He did not know, but he knew that he had missed one of the simple pleasures of being alive. What he had missed! And why? He felt degraded by the destructive self-pity which he had allowed to consume him, and angry that he had surrendered so readily and so willingly.

He stripped himself of his clothes and his humiliation as he went up the stairs, two at a time.

He found a freshly laundered shirt and pulled it over his head. It smelt good, like Maria's apron, but the memory was neither painful nor morbid. He shook the creases out of his black velvet suit – the one he wore at Ottavia's funeral – and put it on. The past could hurt him no more; he had rejoined the present.

He left the house and became a part of the city he loved.

The bell of the Madonna dell'Orto announced the office of vespers.

Pigeons settled themselves on roosting ledges, hiding their coral feet under their plumage.

Wicker cages of silent songbirds were lifted from hooks and taken inside.

Shutters closed.

Thin wisps of smoke drifted slowly into the fading orange sky.

It was dusk in the Most Serene Republic of Venice.

Printed in the United Kingdom
by Lightning Source UK Ltd.
1712

9 781844 260270